"SO YOU WERE GOING TO RUN OFF AND LEAVE ME AT THE ALTAR?"

Cabot rendered, finally, a twisted, sardonic smile. "I thought it preferable to marrying you."

Lady Barbara slapped him then, quite hard. "Is there some other wench you are in love with?"

Again he gave the twisted smile.

"I demand you tell me."

The smile broadened. "There is no one else, milady, no one I can marry, at least. I am motivated solely by abhorrence of you."

She seemed to swell up with air. "Very well. Think what you please. But you will marry me on Saturday next. Make no mistake about that. I will not be disgraced and shamed by the likes of you."

The VIRGINIANS

ELIZABETH BRIGHT

CHARTER BOOKS, NEW YORK

THE VIRGINIANS

A Charter Book / published by arrangement with
the author

PRINTING HISTORY
Charter Original / July 1984

ISBN: 0-441-86482-1

Charter Books are published by The Berkley Publishing Group,
200 Madison Avenue, New York, New York 10016.
PRINTED IN THE UNITED STATES OF AMERICA

CONTENTS

PART III Smoke

PART I

Visitors to Eden

ONE

A Golden Moment

THE STENCH OF bilge water rose as a miasma, sour, musty, pervading everything aboard the *Sarah Constant*. The clatter of pumps, throwing back the sea that seeped through the ruptured planking, was a rhythmic accompaniment to the creaking of tortured rigging and the screams of anchor cables. Moored in the English Channel, battered incessantly by wind and wave, the *Sarah Constant* was more flotsam than ship, pitching and rolling constantly, sickening all those aboard her. And it had been going on for six tormenting weeks.

Cabot North knew none of this. Swaying in his hammock below deck, he had managed to deny the smells, sounds, and violent motion, and in his reverie he left the ship to rejoin a golden moment stolen from time. He was rowing Emily along the River Ryton on an August afternoon, so bright and warm for England. Hazy sunlight filtered through the moving leaves of oak, willow, and acacia trees, speckling the water, making the air shimmer. Yes, a golden day, all glinting and glistening, perfumed with honeysuckle and primrose, filled with the liquid sounds of oar against water, the whisper of leaves, the secret messages of larks.

"We really are terrible—running away from Elizabeth this way."

She was smiling as she spoke, head tilted a little to the side toward the hand she skimmed through the water. Then laughter bubbled out of her, treble in pitch, girlish, revealing her excitement and enjoyment of the game. Emily Fletcher was at this moment an enchantress, and her smiles, every movement

of hand and body showed she knew it. In her homespun gown
of forest green, she was to him a wood nymph, part of the
foliage, and with her bonnet removed, her tawny hair was pure
sunlight.

"She won't even miss us. And if she does, it'll serve her
right." His own laughter, joining hers, showed he didn't mean
it. He loved his sister Elizabeth.

To his right he saw a path along the riverbank, a swath of
golden sand amid lush meadow grass. "Do you want to walk
awhile?"

"If you do."

He did. His arms were tired from rowing. In a moment he
had stepped to the bank and tied the skiff to a tree, then reached
out to help her ashore. Her fingers were cool, smooth, strangely
alive, singularly sensitized. Had he ever taken Emily's hand
before? He must have, but it had not been like this.

It just happened naturally, an accident surely. As she stepped
from the boat to the sand, her skirt caught on the oarlock and
she fell forward into his arms. There was the momentary vision
of sunlit hair, deep green eyes, startled and wide, ripe pink
mouth, slightly open. Now there was only sensation, cool then
hot, soon scalding, moist breaths mingled, a whiff of feminine
perspiration under his nose, a trickle of juices at the rim of his
mouth, curved surfaces against his thighs, pillowy softness and
sharp, penetrating sweetness.

It seemed to last only a moment. Then he was holding her
away, hands on her delicate shoulders, looking at her, surprise
at himself mingling with his own wonder. "I never . . . I didn't
intend—" He swallowed, not without difficulty. "Forgive me.
I'm sorry."

She was smiling at him, laughing really, though no sounds
came from her throat. "Are you truly?"

"Yes. I had no right. I never—"

"Cabot North, I'm fourteen and quite old enough to be kissed
if I wish to be."

Wish to be. He was aware of vivid eyes, shining hair, yet
she was to him all mouth, soft lips, ripe, lightly parted, prom-
ising, inviting. And as he bent his head, extracting the promise,
he felt amid the other sensations a quick, startling stab at his
loins.

• • •

"This 'ere bloody tub'll sink any minute. Praise God it does and quick."

The gruff, blasphemous voice from off to his right, more than the sharp roll of the ship, aroused Cabot North from his reverie. As the *Sarah Constant* righted itself, he felt the queasy roiling in his stomach and the panic of nausea. He might bear the name of a famous seafarer, he might be swinging in a hammock as a member of the crew of a hundred-ton sailing ship, but he was no sailor, never would be. Six weeks at sea, and scarcely a day had passed without his being sick. This was the ultimate humiliation. It was his first voyage, and he did not realize that being anchored in rough seas sickened even veteran sailors. He knew only that *he* was nauseated and loathed himself for it.

"Shuddup yer bloody yappin'. Let a body sleep."

The coarse voices assaulted his senses almost as much as the motions of the ship. As the sixth son of Lord Alfred North, the Earl of Durham, he should rank a cabin to himself, but there was none available. The *Sarah Constant* carried seventy-one passengers, many of them prominent gentlemen, all bound in their folly to colonize a place called Virginia. On the crowded ship he had been relegated to the crew's quarters. He tried to smile. No doubt it would please his father to know his son was being toughened to the rigors of a seafarer's life.

Cabot sighed and thought about going up on deck to escape the stench in this hold. But he couldn't. Even the smell of sea air could not compensate for what he would see. All these weeks at sea and the *Sarah Constant,* together with its tiny consorts, the *Goodspeed* and *Discovery*—had ships ever been more foolishly named?—were still within sight of England. Four days before Christmas, the three vessels had weighed anchor from Brunswick Wharf in Blackwall, several bends of the Thames downstream from the center of London, and sailed as far as the mouth of the river when storms, contrary winds, and vile seas had forced them to anchor at North Downs, off the coast of Dover. A month and a half later the suffering ships were still there, while off to the starboard, tantalizingly near, lay the cliffs of the Kentish shore—and north of Kent lay all he longed for and loved in this life. It was to him the ultimate cruelty visited on him by his father, to be so near and yet so far.

He sighed. No, it wasn't so. Lord Alfred North was demanding and severe, but he wasn't cruel. "This voyage will make a man of you," he had said. His father still thought of him as sickly. And wasn't it true? He was sick, sick to his stomach, sick of the sea and this ship, sick of this endless journey to nowhere. If ever there was an ill-starred voyage, forsaken by God, it had to be this one. At once, he railed at himself for his blasphemy, for his self-pity, for his lack of will and courage. The ship's chaplain, the Reverend Robert Hunt, was deathly ill with the bloody flux. Yet he remained of good cheer and stubbornly refused to leave the ship, although his home was not ten miles away in Kent. Rector Hunt inspired them all, yet here Cabot was full of complaints. When would he ever become a man? Thus Cabot North lay in his swinging hammock, nausea and bitterness alternating with self-loathing, and he had been sloughing through this mental quagmire ever since the ship left London.

Cabot thought he would surely lose his mind were it not for the trick of reverie he had taught himself. By thrusting his mind backward to happy times, he could escape the seasickness, the stench, the horrid food, the insensitive companions. Thus, he willed his mind back to the banks of the Ryton where he held in his arms the girl with the shining hair. He tried to feel her body pressed against his. Again he bent his mouth to hers. Remembering, he waited. Then he sighed. It was gone. He could see and smell and hear, but he could not conjure up the feeling he had before. The game was not working. He would have to start over from the beginning. He lay in the hammock then, his breathing shallow, trying to make himself small. He felt the sway of the ship and listened, straining his ears for the sounds of the summer just past.

"Cabot. Cabot North. Where are you?"

The year was 1606, third in the reign of the Scottish Stuart James I, and Cabot North was seventeen, enjoying the first truly glorious summer of his life. It was a generous summer with many warm, balmy days coming in unaccustomed clusters. But it was not the weather that made the summer special to Cabot. It was freedom, and it was health. His father arranged for Cabot and Elizabeth to visit their great-aunt Harriet, an elderly relative on their mother's side, near Austerfield on the border of Yorkshire and Nottinghamshire. Aunt Harriet was fluttery and frequently forgetful. Supervision was scant and occasionally nonexistent. So they were free to roam the fields, moors, woods, and fens of the whole area, and with the roaming came health to Cabot North. He hated the term "sickly child," but it was the truth. He'd had every childhood disease anyone had ever heard of, and in between them colds, fevers, and repeated bouts of the flux. Doctors stood over him and just shook their heads. And even when he wasn't actually sick, everyone treated him as though he was or soon would be again. His childhood was an abomination of books, boredom, and excruciating loneliness. Then it had all begun to change. He seemed to run out of diseases. Actually, he hadn't been sick in two years, except for a sniffle or two. But everyone had treated him as sickly or "not strong"—until now. This summer of sun and roaming left him tanned, strong, and vigorous for the first time in his life. He felt manly.

"Cabot North. You better answer me."

He sighed. His sister's persistence was only to be expected. He should consider himself fortunate that she had stayed away so long. That morning he and Elizabeth had walked the eight miles or so from Austerfield to Scrooby, for he had a yen to sketch the old Scrooby Manor. Owned by the archbishop of York, Scrooby Manor had once been a great house made of half-timber and containing more than forty rooms. Good Queen Bess had once coveted it, and when James I passed it on the way to London for his coronation, he suggested Scrooby Manor would make an admirable hunting lodge despite its decrepit condition. The archbishop had tactfully ignored the royal remark, for he, too, liked to hunt the surrounding fens. Cabot North now squatted on the earth amid a small copse of trees, two of which formed a suitable frame for the manor house and the great moat surrounding it. At the moment he was drawing some ducks that had nestled in the moat. He had never attempted to sketch such birds before, and the last thing he wanted was to be disturbed by Elizabeth.

"If you don't answer me, Cabot North, I'll cry."

He sighed in surrender. Elizabeth North didn't need anything more to cry about in her life. "I'm over here, Elizabeth—if you must know."

He saw her off to his right. Poor Elizabeth. As fond as he was of her, he always thought of her as unfortunate. For one thing, she had not been physically favored. She had their father's nose, a huge, hooked, disfiguring proboscis. He favored their mother—dark hair, blue eyes, a certain symmetry of feature. But his compassion for Elizabeth did not extend to a desire for her nose. Poor Elizabeth. At age eight, she already knew she was not going to be pretty, and the knowledge of her disfigurement increased her natural shyness and lack of grace.

He saw her coming toward him through the trees and turned back to his sketch, hoping for some quick solution to the problem of the ducks. There was none. He couldn't draw them, for his mind was still on Elizabeth. It was not just that she was unfavored physically. She carried a deeper scar. Their mother, Lady Evelyn, the beautiful, adored second wife to Lord North, had died giving birth to her. Elizabeth, an only daughter, motherless, all but ignored by a grieving father, was reared by nurses and servants. As the youngest son, Cabot had tried to make it up to her. In his own loneliness, she was often his only companion, and they were as close as an older brother and little sister could be. But a brother, no matter how devoted, cannot replace a mother and a father.

"So that's where you're hiding."

"Not anymore, I'm not. Just leave me alone a moment. I'm trying to draw those ducks."

"They're geese, silly."

"I see the geese, but I'm only drawing the ducks."

"The geese would be easier."

"Will you please be still, Elizabeth?"

"Oh, forget your old ducks, Cabot. I want you to meet my new friend."

He sighed, again in surrender, and looked up at his sister, squinting a little against the sun. At once he gasped. Cabot didn't know whether or not he believed in angels, but his instant impression was that one stood beside his sister, for there was a halo around her head. He blinked, then saw what it really was. This girl, young woman really, had removed her bonnet, and the sunlight reflecting off her hair created a golden aura. He rocked forward onto his knees, altering his angle of vision against the sun. Yes, she was just a girl with blonde hair. He lowered his gaze. She was slender and seemed tall, or perhaps it was only because she stood over him. She wore a homespun dress of bright russet. A farmer's daughter, obviously.

"Her name's Emily, Emily Fletcher. She lives here in Scrooby. I met her coming out of the tavern."

She wore a shy, pensive expression as she looked at him, and she seemed all eyes of a vivid green.

"She's very pretty, don't you think, Cabot?"

She had youth more than beauty, and health that rewarded her with clear skin and a straight, slender body. But it was her hair shining in the sun that made him gape at her. He was unaccustomed to seeing blondes. Then he remembered. The Vikings had plundered these coasts. Many in East Anglia had the blood of Danes and Norsemen in them.

The green eyes brightened first. Then a tiny smile of amusement spread her lips. "Elizabeth," she said, "you should never ask a gentleman that."

"Why not? I think you're pretty, Emily, very pretty. Cabot does, too. I can tell."

Emily watched him scamper to his feet, awkwardly, a little nervously, as though he had belatedly remembered his manners, which was true, of course. He was tall. Because of her own exceptional height, it was the first thing she noticed in a man. And he was young, slender, with dark, wavy hair, and blue eyes, deeper than the sky, brighter than still water. Handsome, truly. Prominent brow, such a strong chin with a cleft in the center, and the lips, firm, wide, very manly, yet sensitive, hinting of passion. She liked his mouth. It opened.

"My name is Cabot North."

She knew who he was. Elizabeth's prattle left little to doubt. But she was still surprised at just how much a gentleman he was. He wore a fine doublet of red brocade, graced by a pointed ruffled collar. The shoulders were fully padded, and the sleeves puffed out very fine. His short, stuffed breeches were of matching fabric, and the linen hose on his slender legs were of the finest quality. He was every inch a well-dressed Elizabethan gentleman—and terribly out of place in a sunny glade in the English countryside.

She smiled at him. "Elizabeth told me all about you. You're the sixth son of the Earl of Durham. You and Elizabeth are visiting your great-aunt Harriet at Austerfield. You're a famous artist."

He could not remember when he hadn't drawn. How else did a lonely boy fill his hours? But he was not an artist. She was mocking him, and he bristled at that knowledge.

She read his expression. "I meant no offense, Master North. You are drawing. Does that not make you an artist?" She sought to placate him more, glancing at the drawing in his hand. "Your likeness of Scrooby Manor is very good. I think you will be famous one day."

He heard the soothing tone, saw her smile. Such a lovely smile. She still had good teeth. But he clung to his pique a moment longer. "You frequent taverns?" He had to hurt her back.

Light laughter came from her. "Only in the mornings. I clean for Brother Brewster."

As her laugh brightened, his anger faded. "The postmaster is your brother?" Scrooby Manor lay beside the Great North Road and served as a post house. William Brewster was paid by the Crown to quarter horses for post riders and maintain an inn for travelers.

"He is our brother in the Lord."

Then he knew. "You're a Brownist?"

"If you wish. We do not use the term."

"A separatist then?"

"Not if we don't have to."

"A Puritan?"

"We would like to purify the church, yes."

Her eyes remained bright during the exchange. How frank and honest she was. What good humor she possessed. "I've heard of Postmaster Brewster. He hosts illegal church meetings in his tavern."

Her smile dazzled him. "We do wish that fact was less well known."

"A tavern seems a strange place to hold church."

"Perhaps it is. But God's will can be done in the humblest

abode." She laughed. "Besides, the tavern is the only place large enough for our number. There are more than fifty of us, Master North."

"Cabot, please."

"It is a strange name. Wasn't he—"

"Yes, the sea captain who explored America. My father intended for me to have a life at sea and named me after John Cabot."

Again laughter bubbled out of her. "He should have named you after Sir Francis Drake or Captain Hawkins."

"But Drake North or Hawkins North wouldn't sound as good, would it?" Now thoroughly won over, he allowed his laughter to join hers.

Emily Fletcher became the heart and sinew of that one glorious summer. Cabot and Elizabeth came almost daily to Scrooby to see her, working the fields beside her, milking the cow, tending sheep, walking, talking, living the country life among these simple people. She was to him a blithe spirit, all smiles and laughter and outrageous teasing. She was devoid of pretense, her every thought and action spontaneous and guileless. And all was suffused with a natural gaiety. There was a gentleness, an innate kindness, a generosity of spirit to her that he believed he had never encountered in a human being before.

It was her treatment of Elizabeth that most endeared Emily to him. She offered her total acceptance, never once showing the annoyance he sometimes felt. She was that summer the sister Elizabeth never had. More, she was her mother, hugging her, holding her in her lap, walking hand in hand with her, squealing and screaming over childish games. It was the summer of Elizabeth's first true happiness. Joy resided in her face and in her voice, and to Cabot she became more beautiful and began to show an incipient grace, apparently hidden within her until now. Once he tried to thank Emily for being so kind to his sister. "Don't be silly, Cabot. It's not kindness. I love Elizabeth. She's the little sister I've never had."

"Sister as in the church?"

She smiled. "There really is no difference, Cabot."

Swaying in his hammock aboard the *Sarah Constant,* the queasiness in his stomach now suppressed, Cabot North relived that summer. He pretended to sketch while really watching

Emily and Elizabeth together. He walked through the fen country with them and strolled the woods, mindful for the first time
in his life of every flower and wild creature. He sat with them
at a meal of brown flanker bread and broth, and no food ever
tasted so delicious. And in his remembrances there was an
exquisiteness, a preciousness born of knowing something has
happened but once and is lost forever. Thus, he returned slowly,
savoring every detail, to that golden day on the bank of the
River Ryton, and experienced again that first wondrous ache
in his loins as he held Emily Fletcher in his arms and bathed
his senses in her sweetness. With the second kiss, she gasped
her pleasure and put her fingers to her lips, as though holding
in the sensation. Then she touched his flushed cheek, her eyes
wide with wonder and filled with liquid brightness. She laughed
then, lightly, a little nervously, and the smile that followed
was pure wisdom, replacing all need for words.

She took his arm and guided him along the path, the firm
slope of her young breast against his arm. His heart was pounding, and his whole body tingled. He knew he couldn't speak
even if he knew what to say. But try as he would, he could
not quell his passion, and after a few steps he stopped, turned
to her, and dipped deep again into the well of longing. She
did not protest, but gave again of the waters that quenched no
thirst. Once more they strolled, her arm in his, longer this time.
He watched a bird in a tree, picked a flower and inserted it in
her hair. But inevitably they stopped again, eyes devouring
eyes, fingers being kissed, heads turning, limbs embracing. It
was the memory of this last kiss that made his eyes smart and
his throat ache until he knew longing as physical pain.

The words came to him then, burning his throat. "You can't
marry Worthy Townsend. You just can't."

Her wan smile was all knowledge. "He hasn't asked me,
Cabot."

"He will. I know he will." Worthy Townsend was a member
of the congregation, a quiet, stolid farmer in his early twenties.
Cabot had seen how he looked at Emily when he and Elizabeth
attended the Sunday meetings. "Brewster says you're as good
as promised to him."

"Perhaps, Cabot, only perhaps."

"I won't let you marry him, Emily. You're too beautiful,

too precious, too . . . too everything. You don't belong with a man like him."

Again she smiled. "And where is it I belong, Cabot?"

He touched her face with trembling fingers. "You belong in fine silk, Emily, bedecked with flowers and jewels."

Her eyes brightened at the thought, but her mouth said, "Oh, no, Cabot, never."

"Yes. Yours should be loveliness and happiness always."

Directness of speech was so very characteristic of her; still she surprised him. "You want me to marry you, Cabot, be a great lady?"

"Yes—when we can. We're both young. We can wait."

She looked at him a long moment, her face growing serious. "It would never work. I could not be Lady Emily North. Your father would never accept me."

"He would. I know he would—once he came to know you."

"No, Cabot." She turned away, back along the path. The matter was settled.

Not for him. "Emily, I love you. Is there no way for us?"

She stopped in midstride. Without looking at him she said, "Yes, there could be."

His mind raced. Then he knew. "You mean . . . become one of you, forsake . . ."

She turned to look at him, that wan, knowing smile on her lips. "And that would never work either, would it, Cabot?"

He stared at her, his brain reeling. Become a Puritan? He and Elizabeth had attended "meetings," as they called them, with Emily. They were long, dull affairs, full of endless sermons railing against bishops and vestments, stained-glass windows and ritual. He understood little and cared not at all. Only Emily mattered. "You ask a great deal, Emily."

"I don't ask it of you. It is merely—" She hesitated, biting at her lip. "It is the only way for us, Cabot." There was entreaty in her eyes. "If you could just sincerely believe, become . . ." She shook her head then and turned away, striding back toward the skiff.

He watched her a moment, shock and desire confusing his mind. "Emily, will you give me time to think about it, decide?"

Her step still firm, she said, "Yes, there is a little time."

• • •

A little time. The words stabbed at him. Suddenly the sour hold of the ship closed in on him unbearably, and in one motion he rolled out of the hammock to his feet. He would go up on deck. At least he would see England and feel closer to it.

TWO

Under Sail

THE *SARAH CONSTANT* yawed violently just as Cabot North reached the deck. He lurched, stumbled to his knees, and barely made the rail in time to retch savagely over the side. His stomach was empty, and the spasms were acutely painful, yet he was aware of a hand at the back of his breeches, keeping him from falling overboard.

When he could, Cabot straightened up and, gasping, his eyes watering, faced the man who had helped him.

"I din' wan' you to fall o'erboard, sar."

Still unable to speak, Cabot nodded his thanks, swallowing hard against the vile taste in his mouth. Through swimming eyes, he saw a young man, hardly older than himself, but much more heavily built, broad of shoulder, with strong arms and thick waist. His head fit his body, large, with a mass of dark hair above brown eyes and a squarish face. His mouth appeared lipless, just a line splitting a massive chin. The crack opened.

"If I may, sar, per'aps I can 'elp you wif the sickness."

"Anything. I'll do anything." He could barely gasp the words.

"Me uncle sailed with Drake when he 'feated t'murderin' Spanish in 'eir armada in 'eighty-eight. 'E said t'motion of a ship, sar, is jus' like a baby's cradle." The crag of a face split wider revealing yellowing teeth. "It 'elped me, sar. You might try it, if you wish, sar."

"Anything." Then a new wave of nausea seized him, and he had to hold on to the rail for support.

"Jus' lie down o'er 'ere on t'deck, sar. Try to t'ink of lyin' in yer cradle." He took Cabot's arm. "'Ere, let me 'elp ya."

Cabot let himself be led to a spot of deck near the mainmast, where he lay spread-eagled on the scrubbed wood. At first he felt only nausea and panic. He glanced up at the burly figure above him and felt the sting of humiliation that he was lying at his feet, ready to retch again.

"Jus' feel the ship, sar. Try an' not fight it."

Cabot closed his eyes, struggling against his nausea.

"Sor' o' pleasantlike, ain't it, sar?"

It was anything but pleasant, but Cabot's ingrained courtesy plus his determination not to retch kept him lying there. A cradle. The motion of a cradle. He tried to visualize the cradle in the nursery at home, the one Elizabeth had been rocked in. Yes, he could remember. Imagining had always come easy for him, and he put himself in Elizabeth's place and let himself be rocked. Back and forth, back and forth. Soon he could see his mother, dark hair, blue eyes, so beautiful, standing over the cradle, swinging it. He allowed himself to move with it, telling himself how pleasant it was, and almost at once his stomach began to feel calmer. He found himself enjoying the swaying and without willing it, he fell asleep.

He had no notion how long he slept, but when he tried to get up, the old queasiness returned. Again he lay down, picking up the motion of the ship until his stomach calmed. In a few moments he arose to look for the man who had helped him. He couldn't find him at first. Many passengers had come out on deck. Then he saw him near the stern of the ship.

The crag of a face split into a yellow smile. "Feel better, sar?"

"Yes. I want to thank you." He meant it.

"'Twas nothin', sar. I was sick as a dog meself a couple o' days till I 'membered what me uncle said."

Cabot smiled. "And thank your uncle for me, too."

"If'n I e'er see 'im again, sar, I will."

There was awkwardness then, and Cabot understood why. This fellow was of a far lower station than he, probably a laborer's son. He had been bold enough to help someone retching over the side, but there was no need for help now. And there was nothing to say to him. "I'm Cabot North." He extended his hand in friendship.

The huge, calloused hand was opened, turned, inspected

for dirt, then extended, entirely enveloping Cabot's. "I'm Timothy, sar, Timothy Loudon."

The awkwardness surfaced again, worse than before, and Cabot turned to his left to look at the sea, seeing it for the first time. It was a strange day. The sky was blue and the sunshine brilliant, yet a warm, dry wind blew incessantly from the south, churning the sea into five-foot waves that filled the air with spray and a fine mist. It seemed to him the *Sarah Constant*, harnessed to anchors, would be torn apart by the steady pounding. He raised his gaze, and on the horizon was the gray-green coast of England. A pang of homesickness seized him. More to himself than to Timothy Loudon, he muttered, "Will this damnable ship ever leave England?"

"Soon, sar. A member o' the crew tol' me this 'ere wind should blow 'erself out so we kin 'ead south, sar."

Cabot turned to him, a reply forming on his lips. But his words were lost in a great cracking sound from aloft. It all happened at once, the sound of splintering wood, looking up, pushing Timothy away, then diving head first into a man who stood nearby, pain in his knees and elbows as he hit the deck, the crash of falling rigging. Then ropes were being pulled off him, and Timothy was helping him to his feet.

"You all right, sar?"

His left elbow hurt, but he refused to acknowledge the pain. "I'm fine."

"That was a close'un, sar."

Cabot turned to look at the jungle of rigging and the snapped spar that had caused it.

"I owe you my life, sir."

Cabot turned. The man he had knocked down was on his feet now, helped by others who had rushed to them. He was a short man with a full beard, piercing blue eyes, and a military bearing. Embroidered on his doublet was a crest formed of three heads. Cabot recognized it. "I did nothing, Captain Smith."

"Hardly nothing." He smiled. "That spar would've split even my hard head."

"It was still nothing, Captain. I was mostly saving myself. I'm sorry I had to knock you down."

"Better down than dead. What is your name, young sir?"

"Cabot North, sir."

"Very good, Master North. John Smith does not forget those who save his life." A sardonic smile twisted his mouth. "Although I'm sure there are some among our company who wish you hadn't."

Cabot stared at him, perplexed by his words. Then the moment was gone as sailors began to cut away the wreckage and dump it over the side. With Timothy, he retreated to starboard while Smith headed for the port side of the ship, surrounded by a coterie of men.

"S'cuse me, sar, but is that the Cap'n Smith who fought the Turks, cuttin' off t'ree o' their 'eads pers'nally?"

Cabot laughed. "The very same—and the way he tells it, possessing half the women on the Continent at the same time."

Timothy seemed quite awestruck. "'Magine! And you saved 'is life, sar."

Annoyance surfaced in Cabot. "Look, Timothy, if we're to be friends, you must stop acting as if I'm some kind of hero, which I'm not, and you must stop calling me sir. I'm not sir anybody. I'm just Cabot North."

"But, sar, you's clearly a gennulman."

Cabot sighed. Yes, he was a gentleman. In his case, it came by birthright, but it could just as easily be adopted. The word *gentleman* connoted a certain manner, attire, and speech as well as wits enough to have money without working for it. There were scoundrels who were "gentlemen." Besides, as the sixth son, Cabot knew he would inherit neither title nor much wealth. And his mother had been a commoner. There were people who viewed Elizabeth and him as little more than bastards. "Look, I don't want you to call me sir. I'm just a lowly member of this ship's crew."

"I doubt 'at, sar."

Again Cabot sighed, this time in resignation. There was no point in arguing with the fellow. He would try a new tack. "So you're going to colonize Virginia?"

"Yes, sar. Lookin' for'd to it, sar."

"Do you think you'll like the place?"

"Yes, sar, very much so. I 'ear the land's so rich seeds prac'ly leap out o' t'earth."

Cabot smiled. The stories told about Virginia! If they were half true, the place was a paradise. At least this Timothy Loudon wasn't expecting to find gold nuggets lying on the ground for the picking. "You're a farmer, Timothy?"

"Yes, sar. I was. In Wiltshire, sar."

"What happened to your farm?"

"Fences, sar—and sheep."

Cabot nodded in understanding. The enclosure movement. All over England, common lands were being fenced off and fertile fields given over to the grazing of sheep for the wool trade. Farmers like Timothy were being forced off the land. A major reason for this Virginia adventure was to find employment for them. "So you're looking forward to a new start in Virginia?"

"Yes, sar."

Cabot saw the yellow smile and heard the eagerness in Timothy's voice. He wondered if this lad knew the chances of his owning land in Virginia were remote. He was going as an employee of the Virginia Company, a hired hand. The company had no plans to give or even sell land to settlers. But Cabot decided to say nothing. Let this poor chap enjoy his optimism while he could. "You're not homesick?"

"Yes, sar. I miss m'folks. But I'm eager to get to Virginny."

Cabot looked at him sharply. This Timothy Loudon was about his age, and he was leaving home, family, everything he knew and loved, striking out for the unknown. "How long do you plan to stay in Virginia?"

A shrug of the heavy shoulders was his answer.

"You're going to stay in Virginia, build a whole new life there?"

"Yes, sar." The yellow smile flashed. "I 'ope to, sar."

Cabot looked away from him toward the headland in the distance, feeling—he wasn't sure. Here was a fellow with courage. And what was he? Just someone going on a sea voyage, returning home in a few months. And he couldn't even accept that gracefully. All he did was moan, complain, and retch over the ship's railing.

"Forgive me, sar, but did you say you was a member o' the ship's company?"

Cabot turned to him. "Yes, that's what I am."

"If'n I may say so, sar, you don' look like a sailor."

Cabot smiled wanly. "Obviously, I'm not much of one.

Actually, I signed aboard as a cartographer. I'm supposed to draw maps and sketch Virginia scenes."

"You's an ar'is', sar?"

Cabot's mind leaped back to Scrooby and his meeting with Emily. "Let's say I can draw a little, Timothy. I'm not an artist."

"As you say, sar."

The awkwardness returned, and Cabot looked back toward England. A thought about Emily was half formed in his mind, but it eluded him as he heard Timothy nervously clear his throat. He turned to the sound. "Did you want to say something, Timothy?"

"Yes, sar." He hesitated, obviously uncomfortable, then visibly appeared to button up his courage. "I jus' won'ered, sar, how you come to be 'ere, 'board ship."

Cabot laughed. "It wasn't difficult, I can assure you. My father is Alfred North, the Earl of Durham. I'm his youngest son, his sixth, and I was selected at birth to go to sea. That's how I got the name Cabot." His smile was rather self-deprecating. "I fear I was a disappointment to my father. I was sick a lot as a child, and so any thought of my being a seafarer was discarded—until recently. Then, my father decided this voyage was what I needed. Make a man of me, he said." Cabot shrugged. "I guess it is."

"Thank ye, sar. I unnerstan'."

Cabot looked at him a moment, then back to the shore that beckoned him. No, Timothy Loudon didn't understand. How could he? He hadn't been told the whole truth.

The summer had ended precipitously, the very day after he kissed Emily. Elizabeth and he were summoned back to Graymere, the North estate west of London. Cabot had cooled his heels a couple of days, greatly puzzled over what seemed an ominous turn of events. Then he met his father in his study. It seemed to Cabot to be more like an audience than a father—son chat, for Lord North—and he was every inch a peer of the realm that day—sat behind his desk in the book-lined room. He was as austere as the room. He did not invite Cabot to sit.

"I'm disappointed in you, young man."

Cabot knew better than to speak. Oh, he could have said,

"Yes, sir," but that would suggest agreement, and he had no idea what he'd done to disappoint his father.

He watched his father's eyes, pale blue, a little watery. They were fixed on him, remorseless. Cabot's mind began to play tricks on him. Suddenly he realized he had no idea how old his father was. He was old; that's all he knew. His thin hair was iron gray and had already crept halfway back his pate. His close-cropped chin whiskers and mustache below his hooked nose were of an even lighter shade, and his skin was loose and wrinkled. There was an ugly brown spot the size of a shilling near his left temple. How old was his father? It was suddenly important to know. Fifties? Surely that. Cabot tried to calculate. His half-brother Sir Harold North, oldest of the five sons by the first countess, was almost forty. But how old was their father when he married and begat an heir? He didn't know. Why didn't he know an important thing like that?

"I have received a report on your conduct from your aunt Harriet." Cabot saw him holding a letter in his left hand. "She says you spent the summer in idleness. You and Elizabeth ran off repeatedly by yourselves. You caused a great deal of worry to your aunt. I want to know what you were doing."

Cabot felt keen disappointment in Aunt Harriet. She had seemed so fat, devoted to her palate, and endlessly preoccupied with—what? Her next meal, he guessed. Except for occasional bouts of fussing over them, she seemed not to know of their existence. She certainly had said nothing to him, or to Elizabeth as far as he knew, that registered as disapproval. Why had she written to their father?

"I asked what you were doing."

"Nothing, sir."

"You mean you did *nothing at all?*"

Cabot heard the sarcasm and felt a riling in his stomach. "We went for long walks, sir. I sketched some. We—"

"Oh, yes, you *sketched.*" The word was a profanity the way he said it. "I asked Jacobs to bring me your *drawings.*" He reached behind the desk and produced Cabot's sketchbook. The pain in Cabot's stomach sharpened as he saw it. This was an intolerable invasion of his privacy, but there was nothing he could do about it. "May I say, Cabot, you not only draw badly but your choice of subject matter leaves a great deal to be desired." He slammed the sketchbook on the desk. "I asked what you did this summer in hope—quite in vain, it seems—that you might be man enough not to lie about it."

Cabot bristled. "I do not lie, sir!"

Lord North ignored the protest. "Your aunt Harriet was most concerned about your *extended* absences. She had you followed." He picked up the sketchbook. "Your own pathetic scribblings confirm your aunt's suspicions. You and Elizabeth were consorting with radicals, Brownists. You visited the homes of these heretics. You even attended their illegal church. This ridiculous drawing confirms it. And I assume this one is supposed to be the young woman you were lollygagging with."

Cabot felt physically wounded by his father's words. He could hardly bear the old man's scorn as he turned to the portrait of Emily. It was the best thing he had ever done, almost catching the sunlight in her hair, the laughter in her eyes.

It happened so quickly that Cabot could not even cry out. "At least I can destroy the evidence." Lord North gripped the sketches between his gnarled knuckles and ripped them in half, then in quarters, throwing them into the fireplace. His eyes, fixed again on Cabot, were as cold as his voice. "I am extremely disappointed in you, young man."

Cabot shook with rage. "You have no right. I did nothing wrong."

"You call it *nothing* to fraternize with these godless people. The king has called them snivelers and malicious spirits. He has said, 'I will *make* them conform or I will harry them out of the land.' Those are the king's exact words—and I intend to help him do it!" Lord North, in his anger, had risen from his chair. "And, to think, my son *consorts* with them behind my back!" He glared at Cabot a moment, as though mentally flagellating him. "Have you no respect for me, for my position at court?"

"I did nothing—"

"Silence! You will speak when spoken to." The thunder in his voice seemed to exhaust him, and he surrendered to a bout of coughing. Cabot could only stand helplessly while Lord North expended his lungs into a lace handkerchief. When he recovered, his voice was calmer, as though he were protecting himself from another attack. "What I cannot understand is how

you could make your sister party to your stupidity." He shook his head sadly. "I will not permit heresy in this house. I have employed a proper tutor for her, a man of the cloth. I'm sure he will drum out of her the mischief you have caused." He leveled a cold gaze on Cabot. "As for you, young man, I have one question."

Cabot waited, rage mingling with disbelief.

"Have you begat a bastard by this tavern wench?"

Cabot was shocked speechless. His mouth opened, but no sound came out.

"I demand an answer this instant."

"You have no right to accuse me. I—" Shock and disbelief dulled his protest.

"At least you have a little sense." A hint of a smirk came to his face. "A young man will sow his wild oats, I suppose, but may I remind you of your obligations to this family? It is my fault. I should have arranged a suitable marriage for you before now. But"—he looked away from Cabot—"you were always sick. No one believed you would live, let alone be able to . . . I've hardly had fathers of suitable daughters beating down the doors to offer dowries."

The words were like whiplashes to Cabot. He knew his face had reddened.

"I will take steps to arrange a proper marriage for you— and I assure you it will not be with a tavern wench and most definitely not with a heretic Brownist. Need I remind you of the importance of religion to this family?"

Cabot nodded. Yes, he knew. As a young man, inheriting a minor and impoverished earldom, Alfred North had guessed right in the religious wars that swirled through England. He had abrogated the family Catholicism and wholeheartedly embraced the Church of England. In the War of the Earls, he had sided with the Crown. His reward was favor with Queen Elizabeth and the gift of Graymere. His status at court brought marriage to the daughter of a duke and a huge dowry. Lady Catherine, whom Cabot knew only from a portrait in the long gallery, bore the earl five sons, all of whom made important marriages. Most notable was Sir Harold's marriage to Lady Portia, the daughter of Robert Cecil, Earl of Salisbury, even now chief minister to King James. In his lifetime, Lord Alfred

North had brought his family from near disgrace and poverty to wealth, prominence, and influence. He was not a man to be trifled with, certainly by his youngest son.

"I have decided what must be done with you."

Cabot waited. The thought entered his mind that a condemned man before the bar of justice must feel like this. He was still cringing inwardly when he realized his father's gaze had softened, as had his voice.

"Cabot, my son, you must realize I have a peculiar affection for you."

Peculiar? The strange word pricked at Cabot.

Lord North slumped back in his chair, appearing weary. "Heaven knows, you have done little to deserve it. I suppose it has to do with your mother, the late countess. You resemble her, your eyes, your coloring, many of your mannerisms. She had Irish blood in her, you know."

Cabot felt sudden compassion for his father. With the death of Lady Catherine, Alfred North had married young, beautiful Evelyn Wismer. Much younger than he and a commoner—indeed she had been chambermaid to the woman she replaced as countess—Lady Evelyn had never been accepted among his friends, yet he loved her deeply and still grieved for her.

"I know, sir, I remember her."

"Gave her a spark of fire. She could have a fine temper sometimes. Do you have a temper, Cabot?"

"I don't know, sir."

The earl shook his head sorrowfully. "Now, you wouldn't know. You've spent your whole life cooped up in this house, cared for by nannies and nurses."

Cabot winced inwardly. But wasn't it true?

"Your recent *indiscretions* have helped me make up my mind what to do with you." He paused to clear the residue of a cough from his throat. "I have arranged to remove you from temptations—of the flesh and any other kind. A sea voyage is what you need. It will make a man of you."

"A voyage, sir?" Cabot was surprised he could speak at all.

"Yes. Among my other duties I am a director of the Virginia Company of London. We have a royal charter to establish a colony in America, a place called Virginia. It is a great undertaking to increase the glory of His Majesty, propagate the faith, and keep the Papist Spaniards from claiming the whole New World as their own. As a director I have prevailed upon Captain Christopher Newport, who commands the expedition, to take you on as a member of the crew of his flagship. You sail in two months."

"I do believe the wind's achangin' already, sar."

The voice of Timothy Loudon grated against Cabot's ears, snapping him from his reverie. He turned and saw Timothy grin as he felt the wind against his moistened index finger. Then, as if it had received a cue, the *Sarah Constant* burst into activity. Orders were barked, all of them smattered with oaths and threats, and on the bridge he saw Captain Newport speak to an aide. Barefoot men ran over the deck to scamper aloft and man the winches to hoist the sea anchors. Cabot caught a few words, "mainsail" and "foresail," but none of it had meaning to him. He felt the result, however. The ship seemed to take on a life of its own. As more sail was hoisted, he could feel the *Sarah Constant* shudder. It seemed to groan as wooden masts bent to a new wind, and the vessel slowly turned in the water, heading south, away from England.

"'Citin', ain't it, sar? We's on our way at last."

There was excitement in Timothy's voice, and his eyes were bright with it. Then Cabot could hear others cheering around him. After six weeks of storms and wallowing along the coastline, the voyage was at last beginning. Without willing it, Cabot turned back to the railing and the horizon. The coast of England was already receding. It would soon disappear from view. Would he ever see England again?

As soon as the thought came to him, he squelched it as unworthy. He should be happy like the others. They were at last making headway toward Virginia.

He raised his gaze for a last look at the rapidly shrinking shore. He remembered. His father's words, dispatching him to Virginia had stirred him. A sea voyage to a far-off land. Virginia! The very name was exotic. Such an adventure it would be! He wanted to be part of it. Yet he was appalled. So far away. Gone so long. He thought of Emily. *A little time.* He had written to her, telling her he was going to Virginia and asking her not to make a hasty decision but to wait until he returned. "In a few weeks," he had written. Six weeks had passed and they were only now leaving England. Would she wait for him? She had to. She had to. Then, as he stood against the railing, looking out over the turbulent Channel, he remembered, not without pain, his last glimpse of Elizabeth, shrunken within herself, gaiety gone, the frocked tutor, stick in hand, standing over her, the forsaken, defeated look in her eyes as he turned away from her, unable to help.

"Master North." Cabot turned, looked toward the poop deck. "Report to the captain."

In moments Cabot stood before Christopher Newport. He had immense respect for him, the most celebrated English sea captain since Drake. As captain of the *Golden Dragon* in 1591, Newport had sacked four towns on the Spanish Main, losing a hand in the process, and taken or destroyed twenty Spanish vessels. He had then met and captured the *Madre de Dios,* the greatest Spanish treasure ship ever seized.

"Your action with Captain Smith was commendable."

"Thank you, sir."

It seemed to Cabot the steely eyes of the captain softened just a trifle. "Have you found your sea legs now, Master North?"

"Yes, sir, I think so, sir."

A scant smile widened his mouth. "Good. Then perhaps I may have the opportunity to see some of the sketches you will make aboard ship. The company directors want a full record of this voyage."

Cabot felt himself blushing, but hoped it didn't show. "Yes, sir. I'll start sketching right away, sir."

"See that you do."

Not without relief, Cabot turned to bolt from the captain, heading for the hold and his sketchbook. As he passed Timothy Loudon, he heard, "'Tis certainly good to be unner sail at last, sar, isn't it?"

Cabot North stopped, turned to Timothy Loudon, and clapped him on the shoulder. Grinning, he mimicked his new friend. "Yes, sar, certainly 'tis. I think t'will be a fine voyage now, sar."

THREE

Land Ho!

THE AGONY OF THE anchorage past, the *Sarah Constant* and its two consorts turned out to be speedy ships. At least Cabot thought so. It took less than three weeks to traverse the coast of France, skirt Spain—keeping a wary eye out for Spanish warships that might seek to intercept them—and sail past Morocco. By the end of February they had moored at Santa Cruz in the Canary Islands to replace the slimy water in the casks. The vessels were now well out into the Atlantic, swept along by prevailing westerlies, bound for the West Indies.

All this Cabot learned from Sailing Master Isaiah Adams. To fill his days, Cabot asked for and received instruction in seamanship. From Adams and Second Mate Forest Perth, he learned the parts of the ship, the correct nomenclature, and even went aloft to help set sail. The sailing master let him take the wheel for brief periods. He learned to read the compass and gauge, shoot the sun for latitude, and study the charts. Thus, Cabot came to know where they were going and why. Theirs was the long route to the New World, following the wind, as Columbus had over a century before. It was suspected there was a shorter, more direct route through northern latitudes, but neither Captain Newport nor any other captain of the day had yet risked finding it.

Cabot now leaned against the foremast, sketching the elegant form of Edward Maria Wingfield. Cabot had been spending a good part of each day with his pad, and his drawing had improved, his strokes becoming longer and more confident. He had discovered he was best off if he freed his mind from the task and just let the eye and hand do the drawing. Thus, as the form and likeness of Wingfield took shape on the paper, Cabot's mind was on other matters.

He was now sincerely grateful he was a member of the crew and not one of the passengers. Wingfield was attired as a proper gentleman, ruffled collar, doublet, breeches, hose, and buckled shoes. He was also immensely uncomfortable and sweating profusely in the sun. Long before, Cabot had adopted the garb of the sailors, loose breeches and a simple shirt. On this fine, hot day, he had discarded the shirt, and he enjoyed the warmth of the sun on his bronzed back and bare feet. The sweltering gentlemen looked at him askance, but Cabot truly had no great love for this breed of men and didn't care what they thought.

"I tell you Smith plotted mutiny and belongs where he is."

The voice of Wingfield, talking with a trio of companions, altered Cabot's thoughts. Soon after they left the Canaries, Wingfield and his faction accused John Smith of planning to usurp the government of the new colony and make himself king. It seemed a ridiculous charge to Cabot, but he understood that Captain Newport had no choice but to confine Smith to quarters. At least he hadn't put him in irons.

The clash between Wingfield and Smith had divided the colonists before they were even halfway to Virginia. Cabot thought it so stupid. Here were gentlemen adventurers, risking their lives to colonize an unknown continent full of heathen and possibly hostile natives. Yet, on this ship they engaged in the most petty rivalries. Cabot knew the cause, and it distressed him to think his father, as a company director, was part of it. The colonists had sailed under sealed orders that were not to be read until landfall was made in Virginia. Everyone knew the colony was to be governed by a council of thirteen, but until the orders were opened no one knew who the councilors were to be. Doubtlessly this was done to prevent any diminution of the authority of Captain Newport as admiral of the flotilla. But it left the settlers to wonder and worry about who their leaders were to be. It was a nearly constant subject of discussion and, most unfortunately, divided the colonists into factions supporting this or that candidate and disparaging others. In Cabot's view, the confinement of Captain Smith was a direct result of all this politicking.

"What are you doing here? You're confined to quarters."

It was the voice of Wingfield, imperious always, addressing Captain Smith who was approaching along the deck.

"I am taking my exercise, as permitted by the captain." Smith's firm, military stride did not alter until he stopped before Wingfield. "Or have you declared yourself *Admiral* Wingfield and now give all the orders?" There was no fear on Smith's face, only taunting insolence.

Wingfield sucked in his breath, reddening. "You, sir, are a scoundrel. I'll have you out on a field of honor."

Smith's laugh rang with sarcasm. "We are at sea, Master Wingfield. There are no fields, as even you should be able to see. It is a fact for which you should be grateful."

Wingfield puffed up as though to burst. Cabot saw his hand reach for his sword. Smith's arm mirrored the action. The whole deck became quiet, tense, expectant. Time seemed suspended.

"Would you please hold your pose, Master Wingfield? I can't draw you if you move around." Cabot's utterance surprised him. He had not thought of what to say, only that something had to be done to stop the fight.

Wingfield stared at him a moment, confusion creeping into his eyes. "The pose?"

"Yes. You were looking toward Sir Thomas on your left."

Wingfield hesitated, obviously disconcerted, then to Cabot's relief turned to his left, obeying. Smith resumed his exercise, winking at Cabot as he did so.

Cabot smiled inwardly. His Majesty's fleet probably had no vessel large enough to hold Wingfield and Smith. They were like flint and gunpowder. Brought together, there was bound to be an explosion. For a moment, Cabot concentrated on his drawing of Wingfield, trying to catch his character. At age forty-seven, he was senior among the colonists, one of eight persons—and the only one aboard—to whom the king had granted the license to colonize Virginia. He was also pompous, arrogant, overly conscious of himself and his family connections. Cabot disliked him instinctively, perhaps because his own mother was a commoner.

He was drawn to Smith, and not just because of the "lifesaving" incident. There was something magnetic about the diminutive captain. The son of an impoverished yeoman, Smith had entered the army, fought the Spanish in Holland, then wandered alone across Europe, eventually fighting and being captured by the Turks. When he returned home, he published a book that fascinated all England. It was a hair-raising tale of war, imprisonment, and escape, of narrow scrapes with death, all of it studded with a bewildering array of amorous affairs. Trouble was, there was no possibility of verifying a word of it, for Smith was alone in his adventures. The most famous tale related his mortal combat with three Turkish duelists. Smith claimed to have defeated and beheaded all three, one after the other, and as proof he had fashioned his own coat of arms bearing the three Turkish heads.

Cabot understood. All this was unbearable to Wingfield, who came from one of England's finer families. He had himself fought in Holland and been taken prisoner. To Wingfield, Smith was a twenty-seven-year-old low-born upstart, bragging about his exploits, fashioning his own coat of arms, calling himself "captain," and acting as though he were a man of importance.

Cabot was amused by the confrontation between the two men. Smith was surely brash, outspoken, and abrasive, supremely confident of his knowledge, courage, and ability. He had a way of pushing himself forward into any situation. He not only told others what to do, he suggested he could do it better than anyone else. Yet, Cabot realized that in a situation of danger, the confident Smith would be a far better leader. The overbearing Wingfield would tell an enemy who he was and show them his family tree, while Smith would draw his sword.

No, that wasn't fair. Wingfield would be all right when the time came. He simply couldn't help his nature, and there was nothing for the passengers to do aboard ship but connive and bicker. Actually, it was a distinguished group chosen to begin this colony. Captain Newport's credentials were impeccable. Then there was Bartholomew Gosnold, captain of the forty-ton *Goodspeed*. In 1602, he had sailed the north coast of America, a place called Massachusetts, discovering and naming Cape Cod, Martha's Vineyard, and the Elizabeth Islands. He had even set up a temporary camp at Cuttyhunk and thus experienced life in the New World. His writings and urgings had led to the whole idea of founding a colony. Cabot didn't know much about the third captain aboard the twenty-ton pinnace *Discovery*. He gave his name as John Ratcliffe, but there was gossip his real name was Sicklemore and he was making the voyage to escape trouble at home. Cabot smiled. Chances were this was true of half the men aboard—himself included.

The colonists included Sir George Percy, the son of the Earl of Northumberland, head of the most powerful family in England. Sir George was the only passenger to rank a private cabin. Captain John Martin had sailed to America twenty years before in command of the *Benjamin* in Drake's fleet when it picked up the stranded remnants of Raleigh's first colony at Roanoke. His father was lord mayor of London and a director of the Virginia Company. Yes, there were many good men beginning this venture.

"That's a good likeness, Cabot."

He turned to the voice. "Thank you, Timothy, but I doubt if it's either good or a likeness of our distinguished future councilor."

"You think he's goin' to be one o' them?"

"Without doubt, Timothy." Cabot turned his attention to his drawing, rendering a few quick flourishes to form the ship's railing behind Wingfield. "Feeling better today, Timothy?" Like many aboard the vessel, Timothy Loudon had been weakened by scurvy.

"I dunno, some maybe."

"Have you been eating those dried peas I gave you?" Cabot was convinced he had escaped scurvy because he kept dried peas in his pocket and nibbled them throughout the day. He couldn't explain or prove why it was so, but he did know he had never felt better in his life.

"I try, but they sure taste awful."

Still at his sketching, Cabot laughed. "They can't taste worse than the maggots in the meat or the weevilly biscuits."

"You know I can't eat 'at."

Cabot nodded. The food was an abomination. Half rations might as well be no food at all. Both young men, still growing and filling out physically, were perpetually hungry. Both had lost weight. With his shirt off, Cabot's ribs showed to an alarming degree.

"Eat the peas, Timothy. It's important, I think." He heard his friend agree he would.

What had begun with Timothy helping a stranger get over seasickness and Cabot pushing Timothy away from falling rigging had by now ripened into a friendship between the scion of a peer and the son of a landless farmer. Cabot recognized that Timothy had almost no education. His interests went little beyond the soil for which he longed. Yet, his simplicity appealed to Cabot. He had not one shred of pretense. This was a sharp contrast to the preening gentlemen to whom Cabot should have been drawn by birthright. More than once, Cabot recognized the similarity between Timothy and Emily. Both were guileless and content within themselves.

For his part, Timothy was amazed at the friendship with a person he considered his better. Cabot's easy manner, his good-humored teasing of him, his many kindnesses, such as with the peas, had won him over. Still, Timothy really couldn't believe Cabot North. He was the son of an earl, no less, yet there he was dressed as a sailor, scampering aloft to help set sail, down on all fours holystoning the deck, laughing with the crew, talking to him—*to him*. Timothy really didn't understand it, but he could not refuse the affection offered by Cabot North.

His sketch of Wingfield finished, Cabot closed the cover on his book and turned to Timothy. "What you been doing today, sar?" It had become a joke between them. Cabot's mimicking of Timothy's accent had worked. The farmer stopped calling him "sar" with every breath and even discarded his obsequious demeanor. This as much as anything made their friendship possible.

Timothy smiled. "Well, sar, I been readin'."

"Reading, Timothy, *reading*. You must say your *g*'s."

It had taken Timothy over two weeks to buttress his courage to confess to Cabot he could barely write his name. He'd always wanted to learn to read and do sums. Since he had all this time on the voyage, maybe he could learn, if Cabot would teach him. Thus, Cabot became his tutor, spending part of every day working with him. Rector Hunt had a trunk of books, but mostly Timothy read the Bible. He liked it.

"What did you read today?"

"Something"—he self-consciously exaggerated the *g* sound—

"called the Sermon on the Mount."

Cabot smiled. One of the unexpected results of Timothy's improved reading was a better accent and grammar. Timothy was an eager pupil, if a little slow to learn. Cabot could not help wondering what he would do with his new knowledge in the wilderness he was heading for. "What did you like about it?"

"I liked what Jesus said about a good tree bringing forth good fruit."

Cabot laughed. "I'll bet you did." He clapped Timothy on the shoulder, feeling the dampness of his shirt on the hot afternoon. "If we don't find you some land pretty soon, I think you'll die."

The yellow smile split his crag of a face. "I've an idea I will, too. When do we get there, Cabot?"

"Virginia? Only God himself knows if we'll ever get there. But the sailing master tells me we should raise the West Indies almost anytime." He shoved Timothy ahead. "Well, sar, shall we get at those lessons now?"

They headed aft and sat on the deck, backs to the rail. Timothy produced his Bible and began to read aloud. Cabot listened attentively for a while, making a few corrections in pronunciation, then under the drone of Timothy's halting reading, his mind began to wander. What was Emily doing now? Could she be sitting quietly someplace reading her Bible? It pleased him to think so.

Emily, dear Emily. He still loved her, more than ever, yet for the most part he had stopped moping over her. Oh, at night in his hammock, he'd think of her. He'd walked beside the River Ryton, her breast pressed against his arm, countless times, and he remembered sweet, aching kisses without number. But much of the time he was able to thrust her from his mind. At least his wanting, his worry about her waiting till he returned no longer kept him from enjoying this voyage, the adventure, the knowledge he was gaining of the sea, the manhood he felt burgeoning within himself.

Strangely, Cabot did not concern himself with his father's threat to arrange his marriage. As the sixth son and with his suspect lineage, no father would invest in much of a dowry. Cabot knew he could probably refuse such a marriage. But could he throw everything away to marry the daughter of a landless farmer who was a Puritan to boot? It would hurt his father so. Might even kill him.

He suddenly realized Timothy had stopped reading. "I'm sorry. I was woolgathering, I'm afraid."

Timothy laughed. "I don' see no sheep 'round here, sar."

"And don't you wish you did? Woolgathering means I was thinking of something else."

"I already knew that." He looked up at the full sails. "At the present rate, you'll get back to yer Emily 'fore you know it."

Cabot hadn't intended to tell anyone about Emily, but in the closeness of the ship, he had confessed his love to Timothy and his worry about losing her. "I do hope so, my mind-reading friend." He laughed. "And that word you have your finger under is *centurion*. That's what Roman soldiers were called. They commanded a hundred men."

After that Cabot gave himself wholly to Timothy's lessons, so much so he was shocked by the cry from the crow's nest: "Land ho!"

To a first-time sailor long at sea no words were ever so thrilling. Cabot and Timothy jumped to their feet to peer over the water, as everyone aboard the crowded ship rushed on deck to study the horizon with haunted, eager eyes. There was nothing to see at first, then off to port, where Cabot and Timothy stood pressed against the rail, a mountainous green isle began to rise from the water, welcomed by cheers from those on deck.

Cabot did not raise his voice, but stared at the island through watery eyes, his throat aching. Why did he want to cry at the sight of land? But the feeling lasted only a moment, and then he surrendered to the excitement around him, shaking hands, even embracing a couple of men. Then he remembered Timothy and turned back to him. There was an expression of pure joy on the rocklike face, and tears were streaming down his cheeks as he stared at the verdant isle.

"There's your land, Tim."

"Yes, sar." The voice was choked. "Mighty purty it is. Is it Virginny?"

"I think it's the West Indies."

"No matter. I can tell the soil is good."

Over an hour passed as the *Sarah Constant*, under reduced sail, approached the isle, which Cabot learned was called Dominica. The Reverend Hunt called for quiet and led the passengers and crew in an extended prayer of thanksgiving to the Almighty for leading them across the trackless seas to a safe haven. When it ended, Second Mate Perth led cheers for Captain Newport. Cabot knew enough about navigation to realize what a remarkable feat Newport and Sailing Master Adams had performed. These seas were all but uncharted, seldom visited by English ships. To make landfall, while keeping three vessels together, was no small accomplishment. Cabot's pride in his captain approached adulation.

"Smell it, Cabot, smell the land."

Cabot smiled. "Yes, Timothy, I smell it." And he did, for sweet, pungent odors wafted toward him. It was heavenly.

The three ships had hardly dropped anchor when dozens of canoes raced toward them. For a few minutes there was alarm they were under attack by savages. Then they saw that the natives brought food—pineapples, oranges, small pigs, great quantities of vegetables. Silence swept the deck as the half-starved men stared in wonder at the laden canoes. Their mouths filled with saliva, then with sound, as cheering broke out to exceed even that when they first sighted land.

To his shame, Cabot saw, not the food, but the people in the canoes. In London he had seen drawings of the naked savages of America, but they had all been of men wearing loincloths. Somehow it never occurred to him the women would be naked, too. So, as he stared down at the natives below, he was severely unsettled. He had never seen a naked woman before, and the sight of bare breasts shortened his breath and made his heart pound. Emily must look like that, and memory of her sweetness and softness as he held her in his arms brought the familiar ache to his loins. At once he railed at himself. These were savages, heathen women. To compare Emily to them was unthinkable. Yet, when the bartering was done and the natives carried the food on board, he could only stare in fascination at bare breasts and buttocks, lean, strong limbs and brownish copper skin. Yes, he could see why they were called "red men." How beautiful they were, so healthy and happy.

"Sappose they'se naked like 'at in Virginny?"

Cabot avoided looking at his friend, fearful his inner thoughts might be read. "I imagine so, Timothy."

The flotilla first sighted land on March 24, 1607. For the next three weeks Captain Newport toured the islands. They stopped at Guadeloupe, where men found a bath so hot they could boil pork in it as easily as over a fire. On the isle of Mona, they found bushes laden with birds, and in three or four hours they snatched up two hogsheads full of them. They also found a great store of eggs, which they carried aboard ship. At Nevis and at the Virgin Islands they feasted daily on tortoise, pelican, parrot, and fish. It was three weeks of paradise for Cabot, Timothy, and the others, filling their bellies, recovering from scurvy and dysentery, and regaining their strength on the lovely islands.

On the tenth of April, Captain Newport steered the *Sarah Constant* through Mona Passage and headed northwest for what he hoped was Virginia. He aimed to raise a large inland body of water known as the Chesapeake Bay. He had seen maps that showed the North American continent narrowing above Mexico as it did below at the Isthmus of Panama. Newport had orders to explore the Chesapeake in hopes one of its wide rivers provided a passage to the Pacific.

Cabot learned from Sailing Master Adams that Captain Newport reckoned the passage to the Chesapeake and Virginia would take seven days. The seventh day came and went without sighting land. The eighth came and went, the ninth, the tenth. Apprehension mounted. They were lost. Virginia could not be found. On the afternoon of the eleventh day, the captains met aboard the flagship. Captain Ratcliffe of the pinnace *Discovery* urged a return to England. If they wandered in these waters too long, the food and water taken aboard in the West Indies would be used up and none of them would ever return. Newport was unwilling to give up after such a long, costly voyage. They would continue to search awhile longer.

About five o'clock that afternoon a savage squall bore down on them, and the ships had no choice but to hull down and ride out the wind. For the next four days, Newport was truly lost. He had no idea where the wind had blown them. He doubled the lookouts aloft, while a hundred pairs of eyes scanned the horizon from deck level. Newport sounded repeatedly, but could find no bottom. For Cabot and eager Timothy, it was an exasperating time, to be so near, yet verging each day on turning around to sail for England.

At four o'clock on the morning of the twenty-sixth of April, Cabot was awakened from his slumber by two words: "Land ho!"

FOUR

An Unfortunate Choice

IN THE EARLY dawn, Cabot could see only the outline of a headland, but as the sun rose, he saw that the three ships were passing between a pair of majestic capes to enter an immensely beautiful inland body of water. On the third day they would erect a cross on the southern headland and name it Cape Henry, after the king's eldest son. The northern point was dubbed Cape Charles after his second son, the future, tragic king.

On this April morning, quiet came over the colonists and crew who crowded the decks of the ships. They believed they were looking at land no European had seen before, primeval, virgin, possessed of a native majesty. The flower-scented odors that came from the land devastated them, and the pious among them felt they were viewing the Garden of Eden.

Cabot turned to look at Timothy. His eyes were bright with wonder, his mouth open in awe. "Well, my friend?"

Timothy could not speak for a time; then he found words. "Is it really Virginny?"

"Yes, sar, that's Virginia."

Again the farmer's eyes feasted on the shore. "My *God*, Cabot. Such a *land*." His voice was husky, strangely full of passion. "A *mighty* land. It makes a man feel small."

Cabot nodded. "That it does."

After anchoring, about thirty men, led by Captain Newport, headed for the southern cape in long boats. Cabot was among them. They reached a place of peerless beauty. Sir George Percy, who was keeping a journal, wrote he was "ravished at the first sight" of the land and the "fair meadows and goodly tall trees." Yes, the trees, reaching for the sky, so huge at the base a grown man could not reach his arms halfway around them, cypresses growing to the water's edge, beech, cedar, the fragrant sassafras, oak, the native live oak, a millennium old and still growing. The immense trees shielded the sun and prevented undergrowth. Cabot heard Percy say, "Why, the king's carriage could be driven among those trees with ease."

There were fields of wildflowers, filling the air with sensual scents, and the vines! Honeysuckle, wisteria, and grape festooned the trees, and at their base some of the vines were thicker than a man's thigh. As they marched inland, they saw cascading water and sparkling streams. They found fruits, many of them ripe for the plucking. And when they came upon a patch of wild strawberries, many fell to their knees to gorge themselves. "Why, they're four times bigger than those grown in England," Percy said.

Sketching as fast as he could, trying to remember everything to finish his drawings later, Cabot was conscious of the beauty of the place. Beneath the trees he felt insignificant, and he had a sense of God's majesty. Yet, he was not without misgivings. This place, however wondrous, was a true wilderness. Were civilized men, accustomed to creature comforts, to make a home here? He couldn't escape a thought: this was God's land, made at Creation. What were mortals doing here? They should tread carefully, lest this be an unforgiving land.

The landing party scouted the area, gathering fruits to carry back aboard. Late in the afternoon, as they prepared to enter the boats, Cabot hung back, working at a last sketch, a woodsy scene with wildflowers and high grass. His eye detected movement. There it was a second time. His first thought was that it was an animal, and he looked eagerly for it. Then there were many movements, bronzed men, Indians, creeping toward them on all fours, spears in hand, bows clamped in their mouths.

As they leaped to their feet screaming, Cabot stared in fascination. They were naked except for loincloths. The sides of their heads were shaved, with the remaining hair worn long and braided down their backs. They wore feathers and many beads—some who saw them would insist they were pearls— and their bodies were tattooed and painted garish colors.

Cabot's artistic impressions were lost in a flight of spears and a hail of arrows. Off to his right a sailor screamed and fell, a pair of arrows protruding from his body. Captain Gabriel Archer, one of the leaders, screamed, hit in both hands. Cabot knew they were under attack, that there was danger and that it was a first for him, yet he was not afraid. He didn't hide, run, or even duck, but just stood there, vaguely conscious of a feeling of utter calmness.

It lasted only a moment. A soldier stood beside him, seemingly transfixed. Cabot took his weapon from him, raised it, aimed at a savage. There really was no hesitation, but at the last moment, he raised the musket, firing into the air.

"That's it, men. Show 'em our lead." It was the voice of Newport. At once, flintlocks belched smoke and fire, the sounds reverberating through the trees. Birds took flight in flocks. The Indians stood transfixed a moment, then began to run, screaming in fright. A few more shots were fired after them, but Newport quickly ordered the men to cease firing and retreat toward the boats, carrying the wounded sailor. Cabot took a last look. He could see no fallen Indians and was glad for that.

Back aboard the ships, there was much storytelling and no small amount of bragging. Cabot's conduct was noted. He laughed, saying he had been too fascinated by the Indians to be afraid. But he could not help noticing the expression on the face of Captain Smith. Still under arrest, he had not been allowed to go ashore. What was in his eyes? Envy? Determination? He was not a man to be denied danger and daring very long.

"Tell me about the land, Cabot. I'm dyin' t'know."

Cabot turned to Timothy and laughed. "I'm sure of that, my friend." For the next couple of minutes he described the trees, the fields of flowers and immense strawberries, the running streams, and he showed his unfinished sketches.

"I know it's bootiful, but the soil. Tell me 'bout the soil."

Cabot knew nothing about farming, but he remembered Timothy's earlier words. "My land-famished friend, the seeds'll prac'ly leap out o' t'ground."

That evening the whole company assembled, and the locked box with the long-awaited orders was opened. In a monotonous voice, Captain Newport read the instructions: establish a colony; deal warily with the Indians, avoiding conflict if possible and representing themselves as visitors rather than permanent settlers. Site for the settlement was to be as far up a navigable river as a bark of fifty tons could sail. This was to prevent a sea attack from the Spanish, much feared by company directors and, Cabot knew, not without reason. The Spaniards had long ago claimed this land, and the pope himself had awarded the whole New World to them.

The site was to be on well-drained ground, free of marsh and forests, with a plentiful supply of fresh water. Marshes were to be avoided for health reasons, forests because they would give cover to attacking Indians and required undue effort to clear for planting. After choosing the site, they were to build a stockade, a church, common storehouses, and houses. The structures were to be laid out around a square, with the streets level, angled to the north and south. Nothing was left to chance in London. But, my God, Cabot thought, none of these people, safely ensconced in England, had the remotest idea what this wilderness was like. It would take three men all day just to chop down one of those trees—and there were thousands of them. The final words of the orders were directly from the royal charter. The settlers would enjoy "all liberties . . . as if they had been abiding within this Our Realm of England." Cabot already knew this from his father, but he saw others nod in appreciation.

At last Captain Newport began to read the list of councilors. The three ship captains were named: Newport, Gosnold, and Ratcliffe. That made sense to Cabot, except that he assumed Newport and perhaps all three were to return to England.

"Edward Maria Wingfield."

Hardly surprising. Cabot watched the great man's face. It hardly registered reaction. The man knew when his due was coming.

"Captain John Martin."

Good. He was a veteran sailor and had been to America previously.

"Captain George Kendall."

That was a surprise. There were rumors he was a closet Catholic. Some believed he was a spy for the Spanish. How on earth could he be named?

Captain Newport stopped his reading. He seemed to stare at the page in shock. Finally he spoke, his voice a little strained. "The company has appointed only seven councilors, not thirteen. The remaining member is"—he paused for the effect he knew he would have—"Captain John Smith."

The gasp from the assembled was clearly audible. Wingfield arose, shaking visibly, his face reddening. "I never . . . It can't be."

Newport turned to him. "I assure you, Master Wingfield, that is the name so written here."

Cabot looked at Smith. The smile on his face was slight, but it conveyed inner amusement, triumph, a touch of pride.

"I will not permit it. He will be returned to England and hanged for the mutineer he is."

Wingfield's words hung heavy over the silence; then Smith's voice, acid with sarcasm, cut through it. "We are all suitably impressed with your importance, Master Wingfield, but you are not judge, jury, king—or even a director of the company that named me to the council."

Wingfield, his face the color of raw liver, turned to Smith. "You, sir, are a blackguard and no gentleman."

Cabot saw Smith's eyes go cold as he reached for his sword.

"Stop it, I say, both of you." Captain Newport's voice was sharp. He rose to his feet. "I am still in command here."

"Yes, the admiral is right. No one has been sworn into the council yet." It was the voice of Captain Archer, a barrister by training. "This is no time for quarrels among ourselves. We have not yet chosen a site."

Bartholomew Gosnold picked up the cue. "I quite agree. Choice of a site is of paramount importance. May I suggest that swearing in of the councilors be delayed until the place is chosen? Do you gentlemen agree that Captain Newport should remain in command until then?"

There were sounds of assent. Wingfield, still very puffed

up, turned away from Smith. "I do agree, of course."

Like many others, Cabot sighed with relief, yet he knew the confrontation between these two men had merely been postponed.

Below deck, the *Sarah Constant* carried a disassembled shallop, a small craft capable of carrying twenty-five men. The following day it was put together, lowered to the water, the staysail and sprit mainsail hoisted, and the explorations begun. Again, as cartographer, Cabot was taken along.

They found only shoal water at first, then farther into the bay, Newport came to the mouth of a wide and mighty river, which he named the James, after his monarch. Busy drawing shorelines, Cabot heard Newport exclaim over a point at the mouth of the river. "An excellent anchorage. We'll bring the ships here tomorrow."

"What shall we name it, Captain?" Cabot asked.

"Point Comfort, I think." He laughed. "Because it puts us in good comfort."

Cabot thought it marvelous to be an explorer and get to name things. Such was his awe of his captain, he thought the place should be named Point Newport. He wondered if any place in Virginia would be named for the man who had discovered it.

A band of five Indians was seen on shore and an alarm sounded. Newport immediately ordered the shallop headed for them. As he stepped ashore, he placed his hand over his heart in a gesture of friendship. The Indians, seeing the muskets that surrounded him, laid down their bows and returned the greeting, inviting them to their village, Kecoughtan. A feast was laid and pipes of tobacco passed, while younger Indians put on a dance. Sir George Percy would describe it in his journal as "shouting, howling and stamping against the ground, with many antic tricks and faces, making noise like so many wolves or devils."

For Cabot it was a confusing experience. Rail at himself he did, but he couldn't get over his fascination with the naked bodies. How could they not be as embarrassed as he was?

"Handsome women, aren't they, North?"

Cabot turned to Percy, at twenty-eight a far more worldly man. There was amusement in his eyes, as though he had been reading Cabot's thoughts. "They are savages, sir."

"Oh, yes, savages, but still fine specimens. Tall, slender, splendid limbs, don't you think?"

Cabot was severely embarrassed now. He only hoped he wasn't blushing.

"Simply marvelous breasts." He laughed. "I think the company will have difficulty enforcing its orders against fraternization with native women."

The conversation was insufferable to Cabot. He sought to change the subject. "I don't understand, Sir George. Two days ago they attacked us. Today they offer food and entertainment."

"Yes. I suspect our flintlocks had something to do with that."

That night Cabot showed his rough sketches to Timothy and tried to describe the Indians. He dwelled not so much on their nakedness, their feathers, and gaudily painted bodies as on their size, posture, and obvious good health. "There's a natural dignity to them, Timothy. Yet, it seems to me they must be terribly afraid. After all, this is their land. They must wonder what we're doing here. And with our costumes and weapons, we must look as strange to them as they do to us."

"Will they fight us?"

"I think they don't know what to do, welcome us or attack." He pursed his lips. "There are too many of them, Timothy. For our sake, I hope they never make up their minds."

The following day explorations of the James River began in earnest. Wingfield, Gosnold, and other members of the council joined Newport, but not Smith. Newport felt it wise to keep him separated from Wingfield. Again, Cabot went along as cartographer.

The purpose of the explorations was to choose a site for the settlement. Newport was extremely thorough in this, landing on both sides of the river, frequently marching inland for some distance to determine if Indian villages were located nearby. They saw few Indians, but several smoky fires, which Newport said warned other Indians of their presence. Cabot thought otherwise. It seemed to him the Indians were merely burning off the grass in preparation to plant. How eager poor Timothy must be to put seeds into the ground.

Each time they landed, Cabot saw gentlemen bend over to examine the ground, overturning rocks, sticking their sword points into the ground. He smiled. They actually expected to find gold nuggets lying around for the snatching. In a way he hoped they would, for that would surely determine which site was chosen. Without it, he feared no agreement would be reached. There seemed to be something wrong with every possible choice—too wooded, too inaccessible, no water. The discussions went on endlessly among the leaders. Day after day passed, and Cabot sensed Newport's growing impatience to found the colony and return to England. The voyage had taken much too long already.

At the outset, all deferred to Bartholomew Gosnold. The company orders embraced his advice on site selection. That was the trouble, Cabot realized. Gosnold could only advise— not decide. And every site he urged was criticized by one of the other council members. Gosnold quickly gave in and looked elsewhere. Cabot realized that Gosnold—a kindly, religious man, liked and respected by his peers—simply was not argumentative enough to defend his convictions. Archer tried to support him, but Archer was too pedantic and alienated the others. More than once Cabot wished Smith were there. He would have made a decision, stuck by it, and not bothered with what anyone thought.

Ultimately, the choice came down to either Archer's Hope, as it was dubbed—high ground, clear of trees, blessed with a free-flowing stream—or a low-lying peninsula sticking out into the James, which Wingfield had selected. It had almost no high ground. Indeed, it was marshy and covered with trees and weeds. There was no fresh water. To Cabot the site was an abomination, and it seemed to him Wingfield advocated it out of contrariness. He cared not about the site, but about establishing his authority over the others. His words confirmed it: "I'm sure you gentlemen will agree my site, the peninsula, is best for His Majesty's colony."

All did not agree, and Cabot knew it. He looked at Gosnold, expecting him to protest, but knew at once the kindly man was retreating into a shell, resigning himself to fate. Cabot looked to Archer, normally argumentative. But he, too, looked like a barrister who had argued his case and lost.

The silence seemed to prolong itself, and Cabot was a trifle surprised when it was broken by his own voice: "Master Wingfield, the peninsula is extremely marshy. Company orders were to avoid such terrain as unhealthful."

Wingfield looked at him as though viewing a gnat. "Young North, I didn't realize you were named a councilor."

Cabot bristled. "My father is a company director."

"Then we will hear from your father, not from you."

The words stung, but Cabot had no chance to react before Captain Newport spoke. "Let him have his say, Edward. He is young, I know. But I was not much older when I captained my first ship."

Wingfield turned a withering eye on Cabot. "Very well. Youth must be served, I suppose. What is it you wish to say?"

Cabot met the gaze squarely. "Not only is the peninsula marshy, Master Wingfield; it is also covered with trees. Great effort will be required simply to clear the land."

Wingfield's smile was pure condescension. "My dear young North, what are the houses, the fort to be built of? Wood. And wood comes from trees. A wooded site is an advantage."

"The vegetation will provide cover to attacking Indians."

Wingfield rendered an expansive gesture. "What Indians, my young friend? We have seen hardly any. There are no villages for miles."

Cabot looked around, hoping for support. He knew it was there, but no one spoke. He turned back to the pompous Wingfield. "But there is no fresh water on the peninsula."

"And what is this?" He pointed to the James River and laughed. "It looks like an ample supply to me." He made a waving gesture at Cabot, dismissing him, and turned to Newport. "Have we served youth long enough, Captain?"

"Do not scoff at him, Edward. What he says makes sense." Newport sighed and turned away. "If you will allow me a moment to consider, I will decide the site."

Grateful for Newport's support, Cabot hoped for a moment he would decide for the high ground. Yet, as he watched Newport, he knew he would not. It seemed to Cabot he could almost read his mind. His words offered no surprise. "I've heard everything you gentlemen have said. I'm convinced now there is no perfect site. I am moved by the need to get the settlement established as quickly as possible. It is now the twelfth of May. We must plant crops. If I choose Archer's Hope—and it is an excellent site, my dear Gabriel—I will have to moor my ships in the middle of the river. Many days will be lost in ferrying our supplies ashore by boat. The peninsula, on the contrary, lies in deep water. I can sail the flagship to shore and moor her to a tree trunk. Weeks of back-breaking work will be saved." He hesitated, looking at Gosnold, Archer, Cabot, an agonized expression in his eyes. "I'm sorry, gentlemen, I choose the peninsula."

Cabot saw Gosnold nod in resignation. Wingfield's smile was pure triumph. For himself, Cabot shrugged. What did it matter anyway? A site was chosen at last. Newport was right. The sooner the cargo was landed, the sooner he could return home to Emily. After all, he was not a settler, just a sailor on a sea voyage.

FIVE

Spangled Rocks

ON MAY THIRTEENTH, the three ships sailed forty miles up the James, inched toward shore, and were tied to cypresses. Everyone disembarked. Members of the council were sworn in and Wingfield elected president, with a second vote to break ties. He rendered a lengthy oration, which Cabot did not listen to. His eyes and mind were on John Smith. The other councilors, cowed by Wingfield, had refused to seat Smith, Wingfield again bringing up the silly charge of mutiny. The little captain seemed not to mind. Indeed, he seemed amused, acting for all the world as though he knew something the others didn't.

"I'm sorry, Captain. It wasn't right."

"Thank you, North, but I've lived long enough to know everything happens in its own good time."

Yes, Smith's time would come, but Cabot couldn't help wondering what folly would transpire before it did.

When Timothy stepped ashore, Cabot saw him kneel. Who

could blame him? The farmer had been cooped up aboard ship for so long. Then Cabot realized he was not kneeling in gratitude. He was examining the soil, lifting a handful, crumbling it within his fingers.

"What do you think, Timothy?"

There was no reply. Timothy walked inland, kneeling every few steps. Cabot watched and followed. This colony would have to grow its own food. Why hadn't the leaders consulted a farmer like Timothy before choosing a site? Timothy's perusal continued until he reached higher ground. He paused, repeatedly sifting the soil.

"Well?"

At last Timothy stood up and looked at him. His pensive expression gave way to a yellow smile. "This is good soil. I will plant here."

Cabot laughed. "Thank God! You had me scared to death."

"But there are so many trees. It will take time to clear the land."

"I'm sure you'll find a way, my friend."

But it was not at all easy. After the stores were taken ashore, tents made of sail were erected, which Cabot assumed was to be temporary shelter. Then Wingfield, now in command, even over Newport, issued orders that Cabot viewed as nonsensical at best and at worst, lethal. Then men were divided and put to work at two tasks. Cedar trees were to be felled, then awled into clapboard for siding and wainscoting. This was to be taken back to England, along with a supply of sassafras roots. Clearly, Wingfield's main concern—Newport's, too—was not the survival of the colony but impressing the company directors back in London. Cedar clapboard and sassafras roots would be a pitiful return on the massive company investment, but it would persuade directors of the industry of Wingfield and Newport.

The second task was to erect a fort. It was to be triangular with a fortified crescent at each point. The storehouse was to be in the center. This made sense, except that Wingfield ordered the fort built of daub and wattle. Smith, who considered himself a military expert, argued vociferously for a palisaded fort of logs. Cabot was so persuaded by Smith that he also spoke up. "Master Wingfield, I thought you chose this site because it had plentiful wood for a fort and housing." It was to no avail.

Wingfield cast a haughty gaze on both men, announced he was in command and giving orders, then stalked away.

In truth, with first priority given to the preparation of cedar clapboard, there were not enough men left to build more than the flimsiest of forts. There would have been enough hands, except that the thirty-six gentlemen contributed nothing. They were content to languish under the sail tents or lie in the shade, bestirring themselves only to "supervise" the laborers or to hunt for gold, which they were certain was there. It maddened Cabot that Wingfield did not force the gentlemen to work. He seemed content to have exported the English caste system to Virginia intact.

There were two notable exceptions to the gentlemanly idleness. One was Cabot North. He couldn't stand around sketching while Timothy Loudon worked. So the very first day he picked up an ax. His hands blistered and bled, and for a couple of days his muscles were so sore he wondered if he would ever move again. But there was something he loved about that ax handle, the swinging of it, sweat lathering his body. It was as though with each blow strength was being driven into his body. He may have been a "sickly" child, but he was making up for it now.

The other exception was John Smith. He toiled as hard as any man, which did not go unnoticed by his co-workers. Cabot mentioned it to him. "The men appreciate your working beside them, Captain."

Smith completed the swing of his ax, then leaned on it a moment. "One leads by example. Never ask a man to do what you are unwilling to do yourself."

Cabot smiled. "Your wisdom does not seem to have rubbed off on our other gentlemen."

"Yes, and it will be the death of us, I fear."

"Perhaps they'll be lucky and find gold."

Smith picked up his ax and began the backswing. "I wonder how digestible gold will be come winter." The blow he struck the tree was particularly savage.

There was the problem. Wingfield acted as though the ship's stores would last forever and gave no priority to planting crops. None would have been sown except for Timothy Loudon. After a full day at assigned tasks, he worked till dark to clear the land and plant some seeds. Cabot, Smith, a few others worked with him, but it was a laborious task performed by tired men. Repeatedly, Cabot railed at Wingfield. The high ground at Archer's Hope had cleared land. Crops would already be planted and growing there. This site was a terrible mistake. Even if Timothy's crops were bountiful, there would not be nearly enough to feed the colony.

On the fourth day ashore, the chief of the Paspahegh tribe, whose land the English now knew they inhabited, showed up at the encampment accompanied by a hundred or so armed braves. Cabot recognized the tenseness of the situation, but apparently the chief—the English called him a *werowance*— came in peace, bearing venison and other food for a feast. Captain Newport, rendering his sign of peace, presented the chief with some brightly colored beads and a hatchet, which seemed to please him. Cabot, growing a little more used to the Indians by now, thought the situation was going to go smoothly.

It was not to be. A brave, seeing another hatchet lying on the ground, sought to make himself a present of it. A fellow, whom Cabot knew as Tenpenny, lunged at the Indian. Tenpenny was a head shorter, but he was also Cockney. "Give back me 'atchet, you bloody thief." Other Indians ran up, fully prepared to beat Tenpenny's brains out. Instantly, muskets were raised, and Cabot thought a skirmish was about to begin. But the chief raised his hand and spoke sharply. The Indians, obviously fearing the colonists' firepower, retreated. But it seemed to Cabot they did so sullenly. He was not the only one to think the whole incident unfortunate and unnecessary. Tenpenny argued loudly that it was his hatchet, but was rebuked in any event.

On the morning of the twenty-first, Newport set sail in the shallop with twenty-five men to carry out his orders to explore the James. Percy went along, as did Cabot. Smith was also invited, Newport still believing it wise to keep him away from Wingfield.

Cabot truly believed the voyage should have been postponed until work was finished at Jamestown, but he gave himself to what was an exciting and eventful trip. They encountered many Indians upriver who were friendly and helpful. On the second day, they met eight natives in a canoe. One of them was extraordinarily handsome and intelligent. He understood their signs, and quickly learned a few English words. His name, he said, was Navirans. When he saw Cabot feverishly sketching him, he borrowed the pad and drew a map of the river. Thereafter, he became their protector, racing ahead in his canoe to prepare for their peaceful reception.

Thus, their journey upriver became something of a triumphal tour, with many greetings from Indians, many feasts. Their gifts of penny knives, shears, bells, and beads were well received. Navirans took them to a village to meet his brother-in-law, Chief Arahatec. When they arrived at the next village, there was Arahatec again, ready to receive more gifts. This was a particularly attractive village, high on a hill, separated from the river by fields of corn, beans, peas, pumpkins, and tobacco. Cabot wanted to be sure to tell Timothy. In proper hands, this land was surely productive.

Cabot could not help noticing how adroitly Smith handled himself with the Indians, quickly learning a few words of their tongue and striking a demeanor of friendship.

"You get along with the Indians very well, Captain."

Smith smiled. "North, they are not much different from the Turks and other heathen. You must be friendly, accepting their customs. But you must also be firm, never letting them know you are afraid." He scowled. "Captain Newport is being much too generous with his gifts. I fear it will make future trade with them difficult—immeasurably so. We give away what should be bartered for."

The voyage ended at a falls in the river. Newport wanted to march several days inland to see where the river went. If it was the passage across the "isthmus" to the South Sea, it would give him immortality as an explorer. But Navirans discouraged the trek, indicated the Indians inland were unfriendly. Newport reluctantly turned back; it was better to please the Indians for now rather than satisfy his own curiosity and that of the company directors. In truth, he was greatly excited by what he had discovered. Beyond the falls he saw a gravelly hillside laced with spangled rocks. Gold! What a sensation it would cause in London when he made his report. On one of the islands below the falls, Newport erected a small cross, claiming the land in the king's name, gold and all. Navirans was curious about the symbol. Newport told him the arms of the cross signified himself and Arahatec bound in friendship. Cabot thought it a blasphemous thing to say. He muttered as much to Smith. "But I suppose the captain felt the need to make friends with this great chief."

"I think he is a chief, North, but not a great chief. I do not understand much of their language as yet, but I keep hearing the word *Powhatan*. I do not know if that is the name of a man or his title. But he apparently is the king, the great ruler of all these lands. I must arrange to meet him."

"Does Captain Newport know?"

Smith smiled. "Right now Captain Newport knows only that he has found gold."

Indeed, Newport was in an expansive mood as they headed down river. When they were welcomed at still another village, Newport was generous with his gifts, which led to a particularly fine feast and many pipes of tobacco. The admiral decided to enjoy the hospitality for the night. It was a village with many comely maidens and some of the men, Smith and Percy among them, disappeared from time to time. Cabot was certain it meant nothing. Company orders were company orders, and these were heathen savages.

Cabot told himself he was now accustomed to the nakedness of the savages. He was bothered only by the attention that attended him in this village. His sketching fascinated the Indians, and also, strangely, his blue eyes. There were other men with blue eyes in the party, but none perhaps were as vivid as his. The natives stared at him, and at one point a group of women, ranging in age from young girls to old hags, gathered about him, staring, chattering, giggling, pointing at his eyes. A few braver ones even touched his face. Soon they took his arm and tried to drag him away. He turned and appealed for help to Percy.

He laughed. "My dear North, just remember the company policy."

Percy's laughter ringing after him, Cabot was first dragged then led to a dwelling perhaps a hundred yards off to his left. The Indian buildings, called "long houses" by the English, were made of hides stretched over a framework of poles, sloped on the roof to permit the rain to run off, and open at an end or side to provide access. The women stopped before a small one of these. Still holding his arms, they began to call a word that sounded to him like *Awotaka*.

In a moment a girl appeared, a maiden obviously, for she wore her hair short on the sides, then plaited down her back. The married women let their hair grow naturally long. At her waist was tied an apron of soft buckskin, fringed at top and bottom. This connoted she was of an age to marry, for children were entirely naked except for a sash at their waist.

Despite his discomfort at his situation, Cabot gasped when he saw the girl. She was like no Indian he had seen. Her skin was not reddish brown, but fairer, a light, golden tan. Her hair was not black or dark brown, but auburn, and her eyes not dark, but blue, as blue as his own. He could only gape at her, dimly aware that she was staring at him, eyes wide, full mouth slightly open. Then he was conscious of heightened chatter and much pointing at his eyes.

"Who are you?" His voice sounded strangely husky. Then he realized no one could understand him. He pointed to himself and said, "Cabot North."

When he pointed to her, she did not reply, but several of the women cried, "Awotaka, Awotaka."

That must be her name. "Where do you come from?" He tried to gesture but helplessly realized he knew no signs to ask the question. She raised her hand and touched his cheek under his eye, then her own. "Yes, we both have blue eyes."

"Well, well, young North. We have come to rescue you." He turned to see Percy and Smith approaching him, both greatly amused. "Company policy, you know." When he turned back to Awotaka, she was gone, back into the hut. He stood there a moment, flustered, confused, then walked over to his compatriots.

"Did you see that girl, fair skin, reddish hair, blue eyes?"

"What of it, my friend?"

"But, Sir George, I've never seen an Indian like that."

"Who said all Indians have to look alike?"

Cabot turned to Smith. "Captain, you don't suppose—you know, the colonists lost at Roanoke?"

Smith clapped him on the shoulder. "That was way south of here and twenty years ago. Percy is right. No reason why an Indian can't have blue eyes. Probably lots of them do."

Cabot sighed. "Doubtless you're right."

He could not put the blue-eyed girl out of his mind, however. The vision of her slender, golden body haunted him. There was something in her eyes, a searching out, a beckoning, that affected him. There had been a moment, so fleeting, as she touched his face, when he felt the two of them were alone in the universe, knowing only each other. He had felt it once before—with Emily.

The party of exploration returned to Jamestown on the twenty-seventh to distressing news. The day before several hundred Indians had attacked the fort, breaking down part of the exterior, shooting arrows through the sail tents. With most of their muskets still unpacked, the colonists were hard-pressed to defend themselves. A boy was killed, a man mortally wounded. Fourteen others were hurt, including four members of the council. An arrow had pierced Wingfield's beard, but he was unhurt. The Indians did not disperse until ordnance from the *Sarah Constant* was fired.

The Indian attack brought a sharp change in priorities. Defense became paramount, and all other work, including housing and planting crops, was set aside. Timothy was aghast. "Don't they know how much we'll need this food?"

Cabot was sympathetic to his friend, but he said, "I guess they figure dead men don't eat."

Wingfield now agreed, however reluctantly, to palisade the fort, as he should have in the first place. At the same time he set the men to marching under the watchful eyes of the gentlemen, who drilled them in the use of weapons. Cabot dutifully shouldered his flintlock and practiced soldiering. No one knew when another Indian attack would come. There could be no doubt simple survival might hinge on self-defense. In truth, he enjoyed the drilling as a new experience—that and teasing Timothy, who was a clumsy soldier at best. His heart just wasn't in it. Crops were everything to him. And, despite his labor on the fort and drill field, he managed to clear and plant more land.

Finally, enough of the fort was finished for cannon to be brought from the ships and mounted in the fort—more exhausting labor.

Captain Newport was clearly chafing to leave. He was long overdue on his return, and the company directors must be eager for a report. He counted on his having sighted gold to offset his miserable cargo. Besides, he carried a quantity of ore, which Captain Martin assured him contained gold.

A first order of business was to settle the bickering among the council members. Newport, with the aid of Rector Hunt, sought to patch up the quarrel between Wingfield and Smith. The president, clearly faced with the popularity of Smith among the colonists, abandoned his mutiny charge, and on June tenth, Captain Smith was at last sworn in as a member of the council. Cabot heard the words of harmony, but he didn't believe a word of it. Wingfield's druthers were to hang Smith, either in Jamestown or in London.

Cabot undertook the preparations for their leaving with mixed feelings. He was eager to be gone from this place and return to Emily. In recent days, he had made up his mind what he must do. He had not tried hard enough to persuade Emily to marry him and live at Graymere. Her fears were groundless. She was merely young, unsure of herself. Once she met his father, gave him a little time to accept her, they would become fond of each other. And she already loved Elizabeth as a sister. Yes, that is what he would do the instant he set foot in England. Emily would listen to reason.

Cabot was saddened to leave Timothy Loudon. He had grown extremely fond of this young farmer, and it appalled him to think of his remaining here. Jamestown was the puniest of settlements in an apparently endless wilderness inhabited by obviously hostile natives. There were now only one hundred three settlers, several of them wounded. Even palisaded, the fort looked as if it could not withstand a single determined charge. And the stores that Newport piled ashore would not begin to get these men through the summer, let alone the winter. The voyage had taken too long. Too much food had been consumed. But he heard Newport tell Wingfield and the council that there was plenty of fish and game, fruits and wild berries. Beside, the corn and barley and other crops were already up and doing well. "Why, you'll eat better than we will aboard ship," Newport said.

"Are you determined to stay?" It was the twenty-first of

June, the afternoon before they were to sail. Cabot was standing in the cornfield with Timothy, determined to make one final attempt to persuade his friend to leave with him.

"I signed up, Cabot. I couldn't leave if I wanted to."

"I could persuade Captain Newport to take you. The crew is short anyway. I know I could."

Timothy showed his yellow smile. "I'm no sailor; you know that. I'm a farmer. I belong here."

"But Tim, it's a wilderness."

"'Tis good land, Cabot, some o' the best I ever see. And there's plenty o' it fer everyone."

Cabot thought about correcting his grammar, but his anguish over the parting kept him from it. "Timothy, you have to know none of this land is yours. It belongs to the company. They'll never let you own any."

"Never's a long time. I'll get m'share." He saw Cabot shake his head and look down at his feet in frustration. "You jus' go on back t'England, sar. Marry 'at purty gal o' yours, and settle down to a good life. I'll be fine 'ere."

Struggling with his emotions, Cabot raised his head. "Oh, Timothy, I wish—"

"I got m'wish, Cabot. I'm where I wan' to be, where I was meant to be." He looked off into the distance, down his row of young corn. "There's goin' to be a great lan' 'ere someday, Cabot. I feel it. I wanna be part o' it. Try to unnerstan'."

Cabot couldn't think of what to say, but he didn't get a chance to speak, anyway. Bucks, the cabin boy, ran up telling him Captain Newport wanted to see him in his cabin at once.

"As you know, Master North, I'm taking the *Goodspeed* with me tomorrow. I'm leaving the pinnace and the shallop behind for exploratory purposes"—he cleared his throat—"and emergency use."

"Yes, sir." Cabot had been told to be at ease, but he still stood at attention before the captain. He had spent a lot of time with Newport, but that didn't make him comfortable with him.

"I'm proud of you, Mr. North. You've become an adept sailor." He smiled. "I hardly thought you would when this voyage began."

"I didn't either, sir." He managed a weak smile.

"Life is full of surprises." Newport's smile faded, and he

averted his eyes. He seemed nervous. "You will be needed to help man the pinnace."

Awareness came slowly to Cabot, like dawn on a dark night. "You mean . . . you mean . . . *stay here?*"

"Yes."

Cabot gasped.

"This is where you're needed, Mr. North."

Cabot found his voice in a rush. "But you *can't*. I came only for the *voyage.*"

"I'm sorry. The decision is made."

"But you *can't*. My father will—"

"Lord North advised me to do this, if I thought it wise."

"My *father?*"

"I will be pleased to report to him what a fine young man you have become and what a valuable member of this expedition you are."

Cabot felt himself withering. His voice choking, he said, "I have to get home. I must. It's terribly important. You don't know what you're doing."

His pleading was to no avail.

SIX

A Face in the Forest

AS CABOT NORTH stood on the shore at Jamestown, watching the *Sarah Constant* and *Goodspeed* raise sail and head downriver to the Chesapeake and home, part of him died. He could not articulate what part of him was lost, but youth, hope, optimism seemed to drain from him, replaced by desolation.

He was emotionally numb. He had already expended his anger, frustration, and outrage toward his father and the captain he had revered, even God. The ships carried no letters from him. In the short time allotted him, he had filled pages with venomous words to his father, then had torn them up. His pride, his horror of self-pity, and his fear of being anything less than manly kept him from expressing his feelings. In the end, he decided saying nothing would be most effective. Lord Alfred North would be left to suffer his own guilt. Nor was he able to write to Emily Fletcher and for the same reasons. His words were so self-serving. Begging her to wait for him hardly sounded masculine. Besides, had he any right to ask? Very soon, he would castigate himself for not sending some word of explanation, showing he cared and still loved her, but the chance for that had floated downriver.

Most of the men on shore stared silently after the vessels, some long after there was anything to see. Cabot did not. To see the departing ships brought him unutterable pain, and he turned away to look at the "settlement." He saw it with terrible clarity, a minuscule "fort" mounting a few cannon. There were no houses, only a handful of canvas tents and lean-tos, most of them rotting and rent with arrow holes. The pathetic hoard of barrels and crates held food for only thirteen weeks—and Cabot knew that estimate was probably unbridled optimism. Jamestown was the tiniest toehold on an unknown continent, a flake of civilization in a wilderness. Did not his father, the king, any of the great lords in London remember what happened to a similar colony at Roanoke? The Lost Colony they called it. What did they think would happen to this one? A handful of men, a few weapons, no shelter, a paltry supply of rotting food. And beyond those trees were hostile Indians, unknown thousands of them. In his clarity of vision, Cabot saw for the first time the true situation. This land belonged to the Indians. The white men, himself included, were invaders, bringing fire and death, stealing what was not theirs. Cabot felt drenched in the folly of it all. It was stupid, so utterly meaningless. And he was part of it. He was here, on this shore, participating in— his inward smile was bitter, sarcastic—this great adventure for the glory of king, God, and country.

He sensed Timothy's presence at his side and turned to him. In his eyes were compassion, instinctive understanding. In silence, his friend was reaching out to him. Cabot nodded his appreciation.

"Captain Newport said he would be back in twenny weeks. 'Tis not s'long."

Cabot merely looked at him. Such optimism. Twenty weeks to cross the Atlantic, load stores, and return was an absurdity. One middling gale and the *Sarah Constant* would sail the ocean bottom. But he said none of it.

"It'll be all right, Cabot. You'll see."

Cabot stared at him a long moment. "Yes, you're right in that." He looked away, toward the fort. "I will survive, Timothy." There was a cold, metallic sound of commitment to his voice. "We both will survive. I will not die here—nor will I let you."

The words were easily uttered. Their promise was a different matter, for as June gave way to July, a terrible pall fell over the camp. It was as though the men reacted with despondency to the ship's leaving. Few seemed capable of any action, contenting themselves to lie in their rotting tents or recline under a shade tree, letting day after lazy day pass without lifting a finger to perform any act except eating and obeying the commands of nature. It may have been the humid heat that fell over the colony like a shroud. Even the usually energetic John Smith seemed lethargic; for life in cool, rainy England had not prepared these men for ninety-degree days and oppressive humidity. The men suffered in their hose, breeches, and heavy doublets, but a proper gentleman would wear nothing else. So, they sweated and panted. Even the slightest exertion exhausted their energy, and they learned to move as little as possible. Days passed into weeks and nothing was done. No houses were built, no streets laid out as commanded in London. Only Timothy and a few others, determined to cultivate this land, accomplished anything. And Cabot, working beside Timothy, Tenpenny, and a couple of others, taught them the advantages of his sailor's garb, stripping to the waist to let heat escape.

But that left them prey to mosquitoes and other stinging insects that rose in clouds from the marshes. Mosquitoes were not unknown in England, but the cool weather kept them suppressed. In Virginia, on this isle barely above sea level, the infestations were a torment, and the Englishmen spent much of their energy swatting, scratching, and cursing.

Then there was the water. In April and May, the James and

its tributaries had run full, and the water was reasonably clear. Under the heat of July, the water level dropped, and the riverbanks became vile-smelling mud flats. The water they consumed was brackish, dark in color, and swarming with creatures.

All of these conditions ranked as inconveniences to Cabot North, for his determination to survive helped him overcome the heat, fatigue, bad food, and brackish water. What rankled him was that so few cared. The gentlemen considered labor beneath them. If they did anything, it was to engage in a bit of desultory mining for gold. The council members were next to useless, busying themselves as near as Cabot could see with quarrels and conspiracies to create more quarrels. Wingfield was a pompous, overbearing ass, much impressed with his leadership role, insolent, arrogant and utterly class conscious. John Smith, still suspect among the other councilors, devoted himself to improving the fort and drilling the "troops." Captain Martin surrendered to an apparently permanent illness. Kendall and Ratcliffe gave themselves wholly to plots against Wingfield. Only Bartholomew Gosnold seemed aware of the problems of survival, and it was he to whom Cabot spoke.

"Sir, I think the men have the shipboard illness, the scurvy, from eating the ship's stores." He saw Gosnold nod in acquiescence. "I was thinking, sir, maybe if greater effort were made to fish and hunt, find fresh fruit, everyone would feel stronger."

The veteran explorer sighed. "You may be right, Mr. North, but . . ." He shrugged. "I suspect it is also the foul water, the insects rising from the marsh. This is bad land. I warned against it."

"I know, sir, and you were right."

Gosnold's smile was wan. "But it is too late now, isn't it?"

"Is there nothing to be done, sir?"

Again the shrug. "Hope for cooler weather. Everyone may snap out of it then."

As Gosnold turned to amble away, Cabot could only stare in disbelief. Hope for cooler weather? Did these madmen think they were in England?

Cabot believed he was right about the scurvy no matter what anyone said. He stole a few extra peas when he could, thus his own energy remained at a fairly normal level. He helped Timothy with his crops. These unfortunately seemed afflicted with the same malady as the settlers. Timothy suffered as he watched his peas wilt and shrivel in the heat. His corn, which had sprouted so well, tasseled before it was two feet tall and produced minuscule ears or none at all. The cabbages bolted to seed when the heads were the size of cricket balls. The barley was clearly going to be a disaster.

"I don't unnerstan' it, Cabot. I simply don't unnerstan'."

It was a daily lament, but Cabot felt powerless to ease his friend's frustration. He suggested more water, and the two men began a daily regimen of carrying water from the river. It disappeared into the ground, but did not aid the plants.

"Timothy, I'm no farmer, but could it be the seeds?" He saw Tim nod. "England is cooler. English plants may not like hot weather."

"I've wondered, too."

"Perhaps if you steal some Indian corn and—"

"It's too late for this season, Cabot. But next year I'll grow crops; you'll see."

Cabot smiled. "You can't keep a good farmer down."

Despite his frustration, Timothy managed a smile, too. "No, sar. Le's keep carryin' water, try to save what we can."

Cabot carried water; he hoed corn, stood guard, did everything required of him and more, for he was determined somehow to survive. His labors were also a device to ward off the realization that he had lost Emily. *A little time.* This was no small amount, but a great, endless reach of time. Love was gone, happiness denied him.

As the oppressive July days ground on, his mind again and again returned to the golden Indian girl, her smooth skin, lithe body, the beckoning in her eyes. Carrying water, hoeing corn, heat suffusing his body and sweat dripping from him, dizzied, he thought of her often. He didn't understand why his mind was on her so much, except that she had become, in his erotic fantasies, the one thing he could desire in this wilderness. Sometimes it was almost as though he actually saw her, golden, shimmering in the heat rising from the soil, calling to him. There, standing alone amid the trees where the peninsula joined the mainland, so beautiful, beckoning. He had to go. He set down his water buckets and headed for the trees. Timothy was forgotten.

It had happened before. He would see her, then blink and she was gone. Once he had even moved a few steps before she disappeared. It did not happen this time. She remained standing there as he traversed the distance, closer, closer. He blinked, but she remained. She really was there, all reddish hair, blue eyes, and golden body. Soon her breasts, festooned with plum-colored nipples, leaped toward him. His pace quickened, his breath shortened, and he was aware of heat in his loins.

He stopped a few feet from her. She wore the fringed apron, a necklace of mother-of-pearl. And she was staring at him, intent on his eyes, as though the blue in them bore some message known only to her. He struggled against his disbelief. Then reality came to him. Some rational, analytical corner of his mind saw she could not possibly be an Indian, at least not all Indian. Her lips were fuller. Her face, though almond-shaped, lacked the high, pronounced cheekbones of other Indians. Again he started to ask her who she was, then realized the futility of it.

She blinked at last, then looked down shyly. She had come to see him, he was sure of that. But so far. He reckoned the distance to her village. They had traveled a whole day in the shallop to reach Jamestown. Then he remembered the map he had drawn. The river curved. If she came overland . . . Still it was a long way. "You came all this way?" His voice sounded husky to him. Then he remembered she couldn't understand him, so he pointed off to the north toward her village.

She seemed to understand, smiled and also pointed. The movement of her breast as she raised her arm stabbed at him. Then she bent, picked up a basket and turned away from him. He watched her walk through the trees. The sight made him quiver, for she was naked to the rear. Her back, waist, slender legs, and joined half-moons stupefied him. In a few steps, she stopped, turned to him, and beckoned with her eyes. He followed, although he was surprised he could walk.

She led him off the peninsula onto the mainland. Obviously, she didn't want to be near the settlement. He followed some distance behind, mesmerized by the movements of her body as she walked, her long, graceful strides, her regal bearing. Soon she followed a path through some undergrowth; then she stopped and began to pick berries into her basket. He recognized them, raspberries, a few blackberries, all of them the largest he had ever seen. But mostly he feasted his eyes on her nakedness as she bent and stooped and reached. Suddenly he was glad he wore his sailor's garb. His own nakedness must not seem strange to her.

She seemed oblivious to him at first. Then she turned to him and smiled, shyly to be sure, but with a hint of—what? Acceptance? Secret, womanly knowledge? It was a nice smile. She had good teeth.

She surprised him, taking a berry from her basket, raising it to him, inserting it between his lips. As the delicious juices filled his mouth, he saw her again smile and motion for him to pick, pointing a little farther along the path. Numbly he obeyed, struggling against his own heat and the pounding in his chest, grateful to be distracted from her. Quickly he filled both hands and turned to her. The basket was on her arm, near her waist. She turned, smiled, and he dropped the berries within. It was the closest he had come to her, mere inches away, and he could feel the heat of her, smell sweet, delicate femininity. To break the tension, he inserted a berry in her mouth. She laughed as she accepted it.

He couldn't help it. Her moving lips, reddened and wet with the juices of the fruit, were all he knew in the world. He kissed her, gently, softly, lingering only briefly, for her lips came open and he heard her gasp. There was surprise in her eyes, even bewilderment. Had she never been kissed before? Again he bent over the basket. Her mouth was drier now, hotter, and he kissed her more deeply, lingering, his lips moving hungrily as he felt the sharp, sweet stabbing in his loins.

He felt her trembling, then heard her gasp as she stepped back. She brought her fingertips to her lips. Suddenly shy, Cabot turned away, quickly filling his hands with berries. When he turned back, she remained as he had left her, open-mouthed, wide-eyed as though transfixed. He dropped the berries in the basket, then took it from her arm, spilling some of the fruit as he dropped it to the ground. He truly embraced her now, sweeping her into his arms, smothering her mouth with his, letting his passion rush through the open orifice. For an instant he saw her blue eyes, wide with wonder, startled, then her lids closed as she sagged against him, trembling. He felt drenched in sensation, her mouth, the sweet freshness and delicacy of her, the ecstatic knowledge of skin, against his chest, under his hands, shoulders, back, the sensuous slope to her waist, all soft, smooth, strangely firm under his hands, then the pillowy roundness at the far reaches of his hands, making them ache. He felt her rise to tiptoe to give him access, then push her hips against his, hard, moving. He had to hold her to stand, for he was shaking all over, his maleness, now a sword, pressed against her thighs.

Then she was gone from him, basket in hand, running swiftly along the path. He followed some distance behind, for his legs were weak and there was a roaring in his ears. He saw her around a curve up ahead, running up an incline. As he stopped to catch his breath, he saw her above him, under trees, scampering up rocks. She reached some sort of landing and turned to look at him. Her hands went behind her back, and she undid her apron, put her hands above her head, turned away, and seemed to dive. He ran after her. He struggled up the rocks, panting, to where she had been. To his left was a small waterfall, perhaps a dozen feet high. So it had not been his ears that roared. Below was a cool green pool into which she had dived. She was there now, waist deep, her skin glistening, laughing at him.

Few Elizabethans could swim. Cabot gave no thought as, in his headlong heat, he stripped off his breeches and dived in after her. The water was cool, refreshing, but he felt momentary panic until he realized he could stand up. He saw only her laughing face, glistening breasts, the hard grapes at the tips as he strode toward her. But when he approached, laughter bubbled out of her, and she swam away to the opposite bank.

The water grew deeper in midstream, and he went in over his head. Panicked, he thrashed with all his might and came to the surface. Coughing and sputtering, expending great energy, he struggled across the pool. When he could stand, she was nowhere to be seen. Then he heard her light laugh and saw her behind the waterfall, smiling, waiting for him.

In the darkness of his tent that night, he tried to feel guilty. After all, he had taken an Indian, a heathen savage. But he honestly could not. He could think only of beauty and wonder, of innocence, ecstatic pleasure and, yes, simple honesty. She took his hand and led him behind the falls into a cave, dark with a bend in it. They emerged into a small stone crypt, lit from above. There must be another entrance. He saw a bed of pine boughs. This must be a trysting place for ... He didn't care. He knew only the beauty of her glistening body, his own desire.

In his tent he trembled with remembrances, all crowding his brain, vying to be paramount in his lexicon of rapture, her willing acceptance of him, her soft mouth opening to him, the satin of her skin, wet, smooth, cool, soon hot, the firm softness of her breasts, their fruit filling his mouth, her fascination with his white skin beneath his tan, the exquisiteness of her touch, the marvel of spread thighs, of being somehow consumed within a hot cauldron, moving hips, gasps, moans, unbearable tension, cries filling each other's mouths as he erupted deep within her arched, welcoming hips. Then came other, sweeter memories, caresses, tender explorations, discoveries marveled at, a waterfall of words from their mouths, both at once, all unknown, yet somehow understood, the wonder of new arousal, less urgent now, sweet in the absence of time.

"Cabot, did you ... with her?"

He heard Timothy's whisper beside him. "Yes." There was silence for a time, filled only by the sounds of the wilderness, the hoot of an owl, the scream of a dying animal, a snore of human sleep from across the way. "It wasn't wrong, Timothy. She is so beautiful, so natural, so ... so innocent. I'm—I'm not sorry I did it." He wondered if he was trying to convince his friend or himself. No, not himself. He was already a believer.

"We're not supposed to, Cabot."

"I know." He raised himself on an elbow, looking toward where his friend lay in the darkness. "She's really not an Indian, Tim. She's fair. She has blue eyes, auburn hair."

"How can that be?"

"I don't know. I think maybe the Lost Colony. I think she's English, Tim, half at least."

"Best stay 'way from 'er, Cabot."

"I know."

He lay staring into the darkness, knowing he would not. Awotaka. Awotaka. He had said it a hundred times, the only

Indian word he knew that she could understand. Awotaka. So beautiful. He wondered how old she was. Fourteen, maybe fifteen. Same age as Emily.

SEVEN

Summer Idyll

"MR. NORTH, where did you go yesterday?"

Cabot turned to see Wingfield standing before his tent, glaring at him. He was attired in his helmet and breastplate over a doublet of richly embroidered wool, green in color. At midmorning, rivulets of sweat were streaming under his ruff. "Go, sir?"

"You heard me, Mr. North. You were gone several hours yesterday, not returning till nearly dark."

Cabot smiled. "I was picking berries, sir."

"Berries?"

Cabot's smile widened into a grin, which he hoped might conceal his inner mirth. He knew full well he could be in serious trouble for running off, and his head could roll for what he had done with Awotaka, but he didn't care. He had awakened happy for the first time since he set foot in this miserable colony. Nothing, not even Wingfield was going to ruin it. A nonsensical refrain kept running through his mind: *If you were picking berries, where are the berries you have picked?* "I thought the men might like some, sir. I'm afraid they aren't quite ripe."

It worked. Wingfield accepted the explanation, but found new disapproval. "May I point out to you, Mr. North, that Indian delegations have twice come here to inquire about our ships. Obviously they fear our cannon. I have told them they will return any day. That alone has kept them from attacking.

I doubt they will believe me much longer. I have ordered everyone to stay close to the fort."

"But the crops, sir."

"You will go no farther."

"Yes, sir." But Cabot knew he had no intention of obeying.

"Mr. North, your costume is disreputable. You might disport yourself half naked under Captain Newport's command, but you are under my authority now. You will attire yourself as a proper English gentleman. I'm sure Lord Alfred expects you, as I do, to set an example for the men."

Cabot stared at him in disbelief. "We are not in England, Master Wingfield, but in Virginia. It is much hotter here, or haven't you noticed?"

"Enough of your insolence!"

"It is not insolence, sir, but fact. We wear attire that is too warm. It oppresses the men. It causes the malaise from which all suffer. We would do well to emulate the Indians."

Wingfield sucked in his breath. "We are not savage. We are English gentlemen."

"I doubt if that fact impresses anyone here."

"Insolence! You will follow my orders."

Cabot smiled. "What I will do is report to my father just how excellently you command this colony."

When he reached the fields, Cabot wore only his breeches. He had no fear of Wingfield. The man was a fool. Three others worked beside Timothy and him. The bellicose cockney, Tenpenny, stood guard, flintlock in hand, should any Indians attack.

Cabot worked happily, telling Timothy of his asinine conversation with Wingfield. Neither young man spoke of what was utmost on his mind. For Timothy it was worry for his friend. For Cabot it was the Indian girl, what they had done. It had been his first experience and he was prey to his own memory. It was to him as though the heat of the sun burned through his flesh, striking at his loins, leaving him constantly aroused. He was filled with anticipation. Oh, it occurred to him that she might not come, that he might never see her again, but, strangely, he had no doubt of her. He could sense her presence out there in the woods even now. Early in the afternoon he saw her.

"Cabot?"

He turned to Timothy. His single word was more negative than question. "I have to, Timothy."

In his eagerness to run to her, it seemed an eternity that his friend looked at him. His eyes were questioning. It was as though he were searching Cabot for answers. Finally, he pursed his lips and nodded, then turned. "All right, chaps, let's fetch some water. You come, too, Tenpenny. You've got one free hand for a bucket." He turned back to Cabot. "This bloody hoe is dull. See if you can find the stone to sharpen it." His craggy face split into a smile.

"Thank you, Timothy."

She waited for him along the path where they had picked berries, so golden and beautiful to him, her eyes shy, pensive as she looked at him. The rise of her young breasts, the slope of her hips made him tremble.

"Awotaka, I knew you'd come. I just knew it."

She replied, unintelligible words flowing from her mouth. Neither understood the other, then both reached for other means of communication. He swept her into his arms, devouring her mouth, crushing her body against his. He was aware his passion was unbridled. He felt boyish in his eagerness, and for an instant he feared he had overwhelmed her, frightened her. No. She gave herself to him, accepting his hands upon her, even as she stroked his hot back, and leaned hard against him. When she began an involuntary movement of her hips, he was truly maddened.

When need for breath forced them apart, she smiled at him, pure sweetness, and words flew from her reddened lips, many of them. They had no meaning to him, but the passion in her eyes did. He knew she was saying something beautiful, love words, but he silenced her with his mouth. She permitted only brief interruption, turning away to speak against his cheek, softly, her breath moistening his ear as he held her, caressing her, delighting in the firm, smooth slenderness of her. Yet, it seemed to him her words, not one of them understood except his own name, were the most thrilling of all. Still chattering, smiling, she led him to the crypt, this time from above, down between some rocks lying innocently in a meadow above the falls.

There began for Cabot North an idyll. She did not come every day. Once she did not appear for three days. But it was often enough, or nearly so, a time of ecstatic happiness, a time of sun and laughter and rapture. Both were young, healthy, and vigorous, greatly enamored of new knowledge, innovative in gathering more. His passion for her was a flame that no amount of fluid would extinguish. Her touch, her nearness, even the sight of her set off conflagrations within him. He told himself, at least in the beginning, that their bodies were their only means of communication. Perhaps that truly did account for the insatiable way they were. He had known no woman other than her, yet he knew instinctively how remarkable she was. She never once opposed him. Oh, she would run from him, through the meadow, across the stream, but that was only to make it sweeter, their bodies slipping and sliding, their breath shortened from the chase as well as passion. She was the most giving, accepting person he had ever known. If she had guilt about her body, its uses, the pleasures she derived from it, she never conveyed it to him.

Yet, it was not their lovemaking that really enchanted him. She was truly a wood nymph, a joyful goddess, full of laughter and happy talk. To him, she was in perfect harmony with this wilderness. No, no longer wilderness: a forest of enchantment. They walked hand in hand or ran side by side through the trees, across meadows, falling down to roll on the grass. She loved hide-and-seek, running ahead—she really could run faster than he—waiting for him to find her, behind a tree, within a thicket. He pretended not to know where she was. Then, when he picked flowers or berries for her, she would laugh and let him come to her, sweeping her into his arms. He gave her a gift of beads, a piece of bright red cloth that delighted her. She fashioned it into a new apron and wore it only when she was with him. She presented him with a loincloth of soft buckskin, richly decorated with stitching she had done herself. When he was with her, he wore it, hiding it in the cave when he left her.

He taught her a few words of English and learned the Algonkian equivalents, parts of the body first, trees, flowers, grass, earth, sky, sun, moon, things that could be touched or pointed to. They developed a repertoire of signs, and understanding grew between them. He came to know what she wanted, when she would return, where they would meet. But expression of the abstract or intangible maddened him. He tried desperately to learn who she was and where she came from. The word *mother*—he never could get her to understand *father*—took a half-hour of frantic gesturing. She saw his frustration and laughed and kissed him, trying to make him happy. When she finally understood, she said a word he assumed was an Indian name. He gathered she knew nothing of her origins beyond the village where she lived, but he remained convinced she was half English, somehow connected to the Lost Colony. Nor was he successful in learning how she was able to leave her village, the route she took to reach him, indeed, why she came, other than what was revealed by eyes and limbs and bodies.

Without even token resistance, Cabot surrendered to his love for her, abandoning himself to happiness, the greatest in his life. Just looking at her brought him such pleasure. Her slender body, honed to health, was unfailingly beautiful to him. There was no fat on her, just long, thin muscle. Her tiny waist and flat stomach excited him, and he was fascinated by the dimple that appeared in her thigh near her groin when she walked. There seemed to him a natural grace to her every movement, her long fluid strides, the effortless way she held her shoulders back, the charming tilt of her head as she smiled and spoke to him. She did something that was consummate sweetness to him. She would touch his lips with her fingertips, her thumb beneath his chin. He understood. Of all the pleasures he brought her, his kisses meant the most. He wasn't sure, but he had an idea Indians didn't kiss.

There was a blemish on his happiness. He was putting an unbearable strain on Timothy Loudon, who had to lie and lie and lie, then tell assorted untruths to account for Cabot's absences. He knew what a hardship it was for Timothy, yet his friend never protested or scolded him, however much he disapproved. Cabot tried to help. In their tent at night, Cabot would concoct the next prevarications to be used to explain where he was. Cabot knew he was fooling no one except, he hoped, Wingfield. Twice an amused Percy covered for him. "Oh, yes, Master Wingfield, I did send young North off to fish for our supper." Even Smith lied for him.

Then, it became easier for him to get away. He was able

to spend longer hours with her, a whole day, even overnight, for events were transpiring at Jamestown that gave Cabot freedom to squander.

The exact time when the sickness began was never recorded, only the deaths: John Asbie on the sixth of August, George Flowers on the ninth. On the fourteenth, Jerome Alikock, Francis Midwinter, and Edward Moris. Edward Brown and Stephen Galthorpe died the following day, Thomas Gower on the sixteenth, Thomas Mounslic on the seventeenth, and on the eighteenth, Robert Pennington and John Martin, son of Captain Martin of the council, Drue Piggase on the nineteenth.

They had no names for the illnesses. They spoke of fevers, the bloody flux, and swellings, surely typhoid fever, malaria, and dysentery. A scrape or a cut felled a man already weakened by a diet consisting of a cup of wheat and barley boiled in water, grains that had been in the hold of a ship for twenty-six weeks and contained as many worms as kernels.

The scourge was no respecter of person or rank. Wingfield became ill, Smith, Percy, Archer, Kendall, all the leaders. The fine garb of the gentlemen became stained with their own vomit and excrement. No one escaped. The only issues were how soon a man went down and how soon he would get up, if he ever did. The morning came when Timothy could not rise, but merely lay on his pallet, holding his stomach, groaning. Cabot arose, but his head was swimming with fever, his bowels a raging sewer. He stumbled out of the encampment toward the woods. There was no one to care where he went.

Awotaka saw him and knew at once. Leaning heavily on her shoulder, he allowed himself to be led to the pool below the falls. She pushed him into the water, then dived in after him to keep him afloat. He knew what she was doing, cooling his fever. Then she laid him against the bank, half in the water, while she ran off, returning with a handful of leaves. These she crumbled in her hands, mixed with a little pool water and forced the bitter concoction down his throat. She helped him to the cave, staying with him for two days until he recovered. She made him understand. The pool water, not the river water. Never the river water. She showed him the leaves she had picked and he took some back to Jamestown. He forced some of the bitter fluid down Timothy's throat, as well as Smith's and Percy's. Others spit it out.

There was another cause of death at Jamestown that one of the colonists could identify. Cabot first encountered it in early August, a few days after Awotaka cured his illness. They were in the meadow above the falls, lying amid the yellow daisies with the black eyes, baked by the sun, swept by a cooling breeze. He wore the loincloth she had given him—he was by now browner than she—Awotaka, her red apron. They lay side by side on their backs, hands clasped, looking at the sky. He was seeing faces and shapes in the clouds, many of them lascivious. He felt rapturously happy, to be with her, to be away from the stench and death of Jamestown for a while. Timothy was sleeping, recovering.

"Cabot."

He turned to her. She was smiling.

"Cabot, Cabot, Cabot, Cabot."

She did it sometimes, just repeating his name, as though practicing it. The word was difficult for her, and she exaggerated the movements of her lips and tongue which, with her throaty voice, made her rendering of his name pure sensuousness. He moved closer to her and leaned on his elbow to look down at her, touching her moving lips with his fingers, brushing a wisp of hair, now so reddish in the sun, from her cheek.

"Cabot, Cabot, Cabot."

He took her there, on the grass, earth soft beneath them, surrounded by sky and wind, lifting her apron, seeing her slender, golden thighs spread in acceptance of him, responding, giving, enjoying both. Even as he reveled in the sensations, marveled at the wondrous doing of it, here, under the sky, heated by the sun, alone in the universe, he sensed the preciousness of this girl. She was this land, this sky, in her own way as majestic as they, accepting, open, filled with life and health, natural in her passions, yet, as now, still as his own storm broke over her.

He was saying all this, knowing she could not understand, when she put her hand to his mouth to silence him. He could sense her listening. He tried, but could hear only wind. Then she was pushing him away, scampering up, running across the meadow toward the woods. What a child she was, running, playing even after this. She stopped, turned, motioned him to follow. He laughed. There was no run in his legs just then. She came back to him, took his hand, pulled him after her. Finally, he realized she was serious.

Barely into the woods, she shimmied up a tree and pulled him up after her. Several limbs higher they went, then huddled in each other's arms. He knew what was happening then. She had heard other Indians coming. Other times they'd hidden in trees, once spending hours in the cave. Always it amazed him how she seemed to sense when they were not alone. He saw her point, then saw a band of Indians, perhaps twenty, leave the trees on the far side of the meadow and begin to cross toward them. From the feathers, the paint on their bodies, he recognized them, Paspaheghs, the tribe nearest Jamestown. They carried bows. Their quivers were full. Silently they passed under the tree where Awotaka held him, hand over his mouth, and walked along the stream. For a moment they were gone from view, descending the embankment beside the falls. Then they reappeared, heading for Jamestown. In the spring and fall the pool overflowed into a second, smaller waterfall that ran into the James River near the peninsula. Now, in summer, only a trickle meandered toward the fort. It was beside this the war party stalked.

He tried to climb down, but she held him. "I must warn them." She shook her head vigorously and gripped him tighter. There was surprising strength in her slender arms. Then it was too late for the warning. He could only stand on the limb, watching through a space amid the branches, as the war party crossed to the peninsula and crept amid the trees into the weeds surrounding the fort. In the distance he saw Timothy's fields, where Cabot knew he should be now, men on duty at the parapet of the fort, others pacing at guard before the tents. One of them turned toward him, clutching his chest, then slowly pitched forward. It seemed an eternity until the sound of his agonized scream reached Cabot. He closed his eyes, then heard shouts, musketfire. That night, back in Jamestown, he would learn that many men had died during an Indian raid, the first of many.

Numbly, Cabot allowed himself to be led to the cave to wait in silence as the Paspahegh braves passed overhead on their return. Then she spoke to him, great intensity in her voice, but he could only shake his head, both because he didn't understand her and in dismay at the attack he had witnessed.

She began to sign, as well as speak. She pointed, formed the outline of the peninsula with her hands. Jamestown. She pointed to him, touched her cheek and chin, made a backward motion of her hands. He understood. Before the men with beards. She made the motions of a deer running and of a bow being drawn. He nodded. Indians had hunted at Jamestown. He heard the word *Paspahegh*. Jamestown had been built on a Paspahegh hunting ground. Again she made the motions of the bow. When her finger came across her throat, he understood. The Indians would kill the white men. He nodded his understanding. She came to her knees and cradled his head against her breast. She loved him. She didn't want him to die. She released him, took his hand, gently pulling on it, pointing off to the north. She wanted him to come away with her, to her village, where he would be safe.

He looked at her, saw her anguish, the appeal she was making to him. He sighed. He couldn't, not now anyway. He tried to explain, but gave up. He knew no way to convey friends, family, duty.

The epidemic continued unabated at Jamestown, with men dying nearly every day, some quickly, others lingering like Bartholomew Gosnold, better one day, in agony the next. He tried to give Gosnold the herb that had cured him, but Wotten the surgeon saw him and threw it away. Cabot knew he couldn't explain where he'd gotten it or why he knew it helped. At least Timothy was getting well. Smith, who was terribly ill, was improving, too. Percy was already up and about.

As one of the few able-bodied men, Cabot did more than his share, feeding and caring for the sick, standing guard duty, and burying the dead. This was done at night, so the Indians would not know how many of them were dying. They were simply thrown into a shallow grave like dogs, their resting place wholly unmarked except in the memory of their comrades.

Despite his extra work, Cabot managed to steal time to be with Awotaka. She was his only haven, surcease from the pain and death of Jamestown. He gave himself to her with heightened ardor, relishing not just her body and beauty, but every nuance of their happiness together. With her, he could forget the folly of Jamestown. She signed to him. She had to stay at her village. Much work. He watched her motions and smiled. She had to help harvest crops. He nodded acceptance. She could not return for—she held up five fingers, then six, seven, maybe eight days. Her eyes saddened, and she flung herself into his arms. There in the crypt they were like two squirrels, storing away love to last while she was gone.

She was absent only five days. He was working in the fields with a weak but stubborn Timothy Loudon. Tenpenny—as far as Cabot knew, he was the one man who never did get sick—stood guard. Cabot saw her, standing in the woods in the distance, and he smiled, his pulse leaping at the sight of her.

It began so slowly, with her running toward him, something she had never done. He saw her waving her arms, her breasts moving as she ran, her apron flapping against her legs. He was startled, transfixed actually, in his surprise at seeing her run as fast as she could toward him.

The panorama began to speed up with terrifying rapidity, until it was a nightmarish kaleidoscope of events. He first heard the high-pitched cries and squeals, then saw the war party, many of them, emerging from the trees, racing behind Awotaka. The fort was being attacked. She was warning him.

"Goddamn bloody savages."

He turned, saw Tenpenny raising his flintlock. He watched in horror. *"No! Stop!"*

Tenpenny did not stop. His finger moved against the trigger. The weapon burst fire, smoke, and thunderous noise. Then Cabot was running, faster than ever in his life, unaware of his own agonized screams, kneeling over her, holding her, aghast at the great, spurting hole in her chest, crying, sobbing, wailing to God not to let it happen, unaware of the cries around him, men running by. He raised his head, looked toward that which had hurt his beloved. Why? She was only warning them, trying to protect them. There was no reason to shoot her. He saw the arrow in Tenpenny's chest, watched him fall, saw Timothy pick up the gun, trying to load it. It seemed to Cabot he watched the very flight of the arrow that struck his friend.

He had no knowledge of his own screams, just of rough

hands jerking him away from Awotaka. He caught a glimpse of upraised hatchet.

A harsh voice, guttural, commanding. He was thrown roughly to the ground.

Cannon from the fort was fired. The Paspahegh ran, carrying the body of Awotaka with them.

EIGHT

Madness

HIS WAS SILENT grief. There was no one who had known her or what she meant to him, and she was an Indian, a savage, forbidden to him by company policy. Thus, he bore within himself that which he felt. He did not cry, at least not for a long time. He engaged in no conscious memories of her, no nocturnal eroticism such as he had with Emily Fletcher. No part of Awotaka was separated from the rest to become more cherished, no moment relived to become dominant in his recollections. She remained whole and simply became part of him.

He never did mark the date of her passing. Later, he would arrive at an approximate date. Bartholomew Gosnold, the gentle, unpersuasive captain who had warned against this infested site, became its victim on August twenty-second. He had still been alive when Awotaka was killed. Nor could he reckon when his idyll with her began. It would shock him, when he could think of it, that he had known her only a few weeks. It had seemed so long.

It was death that saved him, and life. Through the dog days of August, well into September, death rose in clouds from the reeking swamps and mud flats, hanging and buzzing in the sultry air, permeating the rotting tents, hovering always, waiting, accepting new victims. When Christopher Newport had left on June twenty-second, Cabot North made the one-hundred-fourth colonist. By the end of September fewer than fifty were left. No exact count was taken. Death kept Cabot busy. Each night, aided by a couple of men still able to walk, he led the burial detail, digging a pit, always a little farther away from the fort, tossed that day's grim harvest inside, covered them. The dead outnumbered the living. The boneyard had greater dimensions than the encampment.

The life was that of Timothy Loudon. Keeping him on this earth saved Cabot North. The arrow had struck him in the chest, puncturing his lung. Already weakened from dysentery, he had no chance of survival, except that Cabot would not permit him to die. A dozen times it seemed he could not live the night, for he remained unconscious, long past delirium, burning with fever, his wound foaming and hissing in the darkness. That sound, at first so hideous, came to comfort Cabot, for it meant his friend still breathed.

He fought for the life of Timothy Loudon with every ounce of his strength. In a rage, he kept the surgeon from cutting out the arrowhead, pushing him bodily out of the tent, forbidding him to return. Wotten was a butcher. If he cut on Timothy, enlarging his wound, he would surely perish. Instinctively, Cabot realized that whatever else that sharp flint might be doing, it was also acting as a plug. Timothy's only hope was to leave the arrowhead in him and let the wound heal around it.

But, God in heaven, the infection. Timothy's body seemed to swell up, and pus drained from the wound in rivulets. If it was possible for a human being simply to burn up with fever, then that would happen to Timothy Loudon. It was this fever that caused Cabot to go where he didn't want to. Awotaka had cured his illness by pushing him into the pool below the falls to cool him. Cabot knew Timothy needed this, but he had no way to carry him there. *The pool water, never the river water.* He would have to bring it to Timothy.

Thus, leaden feet brought him back to where his happiness lay, along the path, now full of thorns, the berries gone, up the rocks to stand on the landing. The falls was greatly diminished in the dying summer, but the pool remained, cool, green.

He had intended not to linger, just fill his buckets and return to Timothy.

He could not, of course. He stood there, where she had stood, eyes burning, mouth a little open, his mind a wound of sounds and smells and visions. He shook with the effort to still the memories, and failed. *Cabot, Cabot, Cabot, Cabot.*

Quickly he stripped off his clothing and dived into the pool, making his way to the far bank, for she had taught him to swim rather well. He climbed up the path, passed behind the falls into the cave and entered the crypt.

The light still came from the meadow above. The pine boughs remained as they had been. He stepped over them and reached behind a rock, extracting his loincloth, her little red apron made from his gift of cloth. He sighed deeply, gasped as he crushed the fabric in his fist, then brought it to his cheek, touching, kissing what had embraced her thighs. "Oh, God, God. Awotaka, my love." He said her name but once. Nor did he sob into the cloth very long. Tears streaming down his face, he removed the boughs and with his hands scooped out the packed earth. In the space he had made, he placed her apron, his loincloth on top, then stood up, looking down a moment. Weeping less now, he kicked dirt over the garments, tamped it down, and spread the boughs on top. He lingered a moment more, nodding with satisfaction, his breathing becoming more regular. He felt somehow he had buried her. He hadn't realized how much he wanted to do that.

Cabot gave himself wholly then to all that mattered to him, the flicker of life in Timothy Loudon. He bathed him almost continually to cool his fever, changed his bandage, winding it tightly to help seal the wound. He forced the pool water down his throat and spooned as much wheat and barley broth into him as he could. It was all he knew to do, yet Timothy remained unconscious, his once burly body now wasted and ravaged. Cabot tried to tell himself Tim's fever had lessened. His wound seemed to have closed. Yet, Cabot dared not hope.

The summer, with its heat, pestilence, and death, lingered through much of September. Then, it broke with a savage storm. There was lightning and thunder such as Englishmen seldom experienced. Rain came down in torrents. In the midst of it, Cabot picked up the emaciated body of Timothy Loudon, carried him outside, held him in his arms and just stood there, face upturned, letting the deluge fall upon them both, soaking them, washing away filth and pain. Finally, he bore him back into the tent and laid him back down.

"Sar, is it really you?"

The words were almost inaudible. "Oh, God, Timothy, God. Yes, by heaven, it is me, sar."

The storm brought cooler weather, suppressing the mosquitoes. The James River became fuller and clearer, and the sickness began to subside. A new specter arose, however. The colonists faced imminent starvation. Timothy's crops had failed utterly. The sturgeon (one seven feet long had been caught earlier) had left the river. The stores, such as they were, were all but gone. The half a hundred survivors were half-starved and weak. Cabot was rail thin, all ribs and sharp bones, and beneath the black beard he had grown, his face was gaunt. Only eighteen, he felt a hundred years old. He had seen enough death and suffering to last his lifetime. When he glimpsed himself in a mirror, he felt each minute in this miserable colony was etched on his face.

Yet, more than the disease, blood, death, and starvation, it was the folly of Jamestown that enraged him. When he told Timothy of what had transpired during his illness, he referred to events as the "madness."

"We are governed by madmen, Timothy, stark, raving lunatics. Death is all around them. Ravaged men drop to their knees and into their grave from simple hunger—and in a land overflowing with natural abundance. We have no houses. We sleep on the damp ground." He raised both hands in a futile gesture toward their sievelike tent. "Winter is coming. Simple survival will take a miracle. Yet, all these men can do is bicker among themselves. When Nero fiddled while Rome burned, he was a master statesman compared to these . . . these *fools*. We are prey to lunacy."

Cabot was right, though anger perhaps exaggerated the degree of inertia and querulousness he saw around him. The leadership of the Jamestown colony was surely disreputable. With the death of Gosnold, five members of the council remained: Wingfield, Ratcliffe, Martin, Kendall, and Smith. Of these, Martin was chronically ill and Kendall, a born trouble-maker, was clearly endeavoring to destroy the colony. Early in September he was put behind bars on the pinnace.

The simmering quarrel between Wingfield and Smith had burst into the open as they stood over the deathbed of Gosnold. Smith accused Wingfield of hoarding the common stores and helping himself to extra rations. Wingfield called Smith a liar, whereupon Smith replied, "You and I might be equal here in Virginia, Master Wingfield, but in England I would not allow my valet to be seen in public with the likes of you."

The quarrel remained at white heat, but clearly Wingfield's days of leadership were numbered. Martin blamed him for his son's death. Ratcliffe, abetted by Archer, schemed to unseat the president, for he figured to replace him. Ultimately, Smith, in his hatred, joined the plot. On September tenth, Ratcliffe, Smith, and Martin went to Wingfield's tent and served him with a warrant, signed by all three, declaring him "very un-worthy to be either President or a member of the Council, and therefore he was discharged from both." He was turned over to a sergeant and locked up on the pinnace, Kendall being let out to make room for him. Ratcliffe was sworn in as president, Archer named recorder of Virginia, and Smith promoted to cape merchant or chief trader, replacing Thomas Studley who had died.

On September seventeenth, Wingfield was brought up on charges he had libeled John Smith with his mutiny charge back in the Canary Islands and also libeled Jehu Robinson, one of the gentlemen, by saying he and others planned to steal the shallop and run away to Newfoundland. To add to the con-fusion, it was supposedly Wingfield himself they were to run away with. A jury was impaneled and Wingfield found guilty. A hundred pounds sterling was awarded to Robinson in dam-ages, two hundred to Smith. It was during this trial that Cabot first used the word "madman." Would Smith now find his "award" digestible?

He wouldn't have to try. The Indians saved them. With their own hungry time ended by a bountiful harvest, they came to trade, bearing baskets of corn, vegetables, freshly killed deer. They even tried to show the English how to eat the corn from the cob, but it was declared "green corn," unfit for civilized palates. The trading, supervised by Cape Merchant Smith, lasted only a few days. The Indians saw and knew. The bearded men were starving. Let them.

Perhaps it was the additional food that did it, but in October, their sickness behind them, the band of colonists found some energy to erect housing. Led by Smith, who still knew the value of leadership by example, the men began to fell trees and gather thatch for shelter. It didn't take long. There were only forty-five of them.

By this time they had food for only eighteen days. Smith declared they must trade farther afield. With Timothy up and around, although woefully weak, Cabot went along. They headed for Point Comfort and Kecoughtan where they had once been feasted. The Indians were willing to trade, all right, a few nibbles of corn in exchange for a gun, a sword. Cabot heard Smith mutter, "By all that's holy, I will not give them the means of our destruction."

Again Cabot was impressed with Smith's acumen in dealing with the Indians. Rather than accept the offered barter, he simply gave beads and gewgaws to the women and children, then retired to the shallop for the night. The next morning the Indians were ready to trade. He soon had sixteen bushels of corn, as well as fish, oysters, bread, and venison. On the way back to Jamestown, they came across two canoes from Warraskoyack, across the river. Smith traded for another fourteen bushels.

It was a stopgap. Smith reckoned he had delayed starvation another two weeks. Their plight was desperate, leading to various suggestions for solution. Some colonists suggested Ratcliffe and Archer take the *Discovery* and return to England to tell of their plight. Cabot smiled and whispered to Timothy, "I wonder whose idea that was?"

Smith spoke. "We must go to Powhatan, the great emperor of all these tribes. He alone can arrange for trade."

Again Cabot detected self-serving. Smith was fascinated by this Powhatan and determined to find him.

Captain Martin, now on his feet at last, settled the issue. "A voyage to Powhatan will bring quicker results than going to England." Lots were drawn. Smith won. He would go to

Powhatan in the shallop, while the pinnace was being readied with supplies.

Cabot went along as Smith headed up the Chickahominy River, the mouth of which lay six miles from Jamestown. The journey was almost a disaster. The river was shallow, closed in with underbrush, and hard to navigate. The Paspaheghs, who bordered one side, refused to trade for goods other than guns and chased off the shallop. Downriver, Smith managed to trade for a paltry ten bushels of corn before returning. Martin also made two trips, returning with eight bushels one time, ten the next. The "twenty weeks" till Newport's return had been marked off. He was due November ninth. Would anyone be alive to greet him?

On November eighteenth, Smith again headed up the Chickahominy, staying to the right side to avoid the warlike Paspaheghs. He exceeded all his expectations, finding the Chickahominies rich and powerful. They were nominally part of Powhatan's confederation, yet kept a large measure of independence. Smith returned at midnight the following day with the shallop loaded to the gunwales with corn. The following morning he went back to bring a second bargeful.

With full bellies, the perils of starvation eased at least temporarily, the madness returned.

When he left on the eighteenth in the shallop, Smith believed the pinnace would follow him the next day, sailing at high tide. It never did make the trip, becoming stuck in the mud at Jamestown. This seemed strange, for *Discovery* was now outfitted and provisioned for a voyage. It occurred to the suspicious among the colonists that the pinnace could sail for England as well as up the Chickahominy. Had it been run aground deliberately so it wouldn't have to make the river trip? Cabot heard rumors that Kendall and Wingfield planned an escape to England.

The issue came to a head from another quarter. Ratcliffe, who was proving even weaker and more conniving than Wingfield, got into a quarrel with James Read, the blacksmith. What it was about, no one seemed to know. Ratcliffe said Read struck him. Others claimed Read only raised his hand. No matter. As president of the council, Ratcliffe was the king's representative in Virginia. Raising a hand against Ratcliffe was the same as threatening the king. A jury was impaneled.

Cabot listened to the "trial," his disbelief giving way to consternation and finally rage. "Madness, Timothy, nothing else," he whispered. "Those who survive we hang."

He had to speak. But as he arose he deliberately tamped down his anger to be more effective. As a man, a survivor, and as son of a company director, he had gained respect. He should not throw it away by labeling these men as the fools they really were.

"Gentlemen, I beg you not to proceed with this condemnation. Of those who came to these shores, less than half of us remain. I myself buried many of our comrades. They lie in unmarked graves, victims of disease, starvation, and Indian arrows. These are the enemies that still threaten us, even as a bitter winter approaches. Let us not condemn and hang one another. It is the purest folly. I beg you not to pursue this course."

Cabot sat down, hearing a murmur of approval. He saw Ratcliffe open his mouth to reply, but it was the voice of Archer that was heard.

"You cannot believe this colony will survive without discipline, Mr. North. We are governed by the king's laws, and Read has broken those laws by striking President Ratcliffe. The guilty must be punished. As Englishmen we have no choice but to hang him."

The jury, hand-picked by Archer, nodded. In less than a minute, Read was convicted and condemned to hang. Cabot could only gape in disbelief.

Read apparently didn't believe it either. He was almost lighthearted as the ladder was set against a tree and the rope thrown over a limb. He seemed nonchalant as he mounted the rungs. Then, as the noose was placed around his neck, he became a believer and cried, "I ain't guilty. I did nothin'. It's Cap'n Kendall and Master Wingfield. They's goin' t'steal the pinnace and go to England."

Read was brought down, and a new madness ensued. Kendall was put on trial. To Cabot's amazement, he confessed. He wasn't going to England, however, but to Spain to tell His Catholic Majesty Philip II about the colony. Men of his rank could not be hanged. Kendall was shot.

Wingfield somehow escaped, probably because his family was too powerful for the others to risk executing him. Later he would write that he had indeed decided to take the pinnace to England "to acquaint our Council there with our weakness." Smith would later write that Wingfield and Kendall were just setting sail as he returned from his second trip to the Chickahominy. He wrote that he stopped them with cannon fire. When Cabot read it years later, he remarked about Smith's love of embellishing a good tale.

NINE

A Tall Tale

THE EXECUTION OF George Kendall deeply affected Cabot North. When so many had perished, it was pure stupidity to take the life of another. When those who remained clung to a perilous existence, it was unspeakable dementia to engage in plots, silly charges, trials, hangings, and firing squads.

He did not grieve for Kendall, who was at best unlikable, but he saw with terrible clarity the folly of this whole venture. All these men had suffered and died for what? A tiny fort, a speck of land wrested from savages. The Jamestown colony was a handful of decrepit men who had crossed an ocean to no purpose. They built nothing, grew nothing, discovered nothing, in fact did nothing—except die.

These thoughts would not leave him. He ate, slept, endured hunger and the bitter cold that frosted the land in early December, but he moved like an automaton. He had given up on Jamestown.

Timothy Loudon did not consider himself the most perceptive of men, yet he believed he knew what was wrong with his friend. Cabot was having a delayed reaction to the death of the Indian girl. He and Cabot had spoken very little about her, not at all since he was wounded, but he knew Cabot was grieving for her, keeping it all bottled up inside him.

Timothy decided to help, as best he could. "Sar, 'ave I ever thanked you fer savin' m'life?"

They were in their hut, for a freezing rain was falling outside. Their small fire hardly held back the chill, however. Timothy sat in a chair, Cabot on his pallet, back to the wall, arms around his knees. He raised his head. "I did nothing, Tim. You got well yourself."

Timothy smiled. "The way I 'ear it, you prac'ly cut off the surgeon's hands to keep 'im from cuttin' on me."

"I felt your only chance was to leave the arrow in. How does it feel?"

He laughed. "Like there's an arrow in me chest." He increased his laughter, but Cabot would not join in. His head went back on his knees. Uncomfortable, not knowing how to proceed, Timothy said, "The Indian girl was killed?" He knew she had been, but it was something to say.

"Yes." The sound was muffled against Cabot's thighs.

"Tenpenny, he didn't mean to—"

"I know. It just happened, that's all."

Timothy's sigh was of desperation. "I'm sorry, Cabot. I know what she . . ." He let his voice trail off, unable to finish. He cleared his throat, crossed and recrossed his legs. "Do you want to talk about her?"

"No. I know you're trying to help, Tim, but don't, please."

Timothy Loudon knew when he was defeated—or almost. "Everybody says Captain Newport will return any day now." He consciously made his voice brighter, but he achieved no reaction. "Won't be long 'fore you's 'ome with that gal o' yours. What was 'er name? I fergit."

"Emily." The word sounded strange to his lips, and he couldn't remember the last time he'd thought of her—or Elizabeth.

"Sure, Emily. Bet she won't know you, what wif yer beard and all."

Cabot tried to conjure up the old image of the golden day. He couldn't, at least not with any feeling. "I imagine Emily has quite forgotten about me."

"I doubt 'at, sar. She'll be right there waitin' fer ya when ya get 'ome."

"If I get home."

Timothy shook his head in frustration, yet when he spoke his voice had a hard edge of authority. "You know that ain't so, Cabot. You said yerself you was goin' t'survive—me, too."

Cabot raised his head from his knees and looked sharply at his friend, memory of his vow adding a hard glint to his eye. "Yes, I did say that. And we have—we will, you and I."

Delighted to see the change in Cabot, Timothy gave his yellow grin. "You betcha, sar. You'll go 'ome t'yer gal, an' next summer I'll grow real crops. Virginny'll make it, too, you'll see."

Cabot sighed. "If there were a hundred men like you, Timothy, but—"

"No buts, Cabot. This is good lan'. Virginny'll bloom. All it takes is hard work and a li'l gettin' used to."

Cabot stared at him. He thought of the disease and death, the hostile Indians, the stupid leadership, and the shiftless gentlemen, but he said none of it. Instead he smiled, perhaps for the first time in days. "Knowing you, my friend, you are probably right."

And Timothy's grin was at its widest, for he knew he had somehow cheered his friend. "Are you goin' wif Cap'n Smith on his expedition?"

Cabot hadn't planned to, believing himself through with Virginia. Now he said, "Yes. Accompanying Smith is always eventful."

In early December, despite the numbing cold, Smith set out in the shallop. With him were Jehu Robinson, the libeled gentleman; Thomas Emry, a carpenter; George Cassen, a laborer; and six others, including Cabot North. By instruction of the council, they were to go "towards Powhatan" in search of food and to test Smith's belief that at the head of the Chickahominy River lay a great lake and beyond it the passage across the isthmus to the South Sea.

Smith did not halt at any of the villages he had passed before. Rather, he coursed sixteen miles up the Chickahominy, finally stopping at a peninsula called Moysonicke. Above there the river became tortuous, dotted with islands and marshes, but they reached Apokant, the last of the Chickahominy villages upstream. The expedition continued another ten miles upriver until it became impassable for the shallop. The river was no

more than a few feet wide, shallow, the current fast and the
bottom rocky.

Smith turned to Cabot. "We'd better go back to Apokant,
secure the barge and go upriver by canoe."

"Whatever you say, Captain." In truth, Cabot already had
misgivings about the whole expedition. Bartering for corn was
clearly the least of Smith's interests. He seemed all puffed up,
determined to find Powhatan, ready to pay any price for a
meeting with him—either that or discover the passage to the
Pacific, thus stealing Newport's thunder. But these doubts in
no way diminished his pleasure in accompanying Smith. The
man was a born leader, a fearless explorer. Thus, Cabot was
disappointed when Smith, after obtaining a canoe by lying that
he was going "fowling" upriver, ordered him to stay at Apokant
with the shallop.

"But, Captain—"

"I know, North, you don't want to miss out on anything.
But these men are fools. You're the only one I can trust to
look after the barge."

Cabot opened his mouth to protest, but knew it would do
no good. He could only sigh in resignation.

"I'm taking Robinson, Emry, and two Indian guides with
me. You and the other six stay with the shallop. These Indians
are hostile. Stay well away from them. And, for God's sake,
don't let anyone go ashore."

In sorrow, Cabot watched Smith and his party paddle upstream. He could not escape a sense of foreboding.

Why Cassen, the laborer, decided to go ashore against orders
no one knew. Perhaps he spotted a metallic glint in the earth,
or an Indian maiden caught his fancy. Maybe it was simple
curiosity or the boredom of remaining in the shallop. But go
he did, wading toward the bank.

Cabot stood in the shallop, shouting, "Cassen, you fool!
Come back!" But he either didn't hear him or ignored Cabot's
shouts, lurching, stumbling toward the shore. When he climbed
up the bank, he seemed to have second thoughts, turning,
looking toward the shallop as if to obey. Then he couldn't.
Indians burst from the woods and seized him.

It happened quickly then. A second man, Squires, jumped
into the river, wading for shore, apparently to rescue Cassen.

Cabot gave a single shout for him to return, then stripped off his coat and sword and dived into the water.

The frigid water took his breath away, but with strong, practiced strokes he swam after Squires, reaching him halfway to shore. He was screaming for Cassen to come back, but Cabot, standing thigh deep in the water, saw it was impossible now. A score of hands held Cassen. He was being dragged away.

And they were seen, too; Indians were pointing at them, emitting bloodthirsty screams. Bows were raised, pulled. The arrows came as a flight, a storm. Cabot dived into the water, pulling Squires under with him. But when he tried to swim away with him, Squires fought him, breaking away, standing up.

"We gotta save 'im!"

"We can't, you fool!" With a single blow of his fist, Cabot felled Squires, then began to swim with him toward the boat. But the weight was enormous, and in a few feet he had to stand up to rest. Arrows still fell as elongated hail, striking the water all around him. Others clattered over the shallop. "Weigh anchor!" he screamed. "Back off!" Then he felt a sting in his arm. Almost as a curiosity he saw the streak of blood near his shoulder, but no arrow. He had only been nicked.

The barge was at midstream, beyond range, when he at last reached it, handing up Squires first, then allowing himself to be pulled out of the water. Unmindful of his own shivering, he turned at once to look toward shore. Cassen had been dragged some distance away and tied to a tree. Cabot snatched up the long glass to see. What unfolded, now seemingly just before his eye, shook him to his very core. He was appalled, then sickened, but he could not stop watching.

At first, he couldn't see what was happening, for the Indians danced in a circle around the tree. Then through spaces among the savages, Cabot saw—*saw*. They were hacking off Cassen's fingers, his toes, one by one, with what looked like mussel shells and razor-sharp reeds. Cassen's screams of agony rose above the howls of his tormentors.

"God almighty, what are they doin' to 'im?"

Cabot heard the voice at his side, but he could neither speak nor relinquish the shaking glass.

A fire was built, the dismembered parts of Cassen's body thrown into it. Then Cabot saw they were flailing at him with reeds, his face and neck, shoulders, arms, on down his body, until his belly was ripped open. Cabot raised the glass, saw the bloody face of Cassen. Was he alive? He couldn't be.

Slowly, shaking uncontrollably, Cabot at last lowered the glass, unable to register the unspeakable. Only when someone tried to take the glass from him did he find voice. "No, don't look." Then he retched into the boat, his body wracked with spasms. He heard muttering. The men still wanted to rescue Cassen. "No, there's nothing we can do." Nor could they remain here after dark. "We'd better go."

As they hoisted sail, all turned to look back ashore. The Indians had set fire to the tree. It went up like a torch, Cassen's body with it, while the Indians danced around it, whooping demonic cries. The smoke, bearing the stench of burning flesh, swept over the boat. The burning tree seared Cabot's very soul.

Back at the fort, Cabot was compelled to report what he had seen. Deep in shock, he spoke of it desultorily, without feeling, as though it were an item of news. Then he walked away, back to his hut, ignoring the babel of dismayed voices.

It took Cabot several days to come to grips with his horror and revulsion. He couldn't drive the memory of Cassen's agony, the bloody flesh, the burning tree from his mind. It remained with him day and night. Often he awoke screaming. Timothy said nothing, for he had no idea how to comfort his friend. Cabot saw what lay in his eyes. "I'll be all right, Tim."

He knew he had to come to grips with the torture-execution, either that or go out of his mind. So he consciously forced himself to think of it. Why had the Indians done it? They had fought the invaders before, but never had they been so barbaric. Why now? He could only conclude the Indians were setting an example. They knew they were being watched from the barge. Had they wanted him to carry a message back to the fort of what fate awaited the white man? Yes, that must be it.

He tried to equate Cassen's torture with the gentle, loving Awotaka. How could both be true? It preyed on his mind for several days. Then he understood. These savages were no different from other men, certainly not the English. They were a compendium of good and evil. In their fear of the invader, they vacillated between friendship—bringing food, offering assistance, hoping kindness would encourage the white men to leave quickly—and battle, trying to kill the intruders or scare them away. Yes, they had to be confused about what course of action to take. Either that or their numbers included people of both persuasions.

John Smith and his companions, Robinson and Emry, were assumed dead. It seemed to Cabot that Ratcliffe and Archer were hardly saddened to be rid of Smith at last. Then in mid-December, three Indian runners appeared, bearing a letter from Smith. He had been captured by Indians, who planned to attack the fort. The Indian messengers were not to be harmed. Rather, all the ordnance in the fort was to be fired, so as to frighten them witless, then they were to be allowed to return with that message.

Ratcliffe and Archer scoffed at the letter. They were giving the orders, not Smith.

Seething with rage, Cabot turned on them, speaking only three words: "You bloody fools!" Then he turned, stalked to the parapet, and ordered the gunners to fire a salvo. As they did so, he opened the gate for the Indians to escape.

He turned back to Ratcliffe and Archer. "I suppose you want to hang me now, gentlemen."

Archer gave him a look of pure malevolence, but no word was said.

Bitter cold, snowy days passed with no word from Smith. It was again assumed he was dead, a fate that Cabot now knew lay ahead for them all. A bleak Christmas was observed. Cabot was compelled to attend church service, but as he listened to the hallowed words he found, not comfort, but irony. Starvation, frostbite, and the eminent massacre by Indians hardly seemed a demonstration of God's love. He knew he was blasphemous. He couldn't help it. God did not reside in Virginia, only pain, privation, suffering, and death—death to the body, death to the soul of the living. In this way did he mark the first day of the year 1608.

To everyone's consternation, John Smith returned the following afternoon, emerging from the woods, accompanied by a dozen Indians carrying baskets of corn and venison. The food was welcomed. Not so Captain Smith. In his absence, the legalistic Archer, working on the pliable Ratcliffe, had gotten himself named to the council. He now emerged as Smith's chief accuser. Where was Jehu Robinson? Dead, at least thirty arrows in his body. Emry? Gone, assumed dead.

"Captain Smith, you stand accused of gross insubordination." Archer's voice took on a harsh tone of authority, yet Cabot felt he could detect the glee that underlay it. "Your orders were to go up the Chickahominy to barter for food. This you did not do. You were to search for your *alleged* lake"—his voice mocked Smith—"which you claim leads to the Pacific. You did none of this. You abandoned your men, one of whom was tortured to death. Your actions caused the death of your companions. You'd better have a suitable explanation."

To Cabot, Smith looked thin, haggard, and he seemed momentarily nonplussed at his reception. He had obviously expected a hero's welcome, not angry faces and calls for his execution. Then his feisty nature asserted itself. Confronted with danger, he always took on stature and energy.

Smith began to weave an imaginative tale. He had been captured by Indians—only after he had the misfortune to fall into a quagmire—and disarmed. His captor was the redoubtable Opechancanough, half-brother to the great Powhatan himself. For days, his life hung in the balance. He was saved by his compass. The needle, pointing north always, a needle the Indians could see but not touch—they had never seen glass before—fascinated the savages. They believed the compass imbued Smith with magical powers.

He was transferred from village to village, feasted, entertained, yet constantly accosted by priests wearing hideous visages who tested his powers, trying to frighten him with howling incantations and fierce rattles. Always he was questioned. Why was he here? Where were his companions? When were the great ships returning? Smith, determined not to show fear, told them his companions were many and would bring fire and death if he was harmed. His "father," the great Newport, would return any day in his great ships. His wrath would be mighty if his "son" was harmed.

Smith's tale began to earn laughter. Indeed, Cabot wearied of it. But Smith plunged on. At last he had been taken before the supreme chief, Powhatan, in his royal court. The Indian emperor sat on a dais of mats, his neck hung with chains of pearls, a mantle of raccoon skin about him. A fire blazed before him. Young women sat at his right hand and at his left. To either side, his chief men were ranged ten in a row, with as many young women arranged behind him. Through the smoke of the fire, Smith saw a tall, well-proportioned man, gray-haired with a short beard. He looked at least sixty, but might have been much older.

Powhatan received him kindly at first, looking at his compass, listening to Smith's oration about the moon and stars, the great lands beyond the sea, the power of the great emperor in London, the fleets of fire-bearing ships at his command. Again came the questions. What were the English doing here? What was Smith doing here? Again the lies. The English were only visiting. Smith merely hunted the passage to the western ocean.

Cabot could hear the open laughter, cries to "hang him," as Smith arrived at the climax of his tale. Powhatan had decided to kill him. His head was placed on a rock, and warriors stood over him, clubs raised to beat his brains out. Then, a voice was heard and a child, a girl of ten, ran toward him and covered his head with her naked body.

"A child?" Archer's voice rang with mockery.

"Yes. Her name is Pocahontas, and she is the favorite daughter of the Great Lord Powhatan himself. After she saved my life, I was treated with kindness. Powhatan declared me his adopted son, gave me a present of lands so I can build a house near him. He afforded me safe conduct here."

There was silence for a moment, then the voice of Ratcliffe, dripping sarcasm. "This savage girl—a princess, you say— saved your life. Why on earth would she do that?" His laughter was joined by others.

Smith stood his ground. "I don't know. It is perhaps the custom among Powhatan's people."

Archer had found a new insinuation. "And you fraternized with her, then."

Smith's anger flared. "You, sir, may have finagled yourself onto the council, where you have no legal right to be. But you will not insult me. I will have you out on the field of honor."

"It was but a simple question, Captain. I'm sure it fills the minds of others here."

Smith heard the "ayes" that followed. "She is but a child of ten, no more than eleven. She has not yet put on her apron."

"I see."

A strained silence followed. Cabot could see distress rising in Smith's face. "In return for Powhatan's kindness and to earn my release, I promised to . . . to give him two small cannon. These men are to return with them."

"You did *what?*"

Smith steeled himself against Ratcliffe's words. "There are many thousands of warriors under Powhatan's command. He can destroy us with a finger. Two small cannon is a small price for his friendship."

"To use against us?"

Smith turned to Archer. "Cannon that one does not know how to use is the same as no cannon."

The Indians, led by Powhatan's trusted lieutenant Rawhunt, had sat to the side, listening, or seeming to, while the bearded men quarreled. When the armament was brought out, they reacted with keen interest, chattering, running their hands over the iron barrel. But when they tried to carry the gift back to Powhatan, it was not possible to get enough men around it to lift it, for each cannon weighed at least a ton and a half.

"Perhaps we should show them how it works, after all," Smith said.

Gunners loaded the weapon with stones, aiming it at a snow-laden tree. The roar and flash, the falling branches and ice frightened the Indians. They ran in terror. Coaxed to return, the Indians accepted beads and bells and hatchets before departing.

It appeared to Cabot the business with the cannon, everyone's laughter at the frightened Indians had defused the menace to Smith. He underestimated Gabriel Archer. The barrister was determined Smith should be tried for the deaths of Robinson and Emry. Ratcliffe, as president, acquiesced.

Cabot thought it the most ridiculous event of his whole stay in this godforsaken colony. Archer came up with something called "the Levitical law." Robinson and Emry had been Smith's responsibility. He had allowed the men to perish, and didn't the Book of Leviticus say in Chapter Twenty-four, "breach for breach, eye for eye, tooth for tooth?" Cabot listened aghast. If Smith was responsible for two men, who was responsible for all those out in the cemetery?

Ratcliffe pronounced sentence. "Death by firing squad at sunrise."

A booming sound rolled from the distance, as though punctuating Ratcliffe's fateful words. The settlers stood transfixed.

"Was that cannon?"

Another voice was found. "The ship. My God, the ship!"

On feet numbed with cold, they ran to the river's edge, standing in the snow, staring downriver. There they saw the *Sarah Constant* coming slowly toward them. There could be no more beautiful sight. A hush fell over all, sunken eyes gaping at salvation. Each man seemed to react in his own way. Some knelt on the frozen earth. Others wept openly. A few began to salivate and drool at the thought of food. Cabot knew only that his eyes were smarting.

The ship seemed to take endless time to come upriver. A line was thrown, the ship tied to the familiar cypress. Cabot saw Captain Newport on the bridge, peering down at them. There was an expression of disbelief on his face. Then Cabot saw him motioning with his hand. He was counting. Cabot already knew the tally. There were thirty-eight left of the hundred and four.

"Where is the rest of your party?"

Silence spread over the frosted air until Cabot filled it. "Dead, sir. All dead."

TEN

Messages

NEWPORT'S RETURN HAD been delayed—indeed, he nearly didn't come at all—because Martin's "ore" turned out to be worthless dirt. Hard-pressed to explain this failure, Newport pleaded that the wrong ore was put in his flagship. There was gold in Virginia; of that he was certain. He promised Robert

Cecil, the Earl of Salisbury and chief minister to the king, that he would not see him again until he brought "that which he confidently believed he had brought before."

Newport left Gravesend with two ships, the *Sarah Constant*, bearing eighty settlers, and the *Phoenix*, a speedy pinnace, with forty passengers. The purpose of the smaller vessel was to make a quick return with the "correct" ore. Unfortunately, the two vessels were separated in a fog, and the *Phoenix* was assumed lost. It showed up at Jamestown ten days after the flagship left on its return voyage to England.

With both amazement and envy, the bedraggled settlers at Jamestown watched their new compatriots disembark. They looked so healthy, confident, and incredibly well dressed to the band on shore.

"Would you look at them glad rags," Percy said to Cabot and Smith who stood near him. "I fear we are all out of fashion, gentlemen."

"And out of hands to do any work, too." There was bitterness in Smith's voice as he counted the "gentlemen" on the passenger list. "Would you believe it? Thirty-three of them."

Cabot was making another tally. "I count twenty-one laborers."

"The Lord save us," Smith muttered. "Thirty-three useless mouths to feed and only twenty-one pairs of hands to do it with."

The complement of new colonists also included four tailors, one surgeon, two apothecaries, a gunsmith, goldsmith, cooper, blacksmith, tobacco pipe maker, two refiners, a perfumer, and a jeweler.

Cabot's laugh mingled bitterness with mirth. "A perfumer. Just what we need."

Percy reacted heartily. "I have been keeping my distance, young North—or hadn't you noticed."

"You or me?"

The company's choice of artisans clearly indicated that the prime purpose of the colony was to find instant wealth, precious stones—hence the jeweler—and *gold*. The refiners and the goldsmith were expected to be most useful and busy men.

Before Newport could begin his search for the yellow metal, there were urgent items of business to attend to. He quickly countermanded Ratcliffe's order for the execution of Smith, much to the relief of all except Ratcliffe and Archer. Then Newport demoted Archer from his illegal seat on the council back to recorder. A new councilor was sworn in, a man named Scrivener.

Next order of business was the erection of housing for the freezing newcomers. This was proceeding satisfactorily when the ultimate disaster befell the colony, or so Cabot thought. On January 14, 1608, virtually the whole settlement burned to the ground—the church, the storehouse, much of the fort, all but three small houses—the thatched roofs burning like tinder, an icy wind spreading sparks from roof to roof. The men were powerless to prevent the conflagration, and the original settlers were left with only the clothes on their backs. Gone were most of their personal possessions and mementos, Rector Hunt's library, which had filled many a lonely hour—and Cabot's sketches.

Cabot and Timothy watched in dismay as the fire raged. "This is it, Tim, the final blow, the extreme of our extremities. There is nothing to do but abandon Jamestown now."

"Not hardly. There's plenty o' trees. We'll jus' have to rebuild it."

Cabot glanced at his friend. There was determination in his eyes, leaving the disenchanted Cabot to shake his head in disbelief.

Captain Newport was of the same mind—at least partially. He set the men to work at once rebuilding the fort, church, and housing. But in his eagerness to begin mining gold, he ordered the construction to be of a temporary, emergency nature, offering just enough shelter to get the colonists through the winter. Everything could be done properly come warmer weather. The cold persisted till the end of February, however, claiming several more lives from pneumonia and frostbite.

Newport's massive search for gold was to Cabot just another instance of the madness that infected all who set foot in Virginia. Virtually all other activity gave way to digging and shoveling, sifting and panning of the river. No likely spot was left unmined. Councilor Martin, enthusiasm renewing his energies, assured Newport various speckled earths were of high assay. The refiners nodded their heads profoundly, and the ore was confidently loaded aboard the *Sarah Constant* until the ship rode low in the water. The colonists truly believed in alchemy. One man was heard to cry, "When I die I want to be buried in those sands by the river so my very bones will turn to gold."

Cabot's disgust was exceeded only by that of John Smith. "It is fool's gold, North, nothing else. We should be building and planting, planning for survival, and all we do is suffer fools."

Cabot sighed. "Then we should clear the land quickly, so Timothy will have time to plant."

It was not just the search for gold that embittered Smith. This whole first supply of food, so long anticipated, was fast being depleted. At first he sympathized with the half-starved survivors, as they gorged themselves on salt pork, beef and fish, butter, cheese, aqua vitae, and, most wondrously, ale. But the inroad on the stores was enormous.

There was another, larger drain on the food supply. That intended to support the colony was not differentiated from the ship's provisions, giving crew members access to it. They proceeded to barter away a goodly portion of it to settlers for whatever they had to offer—rings, furs, Indian artifacts. Wealthy colonists, such as George Percy, gave sight drafts to their kinsmen in England, thus adding to their private hoard of food—at the expense of the other colonists.

Far more damaging, in Smith's view, was the barter with the Indians. They began coming the day after the "tall ship" appeared, bearing corn, beans, bread, venison for barter. This was at first a vindication for Smith, for these were Powhatan's representatives. Even those from the Paspaheghs, Chickahominy, and other nearby tribes came at the Indian emperor's behest.

But the terms of barter horrified Smith. He had always tried to deal fairly with the Indians, driving a shrewd bargain so as not to deflate the value of their goods. Such subtleties were lost on the newcomers. A hatchet that once would have brought a bushel or two of corn was traded now for a mere handful. Beads, bells, and penny knives were scorned.

Cabot heard Smith say bluntly to Newport, "When you leave, my dear Captain, how will we be able to trade for food?" Cabot did not hear the admiral's reply.

Newport wanted to meet Powhatan himself, for he was

convinced the great chief knew where gold could be found. The fact that none of the Indians—so fascinated by glass, copper, and other shiny objects—were not adorned with gold was lost on him. At the end of February, as the temperature warmed, Newport set out in the pinnace. Smith was his guide. A guard of thirty men accompanied them. They approached Powhatan by water, going down the James to Point Comfort then up the Pamunkey River, finally reaching Powhatan's headquarters.

The party remained for several days filled with ceremony, gift-giving, grandiose lies, and verbal sparring. It was here that Smith became utterly disillusioned with Newport. Where the wily Smith was wary of Powhatan, constantly on his guard for treachery, Newport trusted him. Where Smith knew the importance of hard bargaining and not looking foolish to the Indians, Newport permitted himself to be flimflammed. In dismay, utterly helpless, Smith watched Newport trade copper bowls, immensely valuable to Indians, for a fraction of their worth in corn. That the expedition did not return empty-handed was due to Smith's acumen. Among their trade items were some beads of blue Venetian glass. He sensed Powhatan's fascination with them and exploited it by describing the rarity and magical properties of the baubles. In this way he was able to fill the pinnace with grain.

Most disturbing to Smith was the exchange of "sons." Newport "gave" handsome, blue-eyed Thomas Savage, a lad of thirteen, to Powhatan. The intention was to have Savage live with the Indians, learn the language, and act as an emissary between the colonists and the Indians. Smith could see merit in that. But the crafty Powhatan reciprocated with a gift of his trusted servant Namontack. He was to go to England with Newport to replace his "son." Smith saw a "shrewd, subtle capacity" in the Indian and feared he had sent Namontack only "to know our strength."

Smith groused a lot to Cabot, obviously expecting him to relay his complaints to Lord North. Cabot realized he probably would, if he discussed this miserable colony or anything else with his father. Cabot recognized Smith as the ablest man in Virginia. It was a shame he did not have greater authority. Yet, he also recognized Smith as self-aggrandizing and exces-

sively ambitious. Wingfield, Archer, Ratcliffe, and the others
were pompous, lazy fools, yet Smith had not tried to cooperate
with them. He seemed to thrive on dissension.

Such thoughts, Cabot realized, were a symptom of his
changing attitudes. He was already leaving Virginia, becoming
an observer, not a participant, engaging in a sort of summing
up of this nightmare. What had it all meant, the death, starvation, human suffering, the madness? Again and again he
returned to the same answer. It meant nothing. Virginia was
the purest folly, a zero in the history of mankind. The men
who had died would be forgotten, their bones rotting in unmarked graves. Those who survived would go home. Jamestown would be abandoned to the forest, and this land, forsaken
by God, would return to its rightful owners, the Indians.

Cabot knew he was fortunate to be able to leave. A good,
hardworking person like Timothy Loudon, devoid of wealth or
family connection, had no choice but to remain here to die.
Cabot North, useless son of the Earl of Durham, was going
home. Home to what? He tried to visualize Graymere, his
father, Elizabeth, the life he had once led. Strangely, he couldn't.
It was too distant. Perhaps it would come back to him when
he saw England.

For Timothy's part, he was glad Cabot was going home,
although he would miss him terribly. He simply could not
understand why his friend wasn't happy.

Cabot was roused from his dark thoughts by the visits of
Pocahontas. She was clearly a princess, possessing a regal
bearing even at her young age. She arrived with an entourage
of handmaidens, warriors, and trusted representatives of the
great Powhatan. She also came laden with baskets of food, all
the Indians really had to give. These were for the colonists or,
more accurately, for John Smith, whom she obviously adored.
Worship was perhaps not too strong a word.

The relationship between Pocahontas and Smith caused no
small amount of snickering, particularly among the newcomers,
still unused to Indian customs. Cabot knew such talk was ridiculous. Pocahontas was a mere child. Smith's amusement in
her, his gifts, the games he played with her were expressions
of his fondness for a child who had saved his life—or perhaps
he was demonstrating his acumen. This favorite daughter of

Powhatan might be extremely useful to the colony, come another starving time. Her friendship should only be encouraged.

But then, Cabot could understand the difficulties the settlers had in taking her seriously. She was most unprincesslike, at least by English standards, naked as the day she was born. And she was a blithe spirit. Her name meant Little Wanton, not in the sexual but in the playful sense. That she was, laughing, squealing over little gifts, instantly curious about everything. She wanted to see the ship and was obliged. Soon she was scampering up the rigging. She gamboled with boys in the encampment, besting them at cartwheels across the marketplace.

The sight of her wounded Cabot, for she was to him a younger, darker skinned Awotaka. More than once his mind traveled back to the falls and meadow. *Cabot, Cabot, Cabot, Cabot.* Always he tamped down the thoughts. It was over, a fleeting moment of happiness, never to return. And it had been impossible anyway. Imagine taking a naked savage home to Graymere.

The *Sarah Constant*, laden with "precious ore," was to depart April 10, 1608. Cabot North, now nineteen, hoped to take his leave as quickly and painlessly as possible. He was not wholly successful in this. Men kept coming up to him, pressing letters into his hand, giving oral messages for loved ones. More than one crusty survivor became moist in the eye when saying, "If you should see my mother, tell her—jus' give 'er a 'ug for me." Cabot could only nod his assurance.

Percy gave him a letter for his father, another for a brother. "Anything else?" Cabot asked.

The dapper young peer hesitated. For a moment his veneer cracked; then he quickly shored it up, smiling. "Oh, there are a couple of ladies. I thought about asking you to . . . , but then I couldn't trust you."

Cabot smiled. "You may be right."

Smith had no letters or loved ones. "I would like for you to give an accurate report to your father. Some good may come of it."

"I will, Captain." He felt the need to say more. "I'm sure things will improve." He saw Smith nod, but with no particular conviction. "Captain Smith, I want to thank you for taking me along on your explorations, although I'm sorry I missed Pow-hatan."

"I'm not. You would've been killed." He smiled. "Let's say we're even. By leaving you behind at Apokant I saved your life, just as you saved mine."

The leavetaking from Timothy was the hardest, as he knew it would be. "Do you want me to go see your folks in Wiltshire, tell them you're all right?"

"If you wish, but"—he rendered that yellow split in his face that Cabot had grown to love—"I 'magine you'll be busy with that pretty gal o' yours, sar. Fergit her name."

Cabot was forced to smile, too. "Emily. Why is it you always bring her up but can never remember her name?"

"Never was good at names, sar."

There was awkwardness then, both young men uncomfortable with emotion. "I know I can't talk you into leaving. Will you be all right here, Tim?"

"I'll be fine. I saved some Indian corn, some beans, even some o' what they call squash. I'm eager to be aplantin'."

Cabot smiled. "I know you are. You'll turn this place into a Garden of Eden."

"I hope so, sar. It's good lan'."

Cabot nodded, clapping his friend on the shoulder. Then he felt the choking in his throat, the burning in his eyes. "I guess you know...I've grown...fond of you." He saw the craggy head nodding. "Don't...don't let anything happen to you."

Cabot couldn't tell if the wateriness was in Timothy's eyes or his own. But he saw the smile. "After what we been through this las' year, sar, I think we can stan' anythin'."

That helped, and the two young men managed to embrace without feeling too awkward.

Cabot stood at the railing near the bow looking down at the throng below. There were about as many as had come in the first place. There had been no growth in a year, either in people or in structures. Little had been gained by it all. Then he heard Wingfield's voice behind him. That was a blessing, having Wingfield leave, and Archer, too. Smith wouldn't have their contention to deal with.

He saw Timothy on shore. He didn't wave.

PART II

An Iron Hand

ELEVEN

A Son's Advice

IT WAS NOT actually raining, but leaden skies and a sharp wind made the Channel crossing rough and brought discomfort to passengers aboard the ferry bound for Holland. One seemed unbothered, a tall, slender Englishman who stood at the starboard rail staring off to the south. More than a few passengers, especially women, noticed his penetrating blue eyes and the luxuriant dark beard framing his mouth and jaw. But, more than his appearance, it was the mood he conveyed that attracted attention. He was alone and seemed content to remain that way.

"Excuse me, sir, but aren't you the Honorable Cabot North, late of Virginia?"

Cabot turned and saw a blond, blue-eyed man, a little younger than himself and clearly Dutch. His English was adequate, but somewhat accented. Cabot nodded but did not speak.

"I am Pieter van Stamp of Amsterdam. I've heard of your exploits in Virginia and wondered if I might speak to you for a moment."

Cabot sighed. He had been home over a year, and during that time a certain notoriety had attended him. He was back from Virginia, one of the ancients, a survivor. He had seen the wilderness, encountered the naked savages. Curiosity about the colony was inevitable. Cabot tried to be patient, but he also sought to avoid such discussions as much as possible.

Now he met the gaze of the young Dutchman, seeing his innocence, a quality he had once had. His questions would be predictable: Do the savages really go about naked? Then would come, Is it true there are gold nuggets lying about for a man to pick up? Newport's spangled ore had turned out to be iron pyrites, fool's gold, making him the laughingstock of London. Still, belief in Virginia gold persisted.

Pieter van Stamp surprised him. "I wonder if you would do me the honor of visiting my home in Amsterdam. I know my father would love to meet you."

Cabot smiled then, but mostly at himself and his error. "I'm sorry, but I'm only passing through Amsterdam on my way to Leyden." He hesitated to say more, then realized courtesy demanded it. "I'm visiting friends who have a church there."

"Would that be the Scottish church or the English church of Master Brewster?"

"I didn't know there were two."

"In Leyden, yes. My country has accepted a good many English . . ."

Cabot saw his hesitation in characterizing the Puritans. "Separatists—exiles?" The Dutchman smiled and nodded, and Cabot said, "Yes, I hope to see Brother Brewster and others who were in the church at Scrooby."

"Leyden is but a short distance from Amsterdam. I hope you will reconsider and visit my home."

"I'm sorry."

Cabot watched the Dutchman walk away, then turned back to look at the sea, resuming his thoughts of that nightmarish anchorage off the downs while the Channel raged around them. He remembered Timothy then, wondering if he was all right or even alive, if his crops had failed again. He had heard nothing in over a year. Then he forced Timothy from his mind. He was determined to forget Virginia. A new thought came to him. This wallowing ferry was no *Sarah Constant,* but it did feel good to have a deck under his feet again. How strange. How surprising. He continued to stare out to sea, but try as he would, he could not keep himself from remembering.

He had gone at once to Graymere, riding up the carriageway amid the ancient oaks. He had been touched by the sight of home. The stone manor house seemed so much larger than he remembered. Jacobs, the butler, greeted him, greatly surprised at his coming. Lord Alfred was away. He would be distraught at not being there, but no one had known. Elizabeth? She was in the classroom with the tutor, the Reverend Downing. He would send for her. Cabot said he wanted to surprise her.

He stood in the doorway unseen, for the backs of both Elizabeth, hunched over her desk, and the tutor, standing over her, were toward him. Cabot's smile faded as he heard the cassocked rector upbraiding his sister. Then rage raced through him as he saw him raise his stick and rap Elizabeth across the palm. In three steps Cabot was there, grabbing Downing's arm, wrenching the stick from him. "Hit my sister, will you?" he roared and began to flail the open palm of the frightened clergyman. Then Cabot turned over the hand and rapped him across the knuckles as hard as he could.

Shrieking in pain, Downing fell back against the wall, shaking his hand, his eyes wild with surprise. Cabot extended the stick at arm's length, toward his throat as though it were a saber. "I am Cabot North. If you so much as lay a finger on my sister again, I will beat more than your hand."

"I'll—I'll tell Lord Alfred."

"You may tell God himself, if you wish, but you will account to me."

The homecoming with Elizabeth was all he hoped it might be, filled with tears and hugs, great joy, and a prolonged outpouring of words. With their father away, they talked all that night and most of the next day.

He gave his love to her, wholly, spending part of each day with her. They went for long walks, rode horseback, sailed on the Thames. His devotion to her was, he knew, partly his own need for companionship. But mostly, it was compassion for his sister. It was as though he had returned to release Elizabeth from prison. Downing was the jailer, drumming into her the proper prayers, exorcising the heresy that had infected her at Scrooby. In the process, he had cowed her spirit, killed her happiness. Elizabeth North was filled with pain, the pain of neglect and loneliness, the sorrow of her own disfigurement. She had grown in the year he was away, a great deal more in the year after his return. Now almost twelve, she was tall and slender, showing signs of developing womanhood. But with that beak of a nose, she remained extremely unfavored, despite lovely dark hair, a fine complexion. She had turned inward to find a life she could lead. An important part of Cabot's actions were directed toward somehow finding a way to draw her out by talking to her, accepting her, offering his love.

She confessed her interest in Puritanism. What the cruel

Downing had sought to drum out of her, he had merely imbedded more deeply. She read the Geneva Bible in her room at night. She maintained contact with a Puritan congregation, attending services when she could.

"Do you hate me for it, Cabot?"

"No, Liz. I could never hate you."

"Do you think I'm wrong?"

"No, not if you believe in what you're doing?"

"I do, Cabot, I do."

He hesitated. He had declared his acceptance of her, and he didn't want to undermine it now. "Are you sure?" He saw the vigorous nod of her head, heard her emphatic words. She was young, too young to know her own mind. Her ideas would change with time. "Liz, can I ask one question? Why do Puritans interest you so?"

"I thought you didn't disapprove?"

"I don't. It's just a question."

She looked at him, her pale blue eyes unblinking. "I think you know."

He nodded and looked away. The one glorious summer of her life. He looked back at his sister, his eyes soft upon her. Perhaps that was why he was giving himself to her, trying to provide her some other love than Emily Fletcher. "How is she?"

Elizabeth smiled. "Oh, fine, I think. Did you know she married Worthy Townsend?"

The knowledge brought him no wound. "I'm not surprised."

"They have a child already, a boy named Humble. Such a strange name, but I like it, Humble Townsend. In her last letter Emily said they were poor but happy." She smiled. "Emily asks about you, but I had no news to write. Now I do."

He ignored the reference to himself. "They are in Holland?"

"Yes. They left after that summer or maybe early the next year. It was terrible. They were turned away, the men and women separated, but all managed to reach Holland. They are in Amsterdam now—no longer persecuted."

He only nodded. There was nothing to say.

"You did love her, didn't you, Cabot?"

He smiled, memories of golden hair and sweet kisses echoing in his mind. "Perhaps. But she is better off as Mrs. Worthy Townsend."

In a few weeks he received a letter from Emily, telling of

her life and happiness, her fine husband, her adorable son, the other children she hoped to have. She was so glad he had returned safely. Would he come to visit? Another letter months later. They had gone to Leyden. Please, would he visit? He had shared the letters with Elizabeth. She begged him to go, learn about Emily for her, if not for himself. At last he relented. It was why he was aboard this ferry.

His father had come home on the third day after Cabot's return to Graymere, having delayed in London to hear Captain Newport's report. Lord Alfred embraced his youngest son, then looked at him as though seeing him for the first time. "Newport says of a hundred four only thirty-eight survived."

"Some of them died later, after the supply came."

Still Lord Alfred stared at him. His son might have been an apparition. "My God, son. I had no idea. I—I would never have . . . have placed you in . . . in such jeopardy."

Words resided on Cabot's tongue. It seemed to him they had lived there for over a year. *But you did.* He never uttered them. That look in his father's eyes, his nervous speech. Yes, Lord Alfred North felt guilty.

"You've"—again the strange lack of firmness in his voice—"changed, son."

Yes, he had been right to say nothing. Silence was its own accusation.

"I don't know, you're—well, older." His laugh was nervous. "Of course, you're older. I mean you've . . . grown up. You're more . . ."

Finally Cabot spoke. "More of a man?"

The wound lay open in the old man's eyes. "I only tried to do what . . . what I thought best for you." Then he swallowed, finding it difficult. He seemed suddenly to crumble before Cabot, becoming weary, aging, his mouth going slack, his eyes watery. "I've died a thousand deaths worrying about you— what I did. If anything had happened to you, I don't know what . . ."

Cabot saw the pain in his father's eyes. Then he knew his own anger, the sense of betrayal he had nurtured so long was gone. It didn't matter anymore. Nothing did. "I am a survivor, Father."

Tears running from his eyes, Lord North, peer of the realm, embraced his son again. "Thank God for that. Yes, thank God."

In a moment he released Cabot. "Newport says your conduct
was exemplary. I am proud of you." He tried to smile. "He
even says you are becoming a good sailor."

"As you always intended." At last he could grin. "I do have
an attraction for the sea—at least when the weather's good."

"No. You are hardly a fair-weather sailor."

Father and son spent the next several hours in the study,
the first of many such discussions. As a company director,
Lord North wanted to know all that had happened in Virginia,
as well as Cabot's opinion on everything. He spared Lord North
no detail, save his brief happiness with Awotaka. He told of
the disease, starvation, and death, the uselessness of the gentlemen adventurers, the madness of Wingfield, Archer, Kendall,
and Ratcliffe, the stupidity of Newport's hunt for gold. He had
praise only for Smith "whom the council and Newport refuse
to let govern."

"You are young, Cabot, and don't know. What you call
madness goes on at court all the time. It is a way of life."

"Then move the court to Virginia for a year. See how many
survive."

Again and again Cabot denounced the search for gold. "There
is no gold in Virginia. A blind man should see that if there
were gold, the Indians would wear it."

"But the Spanish found gold."

"Not in Virginia."

Lord North sighed. "The belief in gold enables us to recruit
settlers."

Cabot was relentless. "Why recruit? What you should do is
abandon the colony. Send a ship; bring home those men before
they die."

Again the old man sighed. "Cabot, listen to me. The king
wants a colony in Virginia, as does Lord Salisbury, all the
ministers. We cannot surrender the New World to the Spanish."

"I saw no Spaniards in Virginia. They have more sense."

Distress rose in the father's face, his voice. "There just has
to be some future in Virginia." He gave a litany of possibilities.
There were mulberry trees in Virginia. Perhaps they could
cultivate silkworms. Newport's fool's gold contained iron ore.
Perhaps they could start iron works in Virginia. Vines grew
wild in the forest. Perhaps some vignerons should be sent over

to grow grapes for wine. "My God, Cabot, surely something can be made of the place."

"Yes, a graveyard. But isn't it a long way to go to bury the dead?"

"You are not being helpful, my son."

Cabot sighed, deeply. No, he wasn't being helpful. A vision of Timothy Loudon flashed across his mind, the craggy head, the yellow grin, calling him "sar." No, he wasn't being helpful to Timothy. Or to Smith. And he had promised.

When he spoke, it was with considerable eloquence. "Father, when we first landed in Virginia, men fell to their knees, believing we were in the Garden of Eden. And perhaps we were, trees so huge a man could not reach halfway around them, fields of flowers, all manner of fruits and berries, endless forests filled with wildlife, rivers brimming with fish. It was a land supreme in its bounty, yet our men died of simple starvation."

He looked at his father, awaiting a question, some protest. There was none, and he was grateful.

"There was a man among us, a simple, uneducated farmboy from Wiltshire named Timothy Loudon. I swear to God, Father, there were times when he alone loved Virginia—and he nearly died there—when he above all understood Virginia and its promise for the future. You see, Father, Timothy loves the soil as you and I might love a woman or a child, a house, maybe. And there is good soil in Virginia, far richer than you have ever seen or imagined. Timothy knows that. He may have failed the first year, but he knows what the soil can bring forth and how bountifully his endless toil will be rewarded. Virginia will bloom, he says. I, for one, am not about to argue with him."

Again he hesitated, but saw only Lord Alfred's rapt attention.

"If Virginia had a hundred men like Timothy Loudon, a thousand, ten thousand, then the king would have his colony, the company its dividends. But what did we have? We had Wingfield and Archer and Ratcliffe and Kendall. We had, not farmers, but perfumers and refiners and jewelers. We had gentlemen by the score, men who would lie down and die of starvation before they would lift a finger to do an honest minute's work." He knew his voice was rising, but he made no effort to control it. "We made every mistake in Virginia and did nothing right. The charter was wrong, the company was wrong, the governing council a mistake. We were led by madmen who are little above common murderers. John Smith alone had the capacity to lead and he was given no opportunity. Father, Virginia is a primeval wilderness. It is not England. In my opinion, it belongs to the Indians, and we ought to let them keep it. But if we are going to colonize in Virginia, we cannot try to take England there. It may be the richest of all lands, but it is wholly unforgiving. The idle, the pampered, shiftless, or arrogant will only die there. The only privileges are hard work and opportunity. And many of the hardworking will die, yet a few will succeed. Do you understand what I'm saying? If there are enough Timothy Loudons and enough John Smiths to lead them, then there may be a colony in Virginia that is more than a graveyard."

Lord North stared at him for a long moment. "Will you say this to the company directors?"

"No."

"Why not?"

"Wingfield, Archer, and Newport have their report to give."

The father nodded. "I understand. You are young; they are three. But we must know what you say."

"Then I will say it, but only in private to those prepared to listen."

As he stood on the deck of the ferry bound for Holland in September 1609, Cabot knew he had accomplished something by all his frank talk with his father and others who sought him out. The company had received from King James a second charter that greatly increased the power and authority of the company. Lord Salisbury and the bickering ministers at court were prevented from interfering in company decisions. Better still, Thomas West, the Baron De La Warr, had been named governor and captain-general of the colony, with sole command. Even now a flotilla of nine ships, loaded with settlers, animals, and equipment, was preparing to sail for Virginia under Sir Thomas Gates, the deputy governor. Perhaps such a large infusion of supplies, settlers, and leadership would help Timothy.

Cabot was asked to go along with Gates on his flagship *Sea Venture*. He refused, and he wasn't at all sure why. Knowledge that Newport and Archer were returning with the expedition was an ostensible reason, certainly enough to make him stay away. But there was something else. He knew he wasn't finished with Virginia. Somehow the place beckoned to him. Maybe that's why he refused. The time for him to go back had not yet come.

He turned toward the bow of the ferry, seeing the green coast of Holland rising in the distance. He was making this trip in large measure, he knew, because he was restless, seeking the unknown, even if only a visit to Emily Townsend. Yes, he was restless. The feel of this swaying deck beneath his feet did nothing to alleviate it.

TWELVE

Holland

AMSTERDAM FASCINATED Cabot. Twice the size of London, it was far more prosperous and bustling. There had to be five hundred ships, a forest of masts, in the harbor, and the pretentious homes lining the canals indicated the degree to which the Dutch had profited from world trade.

He went overland to Leyden, enjoying a vista of windmills, dikes, canals, and small, prosperous farms. Having wrested the land from an unforgiving sea, the Dutch were not about to waste a speck of it. Some vegetable or fruit was grown in nearly every inch of soil. These Hollanders were surely an industrious people, healthy, clean, happy in their work and prosperity. One other fact impressed him. The air over these lowlands seemed so clear, almost luminescent, the sky dotted with puffs of clouds, creating a panorama of sunlight and shadow.

Leyden charmed him. It was a smaller city of perhaps fifty thousand, famed for its university, a seat of Protestant thought, and it was a center for the textile industry and handicrafts. Leyden's tree-shaded canals, crossed by arched stone bridges and lined with splendid gabled houses made it a beautiful and distinctive city. He knew of no town in England as lovely. London was a sewer in comparison.

Cabot had no difficulty finding Emily Townsend and the other English separatists. They had settled in the heart of town around the Pieterskerk of St. Peter's, formerly a Roman Catholic cathedral. The university was close by. It was a poor and crowded quarter, full of winding lanes and alleys. On one of them lived Elder Brewster and the Townsends. It was called Stinksteeg—Stink Alley. His regard for the cleanliness of the Dutch notwithstanding, he thought the dark, narrow street aptly named.

She opened the door to his knock and stood there, open-mouthed. "Oh, Cabot!" she cried, then she embraced him, her cheek, wet with tears, against his. He had wondered how she might greet him, how he would react. He hardly trusted himself to see her again. Now, as he held her in his arms, he was aware only of how frail she seemed—and of the protuberance against his midsection. Emily Townsend was pregnant. His embarrassment at such a fervent embrace by another man's wife was not lessened when Townsend came to the door. But he was smiling, extending his hand in greeting. He seemed not to mind.

Emily had changed. That which he remembered the most about her was gone. "Your hair." It was now a brownish color. The golden halo was no more.

She laughed, raising her hand to her head. "It darkened when I had little Humble." Then she smiled. "You must meet my darling." Proudly she brought in a toddler, just over a year old and learning to walk on stubby, uncertain legs. He looked fat and healthy, with golden curls. Emily snatched him up to kiss Cabot.

In other ways, the more important surely, Emily was unchanged. She was still a blithe spirit, full of laughter, her green eyes undulled by the grinding poverty in which they obviously lived. She still had contentment within herself, the generosity of spirit that he so admired. And she was happy as a wife and mother. Of that he was certain. Cabot found himself liking Worthy Townsend. In his mid-twenties, he was hardworking, decent, obviously a good husband to Emily, a doting father to Humble.

Cabot and Emily spoke of themselves only once while Worthy was busy in another part of the house. "You suffered much in Virginia, Cabot?"

"I suppose. Many did."

"I can see it in your face, your eyes." She looked at him most directly, biting her lower lip as she hesitated. "Did I add to it?"

"No. You made it bearable many times."

Still she stared at him, as though trying to divine what he was thinking. Then she looked down at her hands. "Cabot, I couldn't wait. We were persecuted at Scrooby. We had to flee. It was a hardship just to escape."

"I know. Elizabeth told me."

"It wasn't possible, Cabot—not for us."

"I know. You did the right thing."

She looked at him again, smiling. "Friends?"

"Always."

He remained in Leyden five days, much of it filled with a recounting of the past. The Scrooby separatists had paid dearly for their faith, leaving all they possessed, including their way of life, in England. They went first to Amsterdam, joining the Brethren of the Separation of the First English Church, better known as the Ancient Brethren. But a schism had developed. Some item of doctrine, which Cabot didn't begin to understand, caused the split, along with a scandal. George Bixby, an elder, was fornicating with various women of the congregation, or so Worthy Townsend whispered to him. Accompanied by some of the Ancient Brethren, the Scroobyites migrated to Leyden. They still had no church, but they hoped to buy a suitable house in Groenpoort, or Green Gate.

They preferred the charm of Leyden to the bustle of Amsterdam—and certainly they were welcomed by the Dutch and freed from persecution—but they lived in appalling poverty. Except for Postmaster Brewster, all had been farmers and husbandmen. Here in Holland those tasks were denied them, for they owned no land. To exist, they were forced to work long hours at low pay at the most menial jobs in the textile industry. Bradford was a corduroy maker. Brewster's son Jonathan, now sixteen, was a ribbon maker. Worthy Townsend carded wool. Others were finishers of bombazine, felt or silk workers, button makers, drapers, hatters, glovers, leather dressers, cobblers, or in a couple of instances hod carriers. Children as young as six and eight worked in factories, just to fend off starvation.

"Why don't you work at more skilled trades? You can learn them."

Townsend's smile was the sort with which one indulged the ignorant. "It is impossible. The skilled trades are controlled by the guilds. Membership is restricted to Dutch citizens."

"Become a citizen then."

"Some of us are. But a long apprenticeship is required, then an investment in capital to become a guildsman."

During his visit, Cabot dutifully joined the Sunday worship services. They began at eight o'clock, ending at noon, after a three-hour sermon by the Reverend Robinson. Following a meal, the afternoon was filled with "prophesying" by members of the congregation about their religious experiences and the portents of the Bible. It was a stultifying bore to Cabot, and his restlessness became a disease. He could never join this religion. But how could Elizabeth? She had to be attracted only because of her love for Emily. The solution, he now knew, was for Elizabeth to attend a few of these Sunday observances. Only the most godly, persuaded, and trapped could endure them.

Before he left, Brewster, Bradford, Robinson, all the elders met with him to talk about Virginia. They were worried about earning a living, about pervasive Dutch influences and losing their "Englishness." What did he think of their emigrating to Virginia? Thank God he had persuaded them of the foolishness of that idea.

While in Leyden, Cabot received a letter from Hendrik van Stamp, father of the chap he had met on the ferry, inviting him to visit. Cabot decided to stop in Amsterdam on his way home. Perhaps this wealthy burgher could help the impoverished Scroobyites acquire some land or better jobs.

Van Stamp was in his mid-forties, quite corpulent, with fleshy jowls, balding pate, and a reddish mustache and chin whiskers. There was a heartiness and zest to him as he welcomed his English guest.

Cabot believed his father wealthy, Graymere suitably baronial, but he was ill-prepared for the opulent way of life of Hendrik van Stamp. He lived in a five-story medieval town house on posh Herren Gracht. It was not that the dwelling was so large—Graymere could have swallowed it—but so splendidly furnished. The walls were ornamented with breathtaking paintings. He recognized the new Dutch artist Rubens, already being called a master, Hans Holbein, Brueghel, as well as El Greco, Titian. There were tapestries, Chinese screens, teakwood chests, gilded Italian divans, full-length draperies of silk brocade, and everywhere vases, urns, objects of gold, silver and shining pewter. All boggled the eye.

Cabot understood. Van Stamp was obviously a merchant, possibly a shipowner, profiting handsomely from trade with the Far East. Freed with help of English arms from Spanish rule and the yoke of the dreaded Inquisition, the Dutch had launched an energetic trading policy, challenging the Portuguese in Macao and the Spice Islands, threatening their bastions in Africa and Brazil. The Spanish plate fleet from Manila was regularly attacked by Dutch men-of-war. The Pacific trade was no longer wholly Spanish or Portuguese. It was risky business, Cabot knew. Obviously, this corpulent Dutchman was selecting the profitable ventures.

Cabot was invited to sit in a damask settee with gilded arms and legs, and offered wine. To his amazement there was even ice in it, cut from a canal last winter and stored in straw all summer. He was introduced to Henrietta van Stamp, a matronly woman somewhat younger than but equally as corpulent as her husband. She had blonde hair braided and wound atop her head. Pieter he knew and greeted. Reference was made to two other married children.

"Where is Katarina?"

"She'll be along, Hendrik. These things take time."

Cabot saw the mother smile at him as she spoke. Then there was a momentary awkwardness, which Cabot sought to fill. "May I congratulate you on your excellent English, Mijnheer van Stamp." It was true. His accent was barely noticeable. "It is far superior to my Dutch, I assure you."

Van Stamp laughed heartily. "Dutch is an obscure tongue, of value only to those born to it. It is necessary to speak the languages of commerce, French, Spanish, Italian, Portuguese, German and, of course"—he nodded—"English."

"I admire your facility, sir."

"It is nothing. One does what one must to get by on this earth. But I thank you for your kind words. All of my children have learned languages." He glared at his wife. "Where is that infernal Katarina?"

Henrietta van Stamp smiled indulgently. "She'll be along, *liefje*."

Cabot moved quickly on behalf of what he had come for, pleading the cause of the English separatists, asking if there was not some way they could enter the skilled trades.

Van Stamp listened cordially, then replied, "As my admired guest, Mr. North, there is nothing I would not do for you or your friends. But what you ask is impossible. The guilds are all powerful." He made a gesture of helplessness. "I should wish for so much power. The Prince of Orange himself envies them. Their power resides in limited membership and certain rituals known only to themselves. The membership is restricted by citizenship, expertise, and capital. That is why their members are so highly paid."

Cabot sighed. "Then there is nothing to be done for my friends?"

"Not in terms of the guilds. I will do what I can. But I fear it must be in the form of charity." He saw Cabot's frown. "I will be discreet, of course."

Van Stamp then began to ask about Virginia. Cabot delivered a brief and hardly encouraging report on the progress of the colony, stating the mistakes as he saw them, omitting only the names and personalities of the leaders. Wingfield was still a powerful man in England. It would not be politic to have him learn of a libel.

Van Stamp listened attentively, interrupting with frequent questions. When Cabot concluded, he smiled and said, "I'm certain His Most Catholic Majesty King Philip of Spain would be charmed by your account."

"Doubtlessly."

"Have no fear, he will not hear it from these lips. I must tell you that I believe your report. I have heard from other sources that Philip considers the colony at Virginia too weak to be worth the trouble and expense of smashing."

The humiliating words about his country stung Cabot. But wasn't it true? Jamestown was not worth attacking. Even the

Indians figured to starve it out of existence.

His host changed the subject. "Then you think there is no gold in Virginia."

"No, sir, none at all."

"That is a blessing for you English."

Cabot was surprised. "I fear the company directors hardly think so."

"Then Providence has blessed them by denying them their own wishes."

Cabot stared at him, greatly puzzled. "I don't understand what you are saying."

The Dutch merchant smiled. "Few do, I fear. The fact remains that the Spanish are impoverished by the very gold and silver they found in the New World."

"Impoverished?"

"It is true, my friend, however much it may not seem so. Their treasure only enriches others. What is not stolen from them on the passage here"—he smiled—"soon ends up here in Amsterdam or Rotterdam or Antwerp, even London. The Spanish are—well, I should not say all Spanish, for I don't know them all—but the Spanish grandee is a totally useless individual. Using his hand or brain for productive work is beneath him. He rouses himself only for war or conquest, which he believes honorable endeavors." He saw Cabot nodding. "Do you understand what I'm saying?"

"I understand there are men who do not work. We had an abundance of them in Virginia."

"But you still had some men who worked, yourself included, I'm sure. When nothing is produced, everything must be purchased. Spain cannot even feed its own people."

"But they have gold."

"Yes, mountains of it—and that is their problem. The price of everything they buy goes sky high, and slowly"—he laughed—"really not so slowly, the gold leaves the country. One day all the gold will be gone, and the Spanish people will be left only with ruinous prices. I fear His Catholic Majesty will have trouble controlling his subjects when that day comes." He watched what he had said sink in. "So it is good that there is no gold in Virginia."

"But there is also nothing produced."

This led to a discussion, not unlike that with his father.

Cabot reiterated his belief that Virginia, in proper hands, might support itself, but not produce anything of great value to the investors.

Hendrik van Stamp stared at him levelly for a long moment, then looked at his son, then back at Cabot. He seemed agitated. "I'm sorry. I forget my manners." He arose, replenished their wine glasses, then stood over Cabot, looking down at him. "I asked you to come here to give me your report. It is not what I expected to hear, but I believe you speak the truth."

"Only as I see it, sir. I am perhaps wrong."

"Yes, that is possible." He raised his glass to his lips. "I should tell you we Dutch are giving some thought to colonizing America. We see no reason to surrender it to the Spanish—or to you English by default."

Again van Stamp looked at his son, as though seeking approval for his thoughts. Apparently he received it, for he began speaking at once. "I see no reason not to tell you this. The whole world will know soon. Within the last few days one of our ships, the *Half Moon,* returned from the New World. The captain was a man named Henry Hudson, a countryman of yours, I believe, but in our employ. He found an admirable port somewhat to the north of Virginia, and a wide and beautiful river, which he named after himself. He hoped it was the passage to the East, but it turned out not to be so."

"I do not wish to denigrate the discovery of Captain Hudson, but in Virginia every wide river, even the not so wide, is said to be the passage to the Pacific." Cabot shrugged gently, but said no more.

"The passage is not what interests me. While sailing up this river, Captain Hudson saw great numbers of fur-bearing animals, beaver, mink, fox—I hardly know them all. He traded with the Indians for pelts. I can tell you the cargo he returned with has considerable value. Perhaps the wealth of the New World is in furs. Do you have fur-bearing animals in Virginia?"

Cabot tried to think. "I hardly know. There must be some, I'm sure. But I saw no abundance. The summer is long and much too hot for such creatures. The winter I was there was cruel, but brief, only a couple of months."

Van Stamp was nodding vigorously. "Perhaps fur-bearing animals exist in more northerly climes." He began to expound on the feasibility of establishing and maintaining trading posts, the value of furs, the inexhaustible market for them in northern Europe.

Cabot only half heard him, for Katarina van Stamp had entered the room.

THIRTEEN

A Lover's Tale

IT OCCURRED TO her she was being excessively romantic. After all, she had not even met him. But from the first moment Pieter mentioned meeting a man who had been to Virginia—the very word connoted romantic adventure to her—Katarina van Stamp was intrigued. She found a way to ask what he looked like. When Pieter used such words as *English, gentleman, young,* and *handsome,* she hardly discouraged her father from inviting him to visit. When Cabot's letter accepting the invitation came, she believed she felt sensations emanate from the paper. It couldn't be, she knew, still, she took the letter to hide with her keepsakes.

From an upstairs window she saw him approach the house, ask directions from a passerby, hesitate at the front door. Even from above she could see he was tall, wonderfully tall, slender, a fine figure of a man in his doublet and hose. And so dark, his hair, the luxuriant beard. When he looked up at the house and she stepped quickly behind the curtain, she caught a flash of vivid blue eyes.

She gripped the curtain, trying to quell an inner excitement. Crossing her bedroom, she opened the door and listened to the exchange of greetings from below. Such a deep voice, so masculine.

In her anticipation of meeting him, Katarina van Stamp changed her dress three times. She wanted to look her best, and she was uncertain what to wear, for she had entered womanhood so recently and rapidly that she was far from accustomed to the alteration in herself, greater height, the spread of her hips, the pronounced leavening of her breasts. They seemed to grow before her eyes, altering her equilibrium, filling up, and bursting all her garments. Her new, more sophisticated wardrobe had been a necessity. More difficult for her than the physical changes were the strange internal stirrings such as she felt now as she prepared to meet this Englishman.

There was another cause for her yearnings. Her older sister Johanna, recently married to Hans van Oeuyen, had continued her girlhood practice of sharing confidences with Katarina, relating to her intimacies that might better have remained hidden within the van Oeuyen boudoir. For Katarina, this new knowledge was surely unsettling. While virginal and virtuous, Katarina was at the point of possessing the little knowledge that is dangerous.

All these events conspired against her as she descended to the foyer and crossed to the main parlor. He was seated facing her, but did not see her at once, as he was looking up at her father standing over him. She again had an impression of his handsomeness. He saw her then and immediately arose. Tall, yes, beautifully tall. She smiled, couldn't help it, but not in greeting. In his eyes she saw surprise, the widening of his pupils. He thought her beautiful.

"So there you are Katarina—at last." The elder van Stamp turned to her, then to Cabot. "Mr. Cabot North, my quite tardy daughter, Katarina."

Cabot bowed, struggling to remember the proper Dutch word. "My pleasure Mejuffrouw van Stamp."

"Where have you been, Katarina? I thought you were eager to learn about Virginia?"

She smiled, not in the least unsettled by her father's annoyance. She was his favorite and knew it. "I am, Father, and I will. But a woman has to make herself presentable."

Again Cabot bowed. "May I say you have performed that task most admirably." The smile he earned was surely dazzling.

He would later insist to himself, or try to, that she was not truly beautiful. The artist in him declared her face too round, her mouth too small, the lips perhaps immodestly turned out. But he had no such sober reflections now. Her hair startled him, straw-colored, but old straw, bleached nearly white in the sun, shining with dew. She wore it short, just reaching her shoulders, the ends curling out into points. Her eyes were the most remarkable he had ever seen, all irises, set wide apart, devouring him now. The color intrigued him. They were at base dark blue, yet from the black center radiated a sunburst of silvery blue. It was as though her eyes were polished gems, faceted by a master jeweler.

She was conscious of her mother speaking, her father resuming the conversation, something about furs and Indians. But truly she was aware only of him. She felt enveloped by his presence. It was as though she was being seen, really seen, for the first time in her life, and when his gaze lowered, she felt heat suffuse her body.

She wore a gown unlike any he had seen. It must be a new fashion. The bodice, light blue in color, was made of thin, summery silk, cut square at the throat to reveal her creamy skin, and somehow flowing, with long, puffy sleeves snugged to her wrists and banded with ribbons. Beneath a wide belt was a voluminous skirt of dark blue silk. He was startled by the naturalness of the garment. Gone were the immense padded shoulders, the stiffened ruff, the ungainly farthingale. Katarina van Stamp stood before him tall, slender, with shoulders and waist and hips. Beneath the loose-fitting blouse, he saw the sharp rise of her bosom.

"I agree, Mr. North, permanent settlements would prove costly. Trading posts may be the answer, don't you agree? The savages would take less offense. If we dealt fairly with them, they would . . ."

Cabot could not take his eyes off her. Her gaze seemed so direct, penetrating, as though she were looking deep inside him. And there was something familiar about the way she looked at him. What was it?

"Hendrick, don't you think you've talked business quite enough? You will wear out our guest's ears."

Van Stamp laughed and glanced at his wife. "You are right, of course. I do get carried away."

The voices intruded, and Cabot turned to his host. "I am most interested in what you say, mijnheer. If I may, I will suggest to my father the possibility of fur trade in Virginia." He saw van Stamp nod. Setting down his glass, Cabot said, "I must be going now. I have enjoyed meeting—"

"I will hear of no such thing. You must stay a few days at least. The festival begins this evening. It is one of the finest times in the city."

"I'm sorry, I—"

Van Stamp turned. "Pieter, Katarina, convince Mr. North he must stay. Tell him what wonderful times the young people have."

Cabot heard the welcome in Pieter's voice, his descriptions of the festival, the pleading for him to stay. But he saw only Katarina and her eyes. Then he knew. Once before he had seen that expression, in the wilderness, another maiden, so attractive, had looked at him that way, beckoning him. Once more he felt a roaring in his ears.

Her lips moved, widening into a radiant smile. "I fear you have no choice, Mr. North. Pieter will be going with Betje, his betrothed, and my sister with her new husband. I will be quite left out if you do not join us." Her laugh was throaty, deeply musical.

He felt himself bowing, heard the words from his mouth, "As you say, I have no choice. I couldn't be responsible for—"

His words were lost in his own laughter and that of the others. And that laughter, it seemed to him, signaled the start of a memorable week. He was welcomed to the bosom of a warm and loving family, greatly expanded by the married son and daughter, other relatives and friends. It was a time of nearly incessant merriment, parties nearly every night, street dances, fairs, games, minstrels, groaning boards, flagons of ale, smiles, unforced gaiety and seemingly constant laughter. He was shown the city. There were languid rides on canals and rivers, trips to the countryside, hayrides, picnics. The reputation of the Dutch for inventive, uninhibited merriment was surely justified.

Some of the time he was in the company of the elder van Stamps and their friends, or with the oldest son Ernst, his wife Anna, and their three young children. Most of the time he was part of a sextet, Johanna and Hans, Pieter and Betje, Katarina and himself. That he was so openly paired with her, that she was allowed to stay out so late, visiting taverns while unchaperoned, surprised him. It would never happen in England. But then, he told himself, Johanna and Pieter must be chaperoning their sister. For this he was grateful. He did not trust himself to be alone with her.

He was immensely attractive to her, and she basked in the envy of her friends. Johanna looked at her knowingly and whispered both her admiration and a sisterly warning. Katarina replied, "I'm not sure I want to be careful, *liefje*—at least not as careful as he is." In truth, he mystified her. He was a participant in the merrymaking. He laughed and seemed to be having fun. Only he wasn't, not really. He held back. He kept something in reserve within him, which he could not or would not let out. There were times when she felt she had to laugh for two. And she was puzzled by the distance he kept from her. She knew he thought her beautiful. His desire for her was almost a physical force between them. Yet, he hardly touched her. She had to take his hand, if she was to know the sensations the merest touch produced. When she caught him looking at her, he quickly looked away. Why was he erecting this wall between them?

He was inhibited with her, he knew, but he couldn't help it, although he railed at himself for his failing. The simple fact was that Katarina van Stamp aroused lusts in him that he had thought were forever buried in a cave in Virginia. Her beauty and statuesque figure wounded him. Her grace, spontaneity, her seeming lack of self-consciousness about the effect she had on him—didn't everyone see it?—made him fumbling, shy. She was to him the embodiment of femininity. Her slightest movement left him in turmoil. The way she spoke his name— ca-Bawt, heavily accenting the second syllable—was wholly sensuous to him. Everything about her was. When, laughing at the Punch and Judy show, she leaned against him, the pressure of her breasts against his arm made him quiver.

He tried to become involved with Pieter and Hans so as not to be alone with her. Nothing seemed to work. He entered an impromptu rowing contest on the Amstel Canal, each of the men racing with his lady. It was close for a while, but Cabot gradually pulled ahead to win. Kate, as he now called her, squealed, urging him on to victory. In her excitement, she leaped up and hugged him, almost tipping over the boat. He had to hold her tight to maintain his balance.

The first night and the second he lay in his bed at the van

Stamp mansion tormented by his desires and his self-loathing for having them. Repeatedly he tried to will himself to discard his lusts, as he thought of them, and recover the facade of indifference that had sustained him ever since Awotaka. Failing in that, he promised himself to find a way to leave the next day. But that never seemed possible by morning light. Roiling in a corner of his mind was the knowledge that he could probably seduce this Dutch girl. Many a "gentleman" would have done so and not given it a passing thought. But it was a traitorous idea to him. He could not accept a man's friendship, stay in his home, then deflower his daughter. It would be a dishonor he could not bear.

On the afternoon of the third day, Sunday, the whole family sailed on the Zuider Zee, then went ashore for a picnic. Kate wore the *klederdracht*, the peasant costume, and wooden shoes. She looked most natural in it and quite fetching. After dining, she suggested a walk along the dike overlooking the inland sea. He looked for others to join them, but none came and he was alone with his temptation.

They walked along in silence for a time. Finally she said, "May I ask you something, Cabot?"

"If you wish, Kate."

She turned and smiled. "I like to be called that."

"It is the English way."

A few steps farther they walked. Her question, when it came, surprised him.

"What happened to make you so sad?"

His instinct was to raise a barrier. "Sad? Why I'm having a wonderful time with you, your family."

She stopped, turned, looked at him intently. "Do you want me to believe that? Or do you want me not to know you?"

"I don't want you to know me, Kate." He saw the hurt in her eyes, her effort to blink it back before she turned to walk away. He stopped her, taking her wrist. "Kate, I probably have not ever enjoyed myself so much as this week. If I act—" He hesitated, trying to prevent the words from forming in his mouth. "Kate, I'm afraid, afraid of you, of myself with you."

She looked at him then, eyes bright, the smallest of smiles on her lips. What he had just confessed was nothing she had not known, she realized, but his words filled her with profound relief. Her voice was little above a whisper. "Don't be. I'm not." She slid his hand down her wrist and entwined her fingers within his.

"Don't, Kate. It's no good." He extricated his hand. "We'll bring nothing but pain to each other."

"I think not."

He sighed and began to walk along beside her, his mind a turmoil of desire and apprehension.

"I think it was a woman who hurt you."

"You are young and far too romantic. She did not hurt me."

"Then tell me what happened."

It came as an impulse, not thought out at all. "All right, I'll tell you. Then you'll know how unworthy I am of you." Yes, if she knew he'd loved a heathen savage, she would want nothing more to do with him. It was the way to end this infatuation before it began.

They sat on the top of the dike overlooking the sea, studded now with whitecaps, and he told of Awotaka, something he had never told anyone, not even Timothy. He began well enough. "When I was in Virginia, I lay with an Indian girl, a heathen savage." He thought he placed proper emphasis on the last two words.

"You didn't!"

There was surprise in her eyes, shock in her voice. Yes, it was working. "I did—many times."

"How did you meet her?"

He told her then, from the beginning, Awotaka emerging from the hut, her blue eyes, fair skin, auburn hair, how different she was from other natives.

"Then you don't think she was an Indian?"

"No, not entirely anyway." He told his theory of the Lost Colony.

She listened, fascinated, and asked many questions. She suggested perhaps a ship had stopped at some time. "Why, she might even be part Dutch. Our fishermen go to America, I'm told."

"I suppose it's possible."

"Then what happened—between you and her?"

He wanted to make his a terrible story, yet, from the beginning, his effort broke down. He could not convey what he did not feel. "I was working in the fields with Timothy. I saw her standing at the edge of the woods. I knew she was... beckoning me. I—I had to go." He made a tactical error. "When I was closer and could see her eyes, there was... It is the way you look at me, Kate." Too late he tried to correct himself. "And you must stop it."

She smiled. "Was she very beautiful?"

"Yes." He looked across the water, seeing only what was in his mind.

"What was she wearing?"

Her question brought him back to reality. "She was naked." He could not bring himself to look at her, but the quick, audible sucking in of her breath brought him satisfaction.

"She wasn't!"

He told of her apron, beads, how the apron signaled she was eligible to mate.

"And she was very beautiful?"

Again the inner sight, suffused with lushness. "She was tall, even for an Indian, slender, glowing with health, somehow regal of posture. Yes, she was very beautiful." His words masked the sound of her shortened breath. He was not looking at her and did not see the brightness of her eyes.

"What did you do?"

He did not speak for a time, and she did not prompt him, for he was staring off in space, remembering. She understood his need to. When he finally began to speak, his voice was so low she had to listen carefully to hear him against the wind and lapping water. He told of woods, path, berries, basket. Katarina listened, almost afraid to breathe. Clearly, he had forgotten she was there. He was reliving his experience. She knew, because his was no ordinary tale, but one rich in detail. She was stunned by the intimacy of it. Part of her felt she should be embarrassed, stop him. But somehow she knew she should not. Instinctively she sensed his need to tell this. Then she didn't want him to stop, for her own mind began to play tricks on her. It was not an Indian girl who felt the passion of her first kiss, but herself. It was she who ran naked up the path, climbed the rocks, jumped into the pool. It was she, not the golden Indian girl, who laughed from behind the falls. It was she who took his hand, led him to the crypt, who felt hand, mouth, wet skin, she who...

At first she was not aware he had stopped talking. Then silence began to intrude, and she opened her eyes. She was conscious that her mouth was open and that he was looking at her intently.

"I'm sorry. I shouldn't have told you all that. I don't know what came over me."

She was filled with desire. All she wanted to do was throw herself into his arms, feel his kisses, his arms crushing her. Instead she said, "You loved her very much, didn't you?"

He nodded. "Yes." Again he looked away from her. "She was there to give and accept, somehow sustained by the giving and accepting. In her was no right or wrong, just joy—given and accepted. She was a natural part of it all, trees, grass, flowers. She was sky and water."

She felt her eyes fill and had trouble swallowing. Her voice was a little choked as she asked, "How long did you know her?"

"I'm not sure. Not long. Several weeks."

"What did you talk about?"

"Nothing—and everything." He looked at Kate and smiled a little. "She knew no English, and I knew no Algonkian—or hardly any. We used signs a lot." He swallowed and looked away. "But I knew her laughter, her joy, her...her touch." He paused a moment. "Actually she talked a lot, almost incessantly, even when we were..." He sighed. "I didn't understand a word, yet I knew, somehow, what she was saying. I knew everything about her."

She felt her tears spilling from her eyes. She was almost afraid to ask, "What happened to her?"

He lay back against the earth, looking up at the sky. She didn't think he would ever reply. When he did, he spoke for a long time and very quietly. He told of Timothy and the fort, the stupidity and frustration, the planting, the trading, the growing hostility of the Indians. He told of the sickness and how Awotaka had saved his life with the medicine, and Timothy's life, too, and how they had climbed a tree to escape a war party. Until, at last, he came to the final day, Awotaka running to warn them, Tenpenny firing, her falling, his running, arrows, Timothy being hit. "Even in death she saved my life. I think that chief must have known about us and stopped them from killing me."

Through streaming eyes she looked down at him to ask, "W–What...h–happened...to Timothy?"

He told her Timothy still lived with an arrow in him.

Barely able to speak, she sobbed, "She died...you... never"—she struggled for breath—"saw her again?"

"No." He told of going to the cave, burying their garments. "Somehow it made me feel better."

She was shaking with sobs. *"Oh, God, Cabot."* She collapsed onto him, her arms around his head, her cheek against his forehead, weeping, her tears wetting his eyelids. She forgot her English and gasped words in Dutch, which he didn't understand.

Who can say when the emotional alchemy began? She was there, in his arms, her breasts high against his shoulders. Then his mouth was on hers, first salty with tears, now scalding with passion. She was above him, holding his head, kissing him, her body nearly atop his. He couldn't move, didn't want to.

"Oh, *lieveling, lieveling,*" my darling, my love. She was kissing his eyes, his face, descending again to his mouth.

His passion was at flood tide, tearing through him. Still clinging to her lips, he rolled her off him so that he was above her, bending, devouring what was eager to be devoured.

"Lieveling, lieveling."

Never was a word so beautiful—or the utterer. Her eyes, shining with happiness, collected the blue of the sky, and her mouth, repeating the love word as a litany, was pure temptation. Again he kissed her, deeply, then bent to kiss the exposed skin between her breasts.

He was not without caution, however. He raised his head and looked back. Her family was some distance away. Not far enough. He looked around for some place to go.

"I will come to your room tonight, *lieveling.* We can wait that long—somehow."

The rest of the afternoon and evening were endless. His passion inevitably cooled, and he knew her plan to be folly. He was a guest in her father's house. It would be a dishonor to—to even think it. He told her so, or tried to. Her reaction was to nod, smile, and whisper, *"Lieveling."* He didn't know what she meant, but after that she seemed to keep greater distance from him. He tried to immerse himself in conversation with Pieter and the others. She would not come to him. She had more sense. And he surely ought to. If she did come, he would send her back to her room. It was only honorable.

Her distance from him was her time of decision. She would have preferred to continue what had begun on the dike and regretted it couldn't be. She wished he would come to her, insistent, demanding, but she knew it was impossible for him, the unfamiliar house, his unwillingness to take advantage of her. Strangely, she had no doubt she would go. She wanted to, although she had scant knowledge of what would transpire. She wanted to satisfy her desire, she wanted his admiration for her. And she wanted him, just him. His tale of the Indian maiden had affected her deeply. She felt his passion, his sorrow. But more, she felt—what? Compassion? No. She knew. He needed her. She didn't truly understand, but she sensed that his need was far more powerful even than love. No, her decision was not whether to go. She hesitated only in the knowledge she would be making a commitment to him. She hardly knew him, but he was already deeply imbedded in her spirit. If this meeting took place, would she ever uproot him?

The house was long quiet, and he felt relief that she was not coming. He was about to snuff the candle and try to sleep when he heard the merest of creaks outside his door, the turning of the latch.

She wore a robe of fine, blue silk, tied at her waist. She was fully covered, yet the thinness of the fabric only enhanced her womanliness. Her eyes were soft, luminous. He saw no fear in them.

He sat on the edge of the bed in his dressing gown. On bare feet she came to stand over him. "Kate, we can't, mustn't," he whispered. "Go back to your room, *please.*"

She smiled, just a little, and reached out to brush his cheek, run a fingertip across his lips.

"Please, go back." But the words were denied as he took her hand, pressing his lips into the palm.

For an instant, he thought she was going to obey him. She took her hand away and stood there, hesitating. He expected her to turn, leave. Instead, she slowly untied the silken robe, opened it.

"Oh, God, Kate." His throat was dry, and he knew he was shaking. Having seen a forest full of nakedness, having known one body fully, he never would have conceived a woman's mysteries held any further fascination for him. Yet, the breasts of Katarina van Stamp leaped toward him, milky, engorged,

gaudy with bright pink baubles, slightly pendulous, rising above a tiny waist and narrow hips. His mouth opened in wonder.

Somewhere he found another protest. "We mustn't, Kate."

She felt his eyes, knew his admiration. She had wanted that, never doubting. Her voice was nearly inaudible, more air than sound, as she said, "Is it not possible in your lifetime, *lieveling,* that another might want to give joy and accept it?" She saw his gaze, somehow tormented, meet hers, and she heard him groan as she stepped forward, cradling his head within her gown.

It was not so much that he was patient with her, for his passions were at flood, nearly spilling over the levees of restraint, but that he was so utterly fascinated. She held delights that suppressed impetuosity. She was not fat, not at all, yet she seemed so fleshy to him. It was as though his hands were in warm cream. She was all softness and smoothness, straw-filled meadows, dew, and the fresh, sweet smell of response. And when at last he immersed himself in the milky tide and she gave to him, as to herself, the gift of her ultimate mystery, he was merely astonished.

She had come to explore his needs, but discovered her own. From the moment she leaned into him, filling his eager mouth, she felt buffeted by sensation. His every touch thrilled her, and her passion rose exponentially until she could barely suppress her cries as at last he entered her. She had no idea what was to happen to her, but she hardly expected what did. A stillness came over her, more pure than she had ever known. All sensation, all awareness seemed to focus in a single place, known only to her, reachable only by him.

When the stillness began he thought he had hurt her and was alarmed. Then he saw her eyelids open, her jewels now misty, and from her mouth came disordered breathing, then words, *"Ik hou van jou, ik hou van jou,"* before her body began to dissolve into a paroxysm of shuddering. It seemed to go on for the longest time, astounding him.

"Kate, oh, Kate."

"Lieveling, lieveling."

They lay finally in each other's arms, limbs of love entwined, spent. He was filled with wonder. Repeatedly, the stillness had come to her, and the knowledge of her ecstatic response to him had again and again replenished him. He felt

her raise her head from his shoulder. She looked up at him,
eyes bright.

"*Ik hou van jou.*" She smiled. "Do you know what it means?"
He nodded.

FOURTEEN

A Wounded Man

WHEN HE RETURNED to London, he found it devastated by the
news from Virginia, brought by Sir Samuel Argall, a returning
ship captain. The great expedition led by Sir Thomas Gates,
the new deputy governor, had met with disaster. The nine-ship
fleet had been battered by a hurricane. Most of the vessels,
some dismasted, had limped into Jamestown. But not the flagship *Sea Venture*. It was presumed lost. Aboard were Gates,
Admiral Sir George Somers, Colonial Secretary William
Stachey, and Vice Admiral Newport. Unable to agree on pre-
cedence and in defiance of company directives, all the new
leaders of the colony had sailed on the same ship. Lost with
them were the new royal charter and company orders.

With no new instructions, John Smith, serving his one-year
term as council president under the old charter, had remained
in charge. Since Archer had returned to the colony and Ratcliffe
was still there, Cabot had no difficulty imagining the turmoil
swirling around the redoubtable Smith.

Upon his return to Graymere, he tried to give himself wholly
to Elizabeth. He would do with brotherly affection what the
cruel tutor Downing had failed to do. He greatly exaggerated
the poverty and unhappiness of the Scroobyites in Leyden.
Elizabeth only wept. He told, more truthfully, of the long,
boring Sunday of worship. Elizabeth only smiled knowingly.
He continued to worry about her secret interest in Puritanism,
but again told himself how young she was.

Elizabeth did not fill his mind. Nothing did. He even tried

sketching again. It was not so much that his hand was rusty as that he was now aware of how pathetic and amateurish his efforts were. Nothing, it seemed, could take his mind from Katarina van Stamp.

The hearty Dutch breakfast the morning after she came to him was difficult. He was certain her father, mother, Pieter must know, see the radiance of her smile, hear the music in her voice, perceive his own sheepish expectation of disgrace and dismissal. It never came. The hardworking Dutch, having given themselves to the merriment of the festival, merely continued it. He stayed the remainder of the week, then allowed himself to be "convinced" to stay two more.

In truth, he surrendered to her, to himself, happiness. He began to talk, a lot, to laugh, to participate fully in the events of the festival and the family fun. Part of him recognized that he ought to consider the future, where all this was leading, but he didn't care. He also recognized in himself attitudes similar to those he'd had with Awotaka. There might be risk, some terrible price to be extracted later, but he didn't care. He was living for now, for pleasure. She was to him all joy and beauty. They shared an intimacy by day as well as by night. It was surprising, to him at least, how often they found a way to be alone, even in a crowd. Theirs was a secret language of glances and gestures. Across a room of revelers, he could make her look at him, see the beckoning in her eyes. Her lips would move in silent words, *lieveling* or *Ik hou van jou*. Yes, he loved her.

They had an intimacy of the mind. He told her of his mother and father, his suspect birth, of Elizabeth and Emily. He spoke again and again of Virginia, death, and his friendship for Timothy. He confessed his loneliness and how she filled it. Theirs was utter frankness. "Did you come to me because of what I told you about Awotaka?"

She looked at him a long time, as though plumbing herself for truthfulness. Finally came a small smile. "I cannot be her, only myself." She spoke of loving him before she ever met him. He scoffed, but she insisted. "I was excited when Pieter first spoke of you. I held your letter in my hand and knew you were wonderful. When I saw you from the window, I felt I couldn't breathe."

He said it wasn't possible. Again she insisted, smiling at herself, at him.

When he expressed his guilt at dishonoring her father, she said, "My father is a most wonderful person—my mother, too. He has not spoken of it, but I know he would not give me to a man I do not love." She looked at him and smiled. "I'm his pet, you see. He wants me to be more than just a . . . a breeder of heirs. He insists I read, study, become accomplished." She laughed. "I'm not sure what he has in mind for me—but he allows me freedom to be myself. I am most fortunate."

"No, I am the fortunate one."

She smiled. Always she was smiling. "Oh, *lieveling*."

He kissed her lightly, quickly. There was no time for more. "So you don't want to be a mother,"

"Of course I do. I just—" She hesitated, struggling for words in a second language. "There has to be something more. I don't know what. Something that tests me as a person, my abilities. I–I want to find out what I can do—besides love you." She laughed. "That's too easy."

How remarkable she was. How he loved her. "Should I speak to your father about us?"

Her eyes were never more radiant. "You needn't. I think he knows." She laughed. "But if it would make you feel better."

She came to him each night in his room, enveloping him within the silken robe. Their physical attraction remained at white heat, and he marveled more at her repeated response to him than at the draining of his own youthful reservoirs. She seemed devoid of doubt or guilt, a condition he could not quite duplicate, try as he would.

To her, it passed all understanding, herself, the convolutions of pleasure he brought her and, most amazing, the knowledge her fulfillment thrilled him so. How was it possible for her consummate pleasure to cause him to love her more? She knew only that she had captured him.

"How can you give yourself so often, Kate?"

She saw the wonder, the love in his eyes. "I have no other gift, *lieveling*."

"But you do. Yours is the gift of love, laughter, happiness, joy."

She nodded. "I give only myself."

The time came when he had to leave. She pursed her lips,

nodded, forced a smile. "When will you return?"

"I don't know."

She looked deep into his eyes. "I love you, Cabot North."

He nodded. *"Ik hou van jou, lieveling."*

Kate remained with him at Graymere, her words, all they had done filling him with desire and longing. Truly he loved her. Yet, he had a sense of events moving too rapidly. He really had just met this girl. But so great was their physical attraction, he had been propelled into dishonor, repeatedly bedding his host's daughter. He had hoped that if he stayed away from her for a while, his ardor would cool. Enough time had elapsed for him to know that wasn't happening, not at all.

In December 1609, Captain John Smith returned from Virginia, severely wounded. He had gone up the James to the falls. On his return, he fell asleep in the shallop. Someone, apparently lighting a pipe of tobacco, dropped a match. It ignited the bag of gunpowder at Smith's waist. In agony he jumped into the river, saving his life, but he was cruelly burned on the thighs and loins. His term as president ended in any event, and he returned to London for medical treatment.

Eager for any distraction, Cabot visited him at the estate of Sir Thomas Smythe, treasurer of the Virginia Company, finding him hearty of voice and feisty, yet drawn and haggard. He still suffered much pain.

Cabot almost could not bring himself to ask about Timothy, then knew great relief at Smith's reply. "Oh, Loudon is fine, indestructible, one of the few ancients left. Just wish I'd had a thousand like him. When I finally got to be president, I set men to work clearing land. Got thirty or forty acres planted. I had to put a bloody gentleman in charge, but it was Loudon who really ran the farm. Some horses, cattle, chickens, and hogs were brought over in the second supply. Young Loudon really got 'em to multiply." He laughed. "The Indians wanted to trade for chickens—never seen 'em before, you know. If those bloody fools just leave Loudon alone, he'll grow enough to feed the colony."

Cabot beamed. The image of Timothy alive and doing what he loved pleased him inordinately.

Smith wanted to tell his story, not in the restrained, self-serving way he had to the company directors (for trumped up charges were pending against him), but to a friend, someone who had been there and knew. His tale, larded with salty language and slanderous references to his fellow colonists, consumed hours that day and continued the next. Cabot ultimately became bored with the dreary details—Smith could not leave anything out—but out of courtesy, he listened as attentively as he could.

Smith dwelt at length on his two explorations of the Chesapeake Bay. He had gone up rivers bearing such names as Patuxent, Patapsco, and Potomac. He had not been able to prove it, but he was convinced that after a short portage, he would have found the Pacific Ocean. Repeatedly Indians told him it was there. His failure to find the passage was due to his constant scuffles with "treacherous" Indians. With great relish, Smith related each of his innumerable skirmishes and "wars" with the Indians in which he unfailingly won the battle. Cabot had no doubt Smith was an indefatigable explorer, as well as courageous and resourceful in coping with Indians. He just wished he'd get on to tell about Jamestown.

He prompted him. "When were you sworn in as president?"

"On September tenth." It took Cabot a second to realize that would have been in 1608. "I had just returned from my second exploration." He smiled. "I will admit I made the voyage and took six weeks doing it just to be gone from that fool Ratcliffe."

"And you timed your return for your swearing in."

Smith's laugh was hearty. "Yes, I confess I did. Found the place in a state of mutiny. Ratcliffe—the blithering, puffed-up ass—had set the men to building him a presidential 'palace.' Can you imagine?"

Cabot nodded. That would have been Ratcliffe all right.

"I put a stop to that and set the men to work at something useful. I was sick to death o' those bloody gentlemen. I said, 'No work, no eat.' Would you believe some o' them still refused? Ran off and begged from the Indians rather than lift a finger. It'll be the ruination of this whole realm, not just Virginia, I tell you. But I put enough o' them to work, along with the good men like your friend Loudon. We accomplished a lot, repaired the fort, cleared for planting, built a blockhouse to guard the entrance to the peninsula from the mainland, drilled the men. Then I put all to work building housing, for I knew

Newport was coming with the second supply. 'Course, I kept up trading with the Indians, or trying to. Winter was coming and I knew we'd starve without it."

It was self-serving, Cabot knew, but probably accurate. Smith would have worked harder than anyone to get the job done.

"Then that bloody Newport came. North, I know your father is a director. I'll deny it if you say I said it, but between you and me, Newport is an ass. He has hurt Virginia as much as any man. He came this time in a ship called the *Mary and Margaret*. There were seventy passengers with him, including two women—a Mistress Forrest, married to a man named Thomas, and her maid, the young Anne Burroughs. You'll never believe the courting that went on o' her. One o' the ancients, John Laydon, won her and I married them."

Cabot smiled. He remembered Laydon.

"You know what that bloody fool Newport did? He brought over a copper crown for Powhatan. He was to crown him emperor and that's all there was to it. Powhatan wouldn't come to Jamestown, so Newport took it to him. There we were, out there in his imperial village, standing in front o' his dais. Newport wants him to kneel so he can put the bloody crown on. Well, Powhatan already figures he's an emperor, and he's not about to kneel for anybody. Finally, I gave Powhatan a little shove. His head went forward, and Newport stuck the crown on. But that business hurt us a lot. Powhatan turned treacherous after that. He wanted an end to all of us."

"What of the Princess Pocahontas?"

Smith grew silent. There was a faraway look in his eye. "We'd o' starved without her that winter. Time and again she came in the nick o' time, bringing food, for Powhatan had forbidden trade with us. He hoped to starve us out. Nobody would trade, not even the Chickahominies. Oh, I went to see Powhatan, threatening and carrying on to bargain for what I could. But the truth is the Indians had a bad harvest. They didn't have much food to spare. We never coulda made it without the princess. She even came running up once to warn us of a big attack Powhatan planned. I don't think he ever forgave her for that. That there is a colony today is due to Pocahontas."

Cabot nodded.

"Oh, I know, everybody figured she and I . . . But she was always just a child to me, a playful Little Wanton."

Cabot smiled. "But what did *she* think, Captain?"

He laughed. "That could be—maybe. But I'm not the marrying kind. You know that." He grunted. "Particularly now I'm not." Cabot wanted to say something to comfort him, but could think of nothing. "Newport was told not to come back till he found gold, the route to the Pacific, or evidence of what happened to the Lost Colony."

Cabot thought again of telling him of Awotaka. But he would not have believed him.

"He failed in all three. Oh, he took home some more ore and the clapboard I'd had cut, but I know that's why he was demoted to vice-admiral." Smith's derisive laughter revealed his true feelings. "Anyway, he mercifully left—but not without leaving me with a peck o' troubles. He brought along some Poles. They were to build an iron works and a glass factory. They weren't too much trouble. It was the bloody Dutchmen."

Cabot's attention increased at the word.

"God in heaven, North, those Dutchmen. They were carpenters. They were supposed to build Powhatan a proper house with a proper door. You know how the Indians are with a door, sit and swing it open and shut all day. Never saw one before. Well, the damn Dutchmen didn't speak any English. Worse than talking to the Indians, it was. They went off to Powhatan and"—he sighed—"I guess they figured if they had to learn a language, it might as well be Algonkian. Besides, the Indians ate a whole lot better than we did."

"They went over to Powhatan?"

"That they did. Treacherous they were. Kept stealing our tools, swords, muskets, anything they could lay their hands on to give to Powhatan. They even tried to lure me into an ambuscade, but fortunately one of them warned me and I scared them off. I can't tell you o' the trouble I had with them Dutchmen."

"Did the sickness return?"

He nodded. "Always. In the summer and fall the new ones die like flies. Those who survive become adjusted after a while. We ancients weren't bothered too much by it again."

Cabot was glad to know that about Timothy.

Smith told of the arrival of Captain Argall in June 1609,

bearing word of the coming of the Gates's fleet. Smith set to work with a will, preparing additional housing, piling up cut clapboard, and drilling the men. He wanted an orderly, well-run colony to turn over to the new governor. Instead of Gates, he got four battered ships, with others limping in later, four hundred new mouths to feed. Some of them were women and children, most of the rest shiftless, larcenous thieves swept from English prisons. Worse, he got Archer, two contentious new councilors, and perpetual wrangles over Smith's authority to govern.

With nearly six hundred mouths to feed, winter approaching, and Indians refusing to trade, Smith ordered the colony dispersed, a practice long used by the Indians during their own starving times. Part of the settlers went to Kecoughtan at Port Comfort, and over a hundred men under Francis West, younger brother of Lord De La Warr, were sent seventy miles up the James to the falls. Early in September, Smith went to inspect the settlement. On his way back, he was burned. In terrible pain, Smith was kept in Jamestown another three weeks while Archer and Ratcliffe trumped up charges against him to accompany him to England. George Percy was elected president to succeed Smith.

Cabot left Smith in a sour mood. Smith had been the best thing in Virginia. Brash, hardly diplomatic, he nonetheless knew how to deal with the Indians and how to get men to work. Percy was likable, but lacked Smith's skills. And with Archer and Ratcliffe there, God help Virginia, God help Timothy. Why, oh, why had the *Sea Venture* been lost? With it went the new charter and new leadership that he himself had urged. Surely Providence had not aided Virginia. Shaking his head in frustration, Cabot tried to tell himself he had done all he could to help Timothy. In truth, he knew he hadn't.

FIFTEEN

Visit From a Governor

CABOT SPENT THE yuletide with his family, expanded now by the arrival of his three oldest half-brothers.

Sir Harold, destined to be the next Earl of Durham, was principal aide to Robert Cecil, the Earl of Salisbury and the king's chief minister. Sir Harold had arrived at his lofty position at court on his own merits, to be sure, but a highly fashionable marriage to Lord Salisbury's daughter, Lady Portia, had hardly hindered him. Sir Robert North, the next brother, was already rising in the diplomatic ranks, having returned for the holidays from his post in Paris. Sir Albert North was a ranking military officer, said to have a brilliant future in the king's regiments. The two half-brothers next older than Cabot and with whom he felt closest did not make it home. Henry was in the Orient with the East India Company and George was in Russia with the Muscovy Company.

Cabot did not feel comfortable with his three oldest brothers. It was partly a matter of age. He was almost a generation younger than Sir Harold. They were husbands and fathers, settled into their own affairs. More, they were to him a bit pompous and, he had faced it many times, condescending toward him and Elizabeth. Lady Evelyn had been no lady to them, a fact that hardly endeared them to Cabot.

He spent most of the holidays greatly bored, wishing he were with Kate and her family. In comparison with the van Stamps, the Norths were sedate, the meals stuffy, the "fun" ritualized, laughter forced. The conversations were not so much a sharing of ideas as an effort by the brothers to impress each other and their father with their knowledge and importance. Soon to be twenty-one, Cabot was invited to participate. But gossip about court personalities and their intrigues, the pontificating about various diplomatic, military, and mercantile initiatives bored Cabot. He wanted to be elsewhere.

"Father tells me you do not think there is much future in Virginia, Cabot."

He turned to Sir Harold. "Not as presently constituted. I have just seen Captain Smith. He does not see much future for the iron and glass works being built there."

Sir Robert interjected. "Our esteemed Captain Smith would be better off defending himself against mutiny charges than disparaging others."

Cabot looked at his smirking face. The charges against Smith were poppycock, but he got no chance to defend him.

Sir Harold was persistent. "Isn't it premature, my dear brother, to assume failure for industry in Virginia?"

"Perhaps, but even if successful, it is still a long way to travel to make products that are more easily manufactured here."

Sir Robert again spoke. "If you believe Virginia a failure, then why have the French established a settlement at a place called Quebec? Other countries are moving in the same direction."

"Yes. The Dutch are thinking of it, the Swedes, too." Sir Harold cleared his throat. "How can you believe we English have no future in America?"

Cabot argued with them, stating how he believed Virginia could succeed. He knew he was wasting his breath, however.

Christmas night, he and Elizabeth accompanied their father to a party at Hatfield House, the new, elegant Cecil estate. It was a large affair attended by the Norths, the Salisburys and many important guests. But it seemed to Cabot everyone was there to see and be seen. But then his view may have been colored by Elizabeth's becoming upset. She had not wanted to go and was in a state of nervousness. He was at her side when they heard a voice say, "Why that poor disfigured child. With a nose like that she'll put some poor chap's eye out." Cabot stiffened at the words and looked at Elizabeth. She might have turned to stone. He took her arm and led her away, but it was much too late.

His efforts to remain with Elizabeth were thwarted when

Lady Portia descended on him. There were people eager to meet him. He had no choice but to accompany her. He was to meet Lord Salisbury—an old, dyspeptic-looking man, obviously in poor health—and various members of his family. Lady Portia's true purpose became known when he was introduced to her niece, Lady Barbara Cecil. It was not a new experience for Cabot. Even as the untitled, youngest son of the Earl of Durham, he was considered eligible for some daughter of a peer. Cabot could have spent all his time accepting invitations to teas, balls, and cotillions. He refused them all. Instead, he was at this one only at his father's insistence and wished mightily he had not come.

"So this is the famous Cabot North of Virginia."

He guessed she wasn't much older than Elizabeth, perhaps thirteen, fourteen at the most, but in terms of sophistication, Lady Barbara was years beyond his sister. Her honey-colored hair was elaborately coiffed, her almond-shaped face with the hazel eyes, now fixed upon him, carefully powdered and made up. Her gown was in the latest fashion, the ruff most elaborate, the heavy brocade of the gown elegant. From deep cleavage, a sure sign she was a virgin and eligible for marriage, peaked small, hard breasts.

He bowed. "You do me honor, Lady Barbara, but I am neither famous nor from Virginia."

She rendered a brittle laugh. Indeed everything about her struck him as brittle, forced, unnatural. "Cabot North—I should say, the mysterious and inaccessible Cabot North—is all I hear talked about, so that makes you famous. And I know for a fact you have been to Virginia."

He sighed, but only inwardly. "Yes, I made the voyage to Virginia."

A young woman at her side whispered in her ear. "All right, Eleanor." She turned back to him. "Mr. North, this is my cousin Lady Eleanor Burghley. She wants me to ask if it is true the savages in Virginia go about quite *naked*."

As he bowed to the cousin, he heard both young women giggle, for it was a daring question for a proper maiden to ask. "Only in the summer, milady. It is quite warm then."

There was a new outburst of tittering; then Lady Barbara was looking at him boldly. "You must have found Virginia *fascinating*, Mr. North."

Cabot bowed. "I have been charmed, miladies. Now if you'll excuse me." He turned to go.

"You are not excused, Mr. North." He turned to see Lady Barbara smile. It was a flirtatious, strangely cold smile. "Once we have captured the handsome and very *elusive* Cabot North, we are not about to let him go."

He recoiled inwardly but held on to his manners. "I'm flattered, milady, but I must go."

Again her brittle laugh. "It seems some other lady has charmed you."

"Indeed. My sister. I promised to attend her." After another bow he departed.

Letters from Kate sustained him. They were unfailingly short, as though she had difficulty writing in English, yet there was a quality of intimacy to them.

> *Lieveling,*
>
> The holidays are over at last. The whole family gathered, and we did the usual merry things, but I missed you and somehow my heart wasn't in it. I understand. You had to be with your family, but I know that one of these Christmases soon, you and I will be together in our love.
>
> It is cold here now. The canals and rivers are beginning to freeze. Skating will start soon. It is a lovely time of year, all cold noses and warm fires. Please try to come for a visit. We all want you. Father mentioned just yesterday that I should invite you.
>
> Oh, Cabot, I miss you so. Do come.
>
> *Ik hou van jou,*
> Your Kate

As he shoved the letter into his pocket, he realized his eyes were smarting. He had to see her again. He knew he did.

Shortly after the first of the year, Lord Alfred asked him to go riding, an infrequent occurrence. When they stopped to rest the horses, Cabot learned the reason for it.

"So what do you think of her?"

Cabot's thoughts had been of Kate, wondering if she rode. "Who, Father?"

"The Cecil granddaughter. What's her name? Oh, yes, Barbara, Lady Barbara Cecil." He smiled. "Winsome lass. One might even say beautiful."

Cabot's mind flitted back to the Christmas party, the brittle, flirtatious girl. "I suppose. I didn't pay much attention."

Lord Alfred laughed. "When I was your age, I paid more attention to such things."

Cabot looked at him. The idea of his father admiring and wooing women was incongruous to him.

"I can tell you made more of an impression on her. You're being invited to Hatfield House for a weekend. I suspect you'll want to go."

Cabot could only stare at him, puzzled.

"She's young yet, of course, but in a year or two—" Again the forced, hearty laugh. "You'll do yourself proud with her."

Cabot was surprised, but not obtuse. "Father, I'm going to be twenty-one in March. I'll make my own choice in these matters."

Another laugh. "Of course, of course. Don't men always decide these things?" Still another chuckle. "But when you see the size of her dowry . . . Of course, there has been no discussion, but I'm certain it will be substantial. There is the problem of a title for you, but something can always be arranged."

"Father, I won't have you—"

"I'm not doing anything, Cabot, but what is best for you—what you will want. You just go off for your weekend"—his laugh was knowing this time—"and let nature take her course." He dug his heels into his mount and headed for Graymere.

Cabot gave no more than a passing thought to the forthcoming invitation to Hatfield House. Lady Barbara Cecil, however exalted her lineage, was repugnant to him, and he was not about to spend a weekend, a day, or even a second courting her. For a moment he thought of telling his father about Kate. Tell him what? That he had met an attractive Dutch girl who thrilled him in bed? No, not yet. He should return to Amsterdam first, talk to Kate, and decide their future.

Before he could leave, however, he was summoned to his father's study and introduced to Thomas West, the Baron De La Warr, governor of the colony of Virginia. He was thirty-two years old, wealthy, splendidly connected, and obviously deeply interested in Virginia. He was of average height, slender, with a long, aristocratic nose. Indeed, his whole face seemed pinched and elongated. The ear-to-ear beard he affected accentuated this feature.

Lord North let his visitor do the talking. "As you may know, Mr. North, the *Sea Venture* has been lost, along with my deputy, Sir Thomas Gates, and others who were to lead the colony."

"Yes, milord, I knew that."

"I am mounting a relief expedition with all possible dispatch."

"And much of the cost is being defrayed from his lordship's own purse."

Cabot glanced at his father, then back at Lord De La Warr. "Your interest in Virginia is well known, milord."

"It is an important undertaking that cannot be allowed to fail." He hesitated, looking at Cabot intently. "Your interest in Virginia is also well known, Mr. North. You were among the ancients there. Your views concerning . . . improvements in the colony have been reported to me. I am much impressed with your thinking."

"Thank you, milord."

"I would like you to accompany me to Virginia as my aide, secretary if you will. Your experience in Virginia will be invaluable."

He'd had no inkling, and the statement came as a total surprise. He saw the pride in his father's eyes, the expectation in De La Warr's. "I'm most flattered, milord, but I'm sure there are others more qualified. Captain Smith, for example."

"Captain Smith has returned to London, sorely injured. If he had not, he would have been placed in charge of colonial defense under the new charter."

Cabot had not known of the honor to Smith. "I hoped Captain Smith was recovered sufficiently to return to Virginia."

"I fear not." His eyes bore into Cabot. "Then you will accept the post I offer."

He sighed and looked away, his mind racing. Go to Virginia, leave Kate. He had such a feeling of events making his decisions for him. He turned back to De La Warr. "Milord, I would be honored to serve as your aide, doing what I can for Virginia." He sighed, more deeply this time. "But could I ask you for a little time to think about it?"

"What is there to think about, my son?"

"I'd planned a trip to Holland, Father, I—"

"Holland? What on earth will you do there?"

Cabot pursed his lips. It would not do to say there was a girl he loved. "It has to do with the discoveries of Captain Hudson. A wealthy Dutch merchant wants to consult with me—about the possibilities of settlement in—in America." It was a lie, but not too much of one.

Lord De La Warr spoke. "We cannot possibly sail before late March. You will have time to settle your affairs in Holland and still accompany me."

"I suppose that's true, milord."

"Good. I will see you in March." He smiled. "And I will not take no for an answer, Cabot."

He left at once for Holland, knowing he would accept De La Warr's offer and return to Virginia. Part of him didn't want to, for memories of death and pain were still strong within him. Yet, he knew that if he didn't go, he would be abandoning Timothy and the other good men in the colony. As De La Warr's aide, he would be able to put some of his ideas into effect. He would be able to help Timothy and Virginia. Yes, he had to go.

But that decision, easily made on the ferry to Holland, was undermined the moment he saw Katarina van Stamp. She was simply more beautiful than he remembered. He told himself it was the distortion of love and desire, but, no, she had changed in only a few months, taking on confidence and poise. When he mentioned it to her she said, "I've heard love does that."

Her greeting of him amid the family was warm, cordial, yet correct. But when they had a moment alone, she embraced him fervently, her cheek against his. "Oh, *lieveling*, at last you're here."

He clutched her, sensation streaking right to his loins. "I've missed you so."

"Yes, oh, yes." The kiss that followed was all pent-up passion. At its conclusion, she whispered, "I'll come to you tonight."

He waited for her, his mind a turmoil of wanting her and hating these disreputable meetings under her father's roof. He knew he could not refuse her, nor could he abide his own dishonor. His solution to the problem was made suddenly, effortlessly the moment she entered his room. He would marry her now and take her to Virginia with him as his wife.

She was all bejeweled eyes, softness, and desire. Yes, it was the right decision. He had to have her, this night and every night. He couldn't let her get away. Then he remembered, producing a small box. "I brought you a present," he whispered. It was a small but flawless star sapphire, which had cost a significant portion of his allowance. It hung between her breasts on a gold chain.

"Oh, *lieveling,* I never saw anything so lovely."

Eyes bright, he said, "I have. I hoped it might exceed your eyes, but nothing can."

He was sitting on the bed, she standing, and she swept his head within her arms, against her bosom. This action, part of the ritual of their lovemaking, seemed to him now to transcend desire, even his passion. He felt smothered in pure womanhood.

She released him to again hold out the gem. "Oh, Cabot, it's so lovely. I'll wear it always. I'll never take it off, even in death." When she looked at him, he felt drenched in love. "I have no gift for you, *lieveling.*"

"Yes, you do."

She smiled. "I do? What?"

She was to him all beauty, all joy and happiness. "Kate, marry me." He saw her mouth open in surprise. "Marry me now, as soon as we can."

The brightness in her eyes was his truest answer. Her words were unnecessary, "Yes, *lieveling,* yes."

"I'll speak to your father in the morning."

Their miraculous pitcher of passion, stoppered for so many weeks, gushered that night, flowing with the knowledge of love, a belief in a future of happiness. For him, his ardor was sweeter, for he knew he was sweeping away his dishonor.

When he asked Hendrik van Stamp for his daughter's hand in marriage the next morning, the reaction was only what he anticipated, a broad smile, an extended hand, finally a hug from the Dutch merchant. "You have my blessing, of course. You must know of my regard for you, as a man, now as my future son-in-law. I know you will bring only happiness to Katarina and to this whole family."

Cabot beamed.

Wine was produced, poured. Van Stamp raised his glass in

a toast to marriage and happiness. When both had sipped, he said, "You have spoken to your father, of course."

"Not yet, but I will immediately."

"Good. I'm sure he'll be as delighted as I am. I expect to be in England in a few weeks. I'll meet with him then to discuss the dowry."

"A few weeks?"

"Yes, there is plenty of time."

"But I'd hoped we could marry now—as soon as possible."

Van Stamp smiled. "Oh, the impetuosity of youth. You must learn patience, my dear Cabot. A quick marriage would be—well, unsuitable."

"But why?"

The Dutchman's smile was positively avuncular. "I can't tell you what pleasure it brings me to see you and Katarina so much in love. I understand your impatience, but as her father I must consider her best interests. She is young. A year or so of waiting will only intensify her love for you—and make her certain of her choice."

"But—"

He laughed. "And a little patience on your part won't hurt you either, my son."

"But we must marry now."

Again the hearty Dutch laugh. "She'll be just as lovely and your desire as great a year from now, Cabot, believe me."

"You don't understand. I want to marry her now, take her to Virginia as my wife."

"Virginia?"

"Yes, Baron De La Warr, the new governor, has asked me to accompany him as his aide. I feel I must. I have obligations to friends there. I made certain suggestions for improvements and—"

"I understand. You feel a duty to help carry them out. Most commendable. I expect nothing less from you, Cabot."

"We sail in March. Kate and I must marry soon if I am to take her along as my wife."

Van Stamp turned away, replenishing his wine glass and offering some to Cabot, who demurred. "Do you plan to remain in Virginia, become permanent settlers, till the land, that sort of thing?"

Cabot hesitated. He simply had not thought this far ahead. "I don't know, sir. I was thinking of a year or so, this tour of duty."

"I see." He looked at Cabot levelly. "Are there women in Virginia?"

"I know of two, sir, a Mistress Forrest and her maid, who has married one of the ancients. Some wives were aboard the Gates flotilla. I believe other women will be going."

"Going to what, Cabot? You yourself spoke of the deaths among newcomers to Virginia. Disease, hostile natives, even starvation claim many lives. You cannot ask me to put my daughter into such a . . . a threatening situation."

"You know I'll look after her."

"Of that I'm certain." He raised his glass, draining it. But it was an act signaling that he had made up his mind. "You must know, my dear Cabot, that what you ask is impossible. Virginia is no place for Katarina—Kate, as you so charmingly call her. Neither of you should marry in haste. I understand how difficult it is to wait, but"—he smiled—"you will both survive." He clapped Cabot on the shoulder. "By all means, return to Virginia and do what you must. You will be better for it. And Katarina will be waiting for you when you return."

Cabot studied him. "Is that your final decision?"

"Yes. And it has not been difficult to make, Cabot. I know I'm right in this instance."

Cabot sighed in resignation, nodding affirmation as he did so. "Please say nothing to her. I haven't told her yet that I'm going away."

"As you wish." He smiled. "Don't look so glum. I did give my blessing to the marriage."

"Yes, and I thank you for that."

"It is I who must thank you for seeking my daughter's hand." Again he touched Cabot's shoulder. "Believe me, a year will pass quickly."

Her first reaction to her father's decision was to smile and say, "Don't worry. We won't have to wait nearly that long. I'm not his favorite daughter for nothing." Then she saw him frown, heard his deep sigh. "What's wrong, *lieveling?*"

Another deep sigh. "Kate, I have to go away—to Virginia." He told her of De La Warr, his own feeling of having left things unfinished in the colony. "Your father thinks I should go, do what I must, and marry you when I return."

His words lay as a wound in her eyes. "Virginia," she said, as though trying to give the word some meaning. "Virginia. So far away." She looked off into the distance. "How long will you be gone?"

"I don't know, a few months, no more than a year." He touched her chin, turning her face toward his. "Not one second longer than I have to be, Kate."

She nodded in acceptance, then smiled wanly. "Can you stay with me awhile?"

"Yes, as long as I possibly can."

Her smile broadened. "Good—and let's not waste a minute of it in being unhappy over what can't be helped."

And they didn't. He surrendered to her and happiness consciously, quickly, and wholeheartedly. The Dutch winter was all he had been led to believe. She taught him to ice skate, for he had not learned as a child, laughing at his early falls, encouraging his progress, and finally boasting of his prowess. They skated for miles along canals and rivers, hand in hand or arms linked, stopping at bonfires to warm their hands and toes, to refresh themselves with hot drinks. Or they rode in sleighs over the ice, cuddled under furs, their laughter and song punctuated with innumerable stolen kisses. Sometimes there would be thrilling races with Pieter and his Betje, Johanna and Hans, tearing over the ice so fast Cabot feared for their safety. The end of the race was invariably a tavern, the loser buying hot ale for all, and they would sit around a roaring log and sing and drink half the night away. But in many ways, best to him were the quiet evenings at home around the fire, occasionally alone, other times with the family. He taught her to play chess. She often sang to him in her small, clear voice, accompanying herself on the lute. At times they talked incessantly, saying nothing yet everything. He felt they had no secrets. Even sweeter were the quiet times when neither spoke of their certain knowledge.

Their passion for each other remained boundless, their consummations practiced, expert, yet the uniqueness was never lost. If he hoped for familiarity to breed contempt, it was a hopeless exercise.

She understood his reluctance to take her under her father's roof, although it did happen there. She arranged various trysting places, usually at the home of Hans and Johanna, once for three whole days at the cottage of an aunt near Delft. He suspected the thicket of lies told in these conspiracies, but he was so relieved to be out of the house on Herren Gracht that he never opposed any subterfuge.

It was during the peerless days of domestic bliss at the cottage—he hadn't known she could cook so well—that their true parting was made.

"I don't want to go, Kate. You must know that."

They were in bed, he lying on his back, she sitting above him, her legs folded under her, the quilt falling away, unmindful of the cold or her nakedness. "I know."

"But I have to go. I can't explain, but there's Timothy and—"

"I said I understood." She looked at him, deeply, as though cementing this moment in her memory. Then she looked down, fingering the sapphire he had given her as though it held a message known only to her. "I know only, *lieveling*, that I will miss you terribly." She slowly raised her head to look at him. "I know one other thing. There will always be a you and me, an us. We are linked, you and I, bound always. We will find some way to be together."

"Oh, yes, Kate, yes, yes." He embraced her then. He hadn't realized she was crying till he felt her wet cheek against his.

When he returned to England, he accepted Lord De La Warr's offer and threw himself into preparations for the voyage. When at last the expedition sailed from the Isle of Wight, he remembered that once before he had sailed for Virginia, madly in love. That girl had married another. But it wouldn't happen again. Of that he was certain. Yet, he couldn't help noting the date, April 1, 1610—April Fool's Day.

SIXTEEN

The Nick of Time

DYING DID NOT worry Timothy Loudon. As a man of the soil, he knew the seasons of all God's creatures. Seeds are put in the earth to grow, flower, and make new seed before they die, returning to the earth. Timothy hardly felt he had flowered. Certainly he had planted no seed of himself. But he accepted that. Many plants must die young to make room for the strong. His death would be the thinning. Nor did lying in the earth hold any terror for him. It would be as home.

It was the manner of his dying that bothered him. He did not want to just lie down in surrender to death. He wanted to be erect, still growing, still producing. When death came, let it be as the thinning. How to die puzzled him for a time. He could not take his own life. Then he knew. When his time came, he would use the last of his strength to walk away from the fort. He would either fall to the blessed earth or, more likely, an arrow would perform the thinning. It wouldn't matter. He already had one arrowhead in him.

He husbanded his strength. He did not want to misjudge when he should leave.

The injury to John Smith was an imponderable loss to Virginia. Even Timothy Loudon, who did not usually think about such things, realized that. Sir George Percy was a seasoned ancient like himself, but he was no Captain Smith. He had no capacity to deal with the Indians. Archer, Ratcliffe, Francis West were at best divisive, at worst a disaster.

The most serious result of Smith's leaving was the loss of Princess Pocahontas. Time and again she had saved the colony. But she turned her back on it when Smith left. No longer did she come, bringing food, gamboling in the commons. Rumor was that she had left the area, having incurred her father's disfavor for saving the colony. Reportedly she had married an Indian "captain" named Kocoum.

Percy tried, heaven knew, but disaster followed on the heels of catastrophe. Most of the settlement at the falls was wiped out in Indian attacks. Only a handful of men, including Francis West, made their way back to Jamestown. West was then put in charge of the pinnace to go up the Potomac to trade for corn. He was successful in this, but, instead of returning to Jamestown, he sailed for England. A less well connected man would have been hanged. West was later given a ship to return to Virginia.

Ratcliffe led a large expedition of over fifty men to go to Powhatan to trade. The force was ambushed. Only sixteen made their way back to Jamestown. Ratcliffe was captured, tied to a tree. Women and children were set to scraping the flesh from his bones before the tree was set afire. Another force was sent down the James to trade. They were all found dead, their mouths stuffed with corn. To venture outside the fort was to invite death. Many did, however, running in hunger to the Indians. None was ever heard of again. Only their fear of the cannon at the fort kept Powhatan's men from a frontal assault that would have wiped out the colony.

There was a far more lethal, unrelenting enemy at Jamestown: starvation. The stores were rationed, pilfered, finally consumed. To Timothy's outrage, the seed for the next harvest was eaten. One by one the horses, cattle, hogs, and chickens were devoured, then dogs, cats. A rat or mouse became a prize. Slugs, maggots, unknown roots were dug up for food. Graves were opened, the bodies eaten. One man killed his wife and salted her body. Percy had him hanged. Archer died. Men went to sleep at night, never to rise in the morning. Burial was by night, shallow holes, bodies thrown in, covered. No one had the strength to dig deep. Percy himself was so weak he could barely draw his sword. It was called the starving time.

Timothy refused to eat human flesh. If he knew of it, he would not put rat or lizard into his mouth, nor certainly a snake. Slugs did not bother him so much. They were part of the earth. He knew he was dying. His eyes were sunken. Little flesh remained on his bones. He felt long past mere hunger, but he had taken to eating earth. It sustained plants. Why not him? Surely it was better than shoe leather.

The winter somehow passed, the weather warmed, the time for planting came. Timothy looked out over the fields and grieved. There was nothing to plant. He had no strength, he knew. On weakened legs he walked out to the fields, scooping up a handful of earth, shoving it into his mouth. Would the arrow find him now?

He marked the dates, through April, one by one those of May. It was a pleasant time in Virginia, rivers full, flowers blooming, the beginnings of new life. He was dying. How strange to die at seed time.

He hoarded his strength, but the time came when he was afraid to sleep. To lie down was to not arise. This he did not want. At last he came to what he knew was the last day. Brain reeling with dizziness, legs so rubbery he could barely stand erect, he marked the date of his death: May 23, 1610. It was as good a day as any. And a nice day, too, sun shining. Yes, a good day to die.

He glanced around the hut that had been his home. He remembered. Cabot North had shared it with him. Cabot must be well in England, and he smiled at the thought. He opened the door, staggered outside, saw the fort, or what remained of it, sky, trees, the river. There must be fish in it now. Who had strength to throw a line? He looked around. No one was in sight. Were all dead but him?

Slowly, staggering, he turned, headed for the gate, his fields, the forest, oblivion. It would be good to rest, just close his eyes, feel the warm earth over him.

Timothy Loudon truly did not hear the sound of the cannon. But something made him turn. Two ships were in the river, approaching the mooring. He stared, unbelieving. He must already have died, and he must now be in heaven. Words of worship formed in his mind, for through swimming vision he saw the word on the bow of one of the ships: *Deliverance*.

On the bridge, Sir Thomas Gates surveyed the settlement. He had expected a greeting, some activity certainly. But there was nothing. The silence from shore was ominous. And the stench! Mother of God, were they all dead? Then he saw a solitary figure, on his knees, bearded, scrawny, practically a skeleton.

Gates had left London in April 1609, aboard the *Sea Venture*, in command of a nine-ship flotilla bearing six hundred settlers for Virginia. Then the hurricane had struck. The *Sea Venture* was demasted, driven by wind and wave, helpless, to what all aboard knew was certain death. Providence had not willed it. The ship landed on a reef, wedged between two rocks. They were all saved on the shores of an island. Admiral Somers knew it. Bermuda.

It was a paradise for the shipwrecked—uninhabited, filled with wild hogs, an abundance of fruit, and fresh water. Gates sensed this isle was a far more hospitable place for a colony than Virginia. He would tell Lord De La Warr and the company directors that. But first they had to survive, then find a way to complete his mission to Virginia.

Gates took command, building housing for the passengers and crew. Food was gathered and stored for the coming winter. The men were put to dismantling the wrecked *Sea Venture*. From her stout timbers and trees felled on the isle, he had built two small pinnaces, which he dubbed *Patience* and *Deliverance*. On May 10, 1610, he set sail for the Chesapeake and Virginia. The vessels carried one hundred fifty passengers and crew, plus himself, Somers, Stachey, and Newport. The company instructions for the colony were also preserved.

Nothing in his imagination had prepared Gates for the scene he witnessed at Jamestown. The fort was in disarray, much of it fallen down. The houses were in no better shape. Obviously most of them had been used for firewood, the colonists unable or unwilling to venture out for firewood. But where were the people? There had to be more than one kneeling wretch. He ordered the church bell rung. No one came at first, then slowly, disbelieving men began to appear from the huts. They seemed mere anatomies, living cadavers. Their eyes were glazed. Those who had strength cried, "We are starved, we are starved." Sir George Percy, eighth son of the eighth Earl of Northumberland, could barely stay on his feet to surrender his pathetic command.

A count was taken. Of the nearly six hundred men, women, and children who had been at Jamestown when John Smith left in October, only sixty had survived the starving time. Several more perished that night, even after being fed from the ships' stores.

Gates conferred with Somers, Stachey, Newport, and Percy,

but he knew the situation was hopeless. There were sixty wretches, plus one hundred fifty passengers on his two ships. Their stores were wholly inadequate to feed them for more than a short time. Trade with the Indians was impossible. Planting could be done, but all would starve long before harvest. The colony must be abandoned. On June 7, 1610, to the beat of a drum, he led the emaciated survivors aboard the two vessels fashioned in Bermuda, the *Patience* and *Deliverance*. Gates remained till last to stop survivors from burning the settlement. It was still company property. It might have use in the future. That evening he set sail down the James for the Altantic and home.

Timothy Loudon didn't want to go. He wanted to stay, plant his fields. But his protests were unavailing, and he had no strength to prevent two men from lifting him off his feet and carrying him aboard the *Deliverance*.

Cabot enjoyed the crossing despite bad weather. It felt so good to be back at sea, and he gave himself to the lure of sail and pitching deck. His duties were light, Lord De La Warr anything but demanding, and Cabot found himself liking and respecting his employer. Captain Argall was every bit as good a sailor as Newport and far more tractable. Cabot's only complaint was that his position as secretary to the governor kept him from stripping down to his breeches as he once had. His discomfort seemed a small price for what was otherwise a happy time.

He thought of Kate, couldn't help it, but his erotic fantasies were restrained by his determination to stay busy so as to make the time pass quickly.

On the fifth of June, De La Warr's fleet, shrunk to two vessels during a storm near the Azores, sailed into the Chesapeake. Cabot again sensed the beauty of the place, but he also had his old feelings of revulsion at all that had happened. These he thrust aside by dwelling on his anticipation of meeting Timothy. He would be so surprised. On the following day, the sixth, they found the *Hercules*, missing since the Azores, moored off Point Comfort. A reunion took place, with the captain of the errant ship reporting he had encountered the ship bearing Francis West on his flight to England. Cabot saw the disgust registered on Lord De La Warr's face.

The governor was eager to sail up the James to the settlement, but the wind turned contrary, then died. They were becalmed just when they verged on reaching their destination. They waited out the wind the whole next day. Then before dawn on the eighth, De La Warr ordered Captain Brewster to take a long boat upriver to Jamestown to announce his arrival. Cabot was to go along, for he knew the waters.

The early dawn stillness, the rhythmic lapping of the oars lulled Cabot, and he was at the point of dozing when he heard an oarsman say, "Ships, sir." Awake fully now, Cabot peered upriver. He recognized the land looming ahead as Mulberry Point. Then around it, as though riding on the heavy mist, came a ship. He saw two more, a fourth. They might have been apparitions, silently sailing the Styx.

Captain Brewster was not so imaginative. He stood up and cupped his hands to his mouth. "Ahoy there. What ships be ye?"

It seemed an eternity until a voice echoed over the still, misty water. "We are the *Deliverance,* Admiral Somers commanding."

Brewster looked at Cabot, who spoke for all. "Did he say Somers? Wasn't he—"

"The *Sea Venture,* yes. It can't be. It was lost." Brewster again cupped his hands. "Did you say Admiral Somers of the *Sea Venture?*"

"Aye." There was another long pause. "Who is hailing?"

Cabot cupped his hands. "I am Cabot North, secretary to Lord De La Warr. He is becalmed at Point Comfort."

Finally, a different voice sounded over the water. "This is Sir Thomas Gates. Did you say Lord De La Warr is here—in Virginia?"

The four small pinnaces were ordered to anchor, and the long boat stood by until Gates, Stachey, and Somers came aboard, then all were sped downriver to the flagship *De La Warr.* As they came aboard, the greetings were extended and doubtless important. De La Warr's surprise at seeing his long-lost deputy was boundless, and the report of Bermuda, survival, and reaching Virginia time-consuming. Cabot listened to all. Finally, came the report. Jamestown was in ruins. Only pitiful, nearly starved survivors remained. The only course was to abandon the colony.

De La Warr studied him carefully. "I have no doubt you made the wise decision, Sir Thomas, but I must countermand you. My ships are well provisioned. We carry three hundred new settlers. We shall return to Jamestown."

If he was dismayed, Gates's face did not register it. He said only, "The Indians have probably burned it by now."

"Providence has willed my coming. If I had been a day later—even an hour, Jamestown would be finished. God's will brought me here. We shall rebuild."

Cabot saw the deputy nod to the governor in acquiescence. When he could, Cabot spoke, not without agitation, to his employer. "Milord, I had a dear friend at Jamestown. I must know . . . if he . . ."

The Baron De La Warr turned to Captain Argall. "I believe there should be an inspection of the survivors."

Cabot urged the long boat back upriver at all possible speed and climbed aboard the *Deliverance,* first among the four ships, fear stabbing at him. The survivors lay on pallets on the deck, shaded by an awning made of sail. He looked at the wasted, pathetic figures in disbelief, then peered at the bearded faces, looking for the craggy head of his friend. He wasn't there. *Oh, God!* He had to be. Cabot turned to ask if there were survivors aboard other ships.

"Sar?"

Cabot turned to the voice. "Timothy?"

"That it be, sar."

He found him lying toward the rear of the group of huddled figures where he was less visible. "God, Tim, is it really you?" He knelt beside him, appalled by what he saw. Timothy seemed mere skin stretched over bones. Eyes smarting, voice choked, Cabot managed to say, "Thank God you're alive."

"I knew you'd come back, sar."

Cabot managed a smile. "Yes, sar, and just in time it looks like."

"Did you marry that li'l lady o' yourn?" A sort of smile split the shrunken face. "Ne'er can 'member 'er name."

Despite himself Cabot laughed. "No, I never did, my friend. But you rest. I'll tell you everything later."

Cabot remained an hour aboard ship, talking to the ship's surgeon, demanding all possible care for the survivors. He was assured nearly all would live. "They'd better, Doctor."

Still distrustful of surgeons, he turned to the first man he saw, a tall, lanky fellow pulling on a pipe of tobacco. "You, sir. I charge you to look after this man. See that he gets all the food he can eat and is kept warm and comfortable. If you don't, you will account to me." Cabot was aware of how pompous he sounded, but he didn't care as long as Timothy got well.

"I'll look after him for you, sir."

"Good." Cabot looked at him. He seemed sensible and capable. "What is your name?" He made the question less of a challenge.

"Rolfe, sir, John Rolfe."

SEVENTEEN

Stinking Weed

THERE WAS NO doubt in Cabot's mind that De La Warr was a far more able leader than any of his predecessors. He had absolute powers. Gone was the council and its bickering. And, as an important and wealthy peer, Baron De La Warr commanded respect and obedience. He set up what amounted to military rule under martial law. He issued orders to "captains," mostly military men, and each was made responsible for the efforts of fifteen settlers. This way, both the gentlemen and the sluggards swept from English jails were made to bend their backs.

There was no shortage of work to do. The fort and housing had to be torn down and started over, only this time De La Warr insisted it be done right. The fort was enlarged and strengthened, more guns and munitions unloaded from the fleet and put in place. A proper town was laid out, with streets, a marketplace, and a new church. Dwellings were made larger, some of them gabled, with a better fit to the timbers. Borrowing from the Indians, they covered the outsides with tree bark to make them more waterproof and airtight. The interior walls and floors were covered with Indian mats for further comfort. Finally, wide fireplaces and large chimneys added to warmth and reduced the risk of fire.

Cabot was pleased to see that De La Warr understood how unhealthful a place Jamestown was and sought, as Smith had, to disperse the colony. He sent a large force to the old village of Kecoughtan near Point Comfort to build two forts on a little river he named Southampton—later shortened to Hampton. The forts were named Henry and Charles, for the king's sons. From the first, the settlers at Kecoughtan were healthier and more prosperous, if only because they were away from the pestilence of Jamestown.

De La Warr also recognized this colony had no capacity to feed itself, not now anyway, for it was now too late to expect much of a harvest this year. He sent Gates and Newport back to London in the *Hercules* to report the colony's plight to the company directors and raise a new supply. In his instructions, De La Warr gave a long shopping list. Most needed were carpenters and other craftsmen.

Nor did he wait for Gates's return and the vagaries of London policy. He sent Somers and Argall back to Bermuda in two ships to gather food, especially the wild hogs that abounded there. This expedition had mixed results. The two ships separated in a storm, and only Somers, at seventy the oldest man ever to come to Virginia, reached Bermuda, where he became ill and died. Before expiring, he beseeched his men to carry on with the slaughtering and salting of pork for Virginia. They laid in the provisions all right, then sailed for England. Argall ended up off the New England coast, where he caught and salted a shipload of fish, returning to Virginia with it. This became an annual event in Virginia, mitigating if not eliminating future starving times.

Later, Argall made a successful trip up the Chesapeake and into the Potomac River to trade with the Indians, returning with a large amount of grain. Cabot went along and participated in some noteworthy events. Argall ransomed Sir Henry Spelman from the king of the Potomacs, where he had been living for over a year as his "son," successor to Thomas Savage. From Spelman, it was learned that Princess Pocahontas, banished by her father for helping the colonists, was living with the Potomacs.

If Cabot gave all credit to De La Warr's accomplishments as governor, he could not escape the bitter knowledge that the more Virginia changed, the more it remained the same. Death still stalked the place, and the causes remained the same. With the coming of July, heat and pestilence felled the colonists. Smith had dug a well inside the fort, but brackish river water seeped into it, bringing dysentery and other maladies. Insects rose in clouds from the marsh, carrying malaria and yellow fever. A new malady was added. Someone aboard the crowded ships had brought the plague, and its toll began. Jamestown was now overrun with rats, where in the beginning the animal was unknown in America. Of the more than three hundred colonists who came with De La Warr, less than half were alive in the spring, including the ancients.

Baron De La Warr was barely one of them. Soon after he arrived, he succumbed to a "hot and violent ague." This fever was succeeded by the bloody flux, cramps, and finally the embarrassment of scurvy. Cabot admired him for his courage in carrying on despite his poor health, but clearly De La Warr would either leave Virginia or die there. He seemed unable to adjust.

Relations with the Indians worsened. Where Smith had managed to trade with the Paspaheghs, Chickahominies, and other nearby tribes and keep hostilities to a minimum, there now existed only open warfare. Indians picked off colonists when they could and lured even sizable parties of colonists into ambushes. The invariable result was colonial vengeance. Indian villages were attacked and burned in reprisal, as many natives as possible killed. In one sickening raid led by Percy and William West, kinsman of the governor, a Paspahegh town was burned, the chief's queen and her children seized.

Cabot was in the storehouse making a tally, when the Indian captives were taken aboard the flagship where De La Warr lay bedridden with one of his illnesses. From shore, Cabot first heard shouting and commotion but paid no attention until gunfire broke out. He raced from the fort to the riverbank.

What he saw nauseated him. The chief's wife, a young, not unattractive woman, stood on the deck, clutching her children, one a babe in arms. One by one her children were being taken from her, thrown into the water, and used for target practice by marksmen until the James ran red.

"God almighty, *stop it!*" Cabot shouted. But his voice was drowned in the howls of the men on shore. He stared at their faces. They were enjoying the blood and death. Still shouting, he frantically pushed himself forward through the throng. When he finally reached the gangplank, it was to see two more children splash into the water. "Stop it, I say!" He ran up to the deck to face a grinning Percy. "Stop it this instant!"

Percy faced him. "Come now, Cabot. Allow the men a little sport."

"You call murder sport? It's butchery! Stop it, I say."

Again Percy grinned. "It's a little late now, isn't it?"

Cabot turned and saw the babe, the woman's last child, jerked from her arms. He screamed but could not move fast enough to prevent it from being tossed over the side. The fatal gunshots were still echoing when he turned back to Percy, enraged. "Did you order this?"

"No. The governor gave permission."

"He did not. He's too sick to order anything. And if he did, he didn't know what he was saying."

"What's it matter anyway, Cabot?"

Shaking with anger, he said, "Who's the savage, Percy? You or them?" He pointed toward the Indian woman who just stood there, seemingly unmoved, stoically accepting the loss of her children. "In God's name, release her—if you have one shred of humanity in you, Percy."

The young peer eyed him a moment, then shrugged. "I suppose it is getting a bit bloodthirsty, isn't it?" He ordered the squaw taken ashore and let go.

It was not to be. The Indian queen was taken ashore all right, but the men had become a mob, the scent of blood strong now. She was seized. Soldiers hacked her to bits with swords.

Neither Cabot nor Percy, still aboard ship, could prevent it. Shaking with rage and revulsion, Cabot said, "You never answered, Percy. Who are the savages?"

"It was only reprisal for what they do to us, Cabot."

"And this day will bring a new reprisal. When will it end, Percy? When everyone is dead?"

Cabot tried to shrug off the incident, but that stoic look in the woman's eyes as the last of her children was killed haunted him.

Timothy saw and tried to help. "All things die, Cabot, some young, some old. It doesn't really matter when."

Cabot nodded. "I know."

"When I thought I was goin' to die durin' the starvin' time, I din't want to. I was too young, I said. But I thought o' it as the thinnin'. It made it easier."

"Thank you, Tim, but I'll be all right."

His craggy face split into the yellow smile. "Sure you will. Pretty soon, you'll be agoin' back to that gal o' yourn."

And Cabot had to smile, too. "Which one? The one whose name you can't remember? Or Kate?"

"That 'er name, is it? Wanna tell me 'bout 'er?"

Cabot didn't. But under Timothy's insistent questioning— "What's she look like? Pretty? Color 'air?"—he began to speak of his beloved, her family, how they met. He told nothing intimate, of course, but his description of her did not lack superlatives.

Yet he was often badgered by a single thought: What if Kate found someone else while he was gone? The image of Katarina van Stamp in the arms of another became his personal sackcloth and ashes, the rack of his mind.

"So why did you leave 'er?"

"Her father thought we should wait a year or so to marry."

"Tha' ain't s'long. You'll be back wif 'er 'fore you know it, sar."

Cabot smiled. "You know, Tim, you really are the one who talks about women all the time. Have you been—"

Timothy's face reddened above his beard. "Naw. Ain't no women 'ere, an' if they was they wouldn't look at me."

Cabot laughed. "Don't be too sure, sar."

Then, as he had many other times, Cabot felt Timothy Loudon was the only sane person in Virginia. They did not live together as before. Cabot's duties as governor's aide kept him near De La Warr. But he spent part of every day with Timothy, in his fields with the belated crops, or at the home he shared with his new friend, John Rolfe. What had started with Cabot's imperious order on shipboard had blossomed into a most amicable relationship between Rolfe and Timothy.

Cabot simply could not figure out Rolfe. He was a good man, decent, extremely religious, but sometimes wholly reticent. At first Cabot thought that grief had made him so. He had sailed from England with his pregnant wife aboard the *Sea Venture*. After it was shipwrecked in Bermuda, Mrs. Rolfe had given birth to a daughter, who died soon after being named for the island. The wife succumbed shortly thereafter. This double tragedy made Rolfe's silence understandable. But as weeks spread into months and Rolfe remained uncommunicative, it all began to seem strange. In the confines of the colony, with everyone so far from home, men soon learned virtually all there was to know about one another. Not Rolfe. Cabot heard a reference to a landed family in Norfolk, East Anglia, but almost nothing else. At times, Cabot had the impression Rolfe was a gentleman. He had manners and some education. He could read and write. But if a gentleman, he was an uncharacteristic one. He loved the soil, which doubtlessly drew Timothy to him, worked hard, and was responsible in any task given him. Although Cabot could not get close to Rolfe, he recognized that Virginia could use a few hundred more like him.

The most apparent feature of Rolfe was the pipe he smoked every waking moment. Even Timothy became addicted. Cabot took a pipe with them once in a while, but in truth he found neither comfort nor enjoyment in the stinking weed. Indeed, Cabot wearied more than a little of the preoccupation the two had with tobacco. It was too late for planting this year, but Rolfe couldn't wait for spring. He was determined to grow tobacco in Virginia and had ensnared Timothy in his enthusiasm. Cabot was unimpressed. Virginia needed corn, beans, squash, edible food, not some vile weed that dizzied the mind.

Rolfe argued—oh, how many times?—that if tobacco could be grown in Virginia, some money could be made. Ever since Sir Walter Raleigh brought the smoking substance to England a quarter-century before, Europe had gone tobacco mad. London alone was said to have seven thousand establishments dispensing tobacco. Everybody used it, men, women, and children, smoking it or sniffing it up their noses or sticking a wad of it under their tongues to suck on all day. Learned surgeons were ecstatic about the medical properties of tobacco, saying the smoke cleared the nostrils and lungs and drove poisons from the mind. Personally, Cabot felt the smoke made him cough, but then he'd never tried anything but Indian tobacco. It was raw, bitter, and rank.

"If you think that stuff you're smoking will sell in London, John, you are crazy."

Rolfe took another long puff on his pipe and exhaled, adding to the acrid stench that already filled the cabin. "I know it won't, Cabot, but if we can get Spanish tobacco to grow here"— he puffed again—"then . . ."

Spain had a virtual monopoly on the tobacco sold in Europe, a mild, fragrant variety, originally from Brazil, but grown extensively in the West Indies. The Spanish realized they were making more money from the tobacco trade than from the gold and silver plundered from Mexico and Peru. Thus, the trade was heavily protected, the plantations patrolled, the ships bearing tobacco convoyed by warships.

Somehow Rolfe had obtained a small supply of Spanish tobacco seed, *Nicotiana tabacum*. How and where he got the seeds, he never told, not Cabot or even Timothy. But have them he did, hence the excited anticipation of spring.

"Did it ever occur to you smoking fools that neither of you has ever grown one leaf of that filthy weed?"

Rolfe's smile might have been proper for an indulged child. "A body can learn."

"Yes, we can learn. Can't be hard to do."

Cabot shook his head. "Look, you two. Even if it grows here, you don't know anything about drying it. What do they call it—curing."

Timothy had an answer for everything. "The Indians just hang it in the sun."

Another gray cloud escaped Rolfe's nostrils. "I think there might be a better way. The sun dries it too quick, sort of burns it."

"What d'you have in mine?"

Cabot listened to a theory about drying it slowly, inside a building, just letting the air circulate around it. He was sorry, but he just couldn't see any future in tobacco. "Do you tobacco merchants know how much King James hates the stuff you're talking about? He has written a pamphlet denouncing tobacco. He won't allow it in his court. What makes you think he's going to permit his prize colony to grow the thing he hates?"

His answer was a pair of puffs from two men who apparently hadn't heard a word he'd said.

At the start of the Virignia winter, Lord De La Warr, somewhat recovered from his illnesses, led an expeditionary force of a hundred men up the James to the falls. Cabot was left behind to "assist" Percy, who was to take charge of Jamestown. Cabot was glad, for in his view his employer had succumbed to Virginia madness. De La Warr was off to inspect the "mines." Cabot knew better. He was hunting gold.

When he returned in March, De La Warr was a very sick man, wasted from scurvy, and he had lost much of his command to Indian attacks, disease, and starvation. Cabot was hardly sympathetic, nor was he upset when De La Warr decided to leave him behind while he journeyed to Nevis in the West Indies to recover his health. Had Cabot known the fate that was to befall De La Warr, he might have thought differently. The baron ran into a storm and never reached Nevis. Instead, his ship limped into the Azores, much of the crew dead or near dead from scurvy. De La Warr ended up in England. He would remain governor for another half-dozen years, but never set foot in Virginia again.

Most grieved was Percy. He had been in this colony, which he had come to hate, for four years. He was one of four or five survivors from the *Sarah Constant* and wanted nothing so much in this world as to return home. He had paid his dues to king and colony. Yet, a good soldier, he stayed on once again as interim governor until the next supply arrived. It was due any time.

EIGHTEEN

Bloody Dale

A FLEET OF three small ships arrived at Jamestown on the nineteenth of May 1611, bearing three hundred new settlers, a great quantity of stores and munitions, and the imposing figure of Sir Thomas Dale, the new marshal of Virginia, who was to serve as interim governor pending the arrival of Sir Thomas Gates.

The moment Dale set foot in Jamestown—hard-eyed, scowling, attired in breastplate and helmet, sword at his side— it was obvious a formidable leader had arrived. Dale was every inch a soldier, accustomed to issuing commands and having them obeyed. Word had already reached Jamestown of Dale's actions at Kecoughtan downriver, where he spent the previous week. He had imposed martial law, ordered the two forts repaired, and set the colonists to planting more corn than had been put into the ground ever before. Creating the most talk was the tale of Dale's rage at Captain Newport, who was admiral of the fleet. Dale had upbraided Newport for spreading malicious lies in London about the prosperity of the colony. Why, the place was practically in ruins, the men bowling in the streets instead of working to sustain themselves. Nothing was planted. Did Newport expect men to eat trees? In his anger, Dale had even pulled Newport's beard.

Dale attended church, since it was Sunday, then began a thorough inspection of James Fort and James City. Nothing in his countenance or remarks suggested he liked anything he saw. Inspection concluded, he ordered all officers to assemble in the church.

Among those summoned was Cabot North. "You were Lord De La Warr's secretary. You will act in a similar capacity for me."

It was an order, not a question. "Yes, sir."

In his speech to the officers, Dale gave every appearance of being a martinet. This colony was in disreputable shape. The deaths were due solely to the insubordination of the officers and the shiftlessness of the inhabitants. He had not come to Virginia to oversee the demise of His Majesty's colony. Jamestown would be a success, and it would become self-supporting, or these men here assembled would rue the day they were born.

He began to issue orders so fast Cabot was hard-pressed to write them all down. The church, storehouse, fort, and other buildings were to be repaired. Captain Brewster was in charge. A new munitions house was to be erected, along with a stable for the colony's horses, a facility for making brick, a blacksmith shop, and a sturgeon house. The latter was to accommodate a new settler who was expert in curing fish. Captain Lawson was in charge of this work. Oh, yes, his men were also to dig a new well. How these men could drink such unsavory water, while being too lazy to dig a new well, exceeded his understanding. A wharf was to be built immediately so goods could be landed "dry and safe." Captain Newport and his mariners were to build it.

All men not so engaged were to begin planting at once. Seeds should be in the ground already, and it was a disgrace they were not. All men were to work a ten-hour day, and if it required the lash to get them to do so, then so be it. In addition, each man was to maintain a private garden to increase the colony's food supply. His orders were to make Virginia self-sufficient within the year. He had every intention of carrying out his orders.

"I will have posted on the morrow *Laws Divine, Moral and Martial* by which this colony is to be governed. If any man thinks I do not intend to apply these laws severely, he is most sadly mistaken."

When the chastened officers filed out, Cabot was set to taking down Dale's Laws, as they soon became known. Actually they were first formulated by Sir Thomas Gates in 1610 and approved by De La Warr. Dale added a few touches of his own. Every man and woman was to attend morning and evening prayer service. Failure to do so was punishable by a loss of a day's allowance for the first offense, a whipping for the second, and six months in the galleys for a third. Every person must attend church on Sunday morning and catechism on Sunday afternoon. Failure to attend on three Sundays was punishable by death. Death was likewise the sentence for blasphemy of any kind, slighting references to God's holy word, traitorous speech against the king, murder, adultery, sodomy, ravishing any maid or Indian woman, sacrilege, and false witness.

Recoiling inwardly but dutifully scribbling, Cabot listened to the droning voice of the new marshal. Any person speaking against the council in England, any of its orders or duly appointed officers, including the governor, lieutenant governor, marshal, or any captain would be whipped, imprisoned, or, if he persisted, hanged. Trading with the Indians without a permit—death. Trading with any sailors or ships' captains, except on terms of a price list nailed to the ship's mast—loss of wages and court-martial. Killing a bull, cow, calf, mare, horse, goat, swine, cock, hen, chicken, dog, or turkey without permission—loss of both ears, branding of the hand, or death at the discretion of the marshal. Washing or throwing dirty water into the street was punishable by a public flogging. Houses were to be kept clean, subject to inspection by overseers. Work was not a matter of choice. Men were to march to and from the fields or other tasks to the beat of the drum—or know the sting of the lash.

"You disapprove, Mr. North? You think me too severe?"

Cabot, who was still writing, looked up. "I think you are doing what you think best, Sir Thomas."

The officer eyed Cabot carefully, then allowed himself a scant smile through his long, pointed beard. "Thank you for that, Mr. North. I assure you these penalties will provide no hardship for the industrious and law-abiding. The slackers and miscreants may find some discomfort, however."

"I have no doubt, sir."

"Good. I intend to run this colony as a military post. All able-bodied men will be both laborers and soldiers. We will have military discipline." Again he eyed Cabot closely. "There is something on your mind. Say what you wish."

Cabot hesitated, uncertain how frank he dared to be. "I came here the first time with the ancients in ought-seven, Sir Thomas. From the beginning, Virginia has been afflicted by gentlemen who refuse to work. Now we are burdened with the scum of the jails who don't know how to. I can only hope these new, sterner measures will produce results when all other efforts have failed."

"You think these laws will not work? Why?"

Again Cabot hesitated. "If I may speak frankly, Sir Thomas, when life becomes too difficult in the colony, the life of the Indian becomes"—he smiled—"shall I say attractive?"

Dale nodded and smiled broadly. "Be so kind as to add this to your list: any person who deserts his post or takes unauthorized absence shall be publicly flogged, branded, put to the rack, and then hanged. Perhaps that will make the native life less appealing."

Cabot worked well into the night, but by the next morning Dale's Laws were posted, then read aloud by commanders. George Percy was one of the first to read them, then approach Cabot. "He can't be serious."

Cabot shook his head. "I'm afraid he is, my friend."

"Cutting off ears, branding?" Percy sighed. "I've got to get out of here, Cabot. I can't take much more."

"I fear you'll have to. Read the punishment for desertion."

"I think I have been rendered into the hands of a madman."

Few believed Dale would enforce his laws. How many other presidents, governors, and captains had proposed severity as a correction for the colony's ills? At most his attempts at discipline would last only a few days before giving in to the oppressive heat and disease that weighed on all who came to Virginia. It did not take long for the recalcitrant to be persuaded of the error of these views. Jamestown rang with the crack of the lash and the agonized cries of the punished. Men were indeed branded, and ears were actually cut off, and the bang of the gallows's trapdoor became an irregular but frequent rhythm to the grumbling of the settlers. Never was a man so hated so quickly. He became "Bloody Dale."

Cabot was in a difficult position. As the marshal's secretary he wrote down Dale's orders or relayed them orally. He began to feel like a Hermes of bad tidings, a messenger of pain. Not a few settlers came to believe Cabot was issuing the orders himself, and he became subject to verbal abuse and threats. When he was forced to stand with Dale to observe punishment, it was almost more than he could bear to watch a person being brutalized. And deliberately taking a man's life still sickened him.

"I don't know how much more of this I can take, Tim."

Cabot had stopped to speak to him a moment as he worked in the fields. Timothy knew the hateful talk about his friend and had already gotten into a fight in his defense. Now he sought to comfort him. "Aye, he is a harsh man, Cabot." He looked around and made a broad gesture. "But have you ever seen so much plantin', the fields so well tended?"

Cabot nodded. It was true. He had to admit, however grudgingly, that Dale was effective. Never had so much been accomplished in Jamestown. Crops were planted, the fort and town made shipshape, and with better water and sanitation even the pestilence was reduced. The well-tended fields, the sturgeon being salted away in the storehouse all promised a winter without starvation.

Dale's energy amazed Cabot. He left nothing unattended to and drove his subordinates unmercifully. More than anyone since John Smith, Dale seemed to understand what this colony needed to prosper. Jamestown was unfit for human habitation, and he was determined to build a new town. One of his first acts was to send an expedition up to the falls to search for a new and better site on which to build.

In June, a Spanish caravel showed up in the river, creating a tremendous stir. When two Spaniards and an Englishman in the employ of Spain rowed ashore to ask for a pilot, Dale had them arrested and sent out John Clark to act as pilot. He was seized, and the Spanish ship turned tail, causing great alarm that a Spanish fleet would soon arrive. Stachey was dispatched immediately to London to warn the king of the threat. He carried with him a long list of needed supplies and a request for carpenters, bricklayers, and other artisans. Cabot had hoped to go with Stachey. He had already been absent from Kate for over a year. Dale gave him a withering look when he asked.

The Spanish threat only intensified Dale's efforts to defend the colony. To him this meant reducing the menace from Indians, and he fell upon them without mercy. Dale had brought with him a "new" weapon—armor from the Tower of London. No longer used much in the era of gunpowder, the armor could still serve its original purpose of fending off arrows. When Dale led the first foray against the Nansemonds, the Indians stared in stupefaction as their arrows slid harmlessly off the helmets and breastplates of the English. One man was hit in the arm, another in the thigh, and Dale himself narrowly missed taking an arrow in the eye. But the armored men simply marched forward into the hail of arrows. Some Indians threw down their weapons and ran, while others began to dance and howl incantations. One Englishman suggested the Indians were praying for rain, hoping it would rust the armor and make the white men helpless. Dale killed many of the Nansemonds, captured others, burned their town, and destroyed their crops.

He began then a systematic plundering of the whole peninsula, all the way to the falls. "I intend to so overmaster the subtle, mischievous Great Powhatan," he said, "as to leave him either no room in his country to harbor in or to draw him to a firm association with us." Toward this end, he proposed to fortify the whole length of the river.

In August an alarm went out that six tall ships were sailing upriver. The Spanish had come. Dale dispatched forty men to reconnoiter their strength, while alarm bells sounded and all Jamestown residents rushed to arms. Then came the word. The ships were English. Sir Thomas Gates had arrived with a massive supply, including a hundred head of cattle and two hundred swine. With him were three hundred new settlers, including twenty women, Gates's wife and two daughters among them.

Those who hoped Gates's return as deputy governor would mean surcease from Dale's bloody rule were disappointed. Gates and Dale were longtime comrades in arms and staunch friends. Dale, as marshal, had the complete support and encouragement of his superior.

There was the usual dying among the newcomers—Gates's wife and daughters among them—but work proceeded anyway. The "back water" area connecting the Jamestown peninsula to the mainland was fortified with several blockhouses, and the colony spread into the forest, where cattle were grazed. Other forts were built along the river and even across it, where an islet, aptly named Hog Island, was fortified to contain the colony's supply of hogs.

The most notable achievement of Dale was the erection of his new town, named Henrico after the king's eldest son and patron of Virginia. The site chosen was about twelve miles above the falls where the river makes a remarkable loop, enclosing about seven acres of "high and healthy" land on three sides. In August 1611, Dale set out with three hundred men and a great quantity of pales, posts, and rails to build his city. He had a ditch dug across the two-mile land side of the site and erected a fence. When Indians persisted in sending arrows toward the workmen, Dale raided and razed the nearby villages. The entire seven-acre site was fenced in and fortified so cattle could be grazed and farmers tend their fields in safety. Then his town was erected, with a church, storehouse, and three streets of houses, instead of the two at Jamestown. Most remarkable, the buildings were erected of brick made on the spot. Henrico was intended as a fortified town beyond the falls to which the entire colony could fall back in case the Spanish attacked.

By midsummer of 1611, Gates, but mostly Dale, had transformed the Virginia Plantation from a wretched place barely able to survive into a settlement offering, if not prosperity for the investors, at least a hope of permanence. The English controlled the whole James River area from Point Comfort, where two settlements were established, past Jamestown all the way to Henrico. There was relative safety from Indian attacks, for Dale had succeeded in overmastering them, or so it seemed. He attacked the Appomatux tribe, took their town and corn, then annexed the site to the colony "forever." He would build a new town to be called Bermuda. Surrounding land was divided into several "hundreds," which Dale gave such names as Upper Hundred, Nether Hundred, West Shirley Hundred, Rochdale Hundred, Digges' Hundred. Virginia had been organized, rebuilt, fortified. Best of all, the 381 inhabitants now could feed themselves.

None of this was what thrilled Timothy Loudon. In the summer of 1611, he and John Rolfe had grown tobacco. The secret West Indian seeds, timorously planted in their private garden, sprouted, took root, and grew, the broad green leaves unfurling into real, honest-to-God tobacco, which they cured and indeed smoked. When they replanted the next year, it was in anticipation of growing enough to ship some to London to see how it fared in shops there. Both men were beside themselves with excitement, absolutely convinced they had found a way to make money in Virginia.

Cabot found his friends' chatter about tobacco a welcome relief from the tensions of being near Dale and Gates. And he did enjoy teasing them. "Can't you two talk about anything but tobacco? You smoke so much this cabin smells like a pig sty. You ought to air it out."

Timothy grinned. "You may not like it, sar, but I tell you we got a good, mild smoke. You jus' wait till London discovers Virginny tobacco."

"You're right. I can hardly wait." His sarcasm was lost on the two addicted smokers, and he listened to their prattle for a while. In truth, he was intrigued by their successful experiment. There was no doubt tobacco could be made to thrive in Virginia soil, and what they grew was far superior to the Indian product, although not as mild as the Spanish. Nor was there doubt Europe was tobacco mad. There might be a market for Virginia tobacco if enough could be grown. It was a big if.

Cabot waited till Timothy stopped talking long enough to light his pipe. "If I were to grant that you might have something in your so-called Virginia tobacco, exactly where do you propose to grow it?" Both were looking at him. He had gained their attention at least. "That little private plot of yours won't grow enough to keep you two puffing away, let alone the City of London."

Rolfe looked at him intently. "What do you think would happen if we spoke to the governor or marshal about letting us use some of the common lands for tobacco?"

Cabot smiled. "I think you would be tied to the post as slackers. Probably forty lashes would do it."

"I'm serious."

"I was afraid of that." He sighed and tried to be serious, too. "There may be a better way, John. If you two promise not to divulge it"—he saw a pair of heads nod—"I can tell you the point has not been lost on either of our Sir Thomases that the private plots are producing far more food per acre than the common lands. It is obvious a man will work harder and better on his own land than he will for the company, no matter how hard the lash is applied."

"I coulda tol' 'em that."

Cabot nodded. "I'm sure you could have, Timothy. Pity you weren't asked. Anyway, there is talk—and I assure you it is no more than just talk—of giving land to the ancients and all who have been here two years."

The pipe almost fell from Timothy's hand. He stared at Cabot wide-eyed. "You mean . . . I'm to get lan' o' my own?"

Cabot saw the disbelief in the farmer's face. And there was desire, too, almost like the lust men feel for a woman. "I hope so, Tim. I know how much you want it." He shook his head and sighed. "But don't count on it. I told you this is all talk—and, again, don't breathe a word of it."

"Land, Cabot? *Land?*"

"I assure you if it comes to pass there won't be much of it, and you'll be expected to give part of your crop to the common storehouse."

"I'll give it all to 'em as long as the land is me own."

Rolfe spoke. "When do you think this might happen?"

"Next year—if it happens." He saw Rolfe nod thoughtfully. "Meanwhile, I'll speak to Dale about your tobacco experiment—if he doesn't know about it already. Maybe he could be persuaded to let you use some common lands for a larger experiment."

Cabot was receiving grateful thanks when there was a timid knock at the door. Since he was closest, Cabot opened it. At once he smiled. "Do come in, Mistress Barton."

"I brung the laundry."

"Since it is forbidden to have laundry in the street, you'd best bring it inside."

Hannah Barton stepped inside, arms laden with laundry, and looked shyly at the two other occupants. To Cabot's amusement, the craggy face of one of them immediately blushed.

"Don't just stand there gaping, Timothy. If it's your laundry, take it from the poor woman."

As Timothy leaped to the task, obviously nervous and overanxious, Cabot had difficulty suppressing a laugh. That Hannah Barton had contrived to deliver the laundry in person and that Timothy Loudon was more than a little glad to see her was about as obvious as the sun rising in the east.

Hannah fell somewhere between plain and pretty. She had dun-colored hair and light brown eyes and really no distinguishing feature to make her beautiful. Yet, there was also nothing that detracted from her, just pleasant even features, good skin, shining eyes and hair. She was extremely petite and next to the hulking Timothy, she resembled a child. Only she wasn't. Hannah Barton was almost seventeen and already a widow. She and Simon Barton had come to Virginia in Gates's flotilla nearly a year ago. Barton was a farmer, she a farmer's daughter, both from the Cotswolds, and Barton had struck up a friendship with Timothy. When the husband succumbed to the bloody flux, it was natural that Timothy look after his widow. Yes, very natural.

"Won't you sit a spell, Mistress Barton?" Cabot saw her turn to him, shaking her head. "But you must. John, do you have any of that good barley ale left?"

"I can't, sir, honest I can't."

"Are you sure? It would be a pity for you to run off."

Tim finally found his tongue. "Yes, do stay, Hannah." The look she gave him, the tiny smile, belied her protests that she had to leave. There was no convincing her.

"The least you can do, Tim, is walk her to her cabin. God himself doesn't know what terrors this Virginia darkness holds." When Timothy returned—much too quickly, Cabot thought— he could no longer suppress his laughter. "I'm telling you, sar, the whole colony's after that girl. You better get to wooing, my friend."

Timothy blushed more deeply than Cabot had ever seen him. "Aw, Cabot, what've I got to offer a gal like that?"

Smiling broadly, Cabot glanced at Rolfe, then back at his dearest friend. "Yourself, sar—and maybe, just maybe, some land."

The next morning Cabot intended to speak to Marshal Dale about the tobacco project, but never got the chance. Percy was with him. Dale spoke. "Sir George is taking the pinnace *Trial* and ten men to the Chesapeake to fish for our storehouse. He has asked for you as pilot. Would you like to go?"

Cabot looked from his employer to Percy. "How long would we be gone?"

"Just a few days. A little deep-water fishing will do you good." He smiled. "Beside, you're a better sailor than I."

Cabot turned to Dale. "As long as you don't mind, Sir Thomas."

"Not at all, Cabot. You've earned a little holiday. But bring back lots of fish, mind you."

Percy laughed. "Oh, we'll have a good catch, Sir Thomas. Have no fear."

The catch was good, and Cabot enjoyed himself immensely, sailing the beautiful bay, stripping down to his breeches to feel the wind and sun and spray. Being away from the tensions of

Gates and Dale no doubt contributed to his carefree attitude. Too bad the pinnace was nearly full. They would have to return soon.

Cabot's pleasure ended the moment he stared down the barrel of Percy's pistol. "Take her to England, Cabot."

"What are you saying?"

"Sail for England. I brought you along because you can navigate. None of us can."

Cabot eyed him intently. "You know what you're doing, don't you?"

Percy's smile was as jaunty as ever. "That I do, my friend. I'm leaving a place I've come to hate. After five years, it is time I went on to other matters in my life."

"It's desertion. You know the penalty."

Percy's laugh was generous and genuine. "I assure you, my dear Cabot, the son of the Earl of Northumberland is unlikely to hang—or the son of the Earl of Durham, for that matter. Now sail."

PART III

Smoke

NINETEEN

Guest at a Party

THE REVEREND EMANUEL COTTER was, it seemed to Cabot, the embodiment of doom. He surely had the voice for it, pitched low, mellifluous, resounding from the pulpit throughout the meeting hall to hang in the air like a shroud over the Puritan brethren.

"I say unto you, the wrath of God shall fall as a mighty sword upon the idolators, for they bear false witness to the word of God. Those who sin among us shall on the Judgment Day be like the quick and the dead, walking for all eternity among the fires of Hell. Those wicked hypocrites who reign over us while professing the name of God, shall know only the bitter rain of brimstone, and it shall fall upon them forever."

Cabot watched the clergyman's immense Adam's apple move and bob as the doomsaying thundered out of his mouth. Yes, doom. The man even looked like doom, tall, gaunt, pasty skin stretched tight over his bony face. The dark eyes seemed sunk into his head, the thin lips, when in repose, lifeless and unsmiling. And the nose, pronounced, beaked. Why, the man looked like a bird, a hawk or vulture, ready to swoop down upon the sinful as if they were carrion, transporting them to a treasured place, hell.

"Those who adorn themselves in fine raiment shall know at the Day of Reckoning only sackcloth and ashes, for the conceits of the flesh are unsightly to our Righteous Lord."

It was the second reference so far to attire. The Reverend Cotter wore black. Hose, long breeches, tunic, hat were all of that color, relieved only by starched white collar and cuffs. Cabot had not seen this garb before, yet a number of Puritans seemed to be affecting it as a badge of their faith. It surely did make them stand out amid the colorful Elizabethans.

Cabot glanced across the aisle to where his sister Elizabeth sat among the women. Her hands were folded contentedly in her lap, and she was looking at Cotter, her eyes bright, falling upon his every utterance. His denouncement of attire seemed not to have affected her. Perhaps Cotter knew there was no possibility of her wearing that Puritan outfit at Graymere, or even donning it to sneak out to this church service. But she had worn the next best thing: a demure gown of dark green brocade. Without willing it, Cabot shook his head in denial. He shouldn't have brought Elizabeth here, but she had begged him and he knew she would have gone without him. If their father knew she was going to a Puritan church, let alone hearing this fellow Cotter, he would have her in a nunnery immediately. Cotter was making a name for himself. Even by Puritan standards he was a radical. And if he kept calling the king and his bishops hypocrites and condemning them to hell, he was going to have a lively but short career.

Cabot had been surprised by the transformation in Elizabeth. At fourteen, she was now a young woman, tall, slender, with rounded hips and small, firm breasts, which she kept demurely concealed. Someone at Graymere must have recognized her metamorphosis, for she was now outfitted with a wardrobe suitable for an earl's daughter, complete with ruffs, farthingales, and stiff brocade by the yard. Effort had gone into making her look prettier, but her unfortunate nose made all attempts futile.

Cabot was sick with worry about his sister. He still guarded her secret. She was now a committed Puritan. Cabot surrendered all hope of altering that fact when he saw how she spoke of her faith. The same inner peace, contentment, and, yes, joy that he had once admired in Emily seemed to invade Elizabeth. This was in sharp contrast to the shyness, rigidity, and lack of grace that afflicted her in all other social situations. Poor Elizabeth. How many times had he thought those words? Even now, their father was negotiating for her marriage, having prepared a suitable dowry for an unfavored and untitled daughter of an earl. Her world would come crashing down around her soon enough. Elizabeth North seemed doomed to unhappiness, and there was nothing he could do about it.

Dutifully, Cabot tried to listen to Emanuel Cotter, but he was now condemning vestments and stained-glass windows. It was old stuff, and Cabot's mind wandered.

He was unable to dissolve his sense of shame over his flight from Virginia. He had vivid memory of Percy's pistol, and he knew he had been coerced. Yet, he could not escape the feeling he was a deserter from his post. Percy had come home something of a hero. He was a true ancient in the colony, serving five years in service of king and country. At once he had begun to denounce the bloody regime of Dale and Gates, as well as elaborate upon the perils of Virginia. Cabot knew Percy was merely making himself more heroic and important, but he played havoc with recruitment of new settlers. Anyone but the son of the Earl of Northumberland would have been hanged or made to stop this slander. Nothing could be done about Percy. When Cabot last saw him, he had a woman of fashion on each arm. "Now tell me I didn't do you a favor, my dear North." Cabot had once liked Percy. It was now impossible.

Cabot told his father the truth about Dale, progress in the colony, and the circumstances of his pirating the *Trial* and his desertion. Lord North tried to argue his son out of his conscience, then point-blank ordered him never to breathe the word *desertion*, lest he bring ruin to himself and his family. Cabot disobeyed, seeking out Lord De La Warr, still the governor of Virginia, to tell him of his misdeed.

"My dear Cabot, you must stop being so hard on yourself. You have done nothing, except serve His Majesty and myself extremely well. You remained far beyond your allotted time and were unstinting in performance of your duty."

Cabot was exasperated. "But—"

"I will hear no argument, Cabot. The circumstances of your leaving were no more untoward than my own. I sailed for Nevis, not England. I'm sure you were a victim of the same contrary winds that afflicted my voyage."

Cabot knew he had escaped disgrace. He should be glad for it, but he was not. What must Dale think of him, and Timothy and Rolfe? A lingering sense of dishonor pestered him.

He forced his mind to happier thoughts, Kate, the silken arms that awaited him across the channel. He was filled with impatience to see her, yet for two weeks he had forced himself to remain at Graymere, tending to Elizabeth, talking to his father, performing the duties of a son who had come home. He had done it all, and tomorrow he could leave, knowing he had prepared the way for his marriage to Kate and happiness.

He smiled, unaware of how incongruous he was amid the doomsaying of Emanuel Cotter. The correspondence between him and Kate while he was in Virginia had been infrequent, yet it had sustained him. Her letters had been long, newsy, filled with love. Again and again she had referred to a "surprise" she had for him. He had been unable to guess, and his uncertainty about this fueled his anticipations at seeing her. For his part, he had written what he believed to be manly letters about Virginia, what was going on, how Timothy was faring, managing to say, without dwelling on it inordinately, how much he missed her, how distraught he was that the year away had been doubled. And yes, he had let her know there had not been another Awotaka. Couldn't have the woman he loved being jealous.

The morning service ended, quite mercifully to Cabot. He collected Elizabeth and headed for the door. That he be introduced to Emanuel Cotter was inevitable.

"Emanuel, I'm eager for you to meet my dear brother, Cabot, of whom I have spoken."

"Thank you for joining us on the Lord's Day, sir."

The words seemed intoned, the voice mellow. As Cabot accepted the proffered hand, he had the impression Cotter was younger than he looked on the pulpit. Early twenties, he imagined, perhaps even younger than himself. "I am honored, Reverend. I have heard much of your zeal and remarkable sermons." He bowed. "Today's message was proof your reputation is warranted."

It was an elaborate compliment, but Cotter seemed not to register it. "We try only to do God's work." His black eyes seemed to probe into Cabot. "Elizabeth tells me you have just returned from Virginia. I understand one of our brethren has done excellent work there."

Cabot remembered. Rector Whitaker had turned out to be thoroughly Puritan, and his sermons had created an uproar. Virginia, or at least its leadership, was nothing if not loyal to the Crown and thus Anglican. "So I have heard, Reverend Cotter."

."And Elizabeth tells me you have visited our brethren in Leyden."

He thought of Emily. Comparison to this cold fish of a man was odious. "That is true, but not for a couple of years. How are they faring?"

"Not well, I understand. They have difficulty maintaining purity of spirit amid the wicked Dutch."

Elizabeth spoke. "I will not be able to attend prophesy this afternoon, Emanuel. Forgive me."

For the first time there was a hint of softness in Cotter's face as he looked at Elizabeth. "The pure of heart receive their own forgiveness, my dear." The thin lips spread into what Cabot supposed was a smile. "A few extra prayers this evening will maintain you in the spirit of the Lord."

On the way home in the carriage Elizabeth chattered happily. "Isn't he wonderful? Have you ever heard such a thrilling speaker?"

"He does have a way with words." That much was true. The man was a spellbinder, no doubt of that.

"I can't tell you what it means just to know him."

He saw the happiness on her face. Images of Scrooby came to his mind. "How well do you know him?"

She flushed, then smiled shyly. "Not well, Cabot, not well at all."

"But you are on a first-name basis."

Her laugh seemed nervous. "Yes, we are that." She looked at him a long moment. Her eyes were bright but somehow probing. "You do like him, Cabot. Tell me you do."

He smiled. He couldn't hurt his sister, now or ever. "Of course I do." Then he looked away. "Only, you must know what father would say." When he looked back at her and saw her eyes, he regretted his words.

"Yes, I know what father would say."

He wanted to scream at her that she was the daughter of an earl. This very afternoon at Graymere there was to be a garden party at which she would be paraded before suitors, her comeliness measured against the size of her dowry. This was the reality of her life, not Puritan soul-searching and not the ascetic Emanuel Cotter. He said none of it.

The lawn party was an agony for Cabot, if only because he

knew the suffering of his sister. Maids spent two hours fussing over her, and she appeared in a costume that Cabot considered a disaster. The gown was expensive, richly embroidered white silk set with tiny pearls and other gems. Below an immense half-ruff, Elizabeth's young breasts were half exposed for public inspection. She wore an immense double rope of pearls, as well as sparkling earrings, bracelets, and rings, all designed as proof of the wealth of the North family. Cabot recognized them as having belonged to the first countess. He assumed they were now part of Elizabeth's dowry. Her face was whitened with heavy powder, her lips and cheeks reddened. Her dark hair, her most attractive feature, was hidden beneath a broad, feathered chapeau. He told her how lovely she looked. In truth he could hardly bear to look at her, and she knew it.

She sat with Aunt Harriet who had come down from Yorkshire to be chaperone. As many as a half-dozen suitors attended her. They ranged in age from a lad of sixteen or seventeen to a man who looked to be in his forties, Lord Pemberton, balding, obese, obviously gout-ridden. Cabot knew he was a widower and therefore eligible, but what was he doing paying court to a girl so young? The other suitors, while younger and in one or two cases handsome, seemed to Cabot to be of an ilk he had seen so often in Virginia, vain, empty, posturing.

Cabot stayed with Elizabeth for a while, trying to help her by joining in what passed for repartee. But his was a hopeless exercise. Elizabeth, so inappropriately dressed, was devoid of wit, charm, or grace. She forced a smile, nodded, extended a hand, mumbled a word or two. Otherwise she might have turned to stone as punishment for the "conceits of the flesh" Emanuel Cotter had thundered against.

"I told myself you just *had* to attend your own sister's party, Mr. North."

He turned. It was Lady Barbara Cecil, attended by her cousin, Lady Eleanor Burghley.

"You *do* remember me, Mr. North." Laughter bubbled out of her. "And my dear cousin."

He had been surprised, but quickly recovered. "Of course, milady." He bowed to her companion. "Lady Eleanor."

"Your sister is *so* lovely, Mr. North. Doesn't Elizabeth look just divine, Eleanor?"

Her eyes were laughing. It was all sham, a mockery, but

he could do nothing but mumble agreement.

Barbara Cecil wore a gown not unlike Elizabeth's, except for the color, which was a light green, and incidental elaborations. If anything it was more deeply décolleté, nearly revealing her nipples. Yet, she wore it with far more ease. Cabot guessed she must be fifteen, perhaps sixteen, yet she already possessed the sheen of sophistication. She was rich, beautiful, and titled, and she knew it. Men desired her, and she knew that, too.

"Be a love, Eleanor, and fetch us some of that delicious punch." It was a ruse, previously planned. "Now, Mr. North, you must show me your gardens. I hear they are just grand."

He glanced at Elizabeth. There was desperation in her eyes as she pleaded with him to stay. He had no choice but to offer his arm. "Milady."

"Oh, puff on milady, Cabot. Call me Barbara."

He walked with her a few steps. "What would you like to see first, Lady Barbara?" He was damned if he was going to assume the familiarity of first names with her. "The formal gardens?"

"I would like to see you."

She had stopped and turned to look at him directly. "You really do leave a girl no pride, you know."

He blinked. "I'm sorry. I don't understand."

She had been serious; now the laughter returned to her eyes and voice. "A gentleman is supposed to call upon the lady, or so I've been led to believe. I'm sure I'm creating a scandal by coming to you."

Then he knew. This party was not just for Elizabeth. Desperately he sought a way out of the trap. "I'm sorry, but I've been in Virginia."

"Oh, puff, Cabot, you've been home long enough to decline invitations to several parties where I had hoped to see you."

His mind raced for some suitable reply. He was saved by the pressure on his arm. They resumed walking, entering the formal garden. Suddenly he wished they were not there among the box hedges. There was too much privacy.

"You are the shyest man, Cabot North. A girl has to be positively bold with you." She had stopped and was looking at him directly, her hazel eyes flirtatious. "I've waited all this time, Cabot—over two years."

"Waited for what, Lady Barbara?"

The hint of anger in her eyes was so fleeting he couldn't be sure he even saw it. Then it was quickly succeeded by laughter. Or was it mockery? "You leave a girl only shame, don't you? I've waited for *you*, Cabot North. I've turned down several suitors waiting for you to return from that awful Virginia."

He turned away. Hers was a flagrant abuse of courtesy. She was the granddaughter of the Earl of Salisbury, niece of his sister-in-law. To mock him so, while he had no recourse but to remain courteous, was a form of social cruelty.

"Do I discomfort you, Mr. North?"

He turned back to her. "Regretfully, yes."

She laughed. "Then it is only what you deserve."

She surprised him then, highly so, quickly rising on her toes to kiss him. It was just a light brushing of the lips, still it was bizarre. "Do you not find me attractive, Cabot? Is that why you will not pay me suit?"

Then he knew what he must do. At once his jangled nerves calmed. "Lady Barbara, you know you are beautiful. You also know for me to court you would be an absurdity. You are the granddaughter of the Earl of Salisbury, daughter of Viscount Cecil who is destined to be the next earl. You are lady-in-waiting to Queen Anne."

"So?"

"So I am the Honorable *Mister* Cabot North."

She laughed. "Oh, puff on all that, Cabot. Is that what's bothering you?"

"It is not puff, Lady Barbara. I know my station. I also know that I am unworthy of your ladyship and that you are mocking me."

Her laughter died, and she turned away, seeming to inspect the hedge, the maze beyond. "I know I seem frivolous to you. Perhaps I am. But when I saw you two years ago, so handsome, just back from Virginia, I fell in love. I cannot give my heart to another."

"Forgive me, milady, but I doubt that."

She met his gaze then, level, unblinking. "I have spoken to my father. There have been discussions with Lord North. Arrangements are being made. I need only say the word."

Later, he would think of a hundred things he might have

said, and another hundred better ways, including silence, as a solution to an intolerable problem. But what he said was, "For your sake, I pray you do not speak it. I do not love you. Nor will I ever." Perhaps worse, he turned and walked away, not seeing the expression on her face.

Two days later a letter came from Holland. In it was a simple card: The Star Sapphire, 57 Singel, Katarina van Stamp, Proprietress.

The Star Sapphire. What was it, some kind of shop?

Penned in her hand was a single word, *"Lieveling."*

So that was her surprise.

TWENTY

A Visit to Court

SINGEL WAS A canal and street a few blocks from Herren Gracht where the van Stamps lived. The modest sign over the shop was in Dutch, so he couldn't read it. But an emblem on it, a star-filled blue stone on a chain, told him he had the right place. He entered a dress shop, with bolts of fabric on tables and in racks along the walls. Several women, a couple with children in hand, were perusing materials or talking to saleswomen.

He saw Kate at the rear with a stout man, obviously a customer. Cabot could feel his heart pounding, for Katarina van Stamp was immeasurably lovely to him, simply yet elegantly gowned, poised, sophisticated, yet so animated as she chatted with the customer. The star sapphire hung from her neck. She raised her right hand to finger it idly.

In a moment she saw him, her vivid eyes and soft mouth registering surprised recognition, then delight. It lasted only a moment, as she turned back to her companion to resume the conversation. Cabot feasted his eyes on her, the straw-colored hair, faceted eyes, the exquisite movements of her lips as she talked, her statuesque posture as she slowly escorted her customer toward him and the door. Her nearness, the sound of her voice, the aura of femininity that always emanated from her were almost overpowering.

She smiled at him as she approached, but when she spoke it was to introduce her companion. Cabot heard the name as van Groudt. He was a stolid-looking man in his late fifties, rather fleshy. His greeting to Cabot was in Dutch. Then he turned to Kate, kissing her in farewell. Cabot saw the admiration in his eyes. He could hardly be blamed for that.

At last van Groudt was shown out the door. Kate turned to him, eyes glistening, mouth a little open. "Oh, *lieveling.*"

"God, Kate, you're so beautiful."

The urge to embrace him was strong, yet she managed to look around, realize they were not alone and restrain herself. "We close in an hour. Can you come then? I—I want to be alone with you."

"Yes. Shall I go to your father's house?"

"No. I want you to myself first." She smiled. "It will be the longest of all the lonely hours I've waited."

"I know."

She opened the door for him and again smiled. "But you'd better make it an hour and a half—not a second longer."

He passed the time in an ale shop, watching the slow trickle of sand in an hourglass. He didn't understand the dress shop or what she was doing there. He had a thousand questions. But one had already been answered. She still loved him. And, if he had ever doubted, he knew he still loved her. His desire for her was a physical pain.

When he returned to the shop, the shutters were closed and there was a sign on the door which he assumed meant "closed." Then the door opened. She had been waiting for him. He entered. She bolted the door behind him. They were alone.

No words were uttered, not at first, anyway. There was a joining of luminous eyes and extended hands, then a quick, convulsive clinging of bodies and a sweet reunion of starved mouths. Passion seemed to explode within both, and each shook under the onslaught. When at last they separated for breath, consuming each other with their eyes, both tried to speak at once. They laughed then and silenced the other with a new kiss, deeper, more lingering than before.

"At last you're here, *lieveling*."

"Yes, it's been an eternity."

"I know." And the intimate squeezing of his fingers within her hand affirmed her words. Moments longer they looked at each other; then she laughed lightly. "Do you like my shop?"

He released one of her hands and turned toward the interior. "Yes, but why? How?"

"Oh, I know, I'm scandalizing all of Amsterdam. Some people consider me a fallen woman to enter a business reserved for men. That's why I was so careful earlier. I don't want to set tongues to wagging any more than I have already."

"I still don't understand."

"Oh, *lieveling*." She nestled closer to him, her arm around his waist. "I couldn't sit home any longer waiting for you. Time dragged so. I had to be doing something. Finally, I persuaded father to let me open this shop. He put up the money, and he imports most of the fabrics for me. Actually, I've surprised everyone." She laughed. "Myself, too, I guess. Ladies seem to like dealing with a woman. It makes fittings easier, and a woman understands . . ." Again she laughed. "I'm making lots of money, Cabot."

The pressure of her thigh and hip against him, the curve of her breast against his ribs tormented him. He could only manage to say, "That's good."

"Do you mind my being a businesswoman, a merchant?"

"No. At least I don't think so." He smiled. "But I'm a little jealous of all these men coming in, seeing you, kissing your hand."

"Mijnheer van Groudt? He's a wool merchant, a friend of father's."

"I think he's more than that." He laughed. "But who could blame him for wanting someone as beautiful as you."

Her smile was radiant. "I belong only to you, *lieveling*. There will never be another for me."

The embrace that followed was the most fervent yet. But it was brief. They were still building their passion, savoring it. "Come, let me show you." Arms around each other, she led him on a tour of the shop, pointing out fabrics, the fitting room, the area for seamstresses. "I've eighteen girls working for me. Would you believe?"

He turned to face her, taking her fully within his arms. "I'll believe anything, Kate." As he kissed her, he again felt the acceptance she always offered him.

Voice husky, she said, "You haven't seen the best part." She led him to the rear of the shop and opened a door on a small room. There was a bed, dresser, mirror, a small commode.

"You live here?"

"No, I'm still at home. But if I work late, I sometimes sleep here." She turned to face him, her arms resting on his. "Actually, it's for you—us." She looked at him, eyes so bright, then smiled wanly. "I knew we'd want a place to be alone when you came."

He could feel himself beginning to tremble. "Have we waited long enough?"

"Yes. And it's been so hard."

"Oh, God, Kate."

Their lovemaking surprised them both. Separated for over two and a half years, each expected an explosion of passion, a quick surcease from longing. But it was not that way. Both lingered, savoring each caress, each of unnumbered kisses, speaking often, rapturous voices enhancing touch and smell, taste and enchanted vision. With their hands, their bodies, their voices, they peeled away layer upon layer of frustration, confronted desire so frequently denied, until, at last, when the stillness came upon her and she whispered, *"Ik hou van jou,"* theirs was an intimacy of mind surpassing mere flesh or sensation.

Neither slept till dawn, the hours of the evening and night filled with millions of words, the telling of all that had happened, hopes, fears, times of despair. There was joy and laughter in the telling, some tears, too, and all was punctuated with caresses and interrupted with consummations as Katarina van Stamp and Cabot North rediscovered each other and their love. It continued the whole next day and night. She had closed the shop and given her employees a day off.

He confessed to her the manner of his leaving Virginia. She alone seemed to understand his sense of dishonor.

"You think you must return?"

He saw the fear in her eyes. "I don't want to, Kate. You must know that."

"Could you not write to this man Dale, explain what happened? You *were* forced to leave at pistol point."

"I've thought of it." He sighed. "The Northumberlands are a powerful family. To accuse George Percy of desertion would be—"

"Unwise. Yes, I see." She looked at him a long moment, her eyes seeming to drench him in love. "I love you, Cabot North. One reason is that you are a man of honor. If you feel you must return to Virginia and make peace with this man—"

He put his fingers to her lips to silence her. Smiling, he said, "If return I must, it will only be with you as my wife, believe me."

Another time he told her of Elizabeth's agony and, rather scornfully, of his conversation with Barbara Cecil. She asked many questions, what she looked like, who she was. When Kate heard of Lady Barbara's open invitation, she exclaimed, "I never. Such boldness. Surely she would not want marriage to a man who does not love her."

He was leaning against the head of the bed. She was sitting before him, legs folded under her, all ripe flesh and invitation. He smiled, mostly out of happiness at being with her. "As you say, surely not. I may not have been subtle, but I did convey my feelings to her."

But when Kate heard him relate the words, *I do not love you. Nor will I ever,* she felt a sudden chill. He had scorned her. This bold young woman from a powerful family would be very angry. He had made an enemy. She sensed trouble, but had no idea what form it might take.

He remained a month. The fall festival took place, and he again felt welcomed into the family. Pieter had married his Betje. Johanna and Hans von Oeuyen were as yet unblessed with a child. Cabot and Hendrik van Stamp had several long chats, with Cabot relating the considerable progress made in Virginia.

"A strong hand is needed in nearly every enterprise."

"But it is so very a bloody hand."

Van Stamp nodded and gave a small shrug of resignation. "Have you learned the fate of Captain Hudson?" Cabot said he had not. Van Stamp told of Hudson's discovery of an immense northern bay that he was sure contained a passage to the Orient. But he remained too long in his explorations, and his ship was locked in by ice. The next spring his starved crew mutinied after putting Hudson and seven men adrift in a small boat. "They were given no food or water. They have not been heard of since."

"That's terrible!"

"I fear Captain Hudson's hand was not strong enough."

And they spoke of Katarina. "What do you think of her shop?"

"I'm amazed, sir. She is doing so well." Then he blushed. "I'm sorry. I didn't mean that she—"

The Dutchman laughed. "I understand perfectly, my dear Cabot. A woman merchant? Unheard of. I was quite against it at first, but I relented, and I'm glad I did. It is precisely the type of enterprise a woman can run extremely well. I understand one or two others may enter the field. I am most proud of Katarina." He smiled. "And it keeps her occupied while she waits."

The comment was not lost on Cabot. "Mijnheer van Stamp, I still love Kate—Katarina more than life itself. May we marry now?"

"Of course." He laughed. "I don't believe I could bear the wrath of my daughter if I said anything else." He arose, produced wine, and again toasted future happiness. Then he grew serious. "Have you spoken to your father about Katarina?"

"No, not as yet. There seemed no point before I left for Virginia. Since my return—well, I thought it best to come here first and make sure of Kate, her feelings."

"I understand. A wise decision. But you must speak to your father now."

He hesitated. "I know."

Van Stamp was not without perception. "Do you anticipate difficulties?"

A long sigh escaped Cabot. "Perhaps, yes. If I may speak frankly."

"By all means."

"I think my father has for some time fancied that I might marry a young woman who is a member of a powerful family, the Cecils. Perhaps you have heard of them."

"Lord Salisbury. Of course."

"He has in mind Lady Barbara Cecil, his lordship's grand-daughter. I will not marry her, of course. I will make my own decision. I will marry Kate."

"But what if your father opposes?"

"He will not. I want Kate to come to England. When father meets her, I know he will love her as much as I do."

"Yes, a good thought. I'm sure it can be arranged." He was smiling as he raised his glass and swallowed from it, yet his eyes were intent on Cabot. "I am not unaware of your English customs. You perhaps place more importance on titles and advancement through marriage than we Dutch do." He hesitated, clearing his throat. "Would it ease your problems if I said that I admire you a great deal? We have discussed the fur trade. Interest in a Dutch enterprise in America is growing." Again he hesitated. "If you were to enter into such an endeavor with me—indeed take charge of it for me—it would not be because you are my son-in-law, but because you are an able young man whom I can trust. Do I make myself clear?"

"Yes. Thank you, sir."

To Kate he said, "I want you to come to England, see Graymere, meet my father and sister. Then we'll announce our betrothal."

She nodded acquiescence, but said, "I'll be very nervous, *lieveling.*"

"I suspect you'll be the only one who knows it."

She came in early December, her sister Johanna accompanying her as chaperone, staying at Graymere. It all went splendidly, far exceeding his wildest hopes. Kate and Elizabeth got along famously. Not since Emily had Cabot seen his sister so delighted with a friend. And when Elizabeth blurted to him, "She's so *lovely,* Cabot. No wonder you love her," he could only beam with pride.

It was his father who astounded him. There was no doubt Kate had prepared for this venture. She was always exquisitely gowned. Her manners were impeccable. She turned on her charm full force, clearly ensnaring Lord Alfred with smiles and wit and laughter. Cabot simply had never seen him so ebullient. He basked in her attentions, showed her Graymere, took her riding, and talked warmly of the past, the court, his pride in his son. Cabot found himself sitting back in rapturous happiness to enjoy the virtuoso performance by his beloved.

Kate and Johanna remained a decorous five days, then departed amid his kisses, thrilled praise for how well it had gone, and his promises to come to Amsterdam for Christmas to announce their betrothal.

Then he confronted his father.

"What do I think of her? Why, she's charming, utterly beautiful." He smiled. "I am most impressed by your choice in women."

"Thank you, Father."

"Her English is quite good. I hadn't expected that."

"She is most intelligent, Father—and independent. Her father—"

"Yes, you told me, a Dutch merchant, very wealthy."

If Cabot hesitated at all, it was hardly noticeable. "I have asked for Kate's hand in marriage, and she has accepted. We will marry soon."

Lord Alfred's glance at him was sharp, but very brief. He was standing behind his desk. He seemed to take sudden interest in some papers, picking up one to read.

"I said I am going to marry her."

"Yes, I heard you." There was another long pause, somehow agonizing. "As I said, she is perfectly charming, a handsome figure of a woman. I can understand your . . . your infatuation."

"It is not infatuation, Father. I love Kate. I am going to marry her."

Again Lord Alfred gave his son a brief glance before returning to the papers he held. "Yes, I can see you are quite smitten. It was . . . quite charming to see two young people so in love. Made me wish I were young again." Now he looked at Cabot directly, lowering his papers to the desk. "As I said, she is quite beautiful—all the things you say she is. To repeat, your choice in women makes me proud of you. I expect nothing less. She is surely a remarkable young woman, one to love, to . . . to *enjoy*. But one hardly marries a woman like her."

Cabot felt as if he had been slapped. "I will not have you speak of her that way."

It was pure impudence, and anger glinted in the father's eye. Then came a genteel wave of his hand, an act of dismissal of his anger. "Ah, yes, yes, I understand. A young man and his first—"

"I am going to marry Kate, Father. There is nothing you can do about it."

"I'm afraid there is, my son. There are certain financial—"

"Disinherit me if you wish, Father. Hendrik van Stamp has offered me a place in his company."

Silence seemed to hang in the room. "I see."

"I want your blessing, Father. But if—"

The vigorous nodding of the old man's head silenced him. "You needn't threaten, Cabot. I can see how much you are in love." He hesitated. A small smile came to him. "But will you at least wait until your audience with His Majesty on the twentieth?"

"Audience?"

"Yes, the king has asked for you. To have an audience so soon before Christmas is quite an honor."

Cabot was received at Theobalds, the king's country house twelve miles north of London. He had acquired it in 1607 in exchange with Lord Salisbury for Hatfield. Cabot, who still had no idea what all this was about, wore a splendid new red doublet and breeches for the occasion. He was ushered by a chamberlain through massive doors into the long gallery. The sight astounded him. The king sat on a throne on a dais at the far end, Queen Anne beside him. Arrayed before them, indeed thronging the entire room, were the ladies and gentlemen of the court, all splendidly dressed in brilliant colors. Dazed, monumentally embarrassed, Cabot allowed himself to be led forward toward the king along a wide, red carpet. His vision seemed to be swimming, the faces he passed unknown. Then he saw his father, pride registered in every pore, and his brother, Sir Harold. Then other faces swept into his vision, Prince Charles, now heir apparent with the tragic death of Prince Henry; George Villiers, the Duke of Buckingham; Lionel Cranfield, the Earl of Middlesex; Charles Howard, Earl of Nottingham and Lord High Admiral; Chief Justice Sir Edward Coke; Sir Francis Bacon; Baron De La Warr; Sir Thomas Smythe. Behind the queen he saw Lady Barbara Cecil. Yes, she was a lady-in-waiting and belonged there. He noted her black armband. Her grandfather, the Earl of Salisbury, had recently died.

As instructed, Cabot stopped at the foot of the dais and bowed deeply before his monarch. He had never felt more alone in his life, a thousand eyes trained only on him. Then off to his right a chamberlain unrolled a parchment and began to read in a droning voice. Only some of the words had meaning to his reeling brain. "The Honorable Cabot North... Virginia... faithful service... distinguished... extraordinary valor... savage attacks... courageous defense..." It was all lies, horrid lies. He had never killed a single Indian. "Intrepid explorer, increasing His Majesty's realm through discovery of diverse rivers named Potomac, Patuxent." Cabot gasped. Smith had done this, not him. It was all lies, monstrous lies. Through burning eyes he saw the king rise from his throne, his long angular face with the deep-set, hooded eyes solemn.

"Kneel, Cabot North."

Cabot looked at him, pleading with his eyes. Not this. Anything but this. He had no choice but to obey, lowering his head. Eyes smarting, ears pounding, he scarcely felt the blade touch his shoulders or heard, "Arise, Sir Cabot, Knight of the Realm."

Numbly he obeyed, and swimming above him was his monarch, bending. Cabot felt whiskers against each cheek, smelled the sour odor of wine on the king's breath. Then came applause from behind him. He was being turned. Dumbly, he saw clapping hands, smiling faces. His father was beaming with pride. Awareness began to come to Cabot. Sir Cabot North. A knighthood, a sham knighthood, for service never rendered, a falsehood, an absurdity, a mockery. Who was responsible for this? His father?

Then he knew. King James raised his hand for silence.. "I am pleased this day to recognize this valorous gentleman." He extended his hand to his right, the smile on his face positively benevolent. The fingers were long and slender. A woman curtsied. "And I am doubly pleased to announce the betrothal of Sir Cabot and Her Majesty's lady, someone I could not love more were she my own daughter, Lady Barbara Cecil."

Cabot's gasp was unwitting, unwilled. He stared at her, saw triumph in her eyes and something else. What did he see there?

It was a trap of awesome proportions, a sham knighthood and a betrothal to a girl he had refused, announced to the court by the king himself. He looked at her again. Then he knew. Revenge was in her eyes.

Two days after Christmas he signed at the last moment aboard the *Argosy* as second officer. It was bound for Virginia.

TWENTY-ONE

Exile

CABOT STALKED OFF the *Argosy* on to the new pier at Jamestown and marched resolutely to the headquarters building. It never occurred to him that Sir Thomas Dale might not be there. He was. "I am surrendering myself for punishment, sir."

Dale stared at him in genuine surprise. "Mr. North, isn't it?"

"Yes, sir. I am remanding myself, sir."

Marshal Dale felt only confusion, but Cabot's demeanor surely suggested something serious. "Punishment? On what charge?"

"Unauthorized absence, sir, desertion."

Dale was impressed. Where most men skulked, begged, or ran to avoid the consequences of their actions, here was one standing at attention, demanding it. "I see." Again he looked at the solemn face of Cabot North. "Mr. North, no one believes in severity more than I, but—"

"Surely you remember, Sir Thomas. I was assigned to pilot the *Trial* for fishing. I took her to England instead."

The second in command of the colony tried not to smile, but he was not wholly successful. "Oh, that. Lord De La Warr has written me the facts. Anyone can be driven off course. The winds can be treacherous in these waters."

"I was not driven off course, sir. I piloted the—"

"Mr. North, surely you are not suggesting that the governor

of this colony prevaricates. You were driven off course."

"Respectfully, sir, I was not."

Dale sighed. "Mr. North, you have a certain facility, I'm told, for navigation and ship handling. But you are hardly experienced. I'm telling you, you were driven off course by the wind."

Cabot could only stare at him in disbelief. "Sir Thomas, I've returned for punishment. My honor demands nothing less."

Dale could only shake his head. In all his years of service to king and country, he had never encountered the likes of this. "All right, Mr. North. I will investigate the circumstances of your departure. Meanwhile, you will resume your duties."

"Duties, sir?"

"You are my secretary, aren't you? I haven't had a good one since you left."

"But—"

"Mr. North, you are dismissed. Go to your quarters. I expect you back here in an hour. I have orders to dictate." He didn't, but it was something to say.

The hour afforded opportunity for Dale to meet with Captain Mason of the *Argosy*. When Dale learned Cabot had been knighted and betrothed to one of the king's favorites just before leaving London, he was thoroughly nonplussed.

"I apologize. I had not known you are now Sir Cabot." He smiled, extended his hand. "My congratulations, Sir Cabot."

Cabot felt himself withering. "Please, sir, don't call me that."

"Oh, come now, you'll get used to it, *Sir Cabot.*"

He sighed. "Sir, it was a mistake. I shouldn't have been—"

"What on earth are you saying?"

If he had ever been more distressed, Cabot couldn't remember it. "Sir, the king was misled. He mistakenly believed I had—"

"My dear Sir Cabot, His Majesty does not make mistakes when it comes to knighthood."

Again Cabot sighed. "There is a lady, sir, Lady Barbara Cecil and—"

"I received my own knighthood from His Majesty in ought six. Are you suggesting it was in some way—"

"Oh, no, sir, your valor is well known. That's what I'm trying to say—about myself. I—"

"Sir Cabot, the *Argosy* will be leaving cargo, then returning. I suggest that you be on it."

"Oh, God, please, don't send me back. I can explain."

"I think you'd better do just that."

For the next half-hour, Cabot somehow found the words to tell all—Kate, his father, Lady Barbara. Dale was barely able to contain his amusement. An affair of the heart. A young man in love running from an unwanted marriage. Finally he said, "Sir Cabot—and you will be Sir Cabot whether you want to be or not—I have heard none of this. You never breathed a word to me."

"Sir Thomas, don't send me back. I'll only disgrace myself, my family."

"As I was saying, Sir Cabot, I know only that you have returned here out of loyalty and dedicated service to His Majesty's colony in Virginia. That you have done so, enduring the hardship of separation from your betrothed, is merely commendable. I will say so in my next dispatch."

Cabot stared at him, seeing not one hint of a smile. "Yes, sir. Thank you, sir."

To Timothy and John Rolfe he said, "If either of you ever call me Sir Cabot, I will stuff you both with tobacco and smoke you."

He told both his friends of Kate, the undeserved knighthood, the betrothal he had never agreed to. Timothy was confused. Social niceties among the upper classes were lost on him. Rolfe was more aware. "What're you going to do?"

Cabot told him of Dale's commendation for colonial service. "It is a mad world, John. If I can be knighted for something I didn't do, I might as well be commended for dedication I don't possess."

"You can't stay away forever."

"I don't know why not. I might as well become a Virginian, too."

That Timothy understood. "You're not, Cabot. You don't want to be." He saw his friend nod. "And what of your girl— Kate?"

In the silence that greeted his question, Cabot arose and

walked to the open doorway, looking out into the early spring night. "I've written asking her to come to Virginia. We'll marry and remain here. I expect to hear that she is coming soon." Then he turned back to them. "Enough of my troubles. What of you two?"

For the next hour he received a full report. Their expanded tobacco crop of 1612 had been a success and the small quantity of Virginia leaf they had shipped to London sold, perhaps only as a novelty. But sold it had. This summer they planned to plant as much as they could, hoping to make a substantial shipment to London.

"You were right about land, Cabot," Timothy said. "We're to get three acres, the equivalent of a month a year, all in return for two bushels of grain to the common storehouse."

Cabot grinned. "I'm glad for you, sar. At last you're a landowner."

A smiling Timothy nodded his pleasure. "John and I are going upriver to Henrico. 'Most everyone in Jamestown is goin' som'ere else. Jus' goin' to be a fort 'ere and the docks. I'm lookin' at land near Henrico, place called Bermuda Hundred."

"I know. I saw it."

"Lan' is good, already been planted by Indians. Should get the crops in as soon as I get the house built."

The slight reddening of Timothy's face was not lost on Cabot. "I gather the house is not for you and John."

Rolfe laughed. "Not unless I wear skirts and cook a whole lot better'n I do."

The flush on the farmer's face deepened under the laughter of both men.

"I gather you and Mistress Barton are going to tie the knot."

"She's a good woman, Cabot, virtuous, hardworking. She's alone and needs someone to . . . well, look after her."

Cabot's laughter flooded over him. "And you're going to marry her out of the goodness of your heart. She's not a bit attractive. You don't love her one whit." Another deep tinge came to Timothy. Cabot went to him, extended his hand, and pulled him to his feet, embracing him. "Sar, I couldn't be more pleased for you. When are you getting married?"

"Soon as I get the house built."

"Then what are you sitting here for? I'll help you tomorrow."

He didn't, for Dale, believing it wisdom to keep him away

from Jamestown in case the king or the Salisburys sent a vessel to take him back to London, dispatched Cabot with Captain Argall aboard the *Treasurer*, his new 130-ton warship. The alleged purpose of the voyage was to sail up the Chesapeake to trade with the Potomacs, the only tribe in the area who would still place any value on English wares.

Cabot soon realized Argall had a purpose other than trade. The Princess Pocahontas and her husband Kocoum still lived with the Potomacs. Argall was determined to capture her by any means, fair or foul, and return her to Jamestown.

"But why, Captain? There's relative peace with the Indians. Why stir up trouble?"

"Perhaps, but Powhatan and his chiefs have several of our men as hostages—and lots of weapons they stole or captured. We figure to trade his favorite daughter for the lot."

The whole episode was distasteful to Cabot. Argall arranged with the greedy Jazapaws, chief of the Potomacs, to lure Pocahontas aboard the *Treasurer* in exchange for a large copper pot. How Jazapaws, or his wife more likely, got the princess to come aboard no one knew, but come she did. Chances are she was curious to see white men again. Englishmen, beginning with John Smith, had always treated her well. She had no fear.

It wounded Cabot to see her. She was now fifteen or sixteen and quite beautiful, with the erect posture and regal bearing of a princess. In her apron she was a nearly unbearable reminder of Awotaka. The capture was done easily. During a tour of the ship, Argall locked her in the gun room, gave the pot to Jazapaws, and sailed for Jamestown.

Cabot sought her out. He saw both fear and recognition in her dark eyes. She remembered him from her early visits to Jamestown. "Don't be afraid," he said. "I'll let nothing happen to you." He didn't know whether she understood him or reacted to his tone of voice, but he saw her nod.

Dale surprised Cabot, receiving Pocahontas as a princess and issuing orders that any disrespect to her would result in the usual floggings and hangings. His kindness to her was boundless, although Cabot wasn't sure it was kindness to put her into corset, farthingale, and heavy gown and to constrict her feet in shoes. She accepted all with her usual dignity. If she objected, she did not show it.

Dale turned her over to the Reverend Alexander Whitaker,

the Puritan minister who claimed a special zeal to convert the heathen to Christianity. Princess Pocahontas would be his finest achievement, he hoped, the first of many converts. Lest Indians try to recapture her, she was taken to Henrico, a far more secure fortress, and in the church there began daily lessons in English, catechism, and other toils of a proper English maiden. Part of Cabot thought it ridiculous—why couldn't she just be left to live her own life?—but the girl's stoic acceptance of her fate undermined his feeling. Could she like and want this new life?

Shortly after his return from the Potomac, a ship arrived with a letter from Kate. He opened it eagerly, then, as he read, his hand began to tremble, so violently he had difficulty making out the words on the page.

Lieveling,

I am with child—our child.

I have asked father to let me come to Virginia to marry you. He refuses, insisting it is too dangerous for me in my condition. I have begged him. I have wept until there are no tears left in me. He refuses to listen.

Tomorrow I am to marry Pieter van Groudt, the wool merchant you met in my shop. I am devastated, but father insists. I try to tell myself he is thinking only of me, my honor. I have no choice but to obey.

Lieveling, I love only you. Forever and ever it is so. I will have our child—a son, I hope—and raise him to be as strong and loving as his father. And I will continue to believe with all my heart that someday, somehow you and I will be together in our love. Don't grieve. Try to be happy.

Ik hou van jou,
Kate

He wept unabashedly, couldn't help it. He wept for Kate, for himself, their lost happiness. He calculated the time the letter had taken to arrive. Weeks. She was already long married. He could do nothing to prevent it. Then came a vision of Kate, his lovely Kate, in the arms of the fat burgher. He flagellated himself with thoughts of Kate, opening her robe to him, spreading her thighs, the stillness coming over her as she gave the gift that was to be only his.

Then came anger, rage really. He railed at fate, God, his father, the whole Cecil family, king, country, and this god-forsaken colony. He swore vengeance on his father and on Barbara Cecil. But none of it would bring back his Kate or happiness. Even in the depths of his grief, he knew that.

With time came his resolve. Never, under any circumstances, would he marry Barbara Cecil. The king could have his head first. She would get from him only the purest hatred he had ever felt for a human being. And he would stay in Virginia—forever. It wasn't the life he wanted, but he would try to make out of it what he could.

Cabot stood up with Timothy Loudon at his wedding. Hannah Barton Loudon looked quite fetching in her bridal gown, and her obvious adoration for her new husband touched Cabot—almost as much as Timothy's nervous blundering amused him. When the two went off to their new home to consummate their nuptials, Cabot got quite drunk at the wedding party. He was not able, however, to drown his memories, aching longing, and bitter anticipation of a loveless future.

As a wedding present, he gave them land. Cabot qualified as an ancient, at least in Dale's eyes, so he claimed three acres adjacent to Timothy's and told him it was all his to farm.

"I can't accept it, Cabot. It's your land, not mine."

"Technically, perhaps, but what am I going to do with land? I'm no farmer."

"I still can't take it, Cabot."

"Tell you what. You call it your north field—for the direction."

Timothy Loudon was visibly moved. There were tears in his eyes. "It won't be no direction to me, sar."

The gift of land gave Timothy quite a spread. The "three acres" was mostly a fiction perpetrated for the benefit of company directors in England. Each settler staked out what he thought he could farm. With Cabot's land and his own, Timothy must have had fifty acres of prime, cleared land, his house built on a hilltop overlooking the river. If someone told Cabot that Timothy had twice that amount of land, he wouldn't have argued. He had no idea how large an acre was anyway.

Cabot officially moved in with Rolfe, whose land was closer to Henrico, but he spent little time there. He had become deeply involved in what he now knew he did best and loved the most— sailing. With Argall, he embarked on an extended exploration of the Chesapeake Bay, especially of the Eastern Shore, which not even Smith had visited. The *Treasurer* no sooner returned from that trip than the cargo of bartered grain was unloaded and the vessel was off on a mission of war. In northern Virginia the French had made settlements, which had to be destroyed. Actually, the French colony was far north of any land ever claimed in the name of James I, but such legal niceties were lost on the English. Argall relished every second, as he raided the French settlements, burning and looting what little there was. He killed numerous Indians and captured fifteen French-men. Argall made two such voyages. The French presence in North America was destroyed, for the moment at least. The English had done to the French what they feared the Spanish would do to them.

Cabot had no taste for the fruits of these excursions, but he surely did enjoy the voyages and the explorations. On the first trip north, Argall sailed into a beautiful wide bay dominated by a narrow, wooded island. It was the finest natural harbor he had ever seen and a most attractive site for a colony. The Indian name for the isle sounded something like "Manhattan" to him. He figured this was the area Hudson had explored for the Dutch.

In between his voyages, Cabot tried to help John Rolfe, who had fallen passionately in love with Princess Pocahontas, or as she was now known, since her conversion and baptism, Lady Rebecca.

She simply amazed Cabot. He thought that Pocahontas, always pliable, would go through the motions of Christianity, secretly maintaining her pagan ways. But her conversion seemed wholehearted. She was far more pious than those who professed to be. The Reverend Whitaker was beside himself with joy. She even helped make peace between Powhatan and the En-glish. Soon after her capture, Dale had demanded a return of hostages and weapons. Powhatan had sent a token hostage and a couple of rusty flintlocks. Dale then sailed the *Treasurer* up the York River, raiding Indian villages and threatening to burn out Powhatan's capital itself, if anyone could find it. No one had seen Powhatan since 1609. Dale took Lady Rebecca along. She stepped ashore, wearing her English finery, and sent a message to her father. If he loved her, he would not value her less than old swords, guns, or axes. Therefore, she would dwell among the English, who loved her.

The reply sent by Powhatan simply astounded Dale. All the guns, swords, and tools would be brought to Jamestown within fifteen days, along with corn in payment for those lost. Furthermore, Powhatan said his daughter should be Dale's child and live with him always as proof of their friendship. There was to be a general peace throughout his kingdom. Any runaway Englishmen would be returned to Jamestown, and if any of his men stole anything or killed cattle, he would send them to Jamestown to be punished. The Peace of Pocahontas, as it came to be called, would last for eight years. If ever a daughter was loved by her father, it was that Indian maiden.

She was also loved by John Rolfe. To Cabot that seemed only natural. Rolfe was a widower, lonely since Timothy had launched his own connubial bliss. Pocahontas was present at the church, which Rolfe was required under Dale's Laws to attend twice daily. As a literate man, he lingered to help the Indian maiden with her hornbook and catechism. All very understandable, even inevitable, considering the severe shortage of marriageable women in Virginia. Besides, she was a handsome woman with a most pleasing disposition.

Rolfe agonized over his predicament. She was not Christian, but a dark-skinned savage, who had only recently roamed the forest half naked. Trying to hide his amusement, Cabot argued with him point by point. She was no longer pagan, but a Christian woman named Lady Rebecca, wearing plenty of attire. As for her skin color, it was rather attractive, wasn't it? Finally, Cabot told of his own love for Awotaka, omitting only his carnal knowledge of her.

"If she hadn't been killed, I would have tried to marry her. Really, John, that's true."

Rolfe seemed not to have heard him. "You know what the Bible says about marrying *strange* wives."

"All wives are strange, I suspect, some merely stranger than others." Cabot feared for a moment he had expressed too much levity.

Rolfe was still not hearing him. "How can I marry a dark-skinned woman? What would people say?"

"Listen, John, I understand the Spanish and Portuguese men who come to the New World married Indian women and settled down to contented family life. Now I know the Spaniards are Papists, but they still worship the same God. Why shouldn't we English marry Indians?" He had at last gotten the tobacco planter's attention. "Does she love you, John?"

"I think so, yes."

Cabot smiled. "Then there you are."

Rolfe stared at him dumbly. "There I am what?"

"Poca—I mean Lady Rebecca loves you. As you say, she is a heathen savage, barely civilized. Her hold on Christianity is surely tenuous. You have a duty to save her from herself, from backsliding into her Indian ways, from nakedness and corruption." He poured it on as thick as he could. "In marrying Lady Rebecca, you will not only be saving *her* for Christ, but thousands, maybe tens of thousands of her countrymen who will follow her lead. Think of it, my friend, you will be the first Englishman to marry an Indian. How many will follow the daughter of Powhatan into the true church? Rolfe, you have a duty to marry her, nothing less."

Rolfe was on his feet, staring at him wide-eyed. "Yes, Cabot, yes. I do see it now."

Only later did Cabot bring up the real problem in the marriage. Dale's Laws proscribed, under penalty of death, any carnal fraternization with Indians.

"Oh, God in heaven, Cabot, what'll I do? I must have her."

Cabot could not restrain his laughter. "And so you shall. Contrary to what many may think, Dale is a flexible man."

With Cabot's help, Rolfe spent days penning a letter to Dale, telling of his love for Pocahontas and the torment it caused him. He wanted to marry her to save her for the church and to convert other Indians. He was not, heaven forbid, moved by any carnal desires. At Cabot's suggestion, Rolfe added that if he had "such desire," he might better satisfy it "with Christians more pleasing to the eye." Cabot thought it a nice touch.

It worked, as Cabot knew it would. Dale agreed to the marriage, criticizing Rolfe only for marrying above his station. He was a commoner and she was a princess, after all. On April 5, 1614, Rolfe and Lady Rebecca were wed, Powhatan readily agreeing to the nuptials. Indeed, the marriage so helped relations between the English and the Indians that Dale offered to marry another of Powhatan's daughters, the fact he had a wife in England notwithstanding. Powhatan, forever wise, refused.

On this his third stay in Virginia, Cabot discovered that he was no longer as isolated as before. In a voyage in June 1613, Argall had explored a northern, more direct route to Virginia, making the trip in seven weeks. Thereafter, ships stopped more often, many of them bringing mail for colonists. Some were for Cabot.

My dearest betrothed,

I am so proud of you, my darling, enduring the hardship of our separation to serve His Majesty, our patron, in his colony of Virginia. Your sacrifice has not gone unnoticed by His Majesty, my father, or anyone at court. Though I grieve that you are away from my aching bosom, I, too, will make the sacrifice until you return to my eager arms.

Yours in longing love,
B.

Sir Cabot, my dear son,

You have become something of a hero in England, or at least those parts of it that matter. Returning to service on the Virginia Plantation, leaving your betrothed so precipitously is being cast in a romantic aura which there is no need for either you or me to believe, however useful such nonsense may be.

I know you are angry with me for arranging your marriage to Lady Barbara. But I did it for your own good. One day you will thank me. Your flight to Virginia was typically headstrong, but I believe it, too, will be useful. Your *other* infatuation will cool while you are away, and you will come to realize the wisdom of the course I have chosen for your life. Your marriage to Lady Barbara will be a brilliant one, providing you with far greater influence in life than circumstances of your birth would ever have provided.

I should report to you, not in a self-serving way, that I have not been as well as I might like. I fear the sands of time are taking their toll. Knowledge of your early departure from Virginia for home would, I am certain, be a balm for my aches and pains.

Your loving father

My dearest brother,

Oh, how I wish I were a man and could fly with the wind to Virginia, escaping heartache and frustration to bring a new life with some hope for happiness.

My heart is broken, Cabot. Father has betrothed me to Lord Pemberton. Do you remember him, the old one at that last party? Oh, Cabot, what is to become of me? I begged Father not to do this to me. I wept, told him if he had a shred of love for me he wouldn't do this to me. I even said I could not help it that Mother died at my birth. Why was he still punishing me? All was to no avail. I must wed Lord Pemberton, though the sight of him repulses me and I know the flesh will fall from his bones at his touch.

Nor do I find comfort in his society. He is a corrupt man, sinful, ungodlike in demeanor and attitude. I know he is marrying me, forgive me for such sinful thought, because I am young and innocent. He is *old,* Cabot, old enough to be my father. He has no child as young as I. And he is already unwell. His gout pains him terribly. What kind of life will it be for me? Father says I was refused by all others. Was a girl ever so scorned as I? I know it is a mortal sin, but I can only hope my marriage will be a brief one. Then I pray for forgiveness for such thoughts.

Your suffering sister,
Eliz.

Cabot read the letter, deeply saddened for Elizabeth. But there was nothing he could do. There was no point in even attempting a reply.

My dearest brother,

I have managed thus far to forestall my dreaded marriage. I pleaded for time to enjoy a little of my youth. I have feigned one illness after another. But I grow more desperate each day. His lordship has argued with Father.

I've heard them. How much longer I can put off this horrible marriage, I don't know.

Please don't worry about me, Cabot. I really am well. And I am sustained by my *secret life*. I pray, many times a day, for guidance and courage, which Emanuel assures me God will provide. I just do so wish you were here to help me. But I would not wish for your return—for your sake. Lady Barbara is the subject of unrelenting gossip, for she is attended by many men. I am certain she uses her betrothal to you to mask her activities, the nature of which I feel I should not, in Christian love, speculate on.

I have begun a correspondence with your Kate in Holland. She is such a dear, sweet, thoughtful person. No wonder you love her. And she is strong, much stronger than I, and an inspiration to me. Her love for you can never fail. She has told me so. At my urging, she has sent a small note for me to enclose for you, as she is uncertain a letter posted in Holland would ever reach you.

Your loving sister,
Eliz.

Hand shaking, Cabot tore the seal on the letter from Katarina van Stamp.

Lieveling,

We have a son. He has dark hair and bright blue eyes like you. He is strong and healthy, and his nature is most loving. He is such a joy to me, for I feel that through him, you are with me.

I wanted to name him Cabot after you, but thought it unwise. I have named him Philip. I hope you like it.

I am in good health, and I try to find what contentment I can. It helps that I have kept my shop. I am busy, and time passes more quickly when I am occupied.

My husband is generous, loving, and thoughtful, more like a father than a husband. He suffers terribly from gout, and his heart is not strong, so his demands upon me are very little, hardly any in fact.

Cabot, *lieveling*, I worry so about you and your being

happy. Please, I beg you, do not be bitter toward your father or my father or anything that has happened to us. You are forgiving by nature. Please don't change. And we still have our love. Nothing can alter that.

Elizabeth writes that she fears you plan to remain in Virginia forever. If so, I beg you to reconsider. I want to see you. I want you to know our son. With all my heart I still believe we will find a way to be together in our love. But our destiny cannot be fulfilled if you hide yourself in Virginia. Please come back to me. We will find a way.

> *Ik hou van jou,*
> Kate

Cabot never did reply to any of the letters. He was resolved to turn his heart to stone if it was possible for a human being to do so. He recognized that he wasn't very happy, but he was determined to find as much contentment as he could, sailing with Argall, running cargo and passengers between Jamestown, Henrico, and Point Comfort, taking a ship on occasion to fish or perform other errands. And he did find happiness with sail and wind, the pitching deck. He had been aptly named he now knew.

He found pleasure in the families of Timothy and John Rolfe. Timothy and Hannah had a son Henry and another child on the way. Rolfe and Lady Rebecca had a son Thomas. The tobacco crop flourished. In 1616 Rolfe and Timothy sent a significant number of barrels of cured tobacco to London and earned a suitable price.

"Lord almighty, Tim, you are going to be so rich you'll put an earl to penury."

Timothy grinned. "Not very likely, but didn't I tell you this was good land here?"

Cabot ate his own words. Imagine that vile weed turning Virginia into an economic success. Who would ever have thought it? Corn and other foodstuffs were still grown—Dale insisted on it—but every available foot of ground was being planted in tobacco. How many times had Timothy said, "Pretty soon they'll be aplantin' it in the streets of Jamestown"? Tobacco had become the currency of Virginia. A man paid for his food, clothes, any item he wanted in tobacco, and every ship was full of imports that not many years before would have been considered unparalleled luxuries. Virginia was going tobacco mad. King James might decry his colony going up in smoke, but tobacco was more valuable than all the gold, silver, iron, glass, silkworms, and nonexistent grapes—all of which men had come to find and died by the hundreds for. John Rolfe and Timothy Loudon had made Virginia an economic success.

But if his two friends cheered him, they were also an aggravation. Timothy, relishing his contented marriage, seemed unable to ignore any opportunity to urge Cabot to return home and "marry some nice girl."

"This ain't for you, sar. This is farm country now, and you ain't no farmer."

Ultimately, Rolfe did him more damage. He was happy with his quiet, dignified Indian princess. His passion for her was undeniable, yet he could not escape the knowledge he married a "strange" woman. Peace would not come for him until he returned to England with her to meet his relatives.

"John, it's madness. Lady Rebecca won't like it. She isn't used to the climate. It might even kill her."

"A man must do what he must."

It was Sir Thomas Dale who struck the final blow. "My dear Sir Cabot, it is time, past time, you returned home to"— he shrugged—"find out what is going to happen."

"No."

"My young friend, you've done everything to avoid the inevitable. The only thing left is to button up your courage and either marry the girl or not."

"No."

Dale looked at him severely. "Next month I am leaving. My work here is done. Captain George Yeardley will become deputy governor. John Rolfe and Lady Rebecca will accompany me, along with a party of Indians. These are my orders."

Cabot nodded. "I will miss you, Sir Thomas. The Virginia Plantation will miss you."

"I have orders to take you with me. Your father is dying."

In May 1616, an unwilling Cabot North stepped aboard the *Treasurer* for his return to England. He had been in Virginia more than three years.

TWENTY-TWO

Loving Brother

THE LORD ALFRED NORTH who strode out of Graymere to greet his son as he alighted from a carriage had aged and deteriorated in vigor, but he was hardly dying. Even as his father embraced him, Cabot knew he had been tricked into returning home.

"My son, my son, thank you for coming."

"I was told you were dying, Father."

His hands still on Cabot's shoulders, Lord Alfred laughed a little. "As you see, I'm not."

"But Sir Thomas said—"

The laugh deepened. "Sir Thomas was instructed to bring you home, even in irons if need be. His prevarication was surely preferable to chains." Lord Alfred chuckled a moment longer, then again embraced Cabot. "I'm sorry you worried, but I am pleased you thought emough of me to come for that reason."

It was not true. He had returned because Dale ordered him to. And he had been most reluctant, each creak of the *Treasurer*'s rigging an accompaniment to the bitterness he felt toward his father. Now, under the old man's unwanted embrace, he sighed. What was the use? Kate was right. He could not remain unforgiving, bitter. It was not his nature. "Why did you want me to return, Father?"

Lord Alfred's answer was to lead him into the house where Jacobs greeted him formally. There was a flurry of instructions to take care of Cabot's luggage, prepare his room, and bring wine to celebrate his homecoming.

In his father's musty study Cabot again asked why he had been summoned.

"In time, my son. Tell me about Virginia first."

The telling took awhile. Cabot gave an accurate report on the colony's progress, stating his belief that Virginia was now established in place and on the verge of success. He gave maximum credit to Dale.

"I'm surprised. Word of Dale's harshness—he's called Bloody Dale, you know—has reached England. It makes recruitment of settlers all but impossible."

"He has been stern, but only with those who require it."

Lord Alfred smiled. "That is an attitude you would not have expressed a few short years ago."

"I still do not like his methods. The results are undeniable, however. Virginia is now a viable colony."

Father looked at son a little askance. "Did you know the Virginia Company is virtually bankrupt. I have lost a fortune. So have other directors and investors. Our only hope is that the colony in Bermuda may become profitable."

"I think Virginia will." He told him of John Rolfe's tobacco.

"So I've heard. But His Majesty does not like tobacco. He has written a pamphlet denouncing it."

"I don't much care for it either, but how does one attack smoke?"

"And how do I profit from my investment in smoke?"

Cabot hesitated, then spoke the truth as he saw it. "I don't think you can—as a company director." He saw the raised eyebrows of his father. "Virginia has no gold, as I told you long ago, no precious stones, no instant profits for the picking. But it has something far more valuable—land. With hard work, the land in Virginia will produce great wealth."

"What are you saying?"

"Dale's most important act was not his bloody discipline, but his insistence on private gardens, then his grant of three acres to every settler. He made everyone a farmer. Virginia became self-sufficient, able to feed itself. And with tobacco will come wealth. There are doubtless other crops to be grown, too." He saw his father listening intently. "Virginia has almost unlimited amounts of land. The colony will prosper beyond your wildest dreams if settlers are given land, many acres of it, to grow what they will. They will make the land yield wealth in tobacco, corn, wheat. Other men will profit from trade in tobacco and by providing all the other manufactured goods the colonists will need. It is the only way, sir."

"But the company's investment?"

"The company was a mistake. Men will not work nearly as hard on company lands as on their own property. Sir Thomas has proven that." Cabot saw the expression on his father's face and was emboldened. "We call it the New World. I think it is, but in ways none of us expected. Rank and privilege, as we know them, are meaningless in Virginia. The only realistic privilege there is the opportunity to work, and only those who work the land or deal in the produce of the land will profit."

Lord Alfred said nothing for a time, seemingly busying himself with replenishing their wine glasses. "Then you believe in Virginia."

"I do now. I did not in the beginning, as you know. I saw only mistakes, folly, madness, and death. But perhaps it was a learning process. Perhaps the mistakes had to be made to discover the true wealth of the New World. Others will go to America and profit."

Lord Alfred sighed. "Perhaps you are right. But I will not live to see it. I live only to put my house in order before I die."

Cabot saw his opportunity and used it. "Why did you bring me back?"

"I wanted to see you again, make my peace with you." There was sadness in the old man's voice.

"Is that the only reason?"

"You know it isn't."

Cabot braced himself inwardly, expecting him to bring up his marriage to Lady Barbara. His father surprised him.

"Your sister, the stubborn fool of a girl, refuses to marry Lord Pemberton until you return home."

Cabot smiled. Elizabeth was cleverer than he figured. When she ran out of feigned illnesses, she used brotherly love as an excuse to avoid marriage. "Father, she doesn't love him."

"*Love?*" The word was pure scorn.

"And he is much too old for her. Perhaps if you selected a younger man, she might—"

"*Silence!*" His anger flared from out of nowhere. "Elizabeth has no more sense about marriage than you do. I have done what is best for Elizabeth, as I have for you. A younger man, you say. Then you find one who is suitable. Your sister is not the most favored of young women, and she refuses to fix herself up, learn grace, manners, womanly wiles. Accept it, as I have, Elizabeth has nothing to offer a man but her *dowry.*" He thundered the word. "The only young men who courted her were *wastrels.*"

Cabot saw the reddened face of his father, his strained breathing. "Father, please calm yourself."

Lord Alfred paused, looking at him. "Yes, I will." He sat at his desk then and made a visible effort to calm himself. He had some success. "The young suitors wanted only her dowry. They would have stolen it, wasted it. She would have been left with nothing."

It was a telling point, not lost on Cabot.

"I know, Lord Pemberton is—well, he hardly cuts a romantic figure to a young girl. But he is a man of substance. He will not steal her dowry. That is not why he wants her."

"Why does he want her? Because she is young, innocent?"

Father glared at son. "You are a man of the world—or ought to be. I need not answer that."

Cabot recoiled inwardly. "And you would give your only daughter to such a man?"

"Don't be a child, Cabot. He will dote on her. She will have every privilege. She need only comfort him, provide companionship in his old age. She will have every security, every luxury, a social position of importance. She will be able to engage her other interests. She will have gained everything— and at a small price. Believe me, my romantic and very foolish son, I am doing what is best for Elizabeth."

Cabot was silenced. His father's words made sense. He had not thought in these terms.

"You have influence with your sister. I want you to go to her at once, talk to her, convince her to marry Pemberton. His patience is nearly exhausted. The marriage will occur in a fortnight."

"Father, don't do this. Don't ask me."

"Your sister stays almost constantly in the west wing. She no longer joins me at meals, but takes her food in her room— if she eats anything at all. She has imprisoned herself. I fear for her mind. If you love your sister, you will do as I ask. And may I suggest that you no longer indulge her foolishness."

He found her by a window, hunched over some needlepoint.

When she arose, startled to see him, he was shocked by how thin she was, the pallor to her cheeks. She cried his name and ran into his arms, weeping against his shoulder. He held her, stroking her fine hair, patting her fragile back, and uttering soothing words. Over her shoulder he saw the room, bare, ascetic, almost a cell, hardly the bedchamber of an earl's daughter. Then he knew. It was like the Puritan churches, devoid of decoration.

Finally, she could speak a little. "Why did you...come? He—He sent...for you, didn't he?"

Cabot produced a handkerchief for her to wipe her eyes and blow her nose. "Yes, he sent for me."

"Oh, please, Cabot, don't make me marry him."

He smiled. "I have no intention of it, my darling."

Again she hugged him. "Oh, Cabot, I knew you wouldn't. I just knew it."

He patted her back again. "Only you can make your decision."

She raised her head, a quizzical expression in her eyes. "What are you saying?"

"How old are you now? Eighteen? Father may still have the right, but he should not try to force you into a marriage you don't want." He smiled. "Indeed, I think he's learning he cannot. He has sent me to persuade you."

"But you said you wouldn't."

His smile widened, softened. "I'm not even going to try. I can't tell you what to do. No one can—no one on this earth." He saw her look at him, understanding instantly. "Have you prayed for guidance?"

"Oh, yes, Cabot, yes. I pray constantly."

"It is no help?"

"I don't know, Cabot. I don't know what God is saying to me."

She turned from him and slowly went back to the window, chair, her needlepoint. He watched, waiting for her to go on. Suddenly he felt shame. He had scant belief in God or prayer. His words were hollow, a mockery. But she believed, believed with all her heart. Wasn't he just trying to comfort her?

"Emanuel says the same thing."

"Emanuel? Oh, the Reverend Cotter."

"Yes. He tells me to pray. God will guide me. He takes

my hand, and we pray together. Often we do that."

Cabot had an image of the ascetic Puritan on his knees, holding her hand. Yes, he would do that.

"He comforts me. I feel better after we pray. Then I come here, and I am confused again, fearful. I believe with all my heart God will speak to me, tell me what I must do with my life. But when? How long must I wait?"

The theological turn to the conversation made him uncomfortable. He sought to change it. "Would it help if I tell you father loves you."

She had been looking down at her needlepoint. Now she looked at him. There was vehemence in her voice. "He does *not*. You know he doesn't."

"Elizabeth, he is stern, I know, quick to anger, often difficult to approach. But he does love you."

"You call it love to force that wicked old man on me?"

Cabot sighed. It was a turn to all this that he hadn't wanted. "He may be wrong—indeed I believe he is—but he wants only what is best for you—or what he believes is best for you." He saw her start to speak, but silenced her by raising his hand. "Father is old and thinking of death. He only wants you taken care of before he dies. That's all it is, Elizabeth. Is it so awful of him to want that?"

"Words, just twisted words, Cabot."

"All right, so he's wrong. But he believes in his heart he is right. He is afraid a younger man will steal your dowry and leave you alone and penniless. Lord Pemberton is—well, he is rich enough not to rob you of your dowry. He wants only—"

"Stop it, I say!" She arose from her chair, her anger arcing toward him. "I *know* what he wants."

"Are you sure? Father says he wants only comfort and companionship. Those were his exact words."

"Comfort in bed! My flesh crawls at the thought of him, his hands. Is that what you want for me, Cabot?"

He sighed. "I want nothing for you, Elizabeth, save your happiness. Believe me, I am—"

"You are trying to talk me into this marriage, and you said you wouldn't."

He wanted to shake her, but restrained his annoyance and his voice. "I am not. I am only trying to help you understand what Father is thinking so you won't hate him. Is that so wrong?" She hesitated, blinked. He had made a point with her. "Has it ever occurred to you that God will not help you because your heart is full of bitterness toward Father?"

His words seemed to fall on her like physical blows. Her face contorted, and she crumbled into her chair, weeping. He went to stand beside her, stroking her back, her hair. "I would not hurt you, Liz, not willingly." He saw her nod assent. "Father may be misguided, but he is not venal. He knows this Pemberton is too old for you, unattractive. He knows why he wants a young, attractive girl like you."

"I–I . . . am . . . not."

"You're prettier than you believe, my sister. Father knows of the . . . the demands Pemberton will make on you. But he believes they will be—at his age, light, bearable. In exchange you will have a home, social position, security for your whole life, opportunity."

"W–What opor—opportunity?"

She had raised her head to look at him through overflowing eyes. He smiled down at her. "You haven't been thinking clearly, have you? Hasn't it occurred to you that as Lady Pemberton you might have opportunity to engage your every whim?"

"I–I want n–nothing."

"Oh, but you do. You want your conscience. I should imagine his lordship would find it difficult to—shall we say?—regulate your religious practices." Again he smiled. "I should imagine he'll be so delighted with his new wife that he might even want to join her at worship. He would make a convert of renown, one of many you might make."

He saw the effect of his words, the rapid drying of her tears, the beginnings of revelation in her eyes. Part of him recoiled at his own words. None of it was true. At least he believed none of it. But he did have to comfort his sister, didn't he?

"Yes, I suppose—yes. I wouldn't have to hide."

"There would be no need for secrets, lies. You could be true to yourself."

"Yes, yes. I see that now. I could—"

The knock at the door could not have been more inopportune. Cabot flinched at the sound and barked, "Come in."

It was Jacobs. "Pardon me, Sir Cabot, but his lordship asks

me to inform you that Lady Barbara Cecil has arrived."

"She's here?"

"Yes, sir. His lordship had me send word as soon as you arrived."

The conniving old fool. "Thank you, Jacobs. Tell my father I'll come at once."

When he turned back to Elizabeth there was a scant smile on her lips. "Do you know father's reasons for forcing *you* into a marriage you don't want?"

He sighed and nodded.

"Are you going to marry her?"

"Of course not." He saw the glint of mockery in her eyes. "The situation is different, Elizabeth."

"How? Oh yes, you're a man and I'm a woman."

"Yes, and I'm twenty-seven and you're eighteen." The irony lingered in her eyes. "I know what you think, but it is not so. I'm not being a hypocrite. I have free choice—or ought to have. I can make my own way in the world. I surely have in Virginia, where I can easily return. If father disinherits me, it is no great loss. You can do none of these."

"I could open a shop like your Kate."

It was the first mention of her name. It seemed to stab at him. "Dutch society is different. Her father is rich, helped her. She could not have broken convention without his approval."

He watched her sigh, purse her lips, and nod assent. "I know. But, oh, how I wish I were a man." Again she sighed. "What're you going to do?"

"I'm going downstairs and break this ridiculous engagement."

"Cabot, she leads a scandalous life. She pretends to be the lonely, suffering fiancée, but really she is constantly in the company of men. She is being seen everywhere with a Captain William Haversham of the Royal Guards. He is a married man, and London buzzes with gossip."

"The more reason for this betrothal to end. She will probably want to."

"What if she doesn't? What if she insists on marriage?"

"Then I will go back to Virginia."

"They made you return this time. They will again."

He sighed. "Yes. You are obviously right." He hesitated,

making a quick decision. "I will go to Holland. Kate's father offered me a position with his company once. Perhaps he will do so again."

"Do you know she has a son?"

"Yes."

Her face seemed all eyes, searching his. "Is he your son?"

He looked at her a long moment. "Yes." Then he turned abruptly. "I'd better go, face that witch downstairs." He strode toward the door, then paused and turned back to his sister. "Elizabeth, I only wanted to help you make peace with Father. Have I?"

She smiled. "Yes, and thank you. I know I can now go to God with a pure heart. He will tell me what I must do."

He nodded. He felt quite pleased with himself.

TWENTY-THREE

Plans

CABOT PAUSED AT the top of the stairs to compose himself. He hadn't expected her. Again his father and Lady Barbara had concocted a surprise for him. His anger at that prevented any clear thoughts about what he would say to her. No matter, he knew what he must accomplish. The words would come when he needed them.

Halfway down the stairs he saw them in the small parlor, she seated, his father standing over her. They were chatting animatedly. He heard her laugh. There was no question she was a beautiful woman, poised, highly confident, worldly. Her honey-colored hair—why were all the women in his life blondes?—was arranged in tiny ringlets, curls framing her face. She wore what he assumed was a new fashion. Gone were the ruff, the padded shoulders, the farthingale. The bodice was now fitted to the waist with long, natural sleeves. The neckline was cut square to reveal her shoulders, and so deeply that the rounded tops of her breasts were revealed above the lace fringe. The skirt of bright green velvet was extremely rich and voluminous, but pulled back to reveal an embroidered petticoat of stiff silk, light brown in color. The garments resembled those he had seen Kate wear in Amsterdam. England was just catching up to the Continent. He wondered if Lady Barbara Cecil knew that.

She saw him as he entered. She registered mild surprise, smiled radiantly, then rose and came to him. "Oh, my darling. At last." She embraced him, and the kiss she gave him, open, deep, greatly experienced, surprised him with its lasciviousness. To his disgust he felt a reaction in his loins.

"Oh, my handsome darling, is it really you?"

Who else did she think it was? "Yes." He extricated himself from her and bowed. "Lady Barbara, it is good to see you looking so well."

"Oh, puff, Cabot. Don't be so formal." Again she threw herself into his arms and gave him a deeper, more prolonged kiss. Out of the corner of his eye, Cabot could see his father beaming benevolently. Then her cheek was against his, her breath warm against his ear. "It has been so long, my darling. I've died of loneliness a thousand times—on each of the thousand days you've been gone." She pulled her head back to look at him, all smiles and bright eyes. "You see, my darling, I've counted every day."

He didn't believe a word of it, but grudgingly admired her performance.

"We're all so *proud* of you, my darling—going off to Virginia to build the king's colony." Her eyes were bright, the words coming effortlessly. "Why His Majesty asks about you *every* day. I've heard him say how proud he is of you." She turned her head away from Cabot. "We are all *so* proud, aren't we, Father?"

Father?

The old man was beaming. "Yes, my child, we certainly are."

She smiled at Cabot again. "And how handsome you look. Why I shan't let you take *one* step out of my sight ever again."

She moved to kiss him again but, hands on her shoulders,

he held her away. "Would you excuse us, Father. I'd like a few moments alone with Lady Barbara."

"Of course, of course. I quite understand." Chuckling, he began to leave the room. "Ah, to be young again."

Mind racing, he turned from her, but not far or fast enough. She seized his hand in both of hers. "Oh, Cabot, it has been too long." Then she was kissing him again. He tried to prevent it and the hated heat she caused in him, but failed on both counts. "We'll be married soon, darling, real soon. I can't bear to wait longer."

Then he was away from her. "Lady Barbara, I—"

"Don't be so formal." She laughed lightly. "I'm not about to call you Sir Cabot."

"I want to be formal, Lady Barbara. I have something to say." He cleared his throat. "This engagement, our betrothal, is a sham devised by my father and your father. I–I think it should be . . . broken."

"What on earth are you saying, Cabot?"

"I'm saying this charade has gone on long enough. It's time we all came to our senses, most especially you and me."

She was looking at him with what passed for seriousness. "Are you saying you don't love me?"

He sighed. "I don't mean to be ungallant, but I fear that is the truth."

Her serious expression lasted a moment longer before giving way to smiles and a cascade of throaty laughter. "You've been in Virginia too long, my dearest. I hear it is quite—well, barbarous there. You have forgotten yourself, you poor, courageous dear."

"What're you saying?"

Again the laughter. "I'm saying those kisses you gave me were hardly those of a man not in love."

"They meant nothing."

"You may fool yourself, Cabot North, but not me. I know what I felt—and what caused it."

He swore under his breath and turned his back to her. "Lady Barbara, our marriage would bring only unhappiness to you, to both of us."

Her laughter trilled behind him. "Oh, puff, Cabot."

"You know I did not court you. I never asked for your hand or spoke to your father."

"Yes, you really are shy, my darling. It's part of why I love you. I do so hate *bold* men."

His sigh was deep, prolonged. "You know this betrothal was forced upon me. Why do you persist in it?"

There was a moment of silence then. "Please turn around, Cabot." When he had obeyed, she said, "Are you telling me I'm not attractive to you? And here I thought I looked my most ravishing today. I needed no rouge for my cheeks. My excitement at seeing you was quite enough."

Again he sighed, shaking his head. "You are a beautiful woman, Lady Barbara. There is no doubt of that, but—"

She came to him. "Oh, Cabot, my love, why are you being so silly and obstinate. When we're married, you know you'll love me."

He held her away. There would be no more embraces. "I hoped not to be so blunt, but you leave me no choice. I do not love you. I do not want to marry you. I demand you break our engagement."

She looked at him, smiling. A month ago, even a week, deep in her passion with Captain Haversham, she might have agreed. The captain's adroit lovemaking, her repeated fulfillments thrilled her into a form of madness. She was ready to throw away everything to be with him. But her calendar brought her to her senses, then to terror, as the twenty-eighth day passed, then the thirty-fifth, finally the fortieth.

This handsome, anguished man who stood before her was salvation. He had returned in time. "I couldn't possibly, Cabot."

"You must. I demand it."

"It is not yours to demand. The king will never hear of it." She smiled. "Besides, ours will be a very happy life."

Yes, very happy. He was handsome enough. She could bear his touch, might even enjoy it. And he was so gullible. He would believe anything. A vista of happiness spread before her, husband, child, respectability—and freedom. Her smile was dazzling. "Don't look so glum, darling. All of England envies you." She patted his cheek. "And I'm eager to show you why." Her throaty laugh sounded again. "I'll set the date for the earliest we can get Westminster Abbey."

He glared at her, helpless under his fury, then stalked past her, out of the room. Behind him, he heard, "Please visit your tailor, darling. You're quite out of fashion."

Her mocking laughter was still following him as he made up his mind. He would go to Amsterdam at once and speak to Hendrik van Stamp. If nothing came of that, he would sign aboard a foreign ship. Any country's would do. If it meant never setting foot in England again, so be it. He was not going to marry Barbara Cecil.

He lingered three more days at Graymere, despite his impatience to be off, and he did buy a new suit. After three years in Virginia, his clothes were threadbare. He wasn't sure he liked the new style. The loose-fitting jacket, snug at the waist, the wide sleeves slit to show the shirt beneath, the lace collar and cuffs seemed flamboyant to him. The ensemble included full breeches below the knee, with short, lace-trimmed stockings to show above short, wide boots. The wide-brimmed hat with the feather was almost too much for him. But, he told himself, if he was going to become a businessman in Holland, he might as well look the part.

He told Elizabeth of his failure with Lady Barbara.

"I knew she wouldn't release you. She needs you as a cuckold." Her face reddened as she said the word.

He remembered Barbara's kisses, hardly those of innocence. "Yes, I suspect so."

"What're you going to do?"

He pursed his lips. "I told you. I'm going to Holland first to speak to Kate's father. Failing in that—" He made an expansive gesture with his arms. "Let's just say there is a great big world out there. England is really a small place."

"You'd become an exile?"

"If need be."

"And you'd forsake your title, your inheritance?"

"Yes. My knighthood was a sham, trumped up by Barbara and Father. And, as the youngest son, my inheritance wouldn't be much anyway."

She looked at him, as though trying to grasp all he was saying. "Are you going to tell Father?"

"Not before I go. I'll write from Holland or wherever, try to make him understand."

"He'll be heartbroken, Cabot."

"Better him than me." He regretted the words. There was

cruelty in them, but he could think of no way to retract them. "Have you made a decision?"

"Yes." She smiled. "You helped me know what to do."

"I doubt that. But your prayers helped?"

"Oh, yes, yes, God has spoken. I am certain in my heart. Emanuel is, too. We have prayed together. He is convinced of God's will."

"I'm glad for you." He was almost afraid to ask. "What've you decided?"

It seemed to him her dark eyes were never larger, more penetrating. "I will marry Lord Pemberton."

He had seen her hesitation. "Are you sure, Elizabeth?"

"Yes, extremely sure."

Again he saw the hesitation. "This is what God has told you to do?"

She smiled. "I am sure in my own mind of what I must do." Her eyes held him a moment longer. "Come, let's go tell Father."

In his study, Lord Alfred North heard the most welcome news, but not without a measure of disbelief. "What made you change your mind?"

Elizabeth stood before her father's desk, erect, calm, her gaze meeting his. She was resolute, and it seemed to Cabot she had grown up overnight. Gone was the shrunken girl, frightened of life. He had never been so proud of her.

"Cabot talked to me, Father. He made me understand your reasons for wanting this marriage. I know now you have only my interests at heart. I am sorry I doubted your intentions or your love." Only now did she turn her eyes downward. "I beg your forgiveness."

She did not see her father's face, but Cabot did. Tears flooded his eyes, and his jaw began to tremble. A sound, half sob, half cry, escaped him as he arose and went to her. "My daughter, my only daughter." Greatly moved himself, Cabot believed it the first time he had ever seen his father embrace Elizabeth. As they wept in each other's arms, his own eyes were smarting.

It didn't last long. Lord Alfred, wiping and blowing, recovered himself. "Then you will marry Lord Pemberton?"

"Yes, Father, as you have arranged, ten days hence."

He looked at her a moment, his disbelief slowly expiring within him. Then there was a happy smile, a cry of laughter. If less infirm, Lord Alfred might have attempted a Scottish jig. "Do you hear, Cabot? Elizabeth will marry Pemberton. And you will wed Lady Barbara. This is the happiest day I've had in years. All my children are taken care of. I'll be able to join my Maker in peace." He shouted to Jacobs to bring wine, even as he embraced both his youngest children at the same time.

Cabot's lie, the traitorous deed he contemplated, was bitter in his mouth, but he was determined not to spoil this day for his father. His dishonor was the price of what he planned to do. And part of the price, too, was the haunted look in Elizabeth's eyes as he surreptitiously shook his head, warning her to say nothing.

Lord Alfred's cup of happiness overflowed when a messenger brought news that Lady Barbara had set the day for three weeks hence. She and Cabot were to be married, not at the Abbey, but at the Palace, the king and queen, the entire court in attendance. He was to be married ten days after Elizabeth.

Cabot made a quick calculation. He planned to leave on the morrow for Holland. He would return for Elizabeth's wedding, then leave forever. Walking out on a palace wedding would only add to his disgrace and his father's wound, but he would not marry Barbara Cecil.

The Channel ferry was buffeted by a summer squall and vile winds. Cabot was grateful, for the act of standing on the pitching deck while noting the handling of the ship helped to keep his mind from what he didn't want to think about—Kate. Thoughts of her, knowledge of his longing, frustration, and pain, were with him constantly. But in three years he had become relatively successful in tamping them down, submerging his feelings, not letting himself be hurt again. It was as though in his mind he erected a high wall around Kate, this whole episode in his life. Now, as he approached Holland, he could feel the wall weakening, threatening to crumble. He would not let it happen. Under no circumstances would he see Kate.

Avoiding the shop on Singel, he went directly to Herren Gracht, finding Hendrik van Stamp at home. In his eyes were surprise, delight, something else. Guilt, perhaps, or sorrow. Then he embraced Cabot warmly. "Thank God you're here. I thought I'd never see you again."

Cabot tried to keep it light. "I could not allow you to be so fortunate, sir."

The Dutchman stood back, beaming. "Cabot, my son, it is so good you're here. Have you seen Katarina?"

"No. I don't plan to."

"But why? She waits for your return. She lives only to see you."

"I doubt that, sir. She is a wife and mother. She has a new life. My seeing her would not contribute to her happiness or certainly not to mine. It is better this way."

Van Stamp studied his face a moment. "Don't be angry with her, Cabot. I did it. I simply could not permit her to go off to Virginia as she wanted. Be angry with me, not Katarina."

"I am not angry at her or you. I understand why you did what you did. Had I been in your position, I would have made the same decision."

His eyes filled. He seemed nearly on the verge of tears. "Thank you for that, Cabot. You don't know what it means to me after all this time." Then he abruptly shook off his emotion and smiled. "Step into the parlor, while I fetch some wine. I'll only be a moment."

Cabot obeyed, entering the familiar room. Nothing had changed. Then he saw the usual decanter of wine. Why had van Stamp gone for more?

The merchant read his mind as he entered. "I thought your visit deserved a fresh bottle at least." He uncorked, poured, and both drank. "Now, tell me about Virginia."

Cabot gave a brief report of Dale's activities, dispersal of the colony, private ownership of land, and the cultivation of tobacco. "Virginia will be a success now."

"Good, and I'm sure you contributed to it. Do you plan to return?"

"No, I can't." He told of his betrothal, the plans for a forced marriage, and his determination to escape it. "That's why I came to see you, sir. You once offered me a position with your company. Is it still available?"

Van Stamp beamed. "Oh, my, yes, yes. I would like nothing better."

And Cabot smiled, too. "Then I accept your offer."

The Dutchman hesitated. "I do want you. You'll be invaluable. But I don't understand how you plan to work for me and avoid seeing Katarina."

"I hope not to be here. I am a good sailor. I love the sea. I would be useful aboard some of your Dutch East Indies ships. I have never seen that part of the world."

"I see. Avoid both Katarina and an unwanted marriage." He smiled. "There is a better solution, I think. We really do want to open trading posts and develop the fur trade in America. With your experience in Virginia, you would be a natural to lead such an enterprise."

"Good. I look forward to it."

Glasses were raised, drained, a symbolic cementing of their agreement. Van Stamp hesitated, then seemed to plunge ahead. "As a friend, Cabot, I must ask you if you think it wise to exile yourself, disobey your father, and no doubt surrender your title and inheritance?"

"I don't care if it's wise or not." He shrugged. "I haven't known what is wise for a long time."

"Is the woman this bad? Do you dislike her this much?"

"The answer to both questions is yes." He said the word most emphatically.

Van Stamp smiled. "So be it. England's loss is Holland's gain."

Cabot was aware of the sounds of the front door opening and closing, yet he was surprised when Kate entered the parlor, holding a child in her arms. From his left, he heard, "I sent for her, Cabot. I had to. Believe me it's better this way."

She was staring at him, mouth open a little, her eyes, liquid jewels now, filled with surprise, happiness, expectancy. She was inutterably lovely to him, and he felt the walls fencing off his feelings begin to crumble, the pain flooding out.

The little boy in her arms broke it. He saw his grandfather and squealed something in Dutch, squirming to be free of his mother's grasp. She put him down, and he ran to embrace van Stamp.

A moment longer she stared at him. "I wanted you to meet our son." Her voice was surprisingly firm. He knew he would be unable to speak.

She turned to the boy and spoke in Dutch. Cabot understood

the name Philip and his own name. Then she spoke in English. "Say how do you do to Mr. North, Philip." To Cabot she said, "I'm teaching him both Dutch and English."

The boy dutifully crawled down from his grandfather's lap and walked to Cabot. He wore a Dutch costume, a black suit with breeches to the knee, a stiff white collar. He extended a tiny hand. Somberly, formally, he said, "How do you do, Mr. North."

Cabot was looking at a miniature of himself, dark, wavy hair, vivid blue eyes, so big, trusting, somehow soulful. Cabot glanced at Kate. She was smiling proudly.

"He's two years and four months old now, Cabot."

He had had scant experience with young children in his life, and none at all with fatherly love. He was filled with emotion as he met the gaze of his son. His lower jaw was shaking as he extended his hand, enveloping the tiny, soft fingers within his. He had no capacity to speak. Then, hands to his waist, Cabot lifted Philip. He intended to set him on his knee. Instead, he pulled him deep within his arms, against his shoulder, the little face against his beard, trembling, throat constricted, eyes burning with the effort to hold back tears.

His son came to his aid, squirming uncomfortably within his arms. Cabot released him, and he climbed down and ran to his grandfather. Cabot looked at Kate. She was smiling, but her eyes were full of tears.

She spoke, her voice surprisingly normal. "Father, will you take Philip? I want to be alone with Cabot."

"Of course. Don't see enough of my grandson anyway." He arose, holding the boy's hand. "Come, *liefje.*"

Out of ingrained courtesy, Cabot arose, too. Then he was alone with his beloved. They spoke with their eyes, and he was conscious only of her, her beauty, her nearness, the femininity that always emanated from her.

Someone had to speak. "He looks like you, don't you think?"

"Yes."

A moment more they looked at each other. Then she was running into his arms, the longing of hands, bodies, lips overwhelming restraint. But only for a moment. "We mustn't, Kate."

"Oh, *lieveling.*" When she kissed him now, her mouth, moist, open, was like an artesian well for her passion.

He had not, despite three years of effort, turned to stone

after all. The fences of his feeling were now as dust, swept away by the love and pent-up longing that consumed him. Hands, never forgetting, found backs, shoulders, faces. And between fevered kisses, love words came from both mouths at once. *"Lieveling, Ik hou van jou,* darling, my love, dearest, beloved..."* She swept through it all.

At last came something coherent. "Why didn't you come to the shop?"

The query brought reality to him, and he stepped back from her. "I didn't want to see you, Kate."

"Oh, *lieveling—*"

"This is no good, Kate. We're only bringing pain to each other."

Tears were streaming down her cheeks now. "I've waited an eternity for you, *lieveling*—and died...every moment of it."

Her tears were like salt in his own inner wound, but he knew what he had to do and had the strength now to do it. "Listen to me, Kate. I don't have much honor left, but I have enough not to cuckold your husband or let you." He saw her open her mouth to protest. "Think of all the lies, the deception, Kate. It will destroy us both—and our love."

Crying now, she could only nod affirmation. But she recovered quickly, wiping her cheeks with her fingertips. "Oh, *lieveling—*" Again she fought back tears. Finally, she could say, "You didn't come to see *me?*"

He managed a smile, quite to his own surprise. "As a matter of fact, I came to see your father."

"But why?"

"He's offered me a job, and I've accepted."

She brightened at once. "Then I'll get to see you."

"No. I'm going to America to open trading posts."

She found only confusion in his words. "I don't understand."

"It seems I am still betrothed to Barbara Cecil. She, my father, apparently even the king insist I marry her. I will not. I am leaving England to escape her."

Fear rose in her eyes. "Oh, no, Cabot, you mustn't."

Her reaction surprised him. "You *want* me to marry her?"

She appeared to wrestle with her thoughts a moment. "If need be, yes. It's better than—running away, giving up everything."

"Better for whom?"

"I married someone I don't love and found some measure of contentment. So can you."

"It would never work for me, Kate."

"But *lieveling—*"

"No, Kate, listen to me. Do you remember saying that you believed with all your heart that someday, somehow you and I would find a way to be together in our love?"

"Yes. I still do."

"I now believe that, too. I will not marry another. You have waited all these years for me. I will now wait for you—my whole life if I have to."

TWENTY-FOUR

A Letter

LORD ALFRED NORTH had extended himself. Having discovered in the twilight of his life the love of his daughter, he sought now to provide her with a sumptuous wedding. It was to be celebrated at Graymere, and he was determined the great house would belie its name in a manner it had not since the death of Lady Evelyn. Heirlooms, silver, jewels were brought out from half-forgotten caches. Servants were driven to polish and clean and refurbish. The great hall, where the wedding was to occur, was bedecked in flowers and arranged for a glittering wedding. No less than the dean of Westminster was to pronounce the vows. All the North sons and their families were summoned home. The guest list boasted Cecils and Villiers, Cranfields and Howards and Coles. The king and queen would not come, of course. Later, they would honor the marriage of the earl's son.

Highlight of the preparations was a prenuptial ball the night before the wedding. Graymere was ablaze with light. It rang with music and dancing, laughter and florid Elizabethan toasts to the bride and groom, king, and family.

Cabot watched in sadness, although he did his best to conceal it. Lord North had never been so happy, so full of pride and sense of accomplishment. And wasn't it so? From a grubby minor earldom in the North, he had brought his family to this shining moment. Cabot saw his father, his successful family all around him, exuding happiness. The knowledge that he would soon bring disgrace on his family and exile on himself was his secret thumbscrew.

He was quite surprised at Elizabeth. At the ball, she had never looked lovelier. Indeed, he felt that some of those who had scorned her might now wish they had courted the daughter of the Earl of Durham. Her gown was stylish, her hair immaculate, and when she danced with Lord Pemberton, careful to avoid his goutish foot, she seemed more graceful than Cabot had known she could be. The applause that greeted them was only warranted. Her smile was radiant as she accepted the many toasts to the bride. When her own time came, she arose and in a clear voice said, offering her glass, "To the man I am to wed tomorrow." Pemberton, who indeed didn't seem all that bad to Cabot, beamed. Then, Elizabeth excused herself, bidding all to continue their merriment. Everyone understood. On the morrow would come her wedding and deflowering.

Lady Barbara was there, ravishing in a too deeply décolleté gown of indigo and green. Cabot was grateful that she did not make a particular effort to upstage Elizabeth, although her mere appearance made it difficult for her not to. Cabot danced and talked with her, endeavoring to conduct himself as he imagined prospective bridegrooms acted. The knowledge he would abandon her as soon as Elizabeth's wedding was over goaded him to his best behavior.

"I can hardly wait for our wedding, my darling."

"Yes, it will be memorable."

The merriment went on half the night. Lord Pemberton became quite tipsy. He was hardly alone in that. Cabot thought about stealing upstairs for a final chat with Elizabeth, then thought better of it. She needed her rest.

The morning dawned bright, sunny, a perfect day for a wedding. Many of the houseguests at Graymere were not quite so perfect when they appeared at breakfast, but appear they did, all Cabot's brothers and their wives, Lord Pemberton and his best man, Sir Robert Craven. It struck Cabot that Craven was more of an age to be marrying Elizabeth. Pemberton was already dressed for the nuptials in a modish suit of brilliant blue satin. It was not too stained, Cabot noted.

He paid no particular attention when Jacobs appeared at Lord Alfred's elbow. "Excuse me, milord, but there seems to be a problem. The maids cannot awaken Miss Elizabeth."

Lord Alfred looked startled. "Not awaken her? Confound it, the child cannot sleep in on her wedding day. Is she ill?"

"Not that we know, sir. Her door is locked, milord. The maids cannot enter."

"Locked? What on earth for?"

Cabot reacted to head off a crisis. "I'll go, Father. I'm sure it's just a bride's nerves."

"Yes, talk to her, calm her down."

On the second floor in the west wing, Cabot found a gaggle of maids outside Elizabeth's door. They grew silent as he approached. "What seems to be the trouble, Agnes?" Agnes was personal maid to his sister. She looked frightened.

"I don't know, sir. The door's locked, both doors. She doesn't answer, sir."

"Well, get the key."

"We have, sir, but it's bolted from the inside."

Fear suddenly stabbed at him. *I know now what I must do.* She wouldn't take her own life. It was unthinkable. He pounded on the door, calling his sister's name several times. Silence. "When did you last see her?"

"Last night, sir, when I put her to bed."

"Did she seem . . . all right?"

"Yes, sir, in quite good spirits, sir, especially excited, if I may say so."

He studied Agnes's face as though it offered some clue, then faced the door. "Stand back." He tried his shoulder against it, wincing with pain. "The door from your room, Agnes. Is it less heavy?"

"I believe so, sir."

Fear now ranged within him, as he went to the maid's room to the left of Elizabeth's, followed by the knot of servants, Jacobs beside him. Again he pounded and called out with the same result. Then he raised his foot and kicked at the door, feeling it give a little. His fear gave him strength and by the third kick he was rewarded with a splintering sound and he burst into Elizabeth's room. With relief he saw the bed unslept in.

"I thought you put her to bed."

"I did, sir. She must have gotten up and remade the bed." Jacobs's dignified voice rose over the babble of female sounds. "Where can she be, sir?"

"I don't know." He looked around the sparsely furnished room. There seemed no place to hide. "I don't know."

Agnes was at the closet. "None of her things is missing, sir." Then she paused. "Excuse me, sir. One is, the blue gown, the dark blue from her trousseau. She planned to wear it—"

He silenced her with his hand. Suddenly he knew, knew with certainty. He saw the open window. She had left that way. Then he stalked to the stand beside her bed, opening the drawer. Her Bible was missing, the Geneva Bible, fuel for her faith.

"Sir Cabot, there is a letter here, addressed to you."

He turned to Jacobs. "Let me have it." Fingers trembling, he broke the seal, unfolded, read.

My dearest brother,

Forgive me, Cabot.

By the time you read this I will be the wife of Emanuel Cotter. Please do not try to bring me back. You will not find either of us.

Forgive me, Cabot, for my lies and deceptions. I hated to lie to Father, but it was the only way. Emanuel and I needed time for our preparations. The party in my honor will provide the perfect opportunity for me to slip away. With the noise, the many carriages, everyone busy, my departure will go unnoticed. I plan to put in an appearance, then fly to Emanuel who will be waiting in one of the vehicles. I'm sorry, Cabot. I know no other way to find happiness.

Forgive me, most of all, my dearest, for deceiving you. I know you believed I intended to go through with this hateful marriage. I know you think it would have been best for me. Every time I looked at you, I could hardly bear to know I was deceiving the one person who has truly loved me in this life. But I had to, Cabot. Please understand. I knew you would try to stop me. I was afraid you might even tell Father. I couldn't take that chance. Forgive me, please. I shall die if you do not.

I know I am doing God's will. I did not lie to you about that. I searched my soul. Emanuel and I have prayed together. We know with certainty ours is the course God has set for us. I now know that God sent you, dearest Cabot, as his messenger. When you told me my hatred for Father stood like a wall between God and myself, I knew those were the truest words ever uttered. When I cleansed my soul of its venom, rendered unto Father my love and forgiveness, God spoke to me with a clear and shining light. He helped me see, as you had long before, the meaninglessness of wealth, the emptiness of privilege. Each of us was put on earth naked to make our own way, to do his will. When you spoke of your determination to forsake all, running away from your own marriage, surrendering your inheritance, I knew that was the course I must follow, also.

Emanuel needs me as a companion in his ministry. He has helped me see that ours is a love not of the flesh, but of the spirit. Ours will be a communion of the mind. Together we shall carry God's word to the sinful, return the wayward sheep to the true flock of God. I expect to be very happy in his service.

I have tried desperately, but I can find no words to explain this to Father. Do it for me, I beg of you, as I beg for his understanding and forgiveness—and yours.

> Your loving and *faithful* sister
> Eliz.

He realized the words were swimming before his eyes. Dear Elizabeth, happiness denied her all her life, was married to the ascetic Emanuel Cotter. No, God, no. It couldn't be possible.

"Is something wrong, sir?"

Slowly he turned to Jacobs, gradually registering his countenance, the faces of the others in the room, startled, concerned. Through the stricture in his throat he found voice. "Please send the servants to their other duties." He swallowed. "Tell Father, his—his lordship, I will...be down in a...a minute—to explain."

"As you wish, Sir Cabot."

He was not conscious of the servants filing out of the room, their curious glances at him, the buzz of whispers from the hallway. Nor was he aware of rereading the words on the pages he still held in his hand. He knew only that he was seized with guilt, the greatest he had ever known. It was all his fault. He had taken Elizabeth as a child to the church meetings at Scrooby. He had encouraged her friendship with Emily, brought her news from Leyden, skulked away with her to Cotter's parish. Oh, God, not Cotter, so self-righteous, so loveless, consumed by the fires of hell, more interested in damnation than in salvation. He was no husband for Elizabeth. He would squeeze all joy, all happiness from her.

His fault, all his fault. He thought himself so clever, convincing Elizabeth to marry Pemberton, make peace with Father. Oh, so clever. All he had done was place in her hand the sword of misery. She would never have thought of running away, forsaking home, wealth, comfort, and respectability had he not told her of his intentions. God in heaven, what had he done?

Slowly he folded the letter and began to walk downstairs. From the stairs he saw that many of the wedding guests had arrived, and others were entering. He was conscious of Lady Barbara being present.

"What on earth is wrong with you, Cabot? Where is your sister?"

Cabot heard the imperious voice of his father, but couldn't speak.

"I demand you answer. Where is Elizabeth?"

Finally, swallowing hard, he found a choked voice. "May I speak to you...alone, Father?"

"You may not. You will speak here, now, in front of my other sons and Lord Pemberton. Where is your sister?"

He pleaded with his eyes, but heard his father again demand an answer, his voice now thunderous. "She has...run off. She...She has...married Emanuel Cotter."

Never had he heard such shocked silence.

Finally, *"Married?"*

Cabot nodded.

"But—But she is to marry Lord Pemberton."

The jilted would-be bridegroom found voice. "Who is this Cotter?"

Cabot opened his mouth to speak, but the words of Lord Alfred filled the air. "I'll tell you who he is—a sniveling snake in the grass, a cowardly bride stealer, a heretic Puritan bastard." Lord Alfred's anger was in full steam now. "He'll not do this to me. Jacobs! Take Sanders, all the men you can find. Bring them back. I'll beat sense into that ingrate of a daughter. And I'll hang that treacherous, ungodly preacher. I'll see he is strung up if it's the last thing I ever do."

"You'll not find them, Father."

The wrath of the father fell on the son. Face red, eyes bulging, he demanded, "What do you know? Tell me. *This instant!*"

"She wrote a letter."

"What letter? I *demand* to see it."

Cabot dutifully handed him Elizabeth's letter and watched in private agony as his father stuck his spectacles on his nose and began to read, his face growing ever redder, his jaw trembling as he silently sounded each syllable.

Cabot could visualize the letter, the words already burned in his memory. *Forgive me. I know I'm doing God's will.* Yes, he knew every word. Then he gasped. Elizabeth's words leaped toward him. He had made a horrible mistake. He should have burned the letter, torn it to shreds, hidden it, anything but let his father read it. Trembling, now with fear, he reached for the sheets of paper. "I don't think you need read this, Father."

His hand was slapped away.

Then his father was raising his head, looking at him, consternation, disbelief, rage, horror in his eyes. *"You!"* His face became the color of raw liver. His eyes bulged. He seemed to be shaking all over. *"You!* You did this—to *me!*"

The letter fell from Lord North's hand, which came up to clutch at his throat, and he began to sway on his feet. Cabot reached for him, but too late, as other hands grabbed the old peer to keep him from falling.

Someone screamed.

TWENTY-FIVE

A Slight Delay

CABOT SAT IN the hallway outside his father's bedroom, bent over, elbows on his knees, consumed with guilt and worry. He was all but ignored, as a parade of doctors, nurses, clergy, relatives, and servants entered and departed the old man's room. Only a few glanced at Cabot.

He had the impression his father still lived, but was gravely ill. Cabot knew it was all his fault. If only he had remembered the words Elizabeth had written, he might have spared his father knowledge of his traitorous intentions. He sighed, deeply. There was nothing to be done now. His father would die, hating the son he had loved the most.

One spoke to him. "So that is what you planned." He heard the anger in Lady Barbara's voice, but ignored both it and her. "I read the letter after it fell to the floor. My dear, sweet sister Elizabeth"—her voice dripped sarcasm—"let the cat out of the bag, didn't she? How unfortunate for you—you scoundrel." Still he ignored her. "I demand you look at me, or is that too much to ask of a cowardly sneak?"

He felt the pressure of her fingers under his chin, raising his head. She stood before him, full of righteous anger, injured womanhood. "So you were going to run off and leave me at the altar." Her hazel eyes seemed full of fire. "Answer me, I say!"

He rendered, finally, a twisted, sardonic smile. "I thought it preferable to marrying you."

She slapped him then, quite hard actually, but it was nothing to him. "Is there some other wench you are in love with?"

Again he gave the twisted smile.

"I demand you tell me."

The smile broadened. "There is no one else, milady, no one I can marry, at least. I am motivated solely by abhorrence of you."

She seemed to swell up with air. "Very well. Think what you please. But you will marry me on Saturday next. Make no mistake about that. I will not be disgraced and shamed by the likes of you."

Stalking off, she spared him the trouble of making a reply.

Late in the evening, Jacobs came to tell him Lord Alfred was resting. There was nothing to do. He should get some rest himself. Ultimately, Cabot went to his room. Pacing the floor, deep in thought, he realized that all that had happened was that his plan had become known before he executed it. If he had left and written from Holland, the result would have been the same—his father's anger, collapse, and probable death. And with the earl's death would come his own disinheritance, disgrace, and exile. He sighed. At least he was here to see the results of his actions. Perhaps he would get a chance to see his father and explain that he had not intended to hurt him. He only wanted to avoid a life of misery with a woman he detested. And he would tell his father he loved him. Yes. If he had ever doubted, he now knew he did. And he didn't want his father to die.

His brother spoke to him the next day. Sir Harold already had the cast of his approaching earldom, authority, even imperiousness residing within him. "Sir Cabot, I assume you know what you have done."

"Sir Cabot?"

"That's what I said."

Cabot sighed. "Yes, Sir Harold, I am fully aware. Or would you prefer I call you Lord Harold?"

Anger showed on the brother's face. "You will not be impudent with me."

"And what is it I will be?"

"Contrite, sorry for what you have done to our father."

Again a deep sigh. "I am that already. There is just nothing I can do about it."

"But there is. You can wed Lady Barbara as he planned. You can and you will spare him and this family the disgrace you contemplated."

Cabot looked at his brother. "How ill is Father?"

"Extremely. The doctors say he has not long."

Cabot pursed his lips and frowned. "I am sorry for that. You must believe me. But with his death there will be no point to the marriage."

"There is every point, you ungrateful wretch!" For a moment it appeared Sir Harold might strike Cabot in anger. "Even if he dies, you will carry out Father's wishes."

Cabot studied him a moment, then walked away from him to stare out a window, trying to calm himself. He had some success. "Harold—and you are still my brother—I wonder if you know the circumstances of my *alleged* betrothal." He saw Sir Harold open his mouth, but he raised his hand to silence him. "Let me speak, please. I know you are married to a Cecil. Lady Portia is a . . . a gracious, loving wife to you. I'm certain of that, as I am that you are happy in your marriage and your family association. Certainly it has afforded you great wealth, power, and prestige." He sighed. "But you must understand that I have no regard for Barbara Cecil. I quite detest her as much as she detests me. This betrothal was forced upon me, quite against my wishes. Why she wants this marriage, I don't know. I offer her nothing—unless it is the pleasure of her own spite. It is a travesty, Harold—almost as much as my own knighthood was. Surely you must see that."

Cabot's speech had the effect of calming Sir Harold, but it did nothing to change his attitude. "I see only that you are young and incredibly foolish. What does love have to do with marriage? Privately detest each other all you want. The fact remains you will profit greatly from this marriage. This Father knew. And in his misguided love for you, he wanted a sinecure for life for you."

"I don't want to profit from marriage."

Sir Harold laughed. "Oh, but I think you do. You just don't realize how much. Lady Barbara's dowry is quite remarkable. It includes a house in London. There are her jewels, ample personal effects, shares in the East India Company, and enough pounds sterling to guarantee the kind of life to which she is accustomed."

Cabot was already gasping. Shares in the highly profitable East India Company were so closely held that only a handful of people owned them. "You're not serious."

Sir Harold smiled. "I am indeed. You will be a very wealthy

man the moment you take your vows. All England will envy you."

"But why? Why should she do it?"

There was mockery in the brother's laugh. "Believe me, I can't imagine. Who can explain a woman's fancy?"

Cabot thought a moment, then spoke. "I still don't want it. I'll not barter happiness for East India shares and houses."

"My God! How unbelievably foolish you are. How did I ever come to be related to you?"

"We are only half-brothers, remember."

"And you are surely the worst half. Listen, my dear Cabot, you will wed Lady Barbara next Saturday if I have to take you to the palace in chains."

"And what will I do afterward? Live in misery, an impoverished son, forever beholden to the Cecils for whatever crumbs fall from their larder?"

Laughter, genuine mirth this time, cascaded from his brother. "So that's it. I might have known. Didn't Father tell you?"

"Tell me what?"

"It seems our father loves you. Why, I can't imagine. Probably has something to do with the second countess. You do look something like her." He paused, shaking his head. "I should be loved half as much by him as you."

"What are you saying?"

"Father's will provides that you receive Graymere, this very house in which we stand. By rights it should be mine, or Henry's. But I am to receive the estates in Durham, Henry the London house, Robert shares in the Virginia Company. All are taken care of. Graymere is yours, my ungrateful brother. There is nothing any of us can do about it."

Cabot was deeply affected. He had a choking sensation in his throat, and his eyes burned. His father loved him, and he gave in return only betrayal. His father wanted only his happiness and success, and he offered only shame and disgrace. He sighed, then, a second time, as though struggling for breath. Then he could speak. "I hadn't known. I never thought."

Sir Harold nodded. "We do not always understand what our parents desire for us—until it is too late."

Cabot looked at him sharply. "Has he—"

"No. And he's asking for you."

Lord Alfred lay as though in death, on his back, white,

waxen, hands folded across his chest. The doctor stood near the right side of the bed. In the corner of the room a clergyman, holding a Bible, silently uttered prayers.

Cabot went to the left side of the bed and leaned over the old man. "Father?"

Slowly, fluttering, the heavy lids opened. The pale blue eyes were seemingly vacant, unseeing, at first. Then the head turned, and the Earl of Durham recognized his son.

"Why have you done this to me?" There was surprising vigor in the voice.

"I'm sorry, Father. I thought Elizabeth was going to marry Pemberton. Cotter is no one for her. She will not find happiness with him."

Lord North's eyelids closed. He sighed heavily. The nod of his head, a nearly imperceptible movement, denoted agreement. Then the eyes opened and he spoke. "You will marry Lady Barbara."

"I'm sorry, Father, no."

The timbre of the old voice changed. "You will do as I say."

"Please, Father, don't anger yourself."

He spoke to the doctor. "Bring the Bible. Make him swear."

"No, Father. I will not swear. And if you make me, I will break the oath. I will not marry Barbara Cecil."

The earl stared at Cabot a moment longer; then he visibly wearied. The eyelids closed, and he seemed to slump back against the pillow. For a moment Cabot feared the end had come. But he was only resting. "But why? She is a handsome woman."

"Father, I detest her and she detests me. We would bring only misery to each other."

"But her dowry. You'll be rich for life."

Cabot sighed. "I don't want her dowry, Father." He felt an ache in his back from leaning over the bed. He pulled a chair close to the bed and sat. "Father, do you remember my telling you about Virginia, that the only wealth there is land and the opportunity for hard work?" He saw the slight nodding of the head. "You sent me to Virginia. It changed me, Father, as I think it will change the whole world. I don't want her dowry.

I don't want idleness and privilege. I want to make my own way in the world. And I know I can."

"You are ungrateful. Your sister, too."

"No, Father. We both love you very much. We understand what you tried to do for us. But times have changed." He smiled. "In your lifetime, you have made them change."

"What are you saying?"

"Look, you inherited a small, impoverished earldom. By your actions, you have brought it to wealth, power, and importance. I know, the marriage to the first countess was an important step in that process. You believe in the usefulness of marriage." Again he smiled. "But I have no earldom to build. I will bequeath no titles. I have only my own life to live—and I intend, thanks to Virginia, to do it by my own efforts."

Lord North lay against the pillow, eyes closed, for a time. "Why didn't you say this to me before?"

"You wouldn't have listened."

"I might have. I listened to you about Virginia, didn't I?"

Cabot pursed his lips. "You're right. I should not have contemplated running away. I should have stayed, convinced you." He sighed. "I ask your forgiveness for that."

The old man lay silent against the pillow so long that Cabot thought he had fallen asleep. Then he spoke. "I still don't understand. The Cecil girl seems pleasant to me."

"It's an act, Father. Believe me, she is not pleasant with me. Besides, I don't love her, never will."

"Love is not important."

Cabot smiled. "Look who's talking. I understand why you married the first countess. But after she died, whom did you choose? Not some powerful heiress with a large dowry. You chose my mother, a chambermaid. You chose her because you loved her and wanted happiness."

"Yes." The word came out as a deep sigh. "I did love her."

"Then why deny me the same privilege?"

"The Dutch girl?"

"Yes. She became with child, my child. He was born while I was in Virginia. Her father forced her to marry another man. We still love each other. I will wait until she is free."

Father looked at son a long moment. "It is no life for you, my son. You should marry, have many children. The Cecil girl is the one."

"I'll say this, sir. You are persistent." He laughed lightly, but it faded quickly. "Have you never asked yourself, Father, as I have, why she wants to marry me? As you say, she is beautiful. Her dowry is immense, her family powerful. She could have at least a duke, possibly even a royal marriage. Why me?"

"She loves you."

"Nonsense. She is incapable of loving anyone but herself." He hesitated, then plunged forward. "I understand she has been seen in the company of a Royal Guards captain. I believe his name is Haversham. And he is married. You don't suppose she is with child and has to marry, do you?"

"That is contemptible, my son, beneath you."

"Have you not asked yourself why this unseemly haste for the marriage? What is the hurry, after all?"

"She has waited three years for you. She wants—"

"No, Father. That is not what she wants." He smiled. "But there is perhaps a way to prove her . . . her condition. When you feel up to it, invite her in here. Ask her to delay the wedding a few weeks until you are well and able to attend."

"What good will that do?"

"If she does indeed carry another man's child—I assure you it is most definitely not mine—then"—he smiled—"her reactions to a postponement should be interesting."

Lord North eyed him for a moment, then spoke to the doctor. "Send for Lady Barbara."

"Not now, Father. When you are stronger."

"I will never be stronger. I want to know now."

The Lady Barbara who swept into the sickroom was not only stunningly gowned, but every inch the distraught and devoted daughter-in-law. She gave Cabot a quick embrace and peck on the cheek, then fluttered over to the patient. "Oh, Father, I'm so *glad* you sent for me." She bent over him, clasping his waxen hands, kissing his cheek. "You will get better. I know you will. You must *promise* me to recover. I'd just *die* myself if anything happened to you." She kept patting his withered hand. "I'll not hear of anything but your *complete* recovery. You will be good, won't you? Take your medicine? Do *everything* the doctor tells you? You do promise, don't you?"

Once again Cabot felt grudging admiration for what he knew to be a virtuoso performance.

Finally, Lord North could get a word in. "Thank you for coming, my dear. It is good to see you—as always."

This brought another flurry of admonitions not to talk, not to exert himself, just to rest and get well.

The old man waited her out with apparent patience, then said, "I asked you to come here, my dear, to seek a favor. It is a great deal to ask, I know, but—"

"I'll do anything, Father, *anything*—just so long as you get well."

He attempted to speak, but surrendered to a spate of rasping coughing. He motioned for Cabot to speak for him.

"What Father wants to ask, Lady Barbara, is that we postpone our wedding."

"Postpone?"

"Yes, just a few weeks until he recovers. He does so want to attend, and he could not possibly do so in his present condition." He saw the hard glint of anger in her eyes. And something else. Was it fear?

She turned back to the bedside, again assuming her demeanor of sweet solicitude. "Oh, Father, you know I'd do anything for you, but to delay my wedding is—"

Lord North found voice to interrupt. "Only a few weeks, my child, no more than two months, three at the most."

"Three months!" The words seemed to horrify her.

"It is not long, really, my dear."

Cabot helped him out. "I've told him we would of course postpone. Having waited three years for our happiness, my love, we can surely wait three months longer."

She was not fooled one whit. Her anger flared. "You will not do this to me. I will not have it, do you hear? I will be married on Saturday next, and that's all there is to it." In her anger, glaring at Cabot, she even stamped her foot. Then at once she tried to reverse herself, turning to Lord North, forcing a smile. "I can't possibly postpone, Father, the invitations, the king, the—"

"I'll send a message to His Majesty," the elder North said. "I'm sure he'll agree to a postponement so I can attend."

And Cabot spoke. "Yes. I'll deliver it myself. I'm sure the king wants only your recovery, Father."

"Yes." He managed a smile. "And having your wedding to look forward to will only hasten my getting well, my dear son and daughter-to-be."

"Stop it, I say! I will marry Saturday next. I must!"

It was the following spring, when daffodils bloomed at Graymere, that happiness came to Cabot North.

Lieveling,

My husband, Pieter van Groudt, died this Tuesday past. It was sudden, his heart apparently.

I did not love him, only you, *lieveling,* but he was a good man, good to me, good to our son. As much as I long to fly to you, I will not dishonor him by a hasty remarriage. We should wait a few months. In the fall, I think. I know. The festival, when we first met. We will marry then.

I see no reason why a visit or two from you in the meantime would be considered improper.

Oh, *lieveling, ik hou van jou,*
Kate

Cabot now sat at what had been his father's desk in the study at Graymere. Quill in hand, he was reading that portion of a letter he had just penned.

My Dear Sar,

I can't tell you what pleasure it brought me to receive your letter and its most welcome news. My congratulations to you and to Hannah on the birth of your second son. Thomas Loudon is indeed a fine name. I'm certain it will bring only pride to his parents. Almost as welcome was your news of the progress in Virginia, especially your report that your tobacco crop prospered. Of course, it pleases me inordinately to know the north field (not Northfield) did so well.

I will report your news about the tobacco crop and shipments to John Rolfe, whom I see from time to time. I am saddened to report that Lady Rebecca is not adjusting favorably to our English climate. She seems unable to ward off a series of colds and congestions. John is planning to return with her to Virginia, hopefully within the next year. I'm sure her health will improve there. Meanwhile, at the behest of Captain Smith, the king and queen are to receive Lady Rebecca at the palace, since she is deemed an Indian princess. John Rolfe will not be received, as he is a commoner. I know, my friend. Things happen in this world which pass all understanding.

Cabot put down the page, for it was as far as he had written, and picked up Timothy's letter, smiling as he reread it. Timothy had not actually written it, for he lacked confidence in both his penmanship and his literacy. He had dictated it to Hannah, whose education was not much superior. The letter was full of strikeouts and misspelled words, but a letter it was, and a delight to receive.

Cabot then applied his quill to his own letter, reporting the happenings in his own life. A half-hour later, he was reading his efforts.

My father lingered close to a month, then expired peacefully in his sleep. I was grateful I was here, for I spent a great deal of time with him at the last. I know death had to come to him as it must to all, but I feel a sense of loss. I had always known that he was a great and powerful man, but I had not realized until the last how very loving and sensitive he was. I had always believed myself more like my mother. I came to know I was more my father's son. I hope your children do not wait until it is too late to fully appreciate their father.

We buried Father here at Graymere. I can't tell you how it pleased me that my sister Elizabeth came before the end to receive his forgiveness. That is one unhappiness she will not have to bear in life.

Under my father's will, I inherited Graymere, where

I now live. It seems, despite my best efforts, I am to be
something for which I have, as you know, no capacity—
a farmer. I employ men, but, sar, if you ever tire of your
beloved Virginia and long for England, I know some
land you can till to your heart's content.

I am happy to report to you that I finally escaped my
betrothal to Lady Barbara Cecil. She refused to accept
a delay in our marriage and broke our engagement.
Thereafter, she speedily married a gentleman named Lord
Pemberton. I understand she is with child and, I assume,
living happily ever after.

That is a condition I am looking forward to, also. My
beloved Kate has become a widow. We plan marriage
in the fall.

Beyond that, I really have made no plans. I know I
am not cut out for the life of a country gentleman. I miss
the sea more than I ever thought possible long ago when
you held my breeches while I retched over the side of
the *Sarah Constant*. There is a lot of talk of Dutch settlement in America. Kate, our son Philip, and I may
become involved in that. Time will tell.

But I will be surprised if I do not find a way to visit
you and your family in Virginia. I miss the place more
than I once thought possible, as you know. I have an
indelible memory of our landing. It truly was the Garden
of Eden, and we were mere intruders, filled with madness, bringing only destruction—or so I once believed.
But through you, my friend, I came to see the bounty
and promise of the land, the opportunity it afforded, a
place to be free, a place to start afresh in life, a place
unfettered by the past, a place where a man could succeed
or fail by his own efforts.

I envy you, sar. You are an ancient and a survivor.
You believed in Virginia when no one else did. I heard
about Gates's men having to carry you, kicking and
screaming, although you were so starved you were a
mere skeleton, aboard the *Deliverance* when they were
abandoning the colony. And you were only correct, sar.
You were in the absolute beginning of something you
knew, as I now do, too, would turn out to be grand and

well worth doing. Neither you nor I can predict the future. But I am sure it lies with you in the New World, not with me here in the Old. If for no other reason, that is why I want to bring Kate to Virginia or someplace in the New World. We want to be part of the promise of the future.

Believe me when I say I am

Yours in gratitude,
Sar

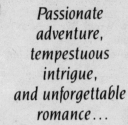

Passionate
adventure,
tempestuous
intrigue,
and unforgettable
romance...

Shana Carrol's PAXTON WOMEN SAGA

continues...